Temples
of
Gold

Also by Corinne Brixton

THROUGH MARTHA'S EYES

ALTARS OF STONE

THE TENT OF FINE LINEN

published by Matador

All profits to Tearfund
Registered Charity No.265464 (England & Wales)

Temples

of

Gold

Book Three of
The Line of Shem Trilogy

Corinne Brixton

Matador
Unit E2 Airfield Business Park,
Harrison Road, Market Harborough,
Leicestershire. LE16 7UL
Tel: 0116 2792299
Email: books@troubador.co.uk
Web: www.troubador.co.uk/matador
Twitter: @matadorbooks

ISBN 978 1805140 597

British Library Cataloguing in Publication Data.
A catalogue record for this book is available from the British Library.

Printed and bound by CPI Group (UK) Ltd, Croydon, CR0 4YY
Typeset in 10pt Aldine401 BT by Troubador Publishing Ltd, Leicester, UK

Matador is an imprint of Troubador Publishing Ltd

For my friends in 'Writers Inc',
who have helped me hone the craft of writing,
and have advised me on anything
from the length of a sentence
to the effort of butchering a heifer.

'Once again, Corinne Brixton has vividly brought to life the world, events and people of ancient Israel. In *Temples of Gold* she encompasses the great sweep of time from King Solomon to the rebuilding of Jerusalem after its destruction by the Babylonian King Nebuchadnezzar. Her great skill is to do this by focusing in on the lives of actual people, 'minor' characters imaginatively fleshed out, persuasively and engagingly portrayed against an impeccably researched background. In doing so, and with a light touch, she airs some of the biggest questions: *What is God's meaning in the things that happen? And what might faithful people yet hope for?*'

J. Gordon McConville, *Professor Emeritus, Old Testament Theology, University of Gloucestershire; author of "Exploring the Old Testament" and "Deuteronomy" (Apollos Old Testament Commentary)*

'Corinne Brixton's characteristically thorough Biblical research and natural story-telling ability combine once more in the climax of this trilogy. *Temples of Gold* gives the reader fresh insights through a compelling narrative that is at the same time both moving and a pleasure to read. A great way to learn more about the unfolding purposes of God.'

Revd. Clive Gardner, *Team Vicar of St Mark's, Wimbledon*

Acknowledgements

I could not have written this book without the careful study of the Biblical text that has been previously accomplished by others, who have published their scholarly findings in commentaries and other books. Many of their insights have been incorporated into the writing of *Temples of Gold,* and I am indebted to them for sharing their learning. The main sources of information are listed in the Bibliography at the end. Thanks also go to: Clive Gardner and Angie Blanche, who read and commented on the manuscript as it was evolving; Geoff Burnes, Sue Dowler and Cairine Hart, for their excellent proof-reading; Peter Warne, for using his extraordinary artistic gifts to create the cover design. I am also indebted to Dr. Ralph F. Wilson for allowing me to adapt his map of Jerusalem at the time of Nehemiah (from www. jesuswalk.com) to use in the book.

In addition to all those mentioned above, I will always and most chiefly be grateful to and in awe of the God who has revealed Himself in Scripture and in the lives of flawed men and women down through history.

Acknowledgements

I would like to thank...

Foreword

The Line of Shem trilogy does not seek simply to retell stories that Scripture has already made memorable. It has a two-fold aim. Firstly, to provide background to and commentary on some of those stories, set in a world far removed from our own culture and time and involving many customs and details with which modern readers may be unfamiliar. Secondly, to build up, over the course of the three books, an overview of the main characters and events of the Old Testament. It does this by taking ten 'bit-part players' from pivotal stories across the fifteen hundred years or so of Old Testament history.

Generally, story-telling in Scripture differs in a number of ways from modern styles. One particular difference is that the Bible is fairly scant when it comes to the internal feelings and thoughts of those involved. *The Line of Shem* has, therefore, deliberately chosen characters peripheral to the main stories to lessen the risk of any unintended misrepresentation of the 'main players' in Scripture. In *Temples of Gold,* we meet the last four characters: Hothir, one of the temple musicians; Joah, a palace official at the time of Hezekiah; Nehushta, the wife of King Jehoiakim; and Uzziel, a goldsmith who helped with the rebuilding of Jerusalem's walls. The book begins in the reign of Solomon and goes through to the return from exile described in Ezra and Nehemiah. Each chapter starts with a quote from a book of the Bible to enable the reader to find the original story in Scripture.

The Biblical accounts on which this book is based have been taken as history. This is, after all, what much of the Old Testament claims to be (the text generally making it clear when it is not). Its events are set in a real geographical setting, with plenty of historical details that relate to the times and places in which those stories are set.[1] As one writer has helpfully pointed out regarding the particular period in question:

> '...the basic presentation of almost 350 years of the story of the Hebrew twin kingdoms comes out under factual examination as a highly reliable one, with mention of own and foreign rulers who are real, in the right order, at the right date, and sharing a common history that usually dovetails together well, when both Hebrew and external sources are available.'[2]

Every effort has been made to be as accurate as possible in the historical details included. However, various assumptions have had to be made at times. Notes at the end of each chapter have therefore been included to indicate, as far as possible, where and why any assumptions or choices have been made, and which characters are fictional. This will hopefully enable the reader to distinguish more easily between what comes directly from Scripture and what is artistic licence or conjecture. The notes also contain, where appropriate, historical or archaeological details. It is not necessary to read the notes to enjoy the book, but hopefully they will enrich the experience and enlighten the reader.

A few additional comments are also worth making. Firstly, the personal name of God, *Yahweh* (which translates the Hebrew YHWH), has been used throughout. In most modern Bible translations, YHWH is rendered *the LORD*, reflecting the Jewish practice of reverencing the name of God by not speaking it. It is not clear when this became common practice among the Jews, but certainly there is nothing within the Scriptures themselves to imply that this was the practice during Old Testament times. Therefore, the characters in the stories use the actual, revealed name of God, although *the LORD* is used in the Bible references at the beginning of each chapter.

Secondly, family trees and maps are included for reference. The family trees only include those mentioned in Scripture. Any scales on the maps are in miles for the convenience of the reader.

Thirdly, it is worth remembering that just because the Bible records something, it doesn't mean it approves of it, even if there is no specific comment to that effect within the text itself. Certainly, within the Old Testament there are things that modern readers will find deeply troubling. Sometimes this is because we *are* meant to be troubled by the behaviour described, as it runs contrary to the revealed will of God. At other times, it may be our modern perspectives that need to be challenged. As always, the whole of Scripture must be our guide.

Fourthly—and most importantly—there is, of course, only one place where these stories are told with complete reliability and without error: the Word of God. Any thoughts, words or actions beyond the Biblical narratives are a work of imagination. Hopefully, however, the stories in this book will leave readers with what has been gained in the writing of them: a deeper love for the Scriptures and for the God who inspired them to be written down.

Notes

1. *See, for example, Kenneth Kitchen's extensively researched book, On the Reliability of the Old Testament (Grand Rapids: Eerdmans, 2003).*
2. *Kitchen, p64.*

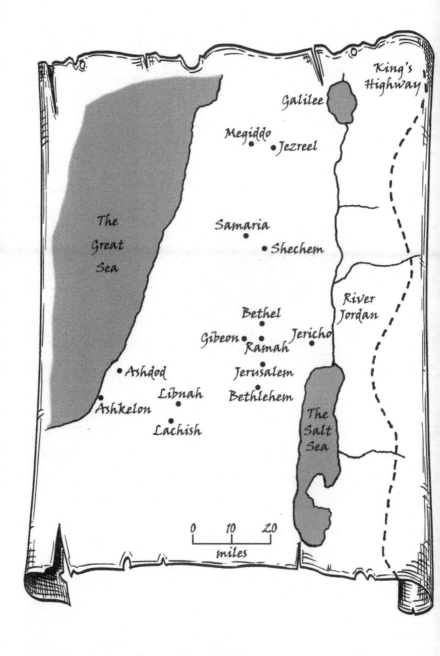

King's Highway

Galilee

Megiddo
• Jezreel

The
Great
Sea

Samaria
• Shechem

Bethel
Gibeon •
Ramah
Jericho

River
Jordan

Ashdod
Jerusalem
Libnah
Bethlehem

Ashkelon
The
Salt
Sea
Lachish

0   10   20
miles

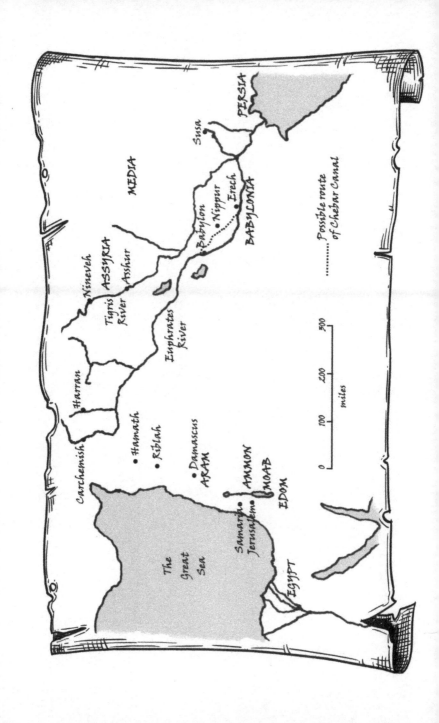

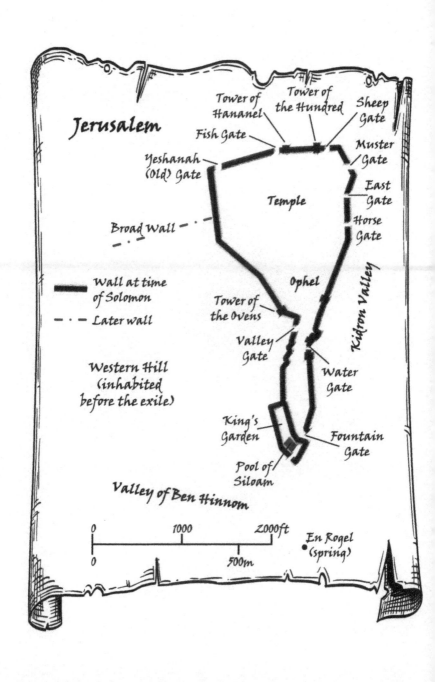

Jerusalem

Tower of Hananel
Tower of the Hundred
Sheep Gate
Fish Gate
Muster Gate
Yeshanah (Old) Gate
East Gate
Broad Wall
Temple
Horse Gate
Wall at time of Solomon
Later wall
Ophel
Kidron Valley
Tower of the Ovens
Valley Gate
Western Hill (inhabited before the exile)
Water Gate
King's Garden
Fountain Gate
Pool of Siloam
Valley of Ben Hinnom

0   1000   2000ft
0   500m

En Rogel (spring)

Hothir

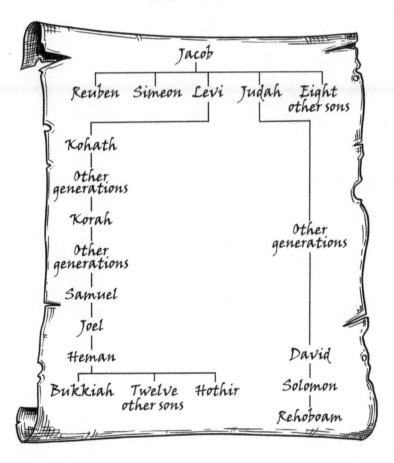

Jacob

Reuben Simeon Levi Judah Eight other sons

Kohath

Other generations

Korah

Other generations

Samuel

Joel

Heman

Other generations

Bukkiah Twelve other sons Hothir

David

Solomon

Rehoboam

I

God gave Heman fourteen sons and three daughters.
(1 Chronicles 25:5)

The day was hot, the coolness of the palace with its stone floors a delicacy to be savoured and enjoyed. It was a rare treat to accompany his father, Heman, to Jerusalem. At just seven years old and with thirteen brothers—all older, save one—there were few privileges or opportunities afforded Hothir. Had he been allowed to roam freely whilst waiting for his father's return, his joy would have been complete. As it was, he had been told—sternly—to stay sitting on the bench and not to move. For a while, he'd stared in awe at the carved cedar panelling and the ornate silver lampstands gracing the hallway. Then his imagination began to conjure up the treasures and secret tunnels that surely lay nearby. His attention, therefore, was not on the task his father had entrusted to him—that of tuning the simple lyre he was now balancing on one knee. His mind wandered as he idly twiddled the tuning pegs. Suddenly, the instrument slid through his fingers and clattered to the ground. It sounded horribly loud on the stone, and the images in his mind's eye of gold gleaming in dark tunnels vanished in a moment. Retribution would surely follow if he'd broken it! Hurriedly he bent down, but his outstretched hands were not the first to reach the lyre. A pair of sandalled feet stopped in front of him—he'd been utterly oblivious of their approach. There were two things that Hothir immediately noticed: clean toenails and the beautiful, embossed patterns gracing the soft leather upon the stranger's feet.

Before he could look up, a hand reached down and picked up the lyre. Hothir's gaze followed the instrument upwards until he found himself staring into the face of a man whom he judged to be of a similar age to his father. The stranger's eyebrows were raised. Then he spoke.

'That is not the way to treat a lyre!' His eyes had a hint of merriment in them, and Hothir dared to hope that he was not about to chided as his

father would have done. The stranger sat down beside him on the bench and examined the lyre carefully. Hothir bit his tongue and waited. 'Fortunately for you, my young friend, it appears that no harm has been done.' He ran his fingers across the strings and grimaced. 'No harm other than to its sound.' He immediately began plucking one string after another whilst twisting the pegs back and forth, causing their pitch to rise and fall. It would have taken all of Hothir's concentration to attempt such a feat, but the stranger conversed easily whilst he tuned the instrument. 'And what is your name?'

'Hothir.'

'And what brings you to the palace today, Hothir?'

'My father is a very important Levite. His name is Heman, and he sings Yahweh's praise at the tabernacle. He's come to see King David today.'

'Ah. And has your father found the king yet?' For reasons that Hothir couldn't fathom, the stranger seemed amused by his own question.

'I don't know. He left me here and went to look for him.'

The lyre's notes began to sweeten under the stranger's touch. 'Is this your first time at the palace?'

'Yes. Usually, one of my older brothers comes. I have twelve of them!'

'Twelve!' exclaimed the stranger. 'I had seven older brothers—and that was bad enough.' There was a twinkle in his eye.

'But I'm not the youngest,' said Hothir quickly. 'I have another brother too.'

'I know.'

Hothir didn't think to ask how he knew. Adults always knew everything, after all.

Rapidly approaching footsteps suddenly drew his attention away from the stranger and the lyre.

'My lord!' There was a look of horror on his father's face.

For the briefest of moments, both the words and his father's expression puzzled Hothir. Then his eyes widened, and his gaze whipped round to the stranger.

'Peace, Heman!' He was holding up his hand, as if to placate the other man.

'I am so sorry, my lord—' continued his father.

'There is no reason for contrition if it is the king himself who chooses to bestow a gift of his time, and to use his hands to help another in the sacred music

with which Yahweh has blessed us.' David paused and a wry smile played upon his lips. 'I know you have many sons to teach, Heman, but this one could do with some training in the tuning of strings!' He winked at the seven-year-old. Hothir grinned and glanced back at his father. Even he was smiling and shaking his head in seeming disbelief. The sweet sound of the lyre drew Hothir's gaze back to the king. Not even his father could make the instrument sing like it was now doing. And with that, Hothir was treated to the king of Israel praising Yahweh with one of his own psalms.

It was not Hothir's earliest memory, but it was his most precious one. But even a score and five years on, remembering his father's mortification as he'd hurried towards the king that day still made him chuckle.

'Hothir!'

His wife's voice pulled him back into the present, the crude lyre he'd held then transforming back into the more ornate instrument that was now in his hands. The smile lingered on his lips.

Deborah was standing with her arms folded. She hadn't finished. 'Is my husband going to spend the entire morning staring at clouds or is he, before he walks to Jerusalem, going to teach his eldest as he vowed he would do last night?'

'I will teach him, if he is now awake and fed.'

'He is just finishing his bread and curds. But as to whether he is awake—' She uncrossed her arms and raised an eyebrow. '—I will leave you to decide.' With that, she turned abruptly and went inside.

Hothir's eyes lingered on the doorway through which she'd disappeared. A smile played on his lips. He sometimes teased Deborah that by the time it came for his father to find a wife for his thirteenth son, all the delicate flowers had already been plucked. Her usual response—after flicking water or wine or whatever was to hand into his face—was to remind him that he was fortunate not to have a wife who easily wilted. *And she was right.* She was not averse to hard work and very little seemed to daunt her. The name of the prophetess who had fearlessly judged Israel some two hundred years earlier had proved apt. She was the fire to his still waters, the clashing cymbal to his gentle lyre. But he loved her, and she had already borne him three boys and a girl.

He turned his attention back to the lyre. Tuning it came as easily to his fingers now as climbing a wall to a lizard's toes. Not that the instrument needed much tuning. He had used it the previous day when he and some of his brothers had played instruments and sung at the New Moon offerings at Gibeon nearby. The tabernacle had resided there ever since the destruction of Shiloh in the days before Saul. It was the same at the start of every month: sacrifices were placed upon the bronze altar made at Sinai in the time of Moses, whilst Levites from the families of Heman and Jeduthun played instruments and sang the praises of the Most High. Their sacred music mingled with the smoke and sweet smells of the burnt offerings rising up into the heavens. David's successor was often in Jerusalem at the New Moon, but not the day before. Solomon had worshipped with them at Gibeon, maybe because its days were numbered, given what was about to happen in Jerusalem.

Hothir strummed the lyre and smiled approvingly. His finger traced one of its smooth arms upwards, following the curve at the top as it curled inwards like a ram's horn, as did the other arm. He was about to start playing when the sound of shuffling fell upon his ears. He looked up. Azarel suddenly stopped when he saw his father. Without a word or glimmer of a reaction, the ten-year-old turned and shuffled back inside before Hothir even had time to say, *Haven't you forgotten something?* Hothir grinned. *If his son was awake, it was barely so.* Azarel reappeared a few moments later, this time carrying a lyre not unlike the one Hothir had used as a boy. Its wood was not decorated, but like his father's, it had two wooden arms of slightly differing lengths on either side of the sound box, with an upper wooden bar that sloped between the tops of the arms. Ten tuning pegs, to which gut strings were attached, ran along the top of the bar, with the other ends of the strings fastened near the base of the sound box, below the thin wooden ridge that raised the strings.

The sun was not yet visible. It would take some time to climb above the walls and roofs of the other buildings in Ramah and for its rays to fall into the courtyard. He edged along the bench so his son could sit beside him. Azarel's unruly hair was sticking out in every direction. Hothir tried—unsuccessfully—to smooth it down. 'Did you sleep well last night—or are you still sleeping?'

'Yes.'

Hothir chuckled for the second time that morning. He suspected that the music lesson might be as fruitless as the small tree that grew in their courtyard. It had yielded a solitary fig the previous year. There was, however, one thing that might rouse his son from his stupor—the thing that had triggered the childhood memory. 'When you have completed today's lesson to my satisfaction, we will go into Jerusalem together.'

It was as if a bronze sistrum had been rattled a handbreadth from Azarel's ear. He immediately sat up. 'To see the building of the temple?'

'Not all of it,' replied Hothir with a laugh. 'But certainly the *start* of the work. I will tell you more on the way there. But first I would like you to show me how well you have practiced the tune *Lilies,* a favourite of your grandfather.'

Azarel's brow furrowed and he pursed his lips together. He slowly began plucking strings.

Hothir sighed and laid his hand over his son's. The strings fell silent. 'But before that, I would like you to show me how well you can tune your lyre…'

Hothir hauled on the rope and the donkey began to move, with Azarel's younger brother Jedaiah sitting astride it. *Not that it had been his intention to take Jedaiah to Jerusalem.* His resolve, however, had been undone by the tears of the seven-year-old when told he was to stay at home. Not for the first time, Deborah duly informed him with a click of her tongue that he was too soft on his sons.

'And you will not forget?' called Deborah after him, bearing Eliel in her arms. Their youngest had been born the previous year and seemed more interested in his mother's milk than in his father's departure.

He half turned as he walked. 'I will not forget.' He then whispered out of the corner of his mouth, 'Remind me, Azarel!' His son grinned. He had promised to buy a trinket in Jerusalem for his daughter. Hannah was two years younger than Jedaiah and stood by the skirt of her mother's tunic, arms crossed and pouting. She was a spark from her mother's fire and knew how to make her displeasure known. *Daughters, however, did not make such trips.*

Hothir would have dearly loved to name his firstborn Samuel son of Hothir, son of Heman, son of Joel, son of Samuel. But being the thirteenth son of his father meant that Heman already had two grandchildren named Samuel and had clearly stated that a third would be one-too-many for his ageing mind. So he had to be content with the knowledge that his firstborn was descended from the great prophet of Israel—the man who had anointed both King Saul and King David—even if he didn't bear his name. They were therefore also descended from Levi and from his eldest son, Kohath, and from Kohath's second son, Izhah. The names of his ancestors flowed through him as naturally as his blood.

He peered up between the houses crowding the narrow street. Clear blue skies graced the second day of the second month of Ziv. *With both the season of rains and the Passover festival behind them, and the warmer summer months ahead, it was a good time to start building.* His musings were cut short.

'Will we see the king today?'

Hothir glanced back at Jedaiah as they passed through the gates of Ramah and onto the track that led southwards towards Jerusalem. 'I expect so. He will want, I am sure, to be watching over the beginning of this great work. His father, David, was planning it for many years.'

'When will the temple be finished?' asked Azarel eagerly.

'Ah. That I cannot tell you, and I am not sure even Solomon himself could answer you. Yahweh alone knows, but it is being built for His glory, and He Himself told King David that his son would build it, so finished it will be and in Solomon's lifetime.' He looked down at his son walking beside him. 'But I would hope it would be finished before Eliel is your age.'

His firstborn was aghast. 'But that's nine years!'

Hothir shrugged. 'Temples are not built in a day—particularly one that needs to be worthy of the God of Heaven.'

Azarel sighed deeply. 'So what will it be like?'

A spirited voice came from behind them. 'It will be made of gold!'

There was scorn in Azarel's reply. 'No, it won't!' He then hesitated and turned to his father. 'Will it?'

'You are both right, my sons. It will be built of stone but decorated with gold aplenty. I am as sure of that as I am that it will be glorious, as indeed it must be as the House of Yahweh. But beyond that, I cannot tell you exactly what it will look like.'

'Why not?'

'Because, my dear Jedaiah, the king has not seen fit to show the plans to me.'

As Hothir continued to lead the donkey south, he listened with amusement as the boys made ever-wilder guesses about the temple, the foundations of which were yet to be laid. Whether there would be lions crafted from solid gold or lampstands bearing a thousand lamps he did not know, although he doubted the former. But he longed for one thing: *a building that would reflect the splendour of the God of Israel, whose exploits had been recounted to him even before he had learned to speak.*

As they passed the place where their track leading south met a turn to the west—the way to Gibeon—his eldest asked, 'Is it true that the sanctuary will be no more once the temple is built?'

'The tabernacle at Gibeon will no longer be needed when Yahweh has a temple in Jerusalem. The ark of Yahweh's covenant is already in the city.'

The words were barely out of his mouth when Azarel asked, 'Is Yahweh no longer at Gibeon then?'

'It is a good question, my son. Yahweh has said that His presence dwells with the ark.' Hothir's eyes danced over the undulating terrain of the hill country, the sun in its brilliance, the clouds that were scattered across the spring skies like sheep across pastureland. 'But Yahweh is also everywhere. How can it be otherwise?' Words and music he had been taught many years earlier began to flow through his mind and out onto his lips. 'As David sang:

9

The earth is Yahweh's, and everything in it,
   the world, and all who live in it.'

He swept out a large arc with his free hand. 'All this is made by
the Creator's hand. He is not confined to a building, and yet He
chooses certain places where we may come before Him with our
worship and our offerings. The tabernacle was one such place and
the temple will be another.'

The words of the psalm stayed with Hothir but for another reason.
'David's words also remind us of the manner of our songs.' Azarel
groaned. 'A lesson as we travel will make our journey pass more quickly.'

'For you.'

Hothir laughed. 'Azarel—you can help your younger brother
with your great learning.' He looked over his shoulder at the donkey
and smiled. Jedaiah's brow was furrowed. *Most likely with doubt. But
his sons were never too young to begin learning their sacred trade.* As he often
reminded them, music was one of Yahweh's greatest gifts, lifting the
heart to heaven when woven together with the treasured truths of the
God of Israel. He turned his attention back to his firstborn. 'Just as
Solomon's temple in all its magnificence will be built by stone upon
stone, how do those words I have sung show us the most common
block from which we build our songs?'

It was imagery that Hothir had used before in teaching his eldest,
and Azarel was ready with his answer: 'We build using pairs of lines;
they both say the same but using different words.'

'Well done, my son.' He turned again. 'So, Jedaiah, listen as your
brother and I sing this psalm. I will sing one line and he will sing the
next. Listen how, as your brother said, our lines will *say the same but
using different words.*' Hothir lifted his voice.

   'The earth is Yahweh's, and everything in it…'
   'The world, and all who live in it,' responded Azarel.
   'For He founded it upon the seas…'
   'And established it upon the waters.'
   'Who may ascend the hill of Yahweh?'
   'Who may…'

When Azarel hesitated, Hothir supplied the missing words: '...*stand in His holy place?*' He turned to Jedaiah once more. 'Do you see?' His younger son nodded solemnly—not unlike the nodding of the donkey as it plodded along the well-worn track—but Hothir doubted he did. He turned forward once more. 'And how do we vary the blocks to make a more beautiful building? Tell me two ways David does this in the psalm.'

'Sometimes the second line adds more meaning to the first—' Azarel thought for a moment. '—so David speaks of those who have clean hands and a pure heart, and then he tells us in the next line who those people are: those who do not worship idols.' He paused again, but then spoke more uncertainly. 'The second line may also contrast with the first?'

'That is true though you will not find it in this psalm. So show me instead from another psalm.' Hothir again supplied the first line.

'*Some trust in chariots and some in horses...*'

Azarel did not hesitate. '*But we trust in the name of Yahweh our God.*'

'We do indeed! But if you are looking for a second precious stone that Solomon's father used to build the first psalm we sang, then you must think of adding lines, where David both repeats an idea and expands it in three or four lines.' Hothir's rich voice rang out across the hill country of Benjamin.

'*Lift up your heads, O you gates;*
   be lifted up, you ancient doors,
   that the King of glory may come in.'

Hothir cast a sideways glance at his son. 'And now I will sing from another psalm of David, a psalm celebrating a famous victory, and you shall sing me the three lines that follow.' Hothir waved his left arm like a banner, as the tune *The Lily of the Covenant* enriched the air around them.

'*God has spoken from his sanctuary:*
   "In triumph I will parcel out Shechem

> *and measure off the Valley of Succoth.*
> *Gilead is mine, and Manasseh is mine;*
> > *Ephraim is my helmet,*
> > *Judah is my sceptre.'"*

Azarel was grinning as his higher, simpler voice continued the song with his favourite three lines:

> *'Moab is my washbasin,*
> > *upon Edom I toss my sandal;*
> > *over Philistia I shout in triumph.'*

But there was an echo from behind them—though slightly less tuneful and as much a shout as a song.

'MOAB IS MY WASHBASIN!'

Hothir chuckled. *It was no surprise that Azarel's brother had picked the line up from him.* 'Thank you, Jedaiah; though I am not sure King David intended it to be sung quite like that!'

The rest of the journey south was passed in Hothir's patient and cheerful tuition of his sons. It was a task he relished, and he often also found himself teaching nephews, when one or other of his brothers despaired of imparting the necessary musical skills to their sons. And it was one of those brothers that Hothir spotted as they neared Jerusalem, making their way past the vast number of workmen's tents pitched on the hills around Jerusalem. A sizeable crowd of onlookers was already there to witness the beginning of the sacred enterprise.

'Hanani! Greetings!'

His brother turned, scrutinising Hothir and his sons before raising an eyebrow. 'Greetings indeed, Brother. Do you make today a feast day for your family?'

'Only for half of them! But have you not also brought your sons to see this great sight?'

Hanani glanced around. 'They are here somewhere—though, unlike you, I have left the young ones at home.'

'Ah, but you are forgetting, Brother: these young ones *are* my older ones!' Hanani was their father's eighth son, and almost ten years Hothir's senior—and often made it known. Hothir went on. 'Has the work on the foundations begun yet?'

'No. Asaph and his sons have sung in praise of Yahweh, but—' He got no further as the sound of trumpets and the blasts of rams' horns rent the air. He only continued when the triumphant peal had faded. 'But I believe it *is* just about to start. Your arrival is timely!'

Hothir craned his neck. Some distance ahead of them, he spotted his fellow Levites, dressed in their white linen tunics, with their instruments now lowered. Beside them was a man whose garments marked him out as royalty and others who appeared to be officials, as well as labourers with tools for digging. Hothir quickly lifted Jedaiah down from the donkey, thrusting its rope into Hanani's hand. 'Here, keep hold of the animal for me. I won't be long.' Before his brother could protest, Hothir was gently worming his way through those in front of him, with Jedaiah's hand in his and Azarel following behind. When there was finally no one blocking the view, Hothir crouched down, his sons on either side of him. He pointed to a man whose arms were raised heavenward. 'Do you see King Solomon?'

'Yes.'

'I see him too,' added Jedaiah eagerly, not to be outdone.

'Is he praying?'

Hothir listened for a moment, but the king was too far away. 'I would imagine, Azarel, he is committing this great work into Yahweh's hands, and asking for the Almighty's blessing and help.'

They fell silent and Hothir strained his ears, but the breeze was bearing the king's words in the wrong direction. When the king lowered his arms, the trumpets and horns were raised once more by the Levites. This time, the blast of the instruments was the signal for the workmen to begin, and picks and shovels were wielded as the laborious task of digging foundations began.

If Hothir had hoped to witness the first of the foundation stones being laid, he soon realised he was to be disappointed. Progress was slow in the rocky terrain around what once had been a threshing floor. The barren, elevated ground to the north of the city walls had been perfect for that purpose. Fairly level rock crowned the top of the hill and there was nothing to impede the winds needed to blow away chaff. The crowds began to mill around, eager to see what they could. With the donkey's rope back in his hand and Jedaiah once more astride the beast, Hothir left Hanani and began working his way to the west of where the foundations were being dug. He glanced south across the area known as the Ophel towards the City of David and stopped.

'Look—it is not only the temple that is being built.' He pointed. 'Can you see the workmen there, Azarel?'

His son squinted in the bright sunlight. 'Are they building a wall?'

'I believe they are. The temple is being built outside the city, but the king will not want it to stay that way. It looks like he is extending the walls of Jerusalem.' But his eyes were drawn away from the sight by a white tunic. A few moments more, and Hothir realised it was inhabited by a familiar face. 'Zaccur!'

The man turned, searching for the one who had hailed him.

Hothir waved. 'Here!' Zaccur's face broke into a smile, and he started making his way towards them. The eldest son of Asaph, one of his father's closest associates, was well known to Hothir. Whilst King David had assigned the task of singing the praises of Yahweh at the tabernacle to the families of Heman and Jeduthun, Asaph's family had been set apart for worship at the tent in Jerusalem in which David had placed the ark. The common calling of the three men wove the families together readily and easily, like the blending of their voices in the songs they sang or of their instruments in the music they played.

Zaccur clapped Hothir on the back when each reached the other. 'Hah! I wondered if any of the sons of Heman would travel here today.'

'I am not the only one of my brothers to do so.'

'And your father?'

'He feels his age—he will come when there is more to see.'

'He is not alone in having passed three score and ten—but my own father has no distance to travel to see the work.' He turned to

Azarel and Jedaiah. 'And have my young friends been practising their music for the day when they will praise Yahweh within the courts of His magnificent temple?' He swept his arm across the open ground behind them, his eyes bright, as if he saw the completed building before him. Jedaiah even twisted his head to look back at the site, as if the temple might have suddenly, by some miracle, appeared out of the spring breeze.

Azarel nodded. 'Yes, Uncle.' Zaccur may not have been one of Hothir's many brothers, but he was treated as such. 'I played *Lilies* for my father this morning on the lyre.'

Zaccur bobbed his head to one side slightly, approvingly. 'Did you, now? That is good.' Azarel flushed.

'He practised and played with more vigour when he learned we were coming here today,' added Hothir.

'We saw the king!' Jedaiah clearly did not want to be left out with nothing to say.

'And did you see his wife?' asked Zaccur.

Hothir smiled wryly. 'Which one?'

'Pharaoh's daughter. I saw her watching from afar with some of her maids.'

It had puzzled Hothir that Solomon should take the daughter of Siamum, king of Egypt, as a wife. He understood that that was the way of kings, forging alliances by marriage with foreign powers— and that even before the death of David, Solomon had an Ammonite wife who had borne him his first son. *But should not such unions be unnecessary for those who ruled under Yahweh? Would not daughters of Israel, who worshipped the same God, make more suitable wives?* Hothir, however, never voiced his perplexities—and wasn't about to start. 'Maybe she wonders if her husband's temple will match those of the gods of Egypt.'

'It will be better!' declared Azarel confidently, despite never having set eyes on Egypt. 'Yahweh is the true God, after all!'

Hothir sighed. 'I fear, however, Azarel and his brother have not seen as much of its building as they would have hoped.'

'Ah, the digging of a hole does not stir the heart greatly, does it?'

'No, Uncle,' replied Jedaiah with feeling.

'Then shall we see if we can do better than a hole for you?' Both boys brightened. 'Why don't you follow me?'

That Zaccur's father, Asaph, regularly mixed with the king's officials meant that their guide had a good knowledge of all that Solomon had done in the three years since the death of King David— and of the best places to see those preparations. The boys were not disappointed, and even Hothir was amazed at what he saw. Although there were no piles of gold to satisfy Jedaiah, the stacks of cedar logs not far from the city could not fail to impress. Hothir and the boys stared at the small mountains of timber.

'The cedar has come all the way from the forests of Lebanon,' explained Zaccur.

'But how?' asked Azarel, wide-eyed. 'That is so far away! Why not use wood from our own forests?'

'To answer your second question first,' began Zaccur, 'we do indeed have wood, but it is not the best—and a temple to honour the God of Israel must have the finest looking and most fragrant panels to adorn it. And no wood is finer than cedar from Lebanon—and no workmanship better than that of the Sidonians.'

'And they willingly give it for the temple?' asked Hothir.

'For a price. Hiram, the king of Tyre, supplied David with cedar, and now he does the same for David's son. But it suits him to do so. Tyre may be rich in both skills and cedar, but it lacks farmland. So anyone who can pay for their wares in wheat and barley, and in wine and oil, is a useful partner.'

'But how do they get the logs here?' asked Azarel once again, with some exasperation. Talk of trade was clearly of far less interest than the wonders of moving such huge logs.

'Peace, Azarel, and I will tell you what I know. After the Sidonians cut the logs, they take them to the Great Sea and lash them together into great rafts that can be floated down as far as Joppa. The overland journey is then more than halved.'

Azarel was still staring at the huge logs. 'But how do they get them from Joppa?'

'Ropes and the sweat of a thousand men.' Zaccur turned to Hothir. 'It is not materials alone that Solomon needs in vast measure. Jerusalem already swarms with workmen. It is said that the king has compelled the labour of one hundred and fifty thousand aliens living in Israel—and seventy thousand of those for carrying alone. Most of the rest are quarrying stone in the hill country. King David may have provided an abundance of gold, silver, bronze and precious stones for the temple, besides timber and stone, but Solomon requires more.'

'But why didn't David build the temple?'

Hothir chuckled. 'My son asks more questions about the temple than his music, but at least he now asks one his father can answer.' He placed his hand on Azarel's shoulder. 'He did not build it because Yahweh told him he could not.'

'Why?'

Hothir raised his eyes to heaven with a little shake of his head and said under his breath, 'And now the younger son asks me to know the mind of Yahweh!' He rested his other hand on Jedaiah. 'I understand that when David charged Solomon to build the temple, he told him that the Almighty did not want hands that had shed so much blood in battle to build His house, but wanted the builder to be a man of peace.'

Zaccur nodded. 'True, Brother, but it was by the hand of David that the kingdom now has rest from its enemies. Solomon can therefore spend his days on building rather than bloodshed and his men can wield saws and chisels rather than swords and spears. David started the work, though it will be Solomon who lays the stones.'

Hothir's gaze drifted to the men digging the temple's foundations, now some distance away. 'And some large stones will be needed.' He turned back to the other man. 'How will they bring the dressed blocks to Jerusalem from the quarry?'

Zaccur's eyes twinkled. 'With exceeding trouble! My brothers and I wonder how they will do it, particularly the foundation stones. But on one thing only are we agreed: it will be a sight to behold!'

Hothir returned his gaze to the labourers, and for several

moments he was silent. Then he spoke. 'But the true foundation of the temple will not be vast blocks of stone. It will rest on Yahweh and His promises to His people.'

There was little point in attempting another lesson on the journey home—a journey that was somewhat delayed by a return to the city when Hothir was reminded by Azarel about the trinket he was meant to be taking back for Hannah. By the end of the visit to Jerusalem, they had learned that the new temple would be not unlike the tabernacle in design, with an altar in the courtyard, a sanctuary with an outer vestibule in which priests would minister, and an inner sanctum—the holy of holies—in which the ark of the covenant would be housed and upon which the Presence of the Almighty would rest. There would also be outer storerooms, and rooms for the priests and Levites when they were ministering there.

The boys were both now on the back of the donkey, with Jedaiah perched between his brother and the animal's head. Their animated chatter rehearsed all that they had seen that day, the torrent of words only stemmed when they paused to fill their mouths from chunks of bread. Hothir had produced the loaf, baked that morning, from the bag slung over his shoulder. It now held only the small string of beads destined to grace his daughter's neck.

Hothir's mind, however, was not so much on the temple as its builder. Despite Solomon's youth—he had seen the passing of not much more than a score of years—few doubted the great wisdom he already possessed. All Israel had heard of how the king's judgment had skilfully resolved a dispute between two harlots and two infants, one living and one dead. Both claimed the child that yet breathed was theirs, but it was only one woman's word against the other. Hothir was sure that neither he nor any other in all Israel would have given the command that had come from the king's lips as he called for a sword: *divide the living child in two, and give half to one and half to the other.* And yet the command had drawn compassion from one woman and callousness from the other, revealing the true mother. Instead of the sword dividing, it had reunited the child with the one who had borne it, who had cried out for it to be given to the other woman rather than slaughtered. The king demonstrated wisdom beyond his years—yet all knew from whence it came: the God who had appeared to the young king at Gibeon, equipping him to bring justice to the low-born and well as the high.

Hothir was now convinced he had seen that wisdom yet again, not in a single judgment, but in the skilful planning and ordering of both men and materials witnessed that day. He remembered hearing that before David died, he had charged Solomon to walk in the ways of God, written in the Law of Moses, so that he would prosper in all things. *Surely there was nothing wiser than to walk before Yahweh in love and obedience—whether you were a humble Levite or the king of all Israel!* The words of his sons' chatter faded in his ears and a melody flowed through his mind. The couplets of the psalm became a prayer in his heart:

Endow the king with your justice, O God,
  the royal son with your righteousness.
May he judge your people in righteousness,
  your afflicted ones with justice.
May the mountains bring prosperity to the people,
  the hills the fruit of righteousness.

Notes

1. *The events in this chapter take place around 967 BC. The dating for the kings in this book is based on the chronology of Leslie McFall (a former lecturer in Old Testament at Belfast Bible College), who built upon the earlier studies of Edwin Thiele. The doctoral dissertation of the latter, 'The Chronology of the Kings of Judah and Israel', was later published in an expanded version as 'The Mysterious Numbers of the Hebrew Kings'. This dating is also largely followed by Kenneth Kitchen and others. Although some criticise the work of Thiele and McFall because of a lack of evidence of the co-regencies upon which their harmonisation of dates*

depends, nevertheless co-regencies are explicitly seen in the cases of David and Solomon, and Uzziah and Jotham. The fact that their harmonisation, as well as following the years of the kings recorded in Scripture, also ties in well with external dates from other ancient Near Eastern sources seems enough reason to adopt it—especially given that any alternative chronologies seem less satisfactory.

2. *Hothir and his father, Heman, are Levites. Heman's genealogy in 1 Chronicles 6:33-38 is traced back to Kohath, one of the sons of Levi. However, the genealogy also includes Samuel the prophet, despite Samuel's father, Elkanah, being described as an Ephraimite in 1 Samuel 1:1. It is likely, then, that the term 'Ephraimite' refers to Elkanah's geographical location or birthplace, rather than his tribal ancestry, given that he is said to come from 'the hill country of Ephraim'. Although Elkanah and Samuel's home, Ramah, is described as being in Benjamin (Joshua 18:25), the reference to Saul travelling to Samuel's city ('in the land of Zuph', a reference to one of Samuel's ancestors) in 1 Samuel 9:4-6, may suggest it is at the edge of Benjamin's territory. Ramah isn't listed as one of the Levitical cities, but the non-priestly Kohathites are allocated four cities in Ephraim (Joshua 21:20-22) at the time of the conquest of Canaan. However, at the time of Samuel, 450 years had passed since the conquest, and migration of the Levites may have occurred, particular after the upheavals in the time of Judges. For example, the Levite mentioned in Judges 17:7 is described as being from Bethlehem, although this was not a Levitical town. Interestingly, however, Jeremiah, who was from a priestly family and who lived around 600 BC, was still living in Anathoth, one of the cities given to the sons of Aaron by Joshua (Joshua 21:18, Jeremiah 1:1).*

3. *It is stated in 1 Chronicles 25:5 that Heman had fourteen sons and three daughters, 'given to him through the promises of God to exalt him'. There is no further information about the nature of these promises, or whether the children were given through a number of wives.*

4. *There are no references in the corresponding Biblical narratives to the ages of any of the characters, including Solomon. The age of Solomon is based on a 'best-guess' chronology of the life of David, including the point at which he married Bathsheba, Solomon's mother. It has been assumed that Solomon was around nineteen or twenty at the time of his accession to the*

throne. The ages of Heman and his sons are chosen to fit in with the limited information known, namely that Heman was ministering as a Levite at the time the ark was brought up to Jerusalem (1 Chronicles 16:37-42), probably around 1001 BC, but was also present at the dedication of the temple in 2 Chronicles 5:12, around 42 years later in 959 BC.

5. *The description of the lyre is based on what has been referred to as the 'Lyre of Megiddo', a depiction of the instrument on a Late Bronze Age (approximately 1600-1200 BC) ivory, recovered by an archaeologist working in northern Israel. The instrument is shown as having nine strings and its player is in Canaanite dress. Remarkably, a similar-looking wooden lyre—believed to be Egyptian and dated to around 1500-1300 BC—was discovered and is preserved in Leiden in the Netherlands, although the strings have, of course, perished.*

6. *That the Levites were required to be trained in singing and that there were both teachers and pupils is referenced in 1 Chronicles 25:7-8. It seems from David's appointment of Heman, Asaph and Ethan (Jeduthun) in 1 Chronicles 15:17-18, that there were other relatives 'next in rank' appointed as musicians and singers under them. Whether these were close relatives or simply other Levites is not clear. However, this may account for how each division of musicians, appointed at the time of David and listed in 1 Chronicles 25:7-31 (including that of Hothir, 'his sons and his relatives'), comprised twelve people.*

7. *It is not clear what state the tabernacle was in at the time of the construction of the temple. 1 Chronicles 21:29 refers to it being at Gibeon, and to the bronze altar of burnt offering also being there. Clearly the ark was already in Jerusalem at this time.*

8. *1 Kings 6:1 fixes the date of the start of the building work on the temple as the second month (Ziv) of the fourth year of Solomon's reign, which is generally taken to be 967 BC. As this is also stated to be 'the four hundred and eightieth year after the Israelites came out of Egypt', this has led to the so-called Early Date for the Exodus as 1446 BC.*

9. *There are scant details on the methods of construction used in the building of the temple. 1 Kings 6:37 speaks of the foundation of the temple being laid, but unlike 1 Kings 7:10, which gives the dimensions of the foundation stones for the palace ('some measuring ten cubits and some eight', i.e. 4.5m*

and 3.6m), there are no details of the size of the foundation stones for the temple, or how they might have been put alongside or upon the existing threshing floor. These dimensions do, of course, beg the question of how such huge stones were moved in the ancient world. The following article from National Geographic has some interesting ideas about such challenges, but given the lack of certainty, it has seemed best to avoid too much speculation in this story. https://on.natgeo.com/3lAhw18

10. No conclusive archaeological remains of Solomon's temple have ever been found, but, as Kenneth Kitchen points out: 'This is hardly surprising, given (1) the thorough destruction of Jerusalem's official buildings by the Babylonians in 586, (2) the reuse of the site in the Persian period, and then (3) the massive redevelopment of the site and total rebuilding of both the temple and the surrounding precincts in Herod's time. Plus (4) Roman destruction and Byzantine and Muslim buildings since then, and (5) the practical impossibility of digging archaeologically in the present precinct.' (On the Reliability of the Old Testament, p122). However, Kitchen goes on to demonstrate that the general size, scale, layout and building materials for the temple, as described in Kings and Chronicles, accord well with what is known of similar structures elsewhere in the world of the ancient Near East during the third to first millennia BC.

11. The pharaoh whose daughter married Solomon (1 Kings 3:1) is likely to be Siamum, who was the last ruler of 21st dynasty (dying in 960/959 BC) whose international standing may have been relatively weak. An alliance with Solomon would have, therefore, been beneficial to Siamun, who in return gave the city of Gezer to Solomon as part of the dowry (1 Kings 9:16). Gezer was a strategic city on a principal road, and so presumably both sides would have seen the alliance as being advantageous, particularly against the Philistines. However, the narrator makes no comment on the alliance. Deuteronomy 17:16 warned the people against returning to Egypt, and yet Egyptian influence is brought by Solomon into Jerusalem. Foreign wives come to exert a serious and detrimental influence over Solomon later in his reign.

12. Capitalisation is following the practices of the NIV Bible translation, which capitalises 'Holy Place' (except in Psalm 24 where it may be more of a general reference), but not 'ark of the covenant'.

13. *The psalms quoted in this chapter (in the order in which they occur) are 24, 20, 60 (or 108, which has some identical verses), and the chapter finishes with a quote from Psalm 72. Although this psalm is attributed to Solomon, it could also be for Solomon.*

14. *Imagined named characters introduced in this chapter are Deborah, Azarel, Jedaiah, Hannah and Eliel.*

Then Solomon summoned to Jerusalem the elders of Israel, all the heads of the tribes and the chiefs of the Israelite families, to bring up the ark of the LORD's covenant from Zion, the City of David. And all the Israelites came together to the king at the time of the festival in the seventh month. (2 Chronicles 5:2-3)

Hothir stood silently in the large courtyard, the lengthy practice for the following day over. The sky above him began to turn from the bright blue of the early autumn day into the softer hues of evening, the white clouds now tinged with the colours of sunset. Men were milling around nearby—priests, other Levites like himself, officials of the king—but none spoke in anything other than a hushed tone. *To do so would feel inappropriate on the holy ground on which they now stood.* The temple may not have been dedicated yet, but it had been built for Yahweh, and, at least in Hothir's mind, should therefore be treated as such.

He had watched the temple grow over the previous seven years, even as his own sons and daughter had grown in stature and their number had been swelled by the births of two more. But now the temple stood as complete as he suspected his family would be, with Solomon having followed exactly the plans revealed to his father David. Some with brooms were sweeping the stones of the courtyard, but he was sure they would be doing so again early the next morning before the ceremony, when hundreds, if not thousands, would stand before the temple to dedicate it to the God of Israel. A lone sparrow caught his attention as it hopped around the ground, searching for any morsel of food, though Hothir doubted it would find any. The approach of a broom drove the little bird into the air in the blink of an eye. Hothir's gaze, however, did not follow it far, lingering instead on the huge doors that stood ajar within the portico that formed the entrance to the temple.

Despite his longing to draw closer, maintaining a respectful distance felt more fitting. To the left and right of the steps leading up to the doors, two massive bronze columns, tall and majestic as cedars of Lebanon, rose up, reaching to the roof of the portico. The tops of both pillars resembled lilies and were decorated with chainwork and pomegranates cast in bronze. An image flashed into Hothir's mind from the previous year. He had taken all his sons north to Succoth and to the plain around the Jordan River. The furnaces for the bronze had been located there; the clay ground had been perfect for making the moulds for casting not only the pillars, but other items for the temple, including Solomon's impressive new altar. At the sight of the molten metal being poured from the crucible into clay casings, Jedaiah had murmured that it was as if the sun itself had been captured by the craftsmen, with the heavens coming to earth for the worship of Yahweh. *He had the makings of a fine poet.*

The two pillars had been called Jachin and Boaz, their names meaning *He establishes* and *in Him is strength*. But it was between them that Hothir now peered. The bronze looked dull in comparison with the gold that overlaid the doors. Each door was made of two cedar panels which could fold in on each other, and each panel was adorned with carvings of the strange-looking cherubim, as well as the more familiar palm trees and open flowers. Thin sheets of gold had then been carefully hammered over all their contours until no wood could be seen. The interior beyond the doors was now dim in the evening light. That, together with its elevation, made it all but impossible to see the treasures within: the ten lampstands looking like flower-covered trees, the altar for the burning of incense and the table for the bread of the presence, all crafted from the finest gold. But Hothir had caught sight of the Holy Place earlier in the day when the bright morning sunlight had streamed inside directly from the east. The brief glimpses had been glorious. The light had reflected off not only the walls but also the doors which led into the

Holy of Holies beyond. Everywhere and everything was gold. He would never walk on the gilded floors beyond the outer doors—only priests were permitted there—but many in Israel would not even come close enough to glimpse what he had seen. *The outer doors, visible to any in the courtyard, were at least, a whisper of the glories within.*

Hothir tore his eyes away from the temple. Although the placing of its stones and the hanging of its doors had been completed almost a year earlier, the furnishing had taken another eleven months, but by design as much as necessity. It meant that the dedication and the accompanying sacrifices could happen just before the Feast of Tabernacles in the seventh month. To Hothir, who was used to singing the praises of Yahweh beside the bronze altar at Gibeon, Solomon's altar on the north side of the courtyard seemed vast—four times the length and breadth of that made by Moses and over three times as high. Whilst the sacrifices at the tent of meeting could easily be laid upon the altar's fire, the temple's altar required a slope leading up to the bronze grating at the top on which fire would be kindled for the burnt offerings.

But now the final lamb had been offered at Gibeon. The evening sacrifice would have been made a short while earlier, with some of Hothir's older brothers singing praises as the smoke and aroma of the roasting meat had risen to heaven. The old bronze altar, the sacred utensils, and whatever else remained of the tabernacle that had served them for five hundred years, were to be borne by priests to Jerusalem where they would be stored within the temple courts. The ark had, of course, already been brought to the city some forty years earlier by David and had dwelt in a tent since then. Its destiny, however, was to rest at the very heart of the new temple. Hothir's eyes then fell on a platform in the centre of the courtyard, erected a few days earlier. It had the same dimensions as the bronze altar at Gibeon—five cubits square and three high—but with a very different function. It would allow Solomon to be both seen and heard by the crowds that would fill the courtyard and beyond.

Hothir started as a hand suddenly clasped his shoulder.

'Come, Brother, we want to eat! All the preparations today have made us hungry!'

He turned to see Mallothi, the brother closest to him in age. 'Is the meal ready?'

'It has been for some time!' His broad smile continued as his gaze left Hothir's face and swept around the temple courts. 'It is a marvellous sight, is it not?'

'A sight to make the heart both soar and thunder.' Both stood in silence for several moments, drinking in the glory of the finished temple.

'But our bellies are thundering too, and the temple will still be here tomorrow when we return. Come, let's join the others and eat.'

Hothir followed his brother out of the temple courtyard and away from the mount on which it sat. They then made their way through the crowds filling the streets of the recently enlarged city, before leaving it through one of the gates set into the new walls. The myriad tents around Jerusalem were no longer those of the army of workmen, but shelters for those who had come to witness the temple's dedication—or take part in it, as was the case for Hothir and his brothers. The families of both Heman and Jeduthun and their relatives were now to join those of Asaph in the task of supplying music and singing to accompany the worship at Jerusalem, and all were to be on duty the following day.

'You found him then, Mallothi.' Mahazioth, Hothir's only younger brother, was crouched over a pot nestling within a small fire.

'It was not difficult.'

Hothir smiled. 'There was no better place to be—and besides, I'd told you where I was going.'

Mahazioth gave the stew a final stir and then rested the spoon in a bowl beside the fire. All around them, evening meals were being prepared in a similar fashion, so that both smoke from the wood and the smells of cooking mingled in the air around them. Rather than the hushed exchanges of the temple courtyard, there was laughter and lively conversation.

The aroma from the pot stirred Hothir's stomach. 'What are we eating?'

'We are eating whatever vegetables and beans my wife gave me to put in the pot, with bread that she baked this morning.' Mahazioth paused to use a sturdy stick to lift the blackened pot by its handle from the arrangement of burning firewood on which it had been carefully balanced. He glanced over to the tents of their older brothers. 'But Hanani has meat in his pot.'

With all fourteen sons of Heman sharing provisions brought from their homes, the meal was more like a feast. It had been some years since they had all eaten together, and they were joined by the sons of Hothir's oldest brothers who were also now of age to serve at the temple. The jubilant mood sprang from joyful anticipation of what lay ahead, and there was wine to gladden their hearts, though prudence prevailed, especially under the eye of Bukkiah, the firstborn among them.

As the meal was concluded by dates that Deborah had packed into Hothir's bag, he suddenly tapped the ground beside him. 'I do not know if I will be able to sleep tonight.'

Hanani spat out the stone from his date. 'If your bones and flesh object to the hardness of the ground, you should have been born into the house of Asaph. They will get to sleep in their own beds tonight in Jerusalem.' Some of his brothers laughed.

'The temple hasn't room enough for all the priests who have travelled here for the dedication,' continued Mallothi, 'let alone for the families of Heman and Jeduthun.'

'Though it is as well that Father has been found a bed there,' added Mahazioth. 'At four score years he would not welcome stony ground this night.'

Bukkiah looked at the youngest across the dying fire. 'Our fathers spent forty years in tents in the desert—and Moses was eighty when they left Egypt. Have we grown so soft that we can no longer sleep out under the stars?'

'The Almighty has given us the Feast of Tabernacles each year to remind us,' replied Hothir, 'and we will still be here for that after the dedication. But hard ground will not be the reason for keeping me awake. Surely tomorrow will be the greatest day in our lives, and our task will never be a more sacred one.' He looked around at his brothers. 'Are any of us truly equal to it?' Each fell silent and Hothir stared at the glowing embers, all that was left of the fire over which Hanani's goat stew had been cooked. The evening was warm and the little heat remaining in the fire was not needed. Somewhere nearby a lyre was being tuned.

'Still, a soft bed would be nice!' The moment of solemnity was passed, and Hothir was the first to laugh at his younger brother's retort.

'Have you seen inside the chambers around the temple yet, Bukkiah?' asked another brother.

'I have indeed. Together they may exceed the sanctuary itself in size. The temple needs not only to accommodate those serving there, but also to store all that is needful for worship, as well as the city's treasures. That is why there are three levels of rooms that wrap around the north, south and west sides of the sanctuary.'

'And why so many of our brothers are now gatekeepers for the temple,' added Hanani. 'They will guard not only its sanctity but also its gold.'

Both David and Solomon had appointed Levites for roles other than worship: treasurers, scribes and judges as well as gatekeepers. Hothir smiled to himself. 'But do not the sons of Heman have the best duty of all—one that is a joy as well?'

'You have spoken truly, my brother,' replied Hanani. And as the sound of a lyre floated into their gathering, his eyes twinkled. 'And is it not time to show those sons of Jeduthun who can handle instruments most ably?'

And before Hothir and his brothers took to their beds, the tents pitched on that side of Jerusalem were blessed with a selection of Israel's songs played and sung by some of its finest musicians.

A full belly had helped Hothir sleep better than he had anticipated, but he still woke before dawn. Any stupor was swiftly dispelled by the import of the day. Mallothi was soon stirring too, and all four who had shared the tent rose as the grey morning twilight began to give shape to the tents around them and the walls of Jerusalem nearby. After a simple and hasty meal of bread, curds and cakes of raisins to sustain them through what would be a long day, they made their way towards the east side of the city and to the spring of Gihon. They were not the only ones washing in the cool waters that left Hothir shivering. Clean bodies were fitting not only for the sacredness of their service but also for the preservation of the pristine linen in which they were to be clothed.

'The city, like us, has awoken early,' commented Hothir, as the brothers made their way back into Jerusalem, instruments in their hands. The streets were already thronging with people.

'Little wonder,' replied Mallothi. 'I doubt it has ever seen a day like today.'

'Or ever will again.' Hothir held his lyre closer to his body. *Now was not the time for it to be damaged by a careless elbow.* 'And Solomon's new streets will never have borne so many feet.' The king had summoned to the city the elders of Israel, the heads of the tribes, the leaders of families—and all the men of Israel. There was little hope that even Solomon's enlarged city could hold so many.

'It is as well we rose when we did,' said Mahazioth. 'The crowds may soon be pressed together as closely as raisins in a cake!'

The mere thought of not being in place in time knotted Hothir's stomach. The temple, now the highest point of the city, was, for the moment, hidden from his view in the narrow streets. But they were moving ever-upward, and suddenly the buildings were gone. They had reached the outer courtyard to the east of the temple, and once again only the expanse of the sky lay above them. The tops of the two bronze pillars flanking the temple porch, now visible above the courtyard wall, were shining in the light of the rising sun. A memory stirred. Hothir recalled his first day serving at the tabernacle in Gibeon; his heart had swelled as he'd walked in through its gates, no longer just a worshipper but a Levite chosen and set apart by Yahweh for His sacred service. Whether his brothers felt that same sense as they passed through the temple gates, Hothir did not know. But all of them fell silent as the temple rose before them in all its glory, its golden doors dazzling in the morning sun.

The moment of awe passed quickly, as faces became familiar and the necessary preparations came to the fore. The temple courtyard was no longer hushed as it had been the previous evening. Priests and other Levites were entering the rooms around the temple, others emerging freshly clad in spotless tunics made of the finest Egyptian linen. Instruments were being tuned, and their sounds mingled with the occasional bleating of sheep and goats tethered to one side along with oxen. The numerous beasts were destined to become the first offerings upon the huge altar, the immaculate bronze of which would not remain unblemished for much longer.

Hothir followed Bukkiah into one of the rooms nearby. Soon he, too, returned to the sunlight, wearing a new linen tunic and grasping his lyre. As their father had pointed out, it was scarcely fitting for the temple to be clothed in cedar from Lebanon and purest gold and yet its servants to be clothed in worn wool. Hothir joined his father and brothers, standing in a group amongst the growing multitude of musicians, made up of both priests and Levites. His palms were already sweaty. His brothers' words washed over him as he ran his fingers over the instrument's strings, checking yet again, if needlessly, that their notes rang true. As he did so, he rehearsed in his mind once more the instructions issued the previous day. It was only when the murmuring around him swiftly died away that Hothir looked up. He followed his brothers' gaze. Azariah, the high priest, had emerged. The gold in his tunic and upon his turban together with his breastplate of twelve gems immediately set him apart from all others.

'Asaph—are you, your sons and your relatives all ready?'

'We are, my father.'

The same question was asked of Jeduthun and received the same answer. But when the high priest came to Hothir's father, he smiled. 'Heman. Are you and your sons ready—all fourteen of them?' The blessing that Yahweh had bestowed upon him was well-known.

'We are, my father—I have counted them myself, together with my grandsons who are of age.' Hothir beamed, and he was not alone in doing so among his brothers.

Soon the three Levite families and those under them were following Azariah and one hundred and twenty priests, also clad in linen tunics but bearing long silver trumpets. The crowds parted for them, even if with some difficulty, as they processed down through the streets towards the city of David—Jerusalem as it had been under Solomon's father. Somewhere in the throng—though whether within the city's walls or without them, Hothir did not know—were his own four sons. *Hopefully all behaving themselves under the watchful eye of Azarel.* Deborah had protested that Joseph, not yet seven, was too young and would likely get lost in the crowd. Hothir had brushed it off, telling her that he knew both the name of his father and his grandfather, and that would be enough for any in Jerusalem who found him wandering to reunite him with his family. He stated firmly that the temple would only be dedicated once, and none of his sons who would one day serve in its courts should miss the occasion. For once, Deborah had no choice but to relent. The face of Michal, their youngest, mimicked perfectly the pout she had learned from her older sister.

Hothir could see his father near the front of the procession, as he had been the last time the ark was moved. Then, his father's years had been much the same as his own. But now Heman was eighty, and yet his step was sure and his frame still erect. Hothir pondered one of David's psalms of praise, which spoke of youth being renewed like that of the eagle. *Was he seeing the truth of that in his father's life?* The thought was fleeting.

Hothir craned his neck slightly as they came to a halt near the place where the ark had dwelt for over forty years. Smoke was rising to heaven as sacrifices were being offered before the final journey of Israel's precious treasure. He soon picked out Solomon, dressed in his robes, with Rehoboam, his thirteen-year-old firstborn at his side. But it was another sight that held his gaze. He drew in a sharp breath. The ark, draped in a bright blue cloth, was being lifted to shoulder height on long golden poles by the four priests who were to bear it the short distance to the temple. His heart leapt. *Here was the ark, crafted under Moses, which held the two stone tablets upon which the finger of Yahweh had written the commandments that formed the heart of His covenant with Israel!*

They waited and then turned about as a trumpet sounded. Hothir fingered his lyre as they waited once more, desperately hoping he would not forget any of the instructions they had been given.

If the downhill procession had been largely silent, the return to the temple could not have been more different. Silver trumpets were lifted to the mouths of the priests, and as the blasts rang out, they began to move forward. Although it had not been heard for many years, the shout that had, from the time of Moses, always accompanied the setting out of the ark rang out loudly: *Rise up, Lord! May your enemies be scattered; may your foes flee before you.*

Hothir's fingers began plucking the strings of his lyre. Zaccur son of Asaph clashed loud cymbals together again and again. The sound was as a slow heartbeat, and the only thing that kept Hothir's instrument in time with the others, given the blasting of the trumpets and the enthusiastic shouting of the crowd. Every surface upon which feet could stand seemed to be occupied, and where there were windows in upper rooms, women and children waved wildly and added their voices to those of the men below. Even if the heavens had thundered, Hothir was not sure their voice would have been heard above the exuberance of that short journey. His fingers danced over the strings as he picked out the tune. Whether any would hear it or not didn't matter. *He was playing for the glory of Yahweh and only the Almighty's ears needed to hear his playing.* Although his lips were unmoving, his heart took wings and mounted up like an eagle in praise to the God of Israel, the God of all the earth.

It was only when they'd entered the courtyard of the temple, passing the gatekeepers standing both alert and erect, that they stopped as the ark drew level with the altar. Hothir and the rest of the Levites moved to the east side of the altar, facing the temple, as crowds surged into the courtyard and the sacrifices began again.

Hothir had been at Gibeon the day Solomon had worshipped there at the beginning of his reign. It was said afterwards that he had offered a thousand burnt offerings upon Moses' bronze altar. As midday came and went, Hothir was convinced that the sacrifices exceeded those of that occasion. He was also glad that the height of summer had passed, or it might have been unbearable, given the heat from the altar fire. Although his fingertips had been toughened by decades of playing, they began to feel sore. He had never played for so long at once and with such vigour, and he was relieved when the sacrifices were finally over—at least for the moment—and his fingers and voice could have some respite, though it would not be for long.

A sacred stillness descended upon the courtyard. Somehow it seemed to spread out from the temple over the whole city. The moment had come for the priests to lift the ark aloft for the last time. Now that the land finally had rest from its enemies and was secure, the sacred chest was to be carried to its own final resting place. Still covered in the blue cloth that would only be removed away from any onlookers, the ark was raised once more on its poles. The weight of the moment was not lost on Hothir. The small box, which not only carried the covenant between the God of Israel and His people but also symbolised His presence, was to disappear from view forever. From the moment its bearers deposited it within the holy of holies, it would be hidden from all but Azariah and the high priests who would follow him. And even then, they would only see it once a year on the Day of Atonement.

Suddenly an intense ache that he barely understood gripped Hothir's heart. *God would be in their midst within Solomon's temple, and yet beyond the reach of sinful men and women. Dwelling with them and yet apart from them. Near to them and yet remote. Could it ever be otherwise?* To Hothir, his question seemed answered already—and yet it lingered deep within.

After a few brief moments, the priests disappeared between the golden doors—and the ark was gone. As they waited and the stillness lingered, a tiny movement caught Hothir's eye. A swallow swooped down upon the temple, disappearing from his sight behind the top of the porch. It didn't reappear. *Had it nested earlier in the year somewhere on the temple's roof? Did the Almighty allow the tiny bird to dwell closer to His presence than any human?* The thought went no further, for in that moment, the four priests emerged into the courtyard. Those bearing the trumpets lifted the instruments to their lips once more. It was the signal for the praise to begin again and the worship within the sanctuary to commence. Once again, Hothir lifted his lyre, but this time—accompanied by cymbals and timbrels, harps and lyres—the three Levite families sang in unison words that David had taught to Asaph when the ark had come to Jerusalem: *Give thanks to Yahweh, for He is good; His love endures for ever.*

Priests began making their way up the steps to begin their duties within the temple: lighting the lamps on the lampstands, setting out the sacred bread on the table and offering the sweet-smelling incense on the altar of gold. But they never entered. As the words *endures for ever* left Hothir's lips, a shout suddenly went up. The trumpets stopped as did the fingers of Hothir and his brothers. He looked up sharply, turning his face towards the point on which every eye seemed to be fixed: the entrance to the temple. The priests, bearing the firepans filled with live coals for the altar of incense, were hurrying down the steps, wide-eyed, as were those carrying the bread of the presence and the vessels holding the precious incense. Their faces bore some mixture of astonishment and alarm. Whispers rippled around the courtyard, like the rustling of wind through the leaves of a tree.

From where he was standing, Hothir could see the left-most golden doors of the Holy Place, folded back, though not much beyond them. The skin on the back his arms suddenly became as uneven as that of a plucked bird, and its hairs stood erect as he heard the exclamations of the priests: *The cloud!* He needed no further explanation—it was Yahweh's glory filling the temple, just as it had the tabernacle at its dedication. *Yahweh Himself had come!* The whispers rapidly petered out, and a holy hush enveloped the gathering. This was the sign of Yahweh's presence with His people, just as their forefathers had seen the cloud that led them for forty years from Egypt to the Promised Land. *Surely the temple was now truly complete!*

Hothir stood transfixed—until the king mounted the platform in the middle of the courtyard. He stood facing the temple and called out in a loud voice, 'Yahweh has said that He would dwell in a thick cloud. I have built You a magnificent house, a place for You to dwell for ever!' Then Solomon turned to face them all. 'Blessed be Yahweh, the God of Israel, who with His own hand has fulfilled what His own mouth spoke to my father, David.'

As Solomon spoke of Yahweh's choice of not only Jerusalem but also the House of David, and the fulfilment of His promise to David that his son would both sit on his throne and build the temple, Hothir's eyes were not on the king. They rested on the entrance to the temple, beyond which was the wondrous yet fearsome sign that the living God was in their midst.

Then, in the presence of all those assembled, Solomon faced the temple again and knelt. He spread out his hands towards heaven and prayed to the Almighty. 'O Yahweh, God of Israel, there is no god like You in heaven above or on the earth below, keeping Your covenant and showing love to Your servants who walk before You with all their heart.' Hothir silently echoed the words of the king, that Yahweh would hear the entreaties of His people as they prayed toward His temple. It was not difficult to be stirred by Solomon's prayer. It was like a rich fabric with a recurring pattern: the gold threads of pleas for Yahweh to hear from heaven and to forgive, interwoven with the darker colours of misfortune or judgment. The darkest threads were Solomon's words describing exile in a foreign land, but even these were followed by the gold of gracious forgiveness. As Hothir echoed the words, he struggled to comprehend both how God's people might sin so greatly and yet still be fully forgiven through the mercy of Yahweh.

But his pondering was brought to an abrupt end. Solomon had barely spoken the last words of his prayer when light suddenly flashed, and heat hit Hothir's face. A sound like thunder filled his ears. Blazing fire was falling from heaven upon the altar, consuming in an instant the meat of the sacrifices. Almost immediately, Hothir and every man around him were on their knees with their faces to the ground. Hothir's heart pounded. *He had seen the hand of Yahweh with his own eyes!* Above the roar of the flames, the words that he and his brothers had sung only a short while earlier began to be taken up by the lips of the prostrate worshippers, and the chant grew and grew: *He is good; His love endures for ever!*

As Hothir's forehead rested on the stone of the courtyard, cooling the heat of his reddened face, wonder and thanksgiving overflowed within, like a cup running over. *Yahweh Himself had both accepted their offerings and given His approval to Solomon's temple.* But as Hothir worshipped and marvelled and trembled at the God of Israel in their midst, words from the king's prayer lingered in his mind, for their truth burned within: *Will God indeed dwell on earth? Behold, the heaven and the highest heaven cannot hold You. How much less this house!*

The rest of the day, as well as the week of dedication and the Feast of Tabernacles that immediately followed, passed by in a joyful if exhausting blur of singing and sacrifices, feasting and sore fingers. Hothir was at the temple most days. More of the temple courtyard had to be consecrated for sacrifices, as the new bronze altar simply could not hold the vast numbers of burnt offerings, grain offerings and fat from the peace offerings—an extravagance fitting the God of Israel. Their abundance was matched only by the greatness of Jerusalem's joy.

Hothir's own gladness of heart was magnified by the privilege of being able to stand in the temple courts as he served. At times, he was almost overwhelmed by the honour bestowed on his father's family. *Yahweh Himself had chosen them through David and Solomon!* He had, however, smiled to himself more than once when a lowly sparrow or swallow had entered the courtyard, as if to humble him. *It was those with a pure rather than proud heart who could dwell on Jerusalem's holy hill. Did not one of David's own psalms say as much?*

Despite his fatigue, it was still with some wistfulness that he helped pack up the tent which had been their home for two weeks and load it onto the cart that was travelling back to Ramah with Bukkiah. He would return to Jerusalem soon enough when he was on duty again at the temple—and then he would stay in one of its rooms. But now they had to plunge themselves into the streams of pilgrims leaving Jerusalem and its temple to return to their homes across Israel. Hothir paused to take one final look back over his shoulder as he, Mallothi and Mahazioth began the walk back to Ramah together. His two brothers did the same. Already they were below Jerusalem, with the temple seeming even more elevated than before. The light of the morning sun was catching the east-facing stonework, so that it almost glowed. The top of the bronze pillar named Boaz was just visible above the walls around the temple.

'It lifts the heart, does it not?' said Hothir softly. His question was not one that required an answer.

Then Mallothi spoke. 'It lifts it and draws it.'

Hothir's gaze remained on the sanctuary. 'I have felt the same.'

'Who would not long to walk in the courts of Yahweh?' added Mahazioth.

They stood for several heartbeats before turning to continue along the crowded roads. Hothir suddenly chuckled.

'What is it, Brother?'

'More than once, I saw birds swoop into the temple at will and without a care. It seems that they walk—or hop—in those courts more freely than we do.'

Mallothi smiled. 'If one of those you saw was a swallow, then I saw it too.'

In the moments of silence that followed, Hothir mused upon both the birds in the temple that bypassed its gatekeepers and those who had travelled by foot rather than wing to get there. Suddenly Hothir stopped again, his eyes fixed on the distant hills. Something was stirring deep within. *'How lovely is your dwelling place...'* he murmured.

His brothers, already three or four paces ahead paused and turned. 'What was that?'

Mahazioth's question washed over him as other words formed in his heart. *'How lovely is your dwelling place, O Yahweh of hosts.'* His father had spoken more than once of how the Spirit of Yahweh could come upon them to inspire them to prophesy—to speak words from Yahweh Himself. *Was this what he meant?* But as suddenly as it had come upon him, the moment had passed. He tore his gaze away from the hills and answered his brother's question. 'Just an idea.'

'What sort of idea?'

'An idea for a song. A psalm in praise of Yahweh and His temple.'

'Then share it with us!'

Hothir smiled. 'Maybe it can occupy our journey back home…'

'A worthy use,' replied Mallothi, 'of both the time and skills of the sons of Heman, the son of Levi!'

Mahazioth chuckled. 'Though you have left out many generations—Samuel, Elkanah, Zuph and Kohath, for instance, to name only four.'

'And you know what Father tells us,' added Hothir, raising an eyebrow. 'Yahweh may have exalted Heman and his line in granting him so many sons, and we are honoured to be descendants of Levi, but we must not forget that we are also humbled by coming from the loins of our forefather who rebelled against Moses and was swallowed up by the earth. We are sons of Heman but also sons of Korah…'

Notes

1. *The events in this chapter take place around 959 BC.*

2. *The assumption has been made that Levites do not enter the Holy Place within the temple, but only priests. This seems a reasonable assumption, given the non-priestly Kohathite Levites 'must not go in to look at the holy things, even for a moment, or they will die' (Numbers 4:20). These 'holy things' include, for example, the lampstand and altar of incense in the Holy Place and not just the ark in the Holy of Holies. A similar prohibition is given in Numbers 18:3 so that the Levites 'do not go near'. However, it appears that kings do enter the Holy Place at times, as Hezekiah 'went up to the temple of the LORD and spread [the letter] out before the LORD' (2 Kings 19:14). Uzziah is also struck with leprosy when he enters the temple to burn incense on the altar of incense, but the reason for the*

punishment is given as Uzziah's attempt to burn incense—the preserve of the priests alone—rather than him being in the temple (2 Chronicles 26:16-18).

3. It is not clear to what extent the open doors of the temple allowed those outside to see into the Holy Place—or whether there were steps up to the temple. Given that the second temple had steps leading into it, it has been assumed that this was the case for Solomon's temple too.

4. In 1 Kings 4:2, it refers to Azariah as 'the priest' during Solomon's reign, though in 4:4 it also mentions Zadok (the priest who anointed Solomon as king) serving as priest. It is assumed that this means that Azariah was the high priest during the larger part of Solomon's reign. Azariah is Zadok's grandson, though it is not clear what happened to Ahimaaz, the son of Zadok and father of Azariah (1 Chronicles 6:8,9), who is last mentioned in the historical narrative in 2 Samuel 18.

5. In 1 Chronicles 5:5 it states that the priests 'brought up…the tent of meeting and all the sacred furnishings in it'. This implies that the remnants of the tabernacle (including the bronze altar) were brought to Jerusalem, although it does not say what happened to them. Given the holiness associated with them, it is assumed here that they are stored at the temple—and maybe it is even the extant bronze altar that is used by Solomon in the middle of the courtyard when more space is needed for the huge number of sacrifices at the temple's dedication (2 Chronicles 7:7).

6. Not all the details of the temple structure are clear. The same is true for the subsequent palace and the geography of the two sites. The general layouts and details of the structures have largely been drawn from the ESV Bible Atlas.

7. There is clearly almost a year's delay between the finishing of the temple building and its dedication: 1 Kings 6:38 says the temple was finished in the eighth month of the eleventh year, but its dedication takes place in the seventh month (1 Kings 8:2), presumably of the following year. It is assumed here that the eleven month delay (so that the dedication occurs at the Feast of Tabernacles) was required for the completion of the furnishings and utensils for the temple, as may be implied by 1 Kings 7:13-51.

8. It has been assumed that priests or Levites who had travelled from elsewhere in Israel to serve at the temple would have slept in its external

rooms when on duty there. In 2 Kings 11:2-3, Joash is kept hidden in a bedroom described as being in the house of the LORD, and many English translations of Ezekiel 40:44 (part of Ezekiel's vision of the temple) speak of rooms for the singers at the temple. Herod's temple complex centuries later certainly had accommodation for priests, and in 2 Kings 23:7, Josiah, during his reforms, 'tore down the quarters of the male shrine-prostitutes that were in the temple of the LORD'. Although it is not clear if these were in the temple building itself or in the courtyard, nevertheless it does indicate a practice of those whose 'work' was connected with worship being stationed at the place of worship. Obviously, Samuel and Eli had also slept at the tabernacle at Shiloh (1 Samuel 3:2-3).

9. *It seems reasonable to assume that the Levites would have washed themselves before their duties and that their linen tunics (2 Chronicles 5:12) were new, given the other expense (e.g. the quantity of gold) that was lavished upon the temple.*

10. *How events such as the dedication of the temple were timed is not clear, given it was long before hours existed, let alone clocks. They could obviously organise events according to the position of the sun, with sunrise, midday and sunset being clear points of reference, but there are scant references (if any) in the Old Testament to any more precise timings.*

11. *Scripture does not say that musicians, trumpeters and singers accompanied the ark to the temple—only that they were in the temple for its dedication. However, given their presence when David brought the ark to Jerusalem (2 Chronicles 15:16-28), it is assumed that the same is true here.*

12. *A number of psalms are attributed to Asaph, three others are 'For Jeduthun', but somewhat strangely, none are attributed to Heman. (Heman the Ezrahite seems to be a different person). There are, however, a number of psalms attributed to 'the sons of Korah'. Despite Korah, the relative of Moses, being swept away in judgment after his rebellion, Numbers 26:11 states that his sons did not die out. Exodus 6:24 states that 'The sons of Korah were Assir, Elkanah and Abiasaph. These were the Korahite clans.' Heman's genealogy in 1 Chronicles 6:33-38 shows that he is descended from the line of Abiasaph. Korahites are also mentioned in 2 Chronicles 20:19 praising the LORD with other Levites, implying that they were closely linked with singing Yahweh's praises. It is possible, therefore, that*

the psalms ascribed to 'the sons of Korah' might be from Heman's family and guild of singers.

13. The psalm alluded to at the end of this chapter, with an imagined account of its composition, is Psalm 84.

14. Imagined named characters introduced in this chapter are Joseph and Michal.

3

When the queen of Sheba heard about the fame of Solomon and his
relationship to the LORD, she came to test Solomon with hard questions.
(I Kings 10:1)

Hothir's slumber was slowly driven from him by the sound of his name.

'Hothir!'

His body was still weary—he had only recently returned from serving at the temple during the Feast of Passover. He pushed back the covering that had kept both him and Deborah warm through the spring night. It was still dark inside.

Deborah stirred and murmured, 'What is it?'

But before Hothir could answer, there was banging on the door. 'Brother!'

He recognised the voice. 'I think it's Hanani.' He felt around for his tunic and then hastily pulled it over his head. The banging started again. 'I'm coming!'

Deborah pulled the covering back over her. 'What does he want?'

'I will not know until I ask him.' But he feared he already knew. He pushed aside the curtain that hung over the entrance to their small sleeping area in the long room that ran along the back of their house. The only door was into the courtyard. Hothir fumbled for the latch and pulled it open. There was still precious little light from the new day, but it showed enough of Hanani's expression to confirm Hothir's fears. 'Is it Mattaniah?'

Hanani nodded. 'Yes. He drew his last breath during the night.'

The second son of Heman had brought a fever back from Jerusalem, and Hothir was not surprised at his demise, given what he had heard from the family about his struggles to breathe. 'Is he to be buried this morning?'

'We will gather as soon as the sun is above the city walls.'

'We will be there.'

'I must tell the others.' And with that he turned to go.

Hothir watched in silence as his brother walked through the courtyard and then disappeared out into the street. A deep sigh shook his body. Mattaniah may not have been the eldest, but he was the first of his brothers to die. As so often happened, Hothir found words from the songs of Israel echoing in his heart.

All our days pass away under your wrath;
  we finish our years with a moan.
Our days may come to seventy years,
  or eighty, if our strength endures.

His own years were fifty-eight and Matthaniah's seventy-five. *It was a good age, but his own sorrow was no less because of it.*

A sound drew Hothir's eyes upwards. Joseph, his youngest son, was on the roof over the kitchen area to one side of the courtyard. He and his wife and young daughter lived in their own room above Hothir and Deborah. He was the only one of their offspring who was still with them—and it was likely to stay that way.

'I heard Uncle Hanani's voice—and the news.'

'You will need your lyre again, but today it will sing a lament.' Hothir paused for a moment, his gaze fixed on the clouds as he drew on details etched upon his memory. 'By the mercy of the Almighty, the temple duty this week falls to Zaccur and to one of the sons of Jeduthun the next. The defilement of death will not keep any of us from our duties.'

It had been seventeen years since the dedication of the temple. Even before it was built, lots had been cast in the time of David to determine the order of those who would serve there. The sons of Asaph, Jeduthun and Heman numbered twenty-four in total, each of them heading up a division of musicians made up of their sons and relatives. These matched perfectly the twenty-four divisions of priests from the line of Aaron—sixteen from the descendants of Eleazar, and eight from Ithamar. And each division of priests and Levite musicians served for a week at a time, commencing on the Sabbath. Not that those were the only duties to occupy Hothir and his brothers. When they weren't tending to their small flocks out on the pasture lands allocated to them, they trained not only those in their own families but also other Levites in music and singing—and Hothir was skilled in both.

Hothir sighed deeply again. 'There will be no more lessons in either the lyre or the psalms today, and we must tell our wives that they will have no need of baking bread this morning.' That they would fast until sunset, and would do so for seven days, needed no explanation. It was simply their custom. He turned to go inside but then paused. 'I will play the flute today—no other instrument has a voice so fitting for mourning—and I will suggest to Bukkiah that he leads us in the Prayer of Moses on our way from Ramah to the tomb.'

'*You turn men back to dust,*' murmured Joseph, '*saying, "Return to dust, O children of men."*'

Despite his heaviness, Hothir's heart was lifted by the knowledge that a rich store of Yahweh's words already resided within Joseph. A smile tinged with sorrow graced his face. 'Spoken well, my son.'

The year continued with little else beside the death of his brother to set it apart. Hothir's division had served its first week of duty during the hottest months of summer. The late-afternoon heat during the evening offering would have been almost unbearable, had the altar not been in the shadow cast by the temple by then, though the fire consuming the offering added to the discomfort. Hothir had struggled to keep his lyre in tune. But with both the shortening and cooling of the days and with the Feast of Tabernacles behind them came news that soon travelled the short distance from Solomon's palace to Ramah.

Deborah looked triumphant. 'We must go to Jerusalem!' She set down her newly filled water jar in front of Hothir with such vigour that some of its contents slopped out onto the dirt of the courtyard, staining it dark.

Hothir stopped milking the goat and looked up from his wooden stool, a questioning smile on his face. 'And why is that?'

'The queen of Sheba is coming to visit King Solomon!'

'And you know this because…?'

Hothir did his best to follow the string of friends, relatives and others between whom this news, gleaned from the well, had passed. '…whose brother heard it from one of the king's officials who said that Geber, the governor of Gilead, had sent a message by a swift horseman to Solomon the day before yesterday to tell him that her caravan was travelling along the King's Highway.'

Hothir chuckled. 'Then it must be true…'

'Of course it's true!' The years had done little to quench Deborah's fire. 'It has been said that nothing like it has been seen in these lands before. We must not miss this sight—we must go at once!' And with that, she folded her arms.

In forty years of marriage, Hothir had soon come to know the meaning of that sign—the matter had been settled and his wife's mind would not be changed.

Hothir thought for a moment—but only of all that would need to be taken care of. *If Joseph wished to travel with them, as he might, then his wife could manage the goats as well as the baby, even if they were away for a night or two.* The sigh that followed was one of resignation. 'There is nothing that I cannot change. You have your wish.'

'Then we leave tomorrow morning?'

Hothir turned his attention back to the animal. He pulled on one of its teats and milk squirted into the bowl. 'We leave tomorrow morning.'

'Is she a queen in her own right or the wife of a king?' They had barely left Ramah when Deborah asked yet another question.

'I don't know,' replied Hothir with some exasperation, 'just as I do not have any idea how many camels she will travel with, how many servants she will bring, or how long she will stay!' Joseph chuckled, and Hothir supposed it was because he was used to such exchanges between his parents. Hothir glanced at him. 'And what does my son think?'

'She is the wife of the king of Sheba, she will arrive with twenty-seven camels and fifty-two servants, and will stay exactly nineteen days.'

The lines around Hothir's eyes deepened in amusement. 'I will count them myself when we see them to find out whether my youngest son's speculations are indeed right.'

'But how long will the journey have taken her?' persisted Deborah.

Hothir sighed again. 'I do not know, but camel trains do not generally go faster than a man's walking pace. But from Sheba?' He shrugged. 'I suppose she will not have wanted to depart until the summer heat faded, so maybe two months...or three...' He thought for a moment and then shrugged his shoulders once more. 'Or maybe more. Beyond that I could not say.'

There was a pause. 'Does she speak our language?'

Hothir let out a cry of mock anguish. He wondered how Solomon coped with his many wives—wives that seemed to multiply greatly with the king's age. Hothir suspected, however, that they gave him more respect and deference than his own wife gave him. *But it mattered not.*

The sun had barely risen—Deborah had insisted that they leave early—but the late autumn day was already bright, and the chill of the morning was not unpleasant. It did not take them long to reach the turning that led to Gibeon. Hothir paused, his gaze turning westward. 'It is many years since sacrifices were offered at Gibeon and the sons of Heman sang there.' He turned back to Joseph. 'You never knew that time, but its glories never matched those of the house of Yahweh.'

It was his son's turn to question him. 'Will Solomon show the queen the temple?'

Hothir started south again. 'That, my son, is an interesting question.'

'More interesting than mine?' retorted his wife.

He grinned. 'I did not say that...'

'Hmm.' Beyond her expression of doubt, she held her tongue.

Hothir pondered the question for several moments. 'I have heard that the king kept the daughter of Pharaoh away from where the ark was in the city of David, because that place was holy. I suppose he did not want it defiled by those who worship foreign gods—even if they are his wives. I assume the same will be true of the queen of Sheba.'

Deborah could never stay silent for long. 'But does she worship foreign gods?'

Hothir laughed. 'I do not know. But she will certainly see the temple rising above the city and will see it from the palace courtyard, if not in that of the temple itself.' A few moments of silence passed as Hothir glanced around him. The hills were already becoming greener with the autumn showers.

'So what *will* Solomon show her?'

'Ah! That is a better question…'

'Why is that?'

'Because it is one whose answer I might at least know!' Unlike the temple, Hothir had never walked within Solomon's palace— he had no need to—but he had heard of its wonders, as had all in Jerusalem and far beyond. 'She will, I am sure, see the king's throne, and will never have seen its like. It is said that although it is carved from cedar, it is covered with both ivory and the finest gold. Each armrest has its own lion standing guard beside it—' He paused and thought for a moment. '—I believe they, too, are covered in gold. The throne also has six steps up to it, each with its own lions, and, if that were not enough, there is also a footstool of gold.'

'And the House of the Forest of Lebanon?' suggested Joseph. 'Surely she will marvel at its magnificent cedar pillars. It is little wonder the hall is named after the forest it resembles and from which the wood was hewn!'

'And do not forget the five hundred shields of pure gold that are said to hang there!' Hothir then laughed. 'Not that they will ever be used in battle—though maybe the sight of them would be enough to make any foreign king quake.'

'Surely there is no king on earth greater than Solomon!' exclaimed Joseph suddenly.

'And that, my son, is only because the God of Heaven—our greater King—has made it thus.'

The rest of the journey to Jerusalem passed swiftly, and they reached the city well before noon. They had met others along the road who were also travelling south for the same reason. The three of them found some shade near the road that came from the north-east, as Hothir had assured them that, if the queen had travelled along the King's Highway, then she would most likely have crossed the Jordan near Jericho and would be coming towards Jerusalem from that direction.

As the day wore on, it became clear that, whether or not the queen arrived that day, they would need to stay in the city overnight. Hothir had already considered the possibility. 'We should be able to lodge with Zaccur tonight—or if not, at the house of one of the other sons of Asaph.'

Deborah turned to him. 'Zaccur? Isn't he dead?'

'Dead? No! He was very much alive when I last saw him in Jerusalem.' Hothir suddenly feared, however, that his wife may have heard something he hadn't. *She did, after all, usually spend far more time than was needed at the town's well with the other women.* 'What makes you think that?'

'He is so old. Isn't he older than Mattaniah was?'

'Bukkiah is older than Mattaniah was, but that means neither that he is dead nor should be dead.' And he quoted, as he often did, the words of the sacred songs inscribed upon his heart.

'All the days ordained for me were written in your book
  before one of them came to be.'

'It is Yahweh, is it not, who numbers our days?' added Joseph.

'It is indeed.' Hothir then squinted towards the north-east. 'Although I hope that *this* day will not prove a wasted one.'

They were not disappointed, however, though the sun was low in the sky by the time the caravan came into view. It did not take long for Hothir to lose count of both camels and the queen's attendants. For the most part, those watching stood in amazed silence or, if they spoke, they did so in excited whispers—even Deborah. The camels were clearly carrying vast quantities of wares from Sheba. Hothir guessed that, whatever else she brought with her, the queen would be arriving with many of the spices in which they traded—and with gold.

The queen's camel, when it finally came into view, was easily marked out by its elaborate blanket, saddle and harness—and the very large numbers of spear-bearing soldiers surrounding it. The queen herself was all but hidden from view by the shades held aloft by the attendants that walked alongside her camel. It was only after she had passed that Deborah finally murmured, 'Are you not glad you came?'

Hothir had to admit, it had been just as his wife had declared: *nothing like it had been seen in their land before.*

By the time the last camel had disappeared into the city, sunset was upon them. Hothir hurried them towards the nearest gate before it was closed for the night.

When the door to Zaccur's courtyard was still open and he himself was sitting there, Hothir turned to his wife, an eyebrow raised. He mouthed the words, *Behold! He lives.*

His welcome was warm and generous, made easier by the absence of most of his family who were making a journey to their ancestral home among the northern tribes—a journey that Zaccur, now almost eighty, had declined. As Deborah helped his wife, Jehosheba, with the evening meal, the three men exchanged news of their families in the last light of the day. Before long, all were sitting inside on patterned rugs and cushions. Between them was a basket of bread and a large steaming dish of stew. The addition of more lentils, onions and garlic to the pot bubbling over a fire in the courtyard had swiftly expanded the meal.

'And were you all impressed by our visitor to Jerusalem?' began Zaccur after he had said the blessing over the food.

'Who could not fail to be impressed by such an arrival?' said Hothir with a smile, dipping a piece of bread into the large dish in the middle of the rug. The meal was a welcome one—and well-flavoured.

Deborah paused after tearing some bread from one of the rounds in the basket. 'I would have wished, however, that the queen was not all but hidden from view.'

'Clearly my wife's desires had not been passed on to her,' said Hothir drily. They laughed.

'Maybe we will see her better within the city,' said Jehosheba.

Zaccur bobbed his head to one side. 'Ah—that depends on whether the king will want to shield his guest from the crowds.'

'But he will want to show her the glories of Jerusalem, will he not?'

'Of that I am sure, Joseph.' Zaccur paused. 'But it may be Solomon's fame that has drawn her here—and I do not doubt that his trading has also touched the land of Sheba and caught its ruler's attention.'

Joseph looked up from the pot. 'Meaning?'

'Sheba is a prosperous nation, successful in its trade. But now Solomon's kingdom extends south to the Red Sea at Eloth, eastwards across Ammon and Moab and northwards towards the Euphrates. If Sheba wants to sell its frankincense or gold to Egypt, or to Kue or Aram in the north, then its caravans and goods—like those of many other nations—have to pass through our lands. Solomon can exact his taxes on all their wares, whether perfumed oils or precious stones, costly wood or myrrh, and he is reaping great rewards.'

Hothir nodded slowly. 'True, my friend. And have we not also heard of the fleet of ships that Solomon has built at Ezion-Geber near Eloth, and which sail with the aid of Hiram king of Tyre? Their ships bring bounty by sea, including gold from Ophir, and they do so more easily and quickly than Sheba's camels. I doubt that will please our Arabian friends. I would not be surprised if, while she is exchanging both words and gifts with the king, she also seeks from Solomon an agreement that will favour them both.'

'Indeed. As his power continues to grow, any ruler who has a beka of Solomon's wisdom will want to be his ally rather than his adversary in trade.'

Joseph's eyes lit up. 'Is it true, Zaccur, that the king's ships have brought back apes and peacocks?'

'It is indeed so.'

Jehosheba smiled. 'And if you are in Jerusalem long enough, you will hear the peacocks' cries, and if you are fortunate, you may even see one of the birds on the roof of the palace. I have never seen anything so majestic or beautiful. I doubt even the queen of Sheba could equal their splendour!'

'The king takes delight in discovering what he can about such creatures,' continued Zaccur. 'His officials say he is able to speak knowledgeably about any plant that grows, whether it is the mighty cedar of Lebanon or the humble hyssop that grows out of a wall. His wisdom is equally wide when it comes to beasts: he knows of both the fish in the sea and the birds of the heavens, as well as those walking the land, be they lion, lizard or lamb. I know Elihoreph, one of the king's secretaries, and more than once he has told me that Solomon's understanding is as abundant as the sand on the seashore!'

'And word of it has spread far beyond Israel,' said Hothir, pausing before taking another mouthful of the stew. 'I'm told that many come to hear his wisdom and his proverbs, both from lands nearby and from the ends of the earth. No other nation—not even Egypt or the lands of the east—can match the wisdom that Yahweh our God has bestowed upon him. Any question the queen of Sheba brings will find its answer in the wisdom of his words.'

Jehosheba passed the bread around her guests once more, the flickering lamps casting both their light on the meal and shadows upon the walls. 'Yahweh blesses us with peace and prosperity under Solomon's hand. Our numbers grow from Dan to Beersheba—we hear as much from our family to the north.'

Joseph took another piece of bread. 'Bukkiah says that the king makes silver as common as stones in Jerusalem and cedar as sycamore.'

'Bukkiah is right.' Zaccur fixed his eyes on Joseph. 'The land flourishes as Yahweh blesses us with the fruit of Solomon's wisdom. Whilst it is true that the king understands the rising of a bird on its wing from the earth to the air, he also understands how to raise a nation from privation to prosperity, and does so through trained

52

and trusted officials. Many may eat at the king's table, but they also serve Solomon well. And so there is order rather than disarray in the affairs of the nation. He fortifies our borders and cities, so the fruits of our land and our labours are protected—and also ensures they are well-used rather than squandered. And whether you agree with it or not, the king has deliberately disregarded many of the tribal boundaries in the twelve new districts he established north of Judah, putting Jerusalem firmly at the heart of his administration and maybe weakening the traditional loyalties of the tribes…'

'Though surely strengthening the hand of his own tribe of Judah,' interjected Hothir. 'He frees them from the obligation of having to supply one month's provision for the royal household and for those who sit at Solomon's table.'

Zaccur pushed the dish and its remnants towards his guests. 'You may be right about Judah, and loyalty is certainly worth more than the gold of Ophir. It is of little surprise that two of those placed over his new districts are wed to daughters of the king—although even they still need to give an account.'

'Enough of trade and the court!' interjected Jehosheba. 'Will not Solomon also speak of Yahweh to the queen? It is He, after all, who has placed both Solomon on the throne and wisdom in his heart.'

The soft lamplight illuminated the smile on Zaccur's face. 'You are right to remind us of that, my love. We speak of the work of the hands of men, but how can Solomon not speak to her of all that the hand of Yahweh has accomplished? After all, surely what we see in the land today is, more than anything else, the gracious fulfilment of Yahweh's promises and His faithfulness to His covenants. We are as numerous now as the stars in the sky, as the Almighty swore to our father Abraham, and the land Yahweh promised him is firmly in our hands. King David was assured that his son would reign in peace and security after him, as we see is the case this day. Whatever else the queen of Sheba sees, she will behold the hand of the Almighty, the God above all gods, who in His goodness has made His people the most blessed nation on earth.' He paused. 'Whatever riches the queen has brought with her, she will return home to Sheba with greater treasures.'

As Jehosheba and Deborah disappeared up the steps outside to prepare the upper room for the guests, with Joseph accompanying them, bearing not only a lighted lamp but also cushions and an extra rug, the two older men stood together in the courtyard under the stars. The ashes in the firepit had long-since grown cold and dark, and the city had become quiet. Its silence, however, was far from complete.

'Listen,' said Hothir suddenly, straining his ears. The unmistakable but faraway sound of pipes, lyres and singing drifted through the air.

'The king honours his guest with a celebration at the palace!'

Hothir smiled to himself in the darkness. 'You were not called upon to play?'

Zaccur laughed. 'We have both trained enough others in our time for that not to be needed.'

'Still,' Hothir replied, 'would it not have been something to have seen with our own eyes such a meeting?'

'Hmm.'

They stood in amiable silence for a few moments, as the strains of music continued. But there was a question in Hothir's mind which had lodged there over some years and yet remained unanswered. For once, Hothir felt able to voice it, though with some hesitance. 'Yahweh has indeed blessed Solomon with both wisdom and great riches...' He left the words, softly spoken, hanging.

Zaccur clearly caught the tone of his voice. 'And yet...?'

'You and I are both privileged as Levites to know the Law of Moses better than many.'

'Go on...'

Hothir deliberately kept his voice low. 'Does it not say, when it speaks of kings, that they should neither multiply horses nor wives nor gold for themselves?'

'And yet Solomon has an abundance of each?'

'It is undeniable.' Hothir paused before trying to answer his own question. 'But maybe it is different if it is Yahweh who multiplies those things...though I am not sure that can be said of his wives.'

Both men fell silent for several moments before Zaccur spoke again. 'When Yahweh appeared to Solomon at the start of his reign and the king asked for wisdom, did not our God promise to bestow riches and honour on him also, because he had not sought them? Surely that is what we see. And our king has not only delighted to build a temple for our God, but also observes worship daily, weekly and monthly, as well as celebrating each year the Feasts of Unleavened Bread, Weeks and Tabernacles. If his heart remains true to Yahweh, then Yahweh's gifts will not be a snare.'

At that moment, Jehosheba appeared on the roof above them, lamp in hand. 'All is ready.'

Hothir turned to the older man. 'Maybe Yahweh has blessed you, like Solomon, with His wisdom.'

Zaccur chuckled. 'But unlike Solomon, I am content with one wife!' With that, he laid his hand on Hothir's shoulder. 'And now may Yahweh bless my friend and my guest with a peaceful night.'

Notes

1. *Scripture does not give any timing for the queen of Sheba's visit. This re-telling has assumed it takes place five years after the completion of the palace (it having taken seven years to build the temple and thirteen to build the palace—see 1 Kings 6:38-7:1), i.e. maybe around 942 BC, as 1 Kings 10:4 speaks of her seeing the house he had built (presumably the palace rather than the temple, which it refers to as the house of the LORD in the next verse). This timing gives some years for his fame to extend, but still allows eleven years before his death and for 'the slide' when 'Solomon grew old' (1 Kings 11:4). Solomon could have been around forty-seven years old at the time of her visit, assuming he was around nineteen when he became king.*

2. *David's formation of twenty-four divisions from the three musical guilds (see 1 Chronicles 25:8-31) is regarded by some commentators as a later addition. However, even from its earliest time, the temple must have needed some sort of rota of duties for both priests and Levites. 1 Chronicles 15:17-18 also supplies the extra detail that the three leaders of music had 'with them their relatives next in rank'. It is clear from the names of these relatives*

that they were not sons of Heman, Asaph or Jeduthun, so presumably were from their wider families or from the Levites in general. It seems then that the twenty-four sons, plus their own sons and these other relatives, formed the skilled core of 288 for temple worship (1 Chronicles 25:7), who then trained the much larger number of 4,000 recorded in 1 Chronicles 23:5. It is not unreasonable, however, to think that the organisation of these musicians evolved over time. Also, given twelve months of roughly four weeks in each year, it may be that each division served for two weeks a year plus extra time at the festivals (as seems to have been the case in New Testament times), with the weeks of their duties also gradually cycling through the year. 2 Kings 11:4-7 shows that weekly duties started on the Sabbath, certainly for those who guarded the temple. It is worth noting that the three guilds of temple musicians correspond to the three sons of Levi, with Heman descended from Kohath, Asaph descended from Gershon and Ethan/Jeduthun descended from Merari (see the genealogies in 1 Chronicles 6:31-47).

3. That pipes were particularly associated with mourning may be implied by Jeremiah 48:36.

4. Mourning, it seems, generally lasted seven days (Genesis 50:10) and involved fasting until evening (2 Samuel 1:12), when food would be offered to the mourners to comfort them (Jeremiah 16:7).

5. As with the building of the temple, many details concerning Solomon's palace are unclear.

6. Scripture does not mention onlookers for the queen of Sheba's arrival, but it is difficult to imagine that such a visit would not have caused a stir or drawn spectators in a culture devoid of the manufactured entertainment of today.

7. Although Ethiopia, Eritrea and Sudan have all been suggested as possibilities for Sheba, it seems that the most probable location is the south-western corner of the Arabian Peninsula—possibly modern-day Yemen, around 1400 miles south-east of Jerusalem. That would put Sheba close to trade routes from Mesopotamia, as well as between Africa and India (through shipping across the Red Sea).

8. Many details concerning the queen's visit are unknown, including whether it was planned or unannounced, or whether she was a consort to a king or

a ruler in her own right. There are no details of travel (other than camels being involved—1 Kings 10:2), let alone clothing etc. The trip would have taken many weeks, but there is precedent for ancient monarchs taking trips of such length.

9. A beka is a Hebrew unit of weight (equal to half a shekel) of around 5.7g.

10. The Hebrew of 1 Kings 10:22 is variously translated as either baboons or peacocks. Assyrians kings from the same period certainly had collections of exotic animals.

11. Judah seems to be exempt from the taxes levied by Solomon in 1 Kings 4:7,22-23. Verse 7 refers to deputies over all Israel, and the twelve districts described in verses 8-19 do not seem to include any lands of Judah, but merely touch its border at Beth Shemesh (1 Kings 4:9). This may account for the distinction between 'Judah and Israel' in 1 Kings 4:20.

12. The books of 1 Kings and 2 Chronicles paint a picture of Solomon's wealth and wisdom as God's blessing upon him, something that is also confirmed by the testimony of the queen of Sheba (2 Chronicles 9:8). 2 Chronicles 8:12-13 also specifically records his faithful observance of godly worship at this point in his reign.

13. That the ancestral home of Zaccur could have been in the north of Israel might be supposed from the fact that the sons of Asaph are descended from Gershon son of Levi (1 Chronicles 6:39-43) and the Levitical cities for the descendants of Gershon are among the northern tribes of Israel (Joshua 21:6). That Zaccur's family are away is simply a literary device for avoiding a further multiplication of names for the reader!

14. Aram is the Hebrew name for Syria.

15. The psalms quoted in this chapter (in the order in which they occur) are 90 and 139.

16. The only imagined named character introduced in this chapter is Jehosheba.

4

*As Solomon grew old, his wives turned his heart after other gods, and
his heart was not fully devoted to the LORD his God, as the heart of
David his father had been. (1 Kings 11:4)*

The journey to Jerusalem did not get any easier, with Hothir's sixty-
four years beginning to weigh heavily upon him. Although his week
of temple duty could now be amply supplied by his sons and relatives,
most of whom he had taught himself, he still felt a holy obligation to
ensure that the division of musicians that bore the name of *Hothir*
offered only excellence to Yahweh. It had been a particular joy when
his first grandson had started serving with them the previous year, a
joy further increased by the name that Azarel had bestowed upon his
firstborn: *Samuel*.

Despite his aching bones, Hothir found, as ever, great pleasure in
the company of his offspring as they travelled south together. He had
no need to instruct them on the journey, as in their youth. All were
competent in their skills and knowledge of the psalms. As Jerusalem
finally came into view, they all paused. The sight never failed to
inspire.

'Are we entering through the Sheep Gate, Father,' asked Azarel.

'*I* am entering through the Fountain Gate. *You* may enter
wherever you choose.'

Eliel frowned. 'Why go to the other end of Jerusalem?'

'Because that is the gate closest to the house of Zaccur, and I wish
to see my friend before going to the temple.'

'Then we will go with you too, Grandfather,' beamed Samuel.

Azarel clicked his tongue. 'I am not sure Zaccur will thank us for
the arrival of six guests…'

'I did not mean that—only that we should also enter Jerusalem by that gate.'

'You may each please yourselves in the matter,' responded Hothir. 'Any who wish may come with my grandson and me.' He began walking again—and all followed.

The conversation continued as they descended into the Kidron Valley to the east of Jerusalem. But before they had reached the lowest point, Hothir spotted a sight that puzzled him. Out from the Horse Gate—the gate nearest to Solomon's palace—came a strange little procession of what appeared to be high-born foreign women, given their clothing. They were carrying baskets covered with cloths. Two of them were leading young goats on tethers, and the small party was accompanied by a handful of guards. They reached the bottom of the valley a short distance ahead and began walking south. Hothir and his sons followed them, the city walls rising above them on their right, with the tree-covered Mount of Olives to their left.

'Who are they?' asked Samuel after watching them for some time.

'I would guess wives of Solomon,' began Azarel, 'or some of his concubines.'

'If I did not know better,' continued Jedaiah, 'I would say they bear sacrifices for worship.'

'But the temple is not that way, Uncle…'

'And they are not Israelites.' Hothir's words were followed by silence. The women then turned onto a path leading eastwards up a hill just to the south of the Mount of Olives. 'You may be mistaken about their purpose, Jedaiah.' The pit of Hothir's stomach, however, betrayed the fear that his son spoke the truth.

'Why don't I follow them, Grandfather? Then we will know for sure.'

Azarel looked scornfully at his son. 'You do not know how far they are going.'

'I will go with him,' said Joseph. 'Let us at least go to the top of the hill.'

All looked to Hothir. He thought for a moment. 'The two of you go whilst we wait here. But stay some distance away and do not make it seem like you are deliberately following them. They would not thank you for that.'

Hothir and his three sons stood watching in silence as the two younger men—uncle and nephew, and yet only nine years apart—wandered along the bottom of the valley and then turned up the same path.

Eventually Eliel spoke, though with some hesitation. 'Do you really think they are going to offer sacrifices up there?'

'What else do they intend to do with the goats?' replied Jedaiah. 'Do not tell me that the king's wives have suddenly taken up herding.'

Azarel's brow furrowed. 'Solomon would not allow such worship, surely?'

Hothir held up his hand. 'Before we speak ill of our ruler, let us at least wait until we know more, otherwise our words are but empty speculation.' They fell silent and stayed that way, none seemingly with any appetite for idle chatter to pass the time. Hothir's troubled thoughts were mingled, however, with unspoken prayer: *Lord God of Heaven, let it not be so!*

Just when Hothir had begun to worry and Azarel had asked with some frustration where the pair had got to, Joseph and Samuel reappeared. They were hurrying and arrived slightly breathless.

'They were indeed sacrificing,' began Joseph. 'We stayed back among the trees, but we saw their altar and the goats slaughtered before it. They also burned incense…'

He paused, but Samuel continued. 'The name of Molech was on their lips.'

'Molech?' exclaimed Hothir in disbelief. 'The god of the Ammonites?' The word *detestable* remained unspoken. They had all heard the stories of child sacrifice.

'What Samuel says is true. We heard it more than once.'

'Is not the mother of Rehoboam an Ammonite?' asked Eliel.

'Naamah,' replied Hothir, nodding. 'She is the first one Solomon wed, but she is certainly not the only daughter of Ammon among his wives.' He did not want to speak disapprovingly of the king before his sons, but the truth was that Solomon had multiplied foreign wives as if they were an army to be strengthened—and not only from Ammon but also from Edom, Sidon and others beside.

'Do you think Solomon knows?' asked Samuel.

Hothir found it hard to conceive that the king would be unaware of such a thing, even if he, like Hothir, was growing older. 'I will speak with Zaccur. Those in Jerusalem will know more than us, and it is not fitting for lips that sing the praises of Yahweh to be found with slander or slur upon them. Does not David himself say as much?

Yahweh, who may dwell in your sacred tent?
Who may live on your holy mountain?
The one whose way of life is blameless,
who does what is righteous,
who speaks the truth from their heart;
whose tongue utters no slander,
who does no wrong to a neighbour,
and casts no slur on others.

We will, therefore, speak no more of it until I have seen Zaccur. The rest of you go back to the Horse Gate and to the temple. I will follow you later.' None of his sons questioned his decision, and Hothir did not desire any further discussion. He wanted only to be left to his thoughts and his prayers on the short walk to Zaccur's house.

He watched as his sons turned and set off northward before resuming his own journey, the same prayer on his lips: *Lord God of Heaven, let it not be so.* It was more a plea of desperation than of hope. *Could Solomon really be ignorant of the idolatry occurring within sight of Jerusalem's walls?*

Hothir found his friend where he expected him to be—sitting in the courtyard, though his eyes were closed and his arms folded as he leant back against the wall. His years hung upon his face like a crumpled cloak. One of his daughters-in-law, Ruth, was kneading dough in a trough nearby, and other members of the family were on the roof, chattering away. Zaccur had buried Jehosheba the previous year.

Ruth looked up as he tapped on the door to the street which stood ajar. 'Hothir! Welcome!'

Zaccur's eyes opened. Whether he had been sleeping, praying or merely thinking, Hothir could not tell.

'Welcome indeed, my friend!' said Zaccur, smiling broadly. He turned. 'Ruth—bring Hothir some refreshment after his long journey.'

'Ramah is neither Dan nor Beersheba, though I will admit the walk feels longer than it used to.'

Zaccur chuckled. 'But you are, what? Almost twenty years younger than me?'

'But I am still older than I was!'

As Ruth served olives and beer to the men, they exchanged news of their families. After they finally both paused to drink, Zaccur studied Hothir's face. 'Ah…I know that look.' He lowered his cup. 'What troubles you?' Hothir glanced over at Ruth and then at those on the roof, and Zaccur caught his meaning. 'Let us take some shelter from the sun…' They rose to go inside.

It was only when they were both seated on stools out of the hearing of the others, but with the door left open to give them some light, that Hothir felt able to speak freely, though still in a lowered voice.

'My sons and I saw something that greatly disturbed my heart as we approached the city today…'

'Go on…'

His strange look and soft words gave Hothir gave the impression that Zaccur had some idea of what he was about to say. 'Women— wives of the king, I believe—left the city, taking sacrifices with them. Joseph and Samuel followed them. They witnessed them making offerings to Molech on the hill just south of the Mount of Olives…'

Zaccur's lips tightened. 'They are calling it the *Mount of Corruption.*'

'You know of it then?'

'Yes, though it grieves me to say so.'

'But does Solomon know?'

'*Know?*' exclaimed Zaccur, with a vehemence that Hothir had rarely heard. He lowered his voice, but it was full of bitterness. 'Solomon built its altars!'

Hothir stared at him, incredulous, too stunned to utter another word. He eventually added, 'How can that be?'

The passion suddenly drained from his friend's face, deep weariness taking its place. 'Solomon's affections for his foreign wives only seem to grow with his years. His heart runs after them and so he gives them what they want. And what they want is not Yahweh but the gods of their own people.'

'But Solomon himself still worships Yahweh…' Hothir could not hide the sudden doubt in his tone.

Zaccur drew in a deep breath and let it out slowly. 'He worships at his temple, but he no longer worships Yahweh alone. His wives lead him astray in his older age, so he accompanies them up that accursed hill, bearing his offerings and sacrificing with them on the altars that he himself built. And not only to Molech, but to Chemosh and to Ashtoreth, and, *who knows*, maybe to other vile gods worshipped by his myriad wives and concubines.' He lowered his head into his hands. 'And others follow him.'

Both men sat in silence. Eventually Hothir murmured, 'How can one so wise become so foolish, for only a fool would allow himself to be seduced by the impotent gods of the nations.'

'Those gods may not require undivided worship, but Yahweh is not like them. The price of infidelity to Him is already writ large for Israel, both in the warnings of Moses and in our history. Disaster always followed when our forefathers ignored those warnings and ran after other gods.'

'And Solomon is blessed to know better than most the Book of the Law,' added Hothir. 'So how is it he forgets the way in which Yahweh's judgment fell when the people worshipped the golden calf?'

'Or how the plague killed many thousands when Israel played the harlot and worshipped Baal of Peor on the borders of the promised land?' He shook his head, lowering his voice once more. 'He holds fast to his foreign wives and ends up exchanging wisdom for folly.'

Hothir thought for a moment. 'Do you think the judgment of Yahweh will fall? After all, did He not raise up others to be thorns in the side of Israel when they failed to drive out the Canaanites after Joshua, and began worshipping their gods instead?'

Zaccur sighed deeply. 'It begins to fall already…'

'How so?'

He paused. 'Does the name *Hadad* mean anything to you?'

Hothir looked at him blankly. 'Should it?'

'You remember when David defeated Hadadezer and the Arameans of Damascus in the north…?'

Hothir smiled weakly. 'I know of it, but you forget that I was barely born then.'

'Indeed, I do forget. But Joab, the commander of Israel's army, also gained at that time a great victory over Edom to the south.'

'*Moab is my washbasin, upon Edom I toss my sandal,*' murmured Hothir. 'David wrote that psalm after those victories.'

'You are right again. But it seems a young Edomite of royal blood escaped Joab's sword and fled to Egypt with his father's servants. There he found favour with the king of Egypt at that time and was given Pharaoh's own sister in marriage.'

'And does Solomon know this from his own Egyptian wife?'

Zaccur shrugged. 'I do not know, but what I do know is that Hadad returned to Edom after the death of David. He has caused the king little worry up until now, but his hand is strengthening. And so Solomon's hold over Edom weakens. But there is trouble not only on the southern borders, but to the north as well. In Damascus, a ruler by the name of Rezon is another thorn in Solomon's side.'

'It sounds as if David's victories over the enemies of Israel are being undone…'

'More than that. Both are threats to Solomon's trade—Rezon to that with the Euphrates in the north-west and Hadad to the king's ships on the Red Sea to the south. Yet are not these adversaries only what Yahweh Himself warned of, if His people were untrue to the covenant? Surely He is simply being faithful to His word—to His promise of judgment as well as blessing?' Hothir had no need to answer. 'But that is not all.' Zaccur peered out into the courtyard through the open door, seemingly to check that none were nearby. 'I would not say this to many in the city, but there are rumours—rumours that Solomon's adversaries are not only from outside our borders.'

'Meaning?'

'You know of Jeroboam son of Nebat?'

Hothir nodded. The Ephraimite was an official appointed by Solomon to oversee the annual labour required from the Israelites as a form of tax. The sweat of the sons of Israel had been used to fortify cities such as Megiddo, to strengthen Jerusalem, and to build other cities for storage or for Solomon's many chariots and horses. 'Yes, he is over the forced labour of our brethren, is he not?'

'He was—but he has recently fled to Egypt and again found refuge there.'

The words perplexed Hothir. 'Refuge from what?'

'From the sword of Solomon. It is whispered that our king sought to put him to death.'

'And so he seeks sanctuary with Shishak?'

Zaccur nodded. 'Yes, and Egypt's ruler grants it.'

'But why would Solomon wish to kill one of his own officials? What has made Jeroboam his enemy?'

'That I do not know, and I might not have believed it had not Elihoreph spoken of it to me.'

The mention of Solomon's secretary was sobering. Hothir thought for a moment, conscious of his earlier caution to his sons. 'I will keep your words concerning Jeroboam as those on a sealed scroll. None will hear them from me while Solomon still draws breath.'

'I know, and that is why I can share them with you, my friend.'

Hothir's thoughts returned to the forbidden altars on the hill opposite Jerusalem. 'The Almighty, however, will hear my unspoken prayers for His king and His land as I minister this week.'

Hothir's walk upwards through the streets of Jerusalem towards its temple was not only slowed by the tiredness of his limbs but also by a burden that weighed as heavily upon him as if borne bodily upon his back. *Solomon was younger than him and yet had been drawn away from fidelity to Yahweh by his wives.* Hothir shuddered. It was both unsettling and fearful to think that one who had received so much from the hand of Yahweh, and to whom the Almighty had appeared twice, could nevertheless be lured into unfaithfulness to the one true God. He had never been so grateful to have but one wife who was a true daughter of Israel. Deborah may not have ministered at Yahweh's temple, but she was not slow to speak of her repugnance of foreign gods, particularly those requiring the sacrifice of the fruit of a woman's womb.

As he approached the temple, built by Solomon when his heart was set on Yahweh alone, Hothir once more echoed words written by David as an unspoken prayer within.

Teach me your way, Yahweh,
*   that I may rely on your faithfulness;*
give me an undivided heart,
*   that I may fear your name.*

Notes

1. *The events in this chapter are set around 936 BC, although could be at any point in Solomon's final years.*
2. *There has been debate about the age of service for Levites. In Numbers 4:3, Moses was told that Levites should serve at the tent of meeting 'from thirty years old up to fifty years old', but in 8:23-26 was told 'men twenty-five years old or more shall come to take part in the work at the tent of meeting, but at the age of fifty, they must retire from their usual duties and work no longer. They may assist their brothers in performing their duties at the tent of meeting, but they themselves must not do the work.' Jewish commentators have suggested that the Levites served an apprenticeship for the first five years. However, despite the Levites being counted from thirty years old or more in 1 Chronicles 23:3, in the*

same chapter in verses 24-26, it appears that David changed the rules, counting 'the workers twenty years old or more who served in the temple of the LORD. For David had said, "Since the LORD, the God of Israel, has granted rest to his people and has come to dwell in Jerusalem for ever, the Levites no longer need to carry the tabernacle or any of the articles used in its service." According to the last instructions of David, the Levites were counted from those twenty years old or more.' It appears, therefore, that not only did David decrease the minimum age, but he also possibly removed the maximum age for service, given the fact that physical labour wasn't required any more. Even Levites under Moses were still able to assist at the tent of meeting when older than fifty. Given that Asaph, Heman and Jeduthun were involved when the ark was brought up to Jerusalem, and also when the temple was dedicated forty or more years later, it certainly appears that an upper limit on service no longer applied. This has been assumed here.

3. *It is assumed that Solomon's foreign wives would have been identifiable by their clothing. The daughters of David certainly had distinctive dress (2 Samuel 13:18), and later, in the time of Isaiah, rich women were clearly adorning themselves in many different ways (Isaiah 3:18-23). It may also be the case that different nations had differing styles of clothing.*

4. *Scripture does not condemn Solomon explicitly for polygamy, but for his idolatry and worship of foreign gods. Marrying Pharaoh's daughter may have been an early compromise, but the actual condemnation only comes at the end of his life, when Solomon not only builds the altars for his foreign wives (2 Kings 11:7-8), but is also involved in this worship (11:5). 1 Kings 11:31-33 also states, 'they have forsaken me and worshipped false gods', suggesting that the apostasy also involved Solomon's subjects.*

5. *It is not clear how widely known God's words of warning to Solomon about other gods (in 1 Kings 9:1-9) would have been, or His words of judgment (in 11:11-13).*

6. *Both Rezon and Hadad were enemies of Solomon throughout his whole reign (1 Kings 11:21-25), but the implication seems to be that God raised both of these up particularly as enemies as a result of his infidelity (1 Kings 11:14,23).*

7. *Some of Solomon's other building projects (described in 1 Kings 9:15-19)*

may have occurred at the same time as the construction of the temple and the palace, given there were only sixteen years left of Solomon's reign after the completion of the palace.

8. *It is not exactly clear how it was that Solomon knew that Jeroboam was a contender for the throne (given that Ahijah's prophecy to the latter was delivered in private, in 1 Kings 11:29-39), but that certainly seems to be the implication of 1 Kings 11:40. God did, however, speak to Solomon of the kingdom being torn from him and given to a subordinate (in 1 Kings 11:11), and it may be that somehow Solomon knew this referred to Jeroboam. Pharaoh Shishak (referred to as Shoshenq I elsewhere) came to the throne in 945 BC (the 24th or 25th year of Solomon's reign), so Jeroboam's flight to Egypt must be dated between that year and the end of Solomon's reign (in 931 BC).*

9. *The psalms quoted in this chapter (in the order in which they occur) are 15 and 86.*

10. *The named imagined characters introduced in this chapter are Hothir's grandson Samuel and Zaccur's daughter-in-law Ruth.*

5

Solomon reigned in Jerusalem over all Israel for forty years. Then he rested with his ancestors and was buried in the city of David his father. And Rehoboam his son succeeded him as king. (1 Kings 11:42-43)

'Father!'

Hothir lifted his gaze from his lyre. The smile drawn onto his face by his son's voice faded as swiftly as it had appeared. Joseph's head was crowned with dust and his tunic torn. Hothir froze, every sense suddenly alert. 'Who has died?'

'The king.'

A cry slipped from Hothir's lips. He set down the instrument and then reached lower, sweeping his right hand across the ground. He rose and raised his clenched hand high, letting the dirt cascade down upon his head. He then grasped the neck of his garment and pulled sharply. The seam came apart easily—it had been rent in grief before.

Deborah joined them outside. 'What has happened?'

'Solomon died last night. The news has just come from Jerusalem.'

They stood in silence, Hothir suddenly aware of the sounds of Ramah beyond their courtyard walls. It felt already as if the song of the city had changed, the normal bustle of a new day turned to the muted melody of mourning.

Deborah let out a deep sigh. 'Am I alone in grieving that the king's glory had already faded before his death?'

'The gold of Solomon's temple remains untarnished but not his reign.' Hothir's mind drifted back. 'David died forty years ago,' he murmured, 'and yet I still remember the day clearly. I mourned as if my own father had died, for the flock of Israel had lost its beloved shepherd.' Hothir struggled for a moment to find the right words. 'But gratitude and grief were woven together. How could I not be thankful for the way Yahweh had worked through his king? It was not that I was blind to David's faults—I knew he had sinned greatly. And yet he'd humbled himself before the Almighty and been forgiven, walking with Yahweh until the end.' He turned to his wife. 'So although I grieve today, it is as much over Solomon's unfaithfulness as his death.' *What good was all the gold in Ophir if one's heart turned away from the Living God?* The answer was both obvious and awful.

'How old was Solomon?' asked Joseph suddenly.

Deborah brushed some dust off Hothir's nose. 'Ten years younger than your father—so fifty-eight.'

Hothir thought for a moment. 'His years did not match those of David, though he reigned as long. Now Rehoboam will rule in his place, and he is already forty-one.' The thought did nothing to lighten Hothir's heart. Not that he knew much of Solomon's firstborn, but the way Rehoboam bore himself left him uneasy.

'What sort of king will Rehoboam be?'

Hothir wondered if Joseph had somehow sensed his disquiet. *It would be better to speak of what he was sure.* 'It is said that just before David died, he charged Solomon to walk in obedience to Yahweh and keep the Law of Moses, telling him that if he did so, he would prosper.' He turned to his own son. 'If Rehoboam heeds those words, all will be well.' He declined to draw out what might happen if the opposite were true.

'Why do you think we are heading to Shechem and not Jerusalem?'

Joseph's question, as the men of the family headed north from Ramah, was one that had perplexed Hothir ever since hearing the news of where Solomon's successor was to be crowned king. 'I do not know and have not heard whether it was Rehoboam's desire or the will of the people.'

'The will of the northern tribes, you mean,' interjected Azarel. 'Judah and Benjamin would have been perfectly content for the ceremony to be in Jerusalem.'

'Or maybe Rehoboam knows that he needs to win the support of the other tribes,' suggested Jedaiah, 'given the favour his father showed to Judah.'

Hothir shrugged. 'If Rehoboam seeks the goodwill of the northern tribes, then he will have inherited not only his father's kingdom, but some of his wisdom too.' He briefly looked up from the uneven path. The ominous grey clouds above them held the threat of rain. *Even a king could not choose the season of his death.*

'But the kingdom Rehoboam will rule over,' continued Joseph, 'is diminished, isn't it?' Solomon's enemies had eroded his control over both southern and northern borders in the final years of his reign.

'It is still a great kingdom!' protested Samuel, clearly keen to preserve their nation's honour.

Hothir nodded. 'Yes, it is. But the reason for its greatness does not lie in its borders.' He returned, once again, to his beloved psalms.

> *'Blessed is the nation whose God is Yahweh,*
> *the people he chose for his inheritance.*

That is where our greatness lies.' He then lifted his voice in song, singing the psalm from its start.

> *'Sing joyfully to Yahweh, you righteous;*
> *it is fitting for the upright to praise him.'*

By the time Hothir reached the next words, *Praise Yahweh with the harp*, every son and grandson had joined in. Their singing drew both the attention and smiles of those nearby who were also travelling north. Hothir's heart soared as they sang of Yahweh's unfailing love. *Was there any better way to pass the time than in praise to their God?* But the psalm was even more apt than he had first realised. *No king is saved by the size of his army*, the psalmist had written, and even as he sang, a prayer formed within—a prayer that the new king would know their true Saviour and King.

The land around Shechem had become a sea of tents. It seemed as if all Israel were there, or at least its men. But news soon travelled around the camp of a name he had almost forgotten.

'Jeroboam son of Nebat,' echoed Samuel after hearing his father's words. 'Who is he?'

'He was one of Solomon's officials,' replied Azarel. 'He has been in Egypt for some years.'

'What was he doing in Egypt?'

With Solomon dead, Hothir was finally free to speak of what his friend had once confided in him, though his eyes remained fixed on the distant figure of Rehoboam, clad in his royal garments and waiting to be proclaimed king. 'Zaccur told me before he died that Jeroboam had fled there because Solomon sought to put him to death, though I know not why.'

'Why has he returned now, then?' asked one of Hothir's other grandsons. 'Does he seek restoration from Rehoboam?'

Hothir pondered the question. *What did he, indeed, seek?*

Azarel pulled on his beard. 'I heard that the northern tribes had sent for him.'

'Maybe they want a spokesman,' suggested Jedaiah.

Hothir had always valued the insights of his second son. 'If they do so, then he must have gained their trust when he was over them.'

'Over them?' repeated Samuel. 'How?'

'Adoniram was over the whole of the forced labour, but Solomon appointed Jeroboam from the tribe of Ephraim over the labour of the northern tribes.' Hothir's gaze had drifted back to Rehoboam. There was movement. 'Look! Men are approaching the king.' The conversations around them died away, all attention on Rehoboam. Hothir strained his ears, but the distance was too great to hear what was spoken. But the exchange was swiftly over and the men parted company. Murmuring broke out around them.

'What has happened?' asked Samuel.

'As we have neither the ears of a hare nor the eyes of an eagle,' replied his father drily, 'we will have to wait to find out. But this much is certain: Rehoboam will not be crowned king today.'

The news was not long in coming, however, spreading swiftly through the vast crowds. Hothir's elder brother Hanani had been some way in front of them and delivered the substance of what had taken place. They gathered around him. 'Jeroboam came before the king as the mouth of the men of Israel. He petitioned Rehoboam to lighten the heavy yoke that Solomon had laid upon them.'

Hothir frowned. 'And their acknowledgement of him as king depended upon that?'

'They said they would serve him if he did so.'

'And if he didn't?' asked Azarel.

Hanani shrugged. 'That I was not told. I know only the reply of the king.'

That Rehoboam had walked away filled Hothir with foreboding. 'Which was?'

'He told them to return in three days for their answer.'

'Why does he need time to think about it?' murmured Jedaiah. 'And was it such a heavy yoke?'

Hanani shrugged again. 'It may have been hard service, but from Dan to Beersheba, all Israel enjoyed peace under Solomon.'

'Peace *and* prosperity,' added Azarel. 'They did not labour for no return. Peace meant that they could enjoy the fruits of their own vines and fig trees, with no fear of losing them to raiders. If the northern tribes have forgotten that, then they have short memories indeed.'

'Yet would it not be wiser to gain the good favour of *all* the tribes at the start of his reign?' Before any answer was given, Hothir added, 'After all, Rehoboam has no need to build either temple or palace.'

Jedaiah then raised a troubling question. 'If Jeroboam was a threat to Solomon, is it possible that he is the same to Solomon's son?'

Hothir was old enough to remember the slaughter after Absalom had risen against his father David. 'Strife within Israel will benefit none of Yahweh's people.' But he also remembered the root of Absalom's rebellion: David's sin against Yahweh. *Might Solomon's own sin carry a similar cost?* 'We will return to our tents and petition our God for His favour,' said Hothir eventually. 'We must ask that *His* will be done. Did not the Almighty promise David, after all, that his house and kingdom would endure forever?' But Hothir also knew the warning that had accompanied the promise: that if David's son did wrong, then Yahweh would punish him with a rod wielded by men.

The three days dragged by as slowly as a night without sleep. The sons of Heman passed much of the time in singing and music. Many near their tents joined with them or just sat listening. There was no air of celebration, however; no jubilation such as had filled the air when Solomon had sacrificed at Gibeon shortly after the start of his reign. All knew that much hung on the words that Rehoboam would return to the Israelites. *Would the bonds of kinship hold and the house of Israel stand, or would the stones built together come tumbling down onto the dirt?* Many times during the waiting, Hothir returned to the promise of Yahweh to David. *Was that not the sure foundation on which the future of the kingdom rested?*

When they assembled again on the third day, Hothir could find no peace in his heart. His lips moved almost imperceptibly as he petitioned heaven and fixed his eyes on the distant encounter. Dismay seeped into him like the chill of a damp tunic on a winter's day. Distance did not disguise Rehoboam's haughty stance, or the deliberate folding of arms that resulted, with heads cocked to one side to do only one thing—to spit upon the dirt in disdain. When Jeroboam and those with him abruptly turned their backs on Rehoboam and strode away, Hothir's heart was as heavy as one of the stones of Solomon's temple. A chant grew as more and more took it up: *What share do we have in David? What inheritance in the son of Jesse?* Hothir stood watching, stunned. The cry became like thunder, only to be replaced by another. *To your tents, O Israel! Look now to your own house, David!* The words were not empty ones, for with them, the assembly began to disperse in all directions, like a startled flock. But not all returned to their tents. Some stood seemingly as bewildered as they were, presumably men of Judah or other Levites. Hothir could only pray for Yahweh's mercy.

'With what words did Rehoboam answer them?' asked Joseph eventually.

'We will learn before too long, I fear,' murmured Hothir, staring at the jubilant northern tribes. 'But this is not a new chant.'

'What do you mean, Father?'

Hothir tore his eyes away from the grim spectacle. 'I remember hearing it many years ago, when the people gathered after the defeat of Absalom. A man named Sheba led the northern tribes away from the king, and those words were his rallying cry. But the kingdom was restored to David through the sword of Joab and the wisdom of a woman. In the end, the only thing that was severed for good was the head of Sheba from his body. We must hope that a similar restoration will be granted by Yahweh.'

'Egypt's king will no doubt rejoice when he hears of this,' said Azarel, kicking the ground. 'Maybe Shishak harboured Jeroboam in the hope that one day he would trouble the throne of Israel, and thereby strengthen Egypt's position.'

'Maybe.' The words *the throne of Israel* lingered in Hothir's mind. *Could Rehoboam's throne be called that now?*

Soon, the crowds had dispersed sufficiently for Hothir and his sons to make their way towards the centre of the gathering, where Rehoboam had stood. The king was nowhere to be seen, however, but before they had gone far, Hothir spotted one of the sons of Asaph, downcast, walking against the flow. He hailed him. 'Asharelah!' The other man soon found Hothir's face in the crowd. He nodded and adjusted his path towards them. 'Greetings, Brother. Do you know what happened?'

'Nothing good,' replied the Levite grimly.

'What was Rehoboam's answer to the people?' asked Azarel.

'The rash words of an arrogant fool.' He shook his head slowly, in seeming disbelief. *'My little finger is thicker than my father's loins!'* Asharelah laughed bitterly. *'His little finger!* It is his tongue that has done the damage. He told them that if his father's yoke was heavy, then he would add to it, and claimed that if his father disciplined them with whips, then he would do so with scorpions.' He shook his head again. 'He wanted to appear strong, but all he has done is weaken his throne. He is no son of his father when it comes to wisdom! The only brightness in the gloom is that the tribe of Benjamin still stands with Judah.'

'But is all lost?' asked Hothir. 'Might not he regain the kingdom if he acts swiftly?'

'He has not listened to wise counsel thus far. Maybe seeing the results of his folly will change that.'

Hothir hoped he was right but feared he was not.

That Rehoboam sent an envoy to the Israelites might have brought some hope, if it not been abundantly clear, to Hothir at least, that his choice of a mouthpiece was another act of folly. It had been through Adoniram that the heavy yoke had been imposed upon the northern tribes under Solomon, so instead of extending a welcome to the official, the hands of the Israelites rained down death upon him with rocks snatched from the ground. It seemed a grimly fitting end for one who had imposed labour involving the same unyielding stone. And when Rehoboam fled in fear back to Jerusalem on his chariot, Hothir knew it was time for them all to return to Ramah. It was no surprise when news followed of Jeroboam being made king of the northern tribes.

When Hothir, however, found himself waiting with trepidation for the second time that month, it was, if anything, worse than the first. Although Rehoboam's summons to all the fighting men of Judah and Benjamin did not include the Levites, Hothir's stomach churned at the prospect of Israelites wielding swords against their brothers for the second time in his lifetime. It would be a very high price to pay for regaining the kingdom—if Rehoboam did indeed regain it through blood. Though Hothir's eldest brother had died some years earlier, it was Bukkiah's division on duty at the temple that week, and word of any battle would return to Ramah with them.

If only to divert his troubled mind, Hothir busied himself with re-stringing one of his grandson's lyres, which had had an unfortunate encounter with a goat. He pushed the peg holding one end of a gut-string into the soundbox more firmly and pulled hard on the string. It held, but he was interrupted.

'Father?'

Hothir looked up. Joseph had come down the steps from the roof into the courtyard. 'What is it?'

'There is a question to which I do not know the answer.'

'And you expect me to know it?'

Joseph shook his head. 'No. It is a question to which there is no answer, at least at the moment.'

'Then why ask it?'

He shrugged. 'Because it may be important.'

Hothir was intrigued and set the lyre down. 'Ask it, then…'

Joseph sat down at the other end of the bench. 'Suppose Rehoboam does not regain the northern tribes. After all, Yahweh promised the throne to the descendants of David, and Rehoboam is still a king…'

Hothir, too, had pondered that prospect. Ever since returning to Ramah, his own mind had had no peace, endlessly considering the possible outcomes of the disastrous encounter at Shechem. He sighed. 'In the time of your grandfather, the kingdom *was* divided for seven years. David reigned over Judah and the remaining son of Saul over the rest. But you have not yet asked a question.'

'If that does happen, the people will still have to return to Jerusalem to worship, won't they, if they are to remain faithful to Yahweh? Might not Jeroboam see that as a threat?'

'What passes through Jeroboam's mind only Yahweh knows, but, yes, he might well rue the return of his subjects to Jerusalem for worship. But he has no choice in the matter. Yahweh has made it clear that sacrifices must only be offered on the altar at Jerusalem, and the people are used to worshipping here.' His lips tightened. 'Their loyalty to the House of David may have waned, but we must pray that their loyalty to Yahweh will remain strong.'

The messenger from Jerusalem came later that same day. Samuel arrived in the courtyard red-faced and breathless. 'There is news…'

Hothir rose to his feet, as did Deborah, who had been crouching over a stew. Joseph hurried down to join them. Hothir studied his grandson's face for some clue as to the nature of the news. There was none that he could read. 'Tell me.'

'One of the prophets brought the word of Yahweh to the king.' He paused for breath.

Deborah urged him on. 'And?'

'Yahweh told Rehoboam that he must not fight against his brothers and that all the fighting men should return to their homes.'

Hothir's heart pounded within. 'And did he listen?'

Samuel nodded. 'He did and the army has dispersed…'

Hothir lifted his eyes to the heavens. 'Yahweh be praised! Our king has shown some wisdom at last.' But his smile swiftly faded as his gaze returned to his grandson. 'And yet you do not rejoice.'

'The prophet said more. He said that this thing was from Yahweh.'

'*This thing*,' echoed Hothir slowly. 'What did the prophet mean by that?'

'The division of the kingdom.'

Hothir was silent, and even Deborah did not speak. The news from Jerusalem had been both comforting and devastating. Eventually Hothir drew breath and let it out in a sigh so deep that it spoke more eloquently of his sorrow than any words. 'At least no Israelite blood was shed.' It was all he could bear to say. *The price of Solomon's divided heart had been the severing of God's covenant people.*

As the weeks that followed slipped by, Hothir continued to ponder Joseph's question about worship. But then the rumours began, and rumours so numerous that Hothir knew he had no reason to doubt them. Jeroboam had set up a golden calf at Bethel, not much more than a morning's walk north of Ramah. But the question found its fullest answer one evening when Joseph's wife returned from the well with more than just water in her jar.

She stood at the courtyard door accompanied by a stranger and what appeared to be the man's family. *And* four goats and a donkey. All looked tired, except the animals.

'Greetings, friends,' said Hothir, rising to his feet. His eyes darted to his daughter-in-law.

'These travellers need lodgings for the night,' she began. 'They are fellow Levites...'

Hothir needed no further explanation, although why they were travelling with goats puzzled him. 'Come! You are most welcome. We are shortly to eat, so you have come just in time to share our meal.'

'You are indeed, welcome,' added Deborah, but then headed into the house, followed by her daughter-in-law.

Hothir beckoned the strangers further in. 'I am Hothir son of Heman, and this is my youngest son, Joseph.'

The man smiled. 'You are one of the musicians, then...'

As the introductions continued, the women brought out cups of water for their guests, while Joseph took the animals to both feed them and tether them among their own in the stalls to one side of the courtyard. The wife sat down on the bench, a baby at her breast. She appeared exhausted. Two other young children—a boy and a girl—stayed near her skirts, clearly shy in the presence of so many new faces. It was only when Joseph's three children approached them that they began to venture away from their mother, and all five were soon playing happily together as the evening meal was stretched, a skill that Deborah had learned in her youth.

'Have you travelled far?' asked Hothir, as he stood watching the children with the newcomer at his side.

'From Shechem,' replied the man, who went by the name of Zimmah. 'It has taken us two days.'

'And your destination?'

'Jerusalem...or elsewhere in Judah.' Zimmah paused. 'Probably.'

Hothir was puzzled. '*Probably*?'

Zimmah shook his head. 'I only decided three days ago that we had to leave Shechem—'

'Do you mean for good?'

He nodded. 'Yes. I have a cart with all our belongings. The gatekeeper told us that he would watch over it at the gates this night.' Zimmah was quiet for a moment, staring up into the sky where the ample clouds were darkening. He finally lowered his gaze and met Hothir's questioning eyes. 'Even though Jeroboam has made

Shechem his capital, I could not remain under that man's rule.' He shook his head again slowly. 'Since being made king over Israel, or at least of the northern tribes, he has sought to let it be known that he rules as Yahweh's chosen king, appointed by a prophetic word given whilst Solomon still lived. That the prophet Ahijah spoke to him thus does, at least, appear to be true.'

Suddenly it was as if the pieces of a fractured pot had been put together, the broken shards matching perfectly. 'That must be why Solomon sought to put him to death,' murmured Hothir, 'and why he fled to Shishak.'

'And yet he rules in violation of Yahweh's commands.'

'We heard that he had set up a golden calf at Bethel.' Hothir gave the earth at his feet a little kick. 'Presumably to divert those on the road south, heading to worship at Jerusalem.' He paused and then added in disbelief, 'But a *calf*? Why not simply set up his own altar?'

'He does not have the ark. I can only think that he seeks another symbol that will appeal to his people. It is not just one calf, though. He has set up another at Dan in the north. He claims that they are the gods who brought the people up out of Egypt, as if claiming to stand in the line of those who have gone before!'

Hothir opened his mouth in disbelief. 'Then he will also bring upon himself and his calf the same judgment that went before!' His raised voice momentarily drew the stares of the children, but their attention soon drifted back to their own pursuits when only silence followed.

'But that is not Jeroboam's only abomination,' continued Zimmah in a lowered voice.

Hothir's heart sank. 'What else has he done?'

'He now proclaims a new festival on the fifteenth day of the eighth month.'

'Exactly a month after Tabernacles,' derided Hothir, his tone steeped in scorn. 'So he replaces the festival decreed by Yahweh with one of his own.'

'And not only that. He has appointed priests from all sorts of people—'

Hothir's eyes widened. 'Other than the descendants of Aaron?'

'Even other than those of Levi. Maybe he doubts our loyalty—and he would be right to do so.'

Hothir nodded. 'Yes, we have been appointed by Yahweh and our loyalty is to Him.' He paused for a moment, deep in thought. 'If Jeroboam appoints men himself, they are likely to please him to keep their positions.'

'You are right, I fear. And what is more, Jeroboam appoints these men not only to minister before his golden idols but also at other shrines he has set up on high places.' He shook his head once more. 'He has created a pattern of worship of his own design—'

'And Yahweh will call it false!'

Zimmah sighed. 'I have spoken to others of our tribe. My family is not the only one abandoning the pasture-lands and property that were Yahweh's gift to us.'

'Yahweh will surely reward you for your faithfulness to Him,' answered Hothir softly. 'Rehoboam may have begun his reign in folly, but he has shown that he can heed the word of a prophet and he worships at the temple.' He laid his hand on Zimmah's shoulder. 'Do not fear, Brother. Judah still has abundant land for those who cleave to Yahweh. You have made a costly sacrifice for the Almighty in giving up your ancestral lands, and it will not go unnoticed by Him. *The eyes of Yahweh are upon the righteous and His ears are attentive to their cry.* Our God will not abandon you—the psalms of our father David assure of us that.'

Zimmah finally smiled again. 'Spoken like a true son of Heman.'

A face in the temple crowd seemed familiar. Hothir looked more closely. *No, it was not the man, but not unlike him.* He thought hard for a moment. *No, he couldn't remember the name—such details now melted away as easily as wax in the midday sun.* He turned to Joseph standing beside him and clad, as he was, in the white linen tunic of a temple musician. 'What was the name of the Levite who stayed with us overnight, after Jeroboam prostituted himself with his calf idols?'

'Which Levite? There were a number...'

'Hmm. You are right.' Some five years earlier, they had, indeed, seen—at least for a while—a steady flow of their fellow Levites leaving the northern kingdom to remain faithful to Yahweh. Hothir thought for a moment. 'The first one. He was a fellow Kohathite and Izrahite—a gatekeeper, I think.'

'Zimmah. But he wasn't a gatekeeper—that was one of the others. Zimmah was one of the judges in the land.'

'Ah. That was it.'

'Why do you ask?'

'A face like his stirred a recollection, though my memory is clearly ailing as much as my bones.' His gaze wandered back to the temple rising high above the altar before them. Hothir's seventy-four years had transformed the journey to Jerusalem into a ride on a donkey's back, but the pleasant late summer sun had not only warmed his aching body but his heart for temple service, even though the division that bore his name no longer required his presence. He knew his days were numbered, and that he might not even be drawing breath still when their next duty came around. Besides, the desire to stand in the courts of Yahweh waxed strongly within. He needed a balm for the deep sadness that so often invaded his heart—an invasion as unwelcome as that of Shishak and his Egyptian army only months earlier.

For the first three years of his reign, Rehoboam had seemed to act wisely. Hothir had suspected that the presence of many Levites like Zimmah who had come south had been used by Yahweh for the good of Rehoboam's small kingdom. Judah, as that kingdom had come to be known, had flourished. But then, whether through the influence of his Ammonite mother or not, Hothir did not know, the king had abandoned good sense and gone the way of Solomon. He had walked in the ways of the nations around them, in idolatry and all manner of behaviour condemned by Yahweh—and once again, the hand of Yahweh had turned against His people. Shishak had been His rod of correction this time, and chariots and horsemen had swarmed across Judah like the plague of locusts that had once afflicted Egypt, capturing its fortified cities before reaching the gates of Jerusalem. It was only the repentance of Rehoboam and the leaders of Judah that had saved the city.

'Behold,' said Joseph, his lowered voice breaking into Hothir's thoughts, 'the king comes.'

Hothir looked to his left. Rehoboam was entering the temple courtyard from the flight of stone steps that ascended from the palace. Shishak's invasion seemed to have sped the advance of the king's years. Disaster had snaked its way through Judah to Jerusalem's gates, and it was only by the mercy of Yahweh that the snake had been charmed before its venomous fangs had struck. Yet the word of Yahweh brought by a prophet to Rehoboam had been a bitter cup to drain. Like Nathan's word to David two generations earlier, discipline and mercy mingled within the same divine goblet.

'Look at the shields,' whispered Samuel on Hothir's other side.

Those flanking the king no longer carried the solid gold shields crafted by Solomon, but new ones of bronze. 'That is part of the high price that Rehoboam paid for infidelity,' replied Hothir. 'The Egyptians stripped both temple and palace of their treasures before returning south.'

'Surely Rehoboam was saving Jerusalem by paying Shishak its gold,' replied Samuel.

'It is the same thing. Egypt's chests have been swelled by much of Solomon's wealth.' Hothir fell silent as the king approached for the evening sacrifice. He raised his lyre, and his sons and grandsons followed his lead.

The smoke from the burnt offering was still curling upwards when the king departed and the worshippers started to disperse. Jedaiah turned and looked back at Hothir. 'Are you not coming with us, Father?'

'Not yet, but I will follow shortly.'

Samuel also paused. 'Would you like me to stay with you, Grandfather?'

Hothir smiled. 'That is kind, but not today. I wish to breathe the air of the temple courts with only my thoughts for company.'

Samuel smiled back. 'Do not get cold. The heat of the day will soon wane.'

'But the fire of the altar will not. It will warm me if I need it to.'

His grandson seemed satisfied. 'We will see you soon, then.'

'You will indeed.' Hothir watched the first two generations of his descendants depart for their quarters. It would be some years until his great-grandsons joined them, and Hothir doubted very much that he would see that day. The light of the sky had not yet begun to fade, but it would before too long—like the evening of his own life. Night would soon fall.

He ached from standing for too long and began walking slowly around the altar as priests tended to its fire. He drank in the familiar sights. The impressive stonework of the courtyard floor, and its walls with their course of cedar for every three of stone. The huge altar that dominated the open space, and the temple itself, with its gilded doors. All had remained unchanged in the thirty-five years since Solomon had finished it, but so much was different outside its walls. Solomon's kingdom had first been diminished and then rent asunder, possibly forever. Two golden calves and the idolatry that accompanied them sullied the land to the north, with no sign yet of Jeroboam's repentance. In Judah, Shishak remained a cloud casting its shadow across the land.

Hothir had rejoiced in his youth to witness the rise of the glory of Israel, but his latter days had brought only grief with its decline. *Could that glory ever be restored?* Only Yahweh knew. He stopped in front of the golden doors. They still stood ajar, enabling him to glimpse the Holy Place beyond, but the sun was by now behind the temple and the only light inside was from the ten lampstands of gold. Hothir could make out their glow, but nothing more.

He held his lyre close. *How many psalms had he played in praise of Yahweh?* His heart felt heavy, however, its melody only one of lament. Movement suddenly caught his attention. A sparrow had flown down and it hopped from side to side across the flagstones. It drew a wry smile. '*Even the sparrow has found a home,*' Hothir murmured, remembering the lines of the psalm that he and his brothers had penned so many years before. '*A place near your altar…*' It lifted his heart. *'How lovely is your dwelling place, O Yahweh Almighty!'* He paused with his eyes resting once more on the door of the temple. Words of Moses suddenly impressed themselves upon his heart: *Lord, you have been our dwelling place, throughout all generations.*

Hothir stood unmoving, as though he himself had been cast in the same bronze as the altar. *Yahweh had been with them before the temple had been built, before even the tabernacle had stood on the plain at the foot of Sinai.* It was as if a mist had cleared to reveal the breathtaking majesty of Yahweh's workmanship—not that of a starlit sky or Mount Hermon capped in snow, but the glory of all that He had revealed. *He was unchanging, however much the earth or the kingdom quaked or fell. The nations were under Yahweh's rule alone, and not even Rehoboam's folly could thwart His purposes. And if every stone of the temple were taken away, Yahweh would still remain, as glorious as ever, upon His throne.* The temple, even if its stones were of solid gold, was as nothing compared to the God in whose honour it had been built— of that Hothir was utterly sure.

He suddenly found his heart aching, but not in lament. His eyes returned to the temple and his fingers to the strings of the lyre. He began softly picking out the melody of a psalm that spoke not only of dwelling in Yahweh's house but also of gazing upon His beauty. A silent prayer rose within him. *Yahweh, permit me one day to see your beauty!* There was no voice, no spoken words, but somehow he sensed that he had been heard and his request would be granted.

And then the moment had passed. Hothir drew in the air of the courtyard and breathed out, content. The sparrow was still on the ground near his feet. He swiftly glanced around him and then addressed the little bird in a whisper. 'I will have a place near Him too…'

Notes

1. *The events in this chapter begin in 931 BC, with the death of Solomon, and go through to just after Shishak's invasion which occurred in 925 BC.*

2.   It is unclear whether the ceremony at Shechem was at the people's insistence
     or at Rehoboam's. It does not seem to have happened immediately after
     Solomon's death, as it appears that there was time for the news of the king's
     death to reach Jeroboam in Egypt and for him to return in time for the
     ceremony (1 Kings 12:1-3). It would probably have taken two weeks to
     travel to Egypt, though the journey may have been quicker if made in haste.
     Pharaoh Shishak (Shoshenq I), with whom Jeroboam had sought refuge,
     probably ruled from Tanis, in the eastern Nile Delta, which would have
     meant a shorter journey to Israel than from other areas of Egypt.

3.   It is likely that Solomon's kingdom would have been diminished in his
     final years. Kitchen writes, '…before his death, Solomon had most likely
     lost control over Aram completely (and Hamath with it), and probably
     of outlying Edom, threatening the Red Sea trade via the Gulf of Aqaba.
     He would have been left with Judah/Israel (with Gilead) and probably
     Ammon and Moab as vassals – a much reduced realm' (pp87-88).

4.   Psalm 33, quoted in this chapter, is without attribution, so it cannot be
     known for certain that it would have been written at this time, but it is
     among the psalms of David in Books I and II of the Psalms (1-72). Only
     16 of these psalms are not explicitly attributed to David, although one is
     attributed to (or possibly for) Solomon. Psalm 33 is the only one of Psalms
     11-41 which doesn't have his name in its title, so it would seem reasonable
     to assume that, if it wasn't written by David, it came from the same period.

5.   It has been assumed that mostly men rather than women would have been
     at the ceremony to make Rehoboam king. Presumably some men would
     have stayed at home for security, and animals would still need to be tended
     in a culture significantly dependent upon its flocks.

6.   It is not known how old Jeroboam was when he became king, only that he
     ruled for 22 years (1 Kings 14:20). He is described as being a 'young man'
     when Solomon put him in charge of his labour force (1 Kings 11:28),
     which seems to be in the period of Solomon's apostasy later in his life, as it
     was around the time of Ahijah's prophecy to Jeroboam (1 Kings 11:29).

7.   The reason for the tribe of Benjamin siding with Judah is not given. It
     may be because of its proximity to Jerusalem, which sits on the border
     between the two tribes. Ultimately, though, the reason is because the Lord
     gave Jeroboam ten, not eleven tribes (1 Kings 11:31). The tribe of Levi is

not counted, and the ten tribes include the two tribes of Joseph—Ephraim and Manasseh.

8. It has been assumed that the word of the Lord through Ahijah to Jeroboam became known after Jeroboam was made king of Israel, as it would presumably have legitimised his rule in the eyes of the Israelites. It has also been assumed that the people of Judah would have heard about the word of the Lord through Shemaiah both when Rehoboam planned to fight Israel (1 Kings 12:22-24) and at the time of the invasion of Shishak (2 Chronicles 12:5-8).

9. Jeroboam's idolatrous innovation with the calves clearly happened early in his reign, as it was the Levites coming south that helped to keep Rehoboam faithful for the first three years of his reign (2 Chronicles 11:17). Archaeological excavations at what is considered to be the location of Dan have uncovered the high place for the idolatrous calf that was constructed by Jeroboam. The area of the sanctuary is about 195ft by 145ft and included an open-air courtyard with a large altar and a raised area for the calf.

10. Ramah appears to have been on the border between Israel and Judah (see 1 Kings 15:17-22, which seems to be a record of a tussle over the city between Asa king of Judah and Baasha king of Israel). It has been assumed that it was far enough south and close enough to Jerusalem that any Levites in Ramah would not have felt any need to move south, as other Levites were doing. Bethel, to the north of Ramah, is listed as territory of Benjamin in Joshua 18:22 (as is Ramah in 18:25), but Bethel clearly was part of the northern kingdom of Israel by the time of Jeroboam.

11. The psalms quoted in this chapter (in the order in which they occur) are 33, 34, 84 and 90.

12. The only imagined named character introduced in this chapter is Zimmah.

Joah

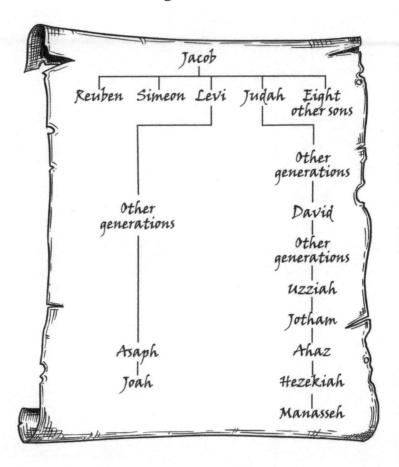

I

The LORD afflicted the king with leprosy until the day he died, and
he lived in a separate house. Jotham the king's son had charge of the
palace and governed the people of the land. (2 Kings 15:5)

Joah rolled the reed pen between his thumb and finger and stared
down at the sheet of papyrus. It still bore some faint ink markings.
Whatever its former use, that purpose had passed; his father, Asaph,
had swiftly and skilfully applied just enough water to wash away
the text without destroying the sheet. The twelve-year-old ran his
hand over the papyrus, trying to smooth the gentle undulations
of its surface. As soon as he lifted his hand, the shallow hills and
valleys returned. A wry smile played across his face. *No matter.* For
a moment, he imagined himself one of the court scribes, sitting—
as his father so often did—in one of the many rooms of the palace.
He straightened his back. No longer was he practising his writing;
now he was chronicling the affairs of the kingdom for all who would
follow. *Perhaps he was listing the tribute paid by the Ammonites before it was*
assigned to the temple treasuries. Or recording the new cisterns or towers built
across the land of Judah, or the materials used for the Corner Gate or the Valley
Gate in Jerusalem. Or even writing an account of the battles waged against the
Philistines or the Arabians! The shouting of his younger siblings in the
courtyard below, however, soon transformed the grand room back
into the flat roof of the family home, and the ornate table into the
small plain one at which he sat.

He adjusted his position slightly on his wooden stool and then
dipped his pen into the small pot of ink. He lifted it out carefully,
wiping away any drips on the already-black rim, and gently brought
the tip of the pen down to the papyrus. The cries of his siblings

faded away like darkness at dawn as he began to write. He was finally progressing beyond the pottery sherds upon which he had oft repeated his letters: *aleph, beth, gimel…* Now, as he moved the pen from right to left, words took shape, a small black dot separating each one on the page.

It seemed almost miraculous to Joah that just twenty-two simple shapes could carry every word uttered, every thought conceived by man. He had no idea—and neither had his father, for Joah had asked him—how these letters had come to them. *Maybe the Almighty Himself had inscribed them upon the mind of their father Joseph, exalted in Egypt, or of the great prophet Moses who had lived in Pharaoh's court. But surely these letters, in whichever mind they had first taken shape, had come as a precious gift!* His father had once shown him a papyrus bearing Egyptian script, telling him of the seemingly countless symbols they employed for writing. And yet in Judah they had only to learn twenty-two. *Elegant* was how his father had described it; to Joah it was both a marvel and a relief.

He reached the left side of the papyrus and lifted the pen. He felt pleased with his first line: *A man's pride will bring him low.* Joah had learned the words from his father's lips almost as soon as he knew the words for *milk* and *bread*. Not that he understood them then. But that was only half of the saying. He returned the pen to the ink and then started on the second line: *but the lowly will be honoured.* He wasn't as pleased with it—the letters hadn't flowed so smoothly. He began repeating the lines, gradually filling the page.

As he returned the pen to the pot yet again, he started slightly at the touch of a hand upon his shoulder. He had been oblivious to his mother's approach.

'You have done well.'

Joah turned his head to face her. The wry smile returned to his lips. 'But how do you know? You cannot read it!'

'I do not need to be able to read to see that it is neat and bears neither corrections nor blots.'

'I should teach you!' Joah could see no reason why anyone would willingly forego such a privilege. *Even a woman!*

Zeruah put her head back and laughed. 'Your father has tried to persuade me many times, and I will ask you the same questions I have always asked him: will being able to read help me to draw water, or mend clothes, or milk goats? Will it aid me in kindling fires or baking bread or giving birth?' Her hand rested for a moment on her swollen belly, as she looked under her eyelashes at her firstborn, amused.

His quick mind darted to other words inscribed upon his heart. 'But does not Father say, *knowledge will be pleasant to your soul?*'

'He does, but not all knowledge is recorded with a pen.' Before Joah's mind could seize upon a clever retort, his mother continued, nodding towards the papyrus. 'But why don't *you* read the words to me instead.' She listened as he repeated the saying about the danger of pride, and then cocked her head slightly. 'And you know why your father impresses the proverb upon you?'

'Yes—it was because of pride in the heart of King Uzziah that Yahweh struck him with leprosy.' It was also the reason that, despite living within the walls of Jerusalem, Joah had never seen the king— but often heard his father's warning. Whilst Uzziah remained confined in separate quarters, it was his son, Jotham, who ruled in his stead and whom Joah's father served.

'You were only two when it happened.' His mother paused, and then smiled, raising her eyebrows slightly. 'But now you are old enough to carry a water-jar.'

Joah groaned. 'But Mother…'

Her eyes returned to the papyrus. She nodded towards it and he knew he was doomed. 'If you are about to protest that it is a woman's work and is therefore below you, then I will ask you to wash all that ink about pride and lowliness from that page.'

With a deep sigh, he stoppered the ink jar, put a smooth stone upon the papyrus to secure it, and followed his mother to the ladder down into the house. As she carefully stepped through the opening in the roof and onto the rungs, Joah asked, 'Why didn't you just call up to me from the courtyard?'

She looked up at him with the exasperated smile he knew so well. 'I did.'

Joah stood with the water jar at the doorway that led from their small courtyard out onto the street. There was a choice to be made. He could walk to the Lower Pool at the southern end of the city, or he could walk to the Upper Pool near the Gihon spring to the east, which fed both pools. Either way, he faced an uphill walk back to the house with a jar filled with water. He decided to head south. Although it was slightly further, it meant that he didn't have to go down the short dark tunnel to reach the water of the Upper Pool. He preferred daylight.

As he ambled down the street, hugging the jar rather than carrying it on his shoulder, he wondered what his father had been doing. Every evening, Joah drank in each detail his father recounted of all that had happened at the palace that day. Asaph considered it part of his son's training to be a scribe. If Joah was to progress, he needed to master not only writing but also the workings of the palace and the king's affairs. And Joah was blessed with both an able mind and a good memory. His father had even started teaching him the language of Aramaic, assuring him that—to serve the king best—it was not enough to know only Hebrew. He must have a command of at least the most common language spoken by the nations around them. Joah took great delight at times in being able to exchange words with his father that his younger brother could not understand—much to the latter's annoyance. His four-year-old sister simply mimicked him in garbled nonsense.

Joah soon reached the Lower Pool. He was relieved to see that he was not the only boy drawing water. He recognised Shebna, of similar age to him and whose father also worked at the palace. Joah grinned to himself—Shebna clearly hated the chore and being there even more than he did. Everything about his posture and expression proclaimed loudly that the task was beneath him—and he did not wait his turn to draw water. The proverb with which he had covered the papyrus drifted back into his mind: *the lowly will be honoured*. While he allowed the women who had arrived before him to use the buckets first, he wondered whether it was wrong to act with lowliness if it was really prompted by a desire to be honoured. He was not sure. *He would ask his father later*. His mind then wandered off, pondering whether the Lower Pool had, in any way, more honour than the Upper Pool. *If anyone deserved honour, however, it was surely those who had first thought to channel the waters of the Gihon alongside the city wall, covering the length of the channel with heavy boulders for its protection all the way down to the Lower Pool.*

He felt a tap on his arm. 'Here.' He turned to see a woman offering him a bucket. He mumbled his gratitude, took the bucket from her and threw it back into the pool. Shebna was nowhere to be seen by now. When he had drawn the bucket up enough times to fill the jar, he hoisted it up onto his shoulder and began the walk home. Just as he was wondering if his father might have returned in his absence, he spotted him in the street ahead. Asaph smiled broadly.

He laid a hand on Joah's free shoulder when they met only a few paces from the house. 'Well done, my son. Did you offer to fetch the water for your mother?'

For a moment, Joah thought of lying to gain his father's greater praise—but knew he would more than likely be found out. 'I went when she asked me,' but then swiftly added, 'I was practising my writing at the time—on the papyrus you gave me.'

'Ah. That is good indeed. And what will I think of my firstborn's labours?'

'You will think that whoever taught him has done an excellent job.'

Asaph chuckled as they entered the courtyard, and he ruffled his son's hair. 'That is a reply worthy of Solomon himself.'

Whilst his father was being greeted by the rest of the family, Joah deposited the jar in the corner of the courtyard. He then hurried up the ladder to the second storey of their home and then up the further ladder leading to the roof, eager to show his father the fruits of his labours. It was only when Asaph was seated and holding a cup of cool water, freshly drawn from the full jar, that Joah could submit his work for scrutiny.

'Good, good…' began Asaph, stroking his beard. 'This is writing fit for the king.'

Joah's heart swelled. It was the praise he longed to hear more than any other. 'I have used up most of the ink, though.'

'Then you shall have to make some more. You do not need *me* to do it for you now.' He laid the papyrus in his lap. 'Fetch what you need, and then I will tell you the day's news.'

Joah studied his father for a moment, wondering at his tone, with shadow rather than sunlight seemingly gracing his countenance. Curiosity hastened Joah's collection of the pot of soot, the small pouch of hardened gum of the acacia tree, and the blackened pestle and mortar he and his father used for the task. Soon he was sitting cross-legged at his father's feet, with the mortar cradled in his lap. The rest of what he needed was scattered around him on the compacted dirt of the courtyard floor. The smell of spiced lentil stew filled the air as the large pot bubbled away over the nearby firepit. Joah's sister sat on her father's knee playing with the edge of his tunic and their mother milked one of their goats to one side of the courtyard. The second son of the family sat nearby, giving the impression of wanting to emulate his older brother—though Joah doubted he ever understood much of what he heard.

Joah began to grind a small piece of the gum in the mortar. It would need to become a fine powder before he could add soot and water.

Asaph sighed. 'Israel has another king.'

Joah stopped grinding and looked up. His father's shoulders were sagging. 'Already? Was it not just two years ago that Pekahiah came to the throne after his father's death?'

'You have remembered correctly. But do you also remember me telling you about one of his generals setting up a rival kingdom to the east?'

Joah cast his mind back. 'Pekah. That was his name, wasn't it?'

His father smiled, though wearily. 'You are right again.' Joah began grinding the hard gum once more as Asaph continued. 'It is being reported that Pekah conspired against the king of Israel, taking with him a band of fifty to kill him. And now he sits on the throne at Samaria in his stead.' He shook his head and sighed again. 'Not that Judah has been free from such conspiracies…'

'The three kings before Uzziah?'

'You have remembered well, my son. Yes, each struck down by the sword. But consider this: during Uzziah's reign here in Judah, there have been, *what*? Six kings of Israel? And now three of those murdered.' He paused. 'But maybe we should not be surprised, for nothing has changed since they seceded from Judah. They still have those accursed bull idols at both Bethel and Dan and bow down to them. How can Yahweh's blessing be upon them when they continue in the sin of Jeroboam son of Nebat?'

Joah glanced up. His father was extricating his sister's fingers from his chin. 'My beard is not a plaything, my little princess.' Joah grinned and returned his attention to the gum. His father went on: 'Still, not all of Judah's kings have walked in the ways of their father David.'

Joah pressed down hard with the pestle, forcing the fragments of gum around the hard, unyielding surface of the mortar. 'But all of them have, at least, been of the line of David. The same cannot be said of Israel's kings!'

'True. Even when men have conspired against a king of Judah, none have sought to replace David's line. *But Israel?* Four generations followed Jehu, but that has been their longest ruling dynasty—and some of their kings did not even manage one son to follow them. It would surprise me little if rivalry between tribes is part of their troubles.' Joah looked up again. His father had a twinkle in his eye. 'But how many sons have followed David to the throne?'

'Ten,' answered Joah, without even a heartbeat's hesitation. 'Or eleven, if you count Jotham who rules whilst his father yet lives. And each descended in a direct line from David.' He grinned. 'Do you want me to name them?' They were all inscribed upon his mind as surely as an ink list upon a potsherd.

Asaph shook his head and chuckled. 'No, I have heard my son recite them often enough already.' He glanced at the dust in the mortar. 'Are there any lumps left?'

'No, Father.'

'Good. Add the soot, then, followed by the water.'

Joah gave all his attention to the mortar, making sure he did not add too much of the finer powder that was blacker than night. After grinding the soot together with the gum, he began adding water, little by little. His father didn't speak, and Joah shut out his sister's chattering which filled the silence. It was only when a smooth dark ink filled half the mortar that Joah looked up again. His father was smiling.

'Good.' He lifted the four-year-old from his knee and gave her a pat. 'Go and see if your mother needs any help.' The youngster scampered off, happily enough. The smile faded from his lips.

'What is it, Father?' Joah placed the mortar carefully on the ground.

'Pekah taking the throne is not the only news from the north—the Assyrians grow stronger. Pekahiah's father may have paid a thousand talents of silver to Tiglath-Pileser for his army's help, but that does not make the ruler of Assyria Israel's friend, especially as there is now a new king in Israel.' The Assyrian king was the third to bear that name.

Joah went quiet. His father had never kept from him difficult truths, whether it was the adultery of David or the idolatry of his son. 'If Assyria is a threat to Israel—' He lifted his gaze to meet that of his father. '—does that also mean it is a threat to Judah?'

Instead of answering him directly, Asaph quoted words of King David, written over two hundred years earlier. '*Some trust in chariots and some in horses, but we trust in the name of Yahweh our God.*'

It was in the summer that followed that Jerusalem was stirred by the news that their king, struck with leprosy ten years earlier, had finally died. Jotham, who had ruled in Uzziah's stead, now sat upon the throne in his own right. To Joah, however, it felt as though nothing had really changed. Of greater import to him was a rumour spreading within the city walls—a rumour that one of Judah's highborn men, living among them in Jerusalem, had had a vision. A vision of Yahweh Himself.

Notes

1. The events of this chapter take place around 740 BC.

2. Joah is named, together with Shebna, in 2 Kings 18:18 (and the parallel passage in Isaiah 36:3) as one of the top officials of Hezekiah.

3. It may be that literacy was fairly widespread in Judah at this time. Alan R. Millard, in his article 'Were Words Separated in Ancient Hebrew Writing?', (Bible Review 8:3, June 1992), states: 'Writing was as much a part of Israelite daily life as it was of Babylonian and Egyptian, with the advantage that anyone who wanted to learn could do so more easily, thanks to the simple 22-letter Hebrew alphabet.' However, this is a matter of some debate. Others think that it was more likely to be confined within certain strata of Israelite society or professions. See also 'The Question of Israelite Literacy', Alan R. Millard, (Bible Review 3:3, Fall 1987).

4. Millard, in the first article above, gives these fascinating details: '... even in early Hebrew inscriptions written in the old Hebrew script, a dot was put after each word as a word divider. This word divider can be seen very plainly in the famous Siloam tunnel inscription... Most texts...were written on papyri that have not survived. Evidence for their existence is clear from the hundreds of clay bullae that once sealed them and bear imprints of the papyrus fibers on their backs.' A bulla (plural, bullae) is a lump of clay stamped with a seal bearing the name of its owner, to create a mark of ownership on, for example, a jar, or to seal or authorise a document.

5. The water system within Jerusalem in the 8th Century BC is much debated, although more recent archaeological research by Ronny Reich and Eli Shukron has undermined the long-held idea that the waters of the Gihon spring were accessed by the inhabitants of Jerusalem via what has been known as 'Warren's Shaft'. It seems that, even before Hezekiah's tunnel, the waters of the Gihon spring were channelled to more easily accessible pools. Isaiah 7:3 (relating to the reign of Ahaz, Hezekiah's father), refers to 'the upper pool'—which probably implies the existence of another, lower pool, and a lower pool is then referred to in Isaiah 22:9, which may or may not be the 'old pool' in 22:11. More details can be found in an article by Reich and Shukron, entitled 'Light at the End of the

Tunnel', (Biblical Archaeology Review 25:1, January/February 1999), or a summary of their work and that of others in 'Life in Biblical Israel', pp213-223.

6. This is a helpful comment on the reigns of Pekahiah and Pekah: 'Pekah... is credited with twenty years of rule. Thiele dates his reign from 752 to 732 BC, thus making him a contemporary of Menahem and briefly Pekahiah. If this is true, then there was more than one person who claimed to be monarch in Israel during this period, which would be consistent with the turmoil described by the writer(s) of 2 Kings. The writer(s) of 2 Kings may have dated Pekah's reign from the establishment of a separate kingdom on the east of the Jordan. This complexity has yet to be unravelled.' (OTBBC, pp401-402)

7. Assyrian records mention tribute paid by 'Menahem of Samaria', the king of Israel before Pekahiah. 2 Kings 15:19 states that this was so that Menahem could gain Assyria's support 'and strengthen his own hold on the kingdom'. This would accord particularly well with there being a rival kingdom (of Pekah) nearby.

8. Although nothing is said about Isaiah's background in Scripture (other than he is 'the son of Amoz', Isaiah 1:1), he is clearly an educated man, given that he is said to have written down all the acts of Uzziah (see 2 Chronicles 26:22). He also seems to have enjoyed ready access to the palace and to the king (see Isaiah 38:5, 39:3). He has traditionally been taken to be from an influential, upper-class family in Jerusalem, or even as being of royal blood.

9. The only imagined named character introduced in this chapter is Zeruah.

2

*Then the LORD said to Isaiah, 'Go out, you and your son Shear-
Jashub, to meet Ahaz at the end of the aqueduct of the Upper Pool, on
the road to the Launderer's Field.' (Isaiah 7:3)*

*He looked on in horror as the walls of Jerusalem crumbled before him as easily
as if they had been a child's precarious pile of pebbles. Through the gaping hole
came a horde of soldiers, armed with sword and spear and surging forward
like a swollen river. He felt only terror as he turned and tried to run. It was,
however, like wading through floodwaters. Every step seemed to take both an
age and an extraordinary effort. Screams began to fill the air behind him, but
still he fought against the invisible tide that sought to slow his escape, fearing
each moment the plunging of a sharpened blade into his back...*

Joah jolted as a hand shook his shoulder.

'Joah! Wake up!'

In a moment he was wide awake, his heart still pounding. Relief
washed over the seventeen-year-old as he found himself beholding
the weary face of his mother rather than a marauding army.

'Did you not hear me call you the first time?'

'No,' mumbled Joah. The truth was that most of the night had
passed drifting between fitful sleep and wakefulness. Only as dawn
approached had he finally fallen into deeper slumber.

Zeruah pulled back his blanket. 'You had better rise straightaway,
or you will not have time to eat before you leave the house.' She
turned and left.

Joah pulled his legs up on the rush mat and rose to his feet, both
the images and the mood of the dream still fresh. *It would not come to
that. Surely.* But despite what he told himself as he pulled his tunic
on, another voice spoke within. The terror of the night would soon

be banished, but not the dread of the day. It weighed upon his mind when not fully occupied with his tasks at the palace.

Fear had spread across the land like an ever-deepening shadow cast by the thunderclouds rising in the north. With the distant rumbles and the growing chill came the question of when the storm might break upon them—and how fiercely it might rage. Except the storm cloud was not the Assyrians. The danger that kept Joah awake at night and stalked his dreams had arisen at a distance that could be travelled in days rather than weeks. Although Tiglath-Pileser had, some three years earlier, brought his army to the land of the Philistines in the west, it was Israel to their immediate north, and Pekah, its king, that had been harrying Judah, as had Aram beyond them. The trouble had started in the few years that Jotham had sole reign after Uzziah's death. But now Jotham's son, Ahaz, ruled the land.

Joah was still chewing a piece of warm bread, with more in his hand, when he and his father walked out through the courtyard door a short while later. In the year or so that he had been accompanying his father to the palace, Joah had learned not to speak until spoken to, unless he wanted a sharp reply. The smiling father of his childhood seemed to have all but disappeared. Under both Uzziah and Jotham, the land had known prosperity and peace, but now the latter had disappeared as readily as damp on the dust in the heat of the day— and with it, his father's easy manner.

And so it was his own thoughts that were usually his company on the short daily walk to the palace. He wondered what the day held for him. Whilst occasionally he stayed with his father, learning from him, most of the time he worked in the stores under Shaul, one of the king's stewards. Joah would list each newly arrived jar of wine or oil, whilst Shaul placed upon it a small lump of clay which he stamped with a seal so that it bore the words *belonging to the king*. Joah faithfully recorded all the provisions purchased for the royal household. It was difficult to entirely forget, however, the numerous beggars he saw in the city as the abundance that the king enjoyed passed through his hands.

But while he made records of flour and figs and raisin cakes as they were counted and weighed, his father had been chronicling the disastrous defeats of Ahaz at the hands of Pekah, king of Israel, and Rezin, king of Aram. War had come close to Jerusalem but had not overtaken it. Joah had never been more thankful to wield a reed pen rather than a sword, and hoped he never had to trade one for the other.

As they neared the palace, his father suddenly held out his arm to stop him, the reason immediately obvious as Joah looked up. The king was striding down the street with one of his wives, his dark green robe, richly embroidered with yellow and blue, swinging back and forth as he walked, his head held high. Guards flanked him and Joah bowed his head, staring at his own sandalled feet as the king and those with him swept past. He didn't need to wonder where they were going. It was the same every morning. Ahaz would be heading down into the Valley of Ben Hinnom that ran along the south side of Jerusalem and in which he burned incense to Baal. It was not the only altar at which he made his offerings to the Canaanite god, but it was the closest.

His father tugged his sleeve. Joah stole a quick look over his shoulder as they resumed walking. It puzzled him. Ahaz's grandfather and father both worshipped only Yahweh, and yet it was in the latter's time that both Pekah and Rezin began to rise against Judah. And now these kings, neither of whom worshipped Yahweh, had inflicted great harm upon their land. *What if there were other gods? Maybe Ahaz reckoned that if he made offerings to his foes' gods then he might gain their favour too. But the law of Moses told them to neither have nor worship any gods beside Yahweh.* The jumbled thoughts troubled Joah, but he was not about to voice them. *It was his place to serve the king, not to question his actions.* It was clear, however, that many in Jerusalem were happy enough to follow where Ahaz led.

They entered the outer courtyard of the palace, but it was only as the cedar doors to the inside loomed before them that his father finally spoke. 'Go and help Shaul again today. Do whatever he tells you, and I will collect you when I am finished for the day.' And with that, Asaph turned and left him. Joah stood for a few moments,

103

staring after his father as he disappeared down the corridor. Then he sighed, turned in the opposite direction and made his way toward the stores.

There was something strange about the palace that day—a different mood in those he passed. And when he reached the stores, he found Shaul seated on a sack of flour with three others whom Joah recognised surrounding him. All turned towards him as he approached.

'Have you heard?' asked Shaul.

'Heard what?'

'Pekah and Rezin have formed an alliance.'

It felt as if one of the scale weights had fallen into his stomach. There was an obvious question but one whose answer he had already guessed. He asked it anyway. 'Against whom?'

'King Ahaz.'

One of the others continued in a lowered voice. 'It is said that they intend to stand together against the Assyrians, but because Ahaz will not join them, they plan to overthrow and replace him.'

Joah's mouth suddenly felt dry. 'Is it not better for Ahaz to stand with them rather than against them?'

Shaul shrugged. 'That depends on how Ahaz views the king of Assyria.' He paused. 'But of this you can be sure: if the Assyrians return and continue their conquest to the north, neither Pekah nor Rezin will want to find themselves attacked by Assyria on one side and by its allies on the other.'

The day passed more quickly than usual, with similar conversations whenever others visited the storeroom. When his father finally appeared at the door, the sun was lower than usual. His sombre expression matched the mood of the palace. Joah yearned to know more of what was happening but had no desire for a swift and sharp rebuke. His father, however, did not need to be asked.

'Tomorrow, you will accompany me in my service of the king.'

'Do you know what we will be doing?' It seemed a safe question.

'The king wishes to inspect the city's water supplies. We will be ready to record any instructions that he gives.'

Joah was sure it must have some connection with the events to

the north. 'Shaul says there is an alliance between Rezin and Pekah…'
He left his words hanging.

'Shaul speaks the truth. If they are to attack Jerusalem and there is
a siege, Ahaz wants our water supplies to be secure and not to aid our
enemies.'

Joah's fear finally freed his mouth. *If it earned him a rebuke, so
be it.* He lowered his voice. 'If Ahaz could defeat neither Rezin nor
Pekah before, how will Jerusalem survive if they come against the
city together?'

Asaph's expression was grim and he looked steadfastly ahead,
avoiding Joah's eyes. 'Help may yet be found elsewhere…'

*There was only one place that his father could mean. The place to which
a previous king of Israel had looked when he had needed his hand to be
strengthened against rivals: Assyria.*

Asaph held out a wooden box to Joah. 'Here.'

Joah took the writing kit, feeling suddenly as if his life had taken
on greater significance. He had never accompanied the king on such
an important task, although he knew his role would simply be to
remain silent and write only if it was required of him. His father
carried an identical kit; Joah deemed them ingenious. The shallow
box was hinged and opened out into two halves. Each half had
a writing surface covered with wax and protected by a small rim
around its four sides. A wooden stylus was stored within the box to
inscribe upon the surface, which would then remain protected when
the box was closed again. It was easy enough to renew the wax when
the words upon it had served their purpose.

The small procession of the king and his officials left the palace,
with Joah and his father at the rear. Joah felt more at ease there. He
had no wish to be conspicuous. They were soon leaving the city
and it was only a short walk to their destination: the end of a water
channel beside the road to the Launderer's Field where cloth was
washed. Joah stood on the edge of the gathering, next to his father.
He copied him as Asaph opened up his writing kit and held the stylus
ready. Joah was soon absorbed in the discussions of the king and his

officials, and even occasionally jotted down a number or a name in the wax as his father directed. Joah suddenly, however, became aware that the discussion around him was petering out. He looked up and saw the gaze of the now-silent king fixed on a point behind him. Joah stole a look over his shoulder, but even as he caught sight of a figure approaching them, his father dragged him to the side to let the young man and the child who was accompanying him have a clear path to the king. 'It's Isaiah,' hissed Asaph, in a barely audible voice.

Joah gawped at the man they were calling a prophet. *Here was the one who had seen Yahweh Himself! Or so it was said.* Then Joah remembered where he was and swiftly closed his mouth. He had heard of the prophet Micah, who had begun speaking in the name of Yahweh some years earlier, but had never seen him. *Here was Isaiah standing within the toss of a stone!* He judged the prophet to be slightly older than the king, who was not much beyond his twentieth year. The boy with him looked around five. No one spoke—not even the king, who simply stood scrutinising the newcomer. Joah's eyes darted between the two men.

Isaiah stopped just a few paces from the king. The child seemed oblivious of the company in which he was standing, staring around him with interest. There was an uneasy silence.

'Take care and be calm,' began Isaiah, addressing Ahaz. 'Have no fear and do not be fainthearted because of these two stumps of smouldering firewood, on account of the fierce anger of Rezin and Aram and the son of Remaliah.'

Joah stared at the prophet who dared to refer to Pekah, king of Israel, merely as *the son of Remaliah.*

Isaiah continued. 'Because Aram, with Ephraim and the son of Remaliah, has planned evil against you, saying, *Let us invade Judah; let us tear it apart and divide it among ourselves, and make the son of Tabeel king over it*, this is what the Lord Yahweh says: *It will not take place, it will not happen.*' The prophet's message continued, predicting that within sixty-five years, the northern kingdom of Israel would be shattered. He concluded the message looking around at them all. *'If you do not stand firm in your faith, you will not stand at all.'*

As silence fell once again, Joah glanced quickly at Ahaz. The king's expression gave no sign of what was within. His face was set like stone. Joah returned his attention to the prophet. *He had spoken of Rezin and Pekah as if they were of little consequence, despite both kings having already bettered Ahaz in battle.* The boy with Isaiah—whom Joah guessed to be his son—continued watching those assembled with both innocence and interest.

Finally, Isaiah spoke again. 'Ask Yahweh your God for a sign, whether in the deepest depths or in the highest heights.'

Every eye was upon Ahaz. They waited. The king's mouth twitched. 'I will not ask; I will not put Yahweh to the test.'

To Joah's ears, the words sounded pious. Isaiah clearly felt otherwise. 'Hear now, you house of David! Is it not enough to try the patience of humans? Will you try the patience of my God also?' The prophet's eyes swept over the officials. 'Therefore the Lord Himself will give you a sign: the virgin will conceive and give birth to a son, and will call him *God with us*. He will be eating curds and honey when he knows enough to reject the wrong and choose the right, for before the boy knows enough to reject the wrong and choose the right, the land of the two kings you dread will be laid waste. Yahweh will bring on you and on your people and on the house of your father a time unlike any since Ephraim broke away from Judah—He will bring the king of Assyria.'

Joah's mind was reeling, the words *the king of Assyria* echoing there as Isaiah went on. *The prophet seemed to be saying that Rezin and Pekah were not the ones to be feared and would both be devastated, but that the real threat was Assyria. And who was the virgin who would give birth to a child to be named Immanuel—God with us?* Suddenly Joah became aware that the prophet had fallen silent. Without waiting to be dismissed, Isaiah simply turned and left, his son trotting happily behind him. The officials glanced at one another, clearly nervous. Ahaz stood tight-lipped, staring after Isaiah. Then, without a further word, he too turned and began walking away, but in the opposite direction. The visit to the water supply was clearly over.

The officials followed a little distance behind the king, murmuring to one another, with Joah and his father behind them. Whatever they were saying was beyond his hearing. For a while, the two walked together without speaking, with questions still swirling around in Joah's mind like chaff in a summer breeze. But one was more puzzling than any other, and he could not even begin to imagine its answer. He turned to his father. 'Why did Isaiah bring his young son with him?'

His father shrugged. 'Maybe he was making a point...'

'What point?'

Asaph sighed wearily. 'I understand that he gave his son a strange name.'

'Which is?'

'*A-Remnant-Shall-Return.*'

The furrow on Joah's brow only deepened. 'A remnant of what? And return from where?'

'How should I know?' snapped his father.

Joah fell silent and decided it was prudent to stay that way as they returned to the palace. Unbidden, some of Isaiah's words came back into his mind, and they troubled him: *If you do not stand firm in your faith, you will not stand at all.*

Within only a few months, Joah found himself with a new job at the palace: not helping to record the arrival of oil or wine for the kitchens, but the departure of silver and gold from the treasuries. The tallies of cups, plates and other precious articles grew ever longer on the sheets of papyri. A similar record was being made at the temple as its stores were similarly depleted—and all of it with the same destination: Assyria.

'One hundred and forty-two shekels,' said Shaul as he removed the gold plate from the scales and added it to a growing pile.

Joah glanced up after recording the number. 'How will the king transport all this to Nineveh?'

Shaul shrugged. 'Quickly, I imagine. He will not want it seized by Pekah or Rezin, though it may not harm the king if they later learn what has gone to Assyria.'

'But he cannot send it north along the King's Highway! That would take it straight to Damascus...'

Shaul shrugged again. 'I imagine it will go east, especially as Judah has now lost the port of Elath to the Edomites. The desert is not an easy route, but it is a less travelled one. And you can be sure that the king's mules will have a heavy guard.' He balanced another plate on the scales and added more weights. 'One hundred and sixty-five.'

Joah jotted it down. 'How much gold will be enough?'

'The greater the amount, the greater the favour he will earn with Tiglath-Pileser.'

Before either could speak again, however, a woman's scream rang out. It was distant but within the palace. Joah looked up sharply. Shaul's hand was frozen in mid-air. Joah strained his ears. More screams followed and then they abruptly stopped, as if the woman had been suddenly silenced. He stiffened.

Shaul put down the scale pans. 'Stay here.' He disappeared out into the corridor and when he returned sometime later his face was ashen.

Joah's heart pounded. 'What has happened?'

'It is what is about to happen that will make your ears tingle.'

'What do you mean?'

'The screams were from one of the king's wives. The king's guard came and forcefully took her baby—one of the king's sons.'

'What for?' Joah feared the answer but could not avoid the question.

Shaul's face darkened. 'It seems that incense is not all that Ahaz will be burning on his altars down in Ben Hinnom…'

Joah's stomach lurched. He looked down at the papyrus again, but the numbers swam before his eyes. 'Gold for the Assyrians,' he murmured, 'and an even higher price to buy the favour of the gods…' For a fleeting moment, his mind glimpsed the face of the young prophet—and wondered what he would say.

'It is time for you to wed.'

Joah stopped chewing the mouthful of lamb stew and stared at his father. He then glanced swiftly at his mother. *She clearly knew what was coming.* His mind raced. *Had his father already decided whom he was to marry?* He swallowed the mouthful but held his peace and waited.

His younger siblings giggled. Joah ignored them, looking steadily at his father instead.

Asaph continued. 'I have been speaking to Joseph son of Nethaniah. His daughter Miriam is now of age.'

Joah knew her. Although his heart did not soar, neither did it plummet. *Whilst she did not have the beauty of Naomi daughter of Izri, she was not unpleasant to the eye.* Joah suddenly realised with a start that beyond her appearance, he knew nothing of his future wife, though her father was known to him as another official at the palace. 'When are we to be betrothed?'

'At new moon,' answered his father, dipping his bread in the pot of stew at the centre of the low table around which they were seated. 'And you will be wed in the month of Tishri.'

Joah was pleased that he wouldn't have too many months to wait. 'What is she like?'

'She cooks well enough and can sew and weave,' began his mother.

'More importantly,' interrupted his father, 'her elder sister has already borne two healthy children to her husband. Joseph assures me that Miriam will also be a fruitful vine to you.'

Joah wondered if that was something a father could know of his daughter. He decided not to ask, as he suspected it would only draw further mirth from his siblings—and he did not want to show his ignorance in front of them. His own father, however, suddenly rose and disappeared for a few moments, reappearing with a skin of wine. It was only then that Joah realised why they were eating meat that evening. *This was a celebration, of course.* But more than the wine, it was his father's mood that gladdened his own heart. In the two years or so since Judah sent its gold to Assyria, becoming its vassal, the army of Tiglath-Pileser had swept in from the north, capturing Damascus, deporting its people and putting Rezin to death. A similar fate had fallen upon Galilee. Pekah, however, had died at the hands of an Israelite named Hoshea who had both conspired against him and taken the crown from him. Joah's dreams were no longer stalked by invaders and the daily walk to the palace no longer marked by a brooding silence.

Joah lay awake later, staring up from his rush mat into the room that was as black as the ink in his pen, his belly satisfied by a joyous mixture of meat and wine. His mind was like a bee in a patch of flowers, both dancing around and sucking sweetness from all upon which his thoughts alighted. He smiled to himself in the darkness, but then he frowned slightly. *Isaiah's words had been true: the two kings that Ahaz had feared had come to nothing. But the king of Assyria rather than Yahweh had brought about their downfall. And yet hadn't Isaiah also spoken of Assyria being a hired razor that would shave off both the hair and beard of Judah? It was true that Ahaz had hired him, and that their king was now the first vassal in David's line. Was that the humiliation of being shaved?* Joah was not sure what to think—so he thought of Miriam instead.

Before the month of Tishri arrived, and with it his marriage to Miriam, there was, however, a change within the city.

'Shaul!'

Joah looked up as an unfamiliar man entered the room, though clearly a temple priest from his dress.

'Yes, what is it?'

'How much silver have you here?'

Shaul smiled wryly. 'Who wants to know?'

'Uriah.'

'And why does the high priest wish to know how much silver the king has, particularly when Ahaz is away in Damascus meeting the king of Assyria.'

'Because Ahaz has sent Uriah a message requiring him to build a new altar for the temple before his return. He has seen the altar at the temple of Hadad in Damascus, and he wishes to have one like it in Jerusalem. He has sent ahead a pattern to be followed, as he desires it to be ready before his return. The silver is to buy the materials and pay the workmen.'

Shaul glanced up at the room's high window through which light was streaming. 'Come back after noon and I will give you your answer.'

The priest seemed happy enough and left. Neither Shaul nor

Joah spoke until he was out in the corridor. 'Why does he want a new altar?' murmured Shaul. 'Is Solomon's altar not enough?'

'Maybe he wants to please the king of Assyria...'

'Or appease the gods of the other nations. Why worship one god when you can worship them all?'

Joah wondered whether Shaul spoke his own mind or what he supposed to be in the king's. He didn't ask.

Notes

1. *The events of this chapter take place between what is thought to be the date of the Israel-Aram alliance against Judah (735 BC), and the fall of Damascus and Hoshea becoming king of Israel (732 BC). However, as many commentators admit, the chronology of this particular period is very complicated and datings vary. Even in the dating of Thiele and McFall, the end of Jotham's reign and the start of Ahaz's reign seems to be particularly problematic, particularly as the Biblical accounts seem to have only Ahaz dealing with the crisis with Rezin and Pekah (around 735/734 BC) although Jotham may not have died until around 732 BC. In three places Jotham is said to have reigned 16 years (1 Kings 15:33, 2 Chronicles 27:1,8), but 2 Kings 15:30 refers to his twentieth year. He may have ruled from 750 to 732, possibly as coregent with his father Uzziah for ten years and with his son Ahaz for three years.*

2. *If the dating of this period is complex, then so also is the understanding of how the records in the different Biblical texts dovetail together. 'There are various, divergent accounts of this complex conflict in the Old Testament, in 2 Kings 15:37, 16:5, Isaiah 7, Hosea 5:8-6:6 and [2 Chronicles 28].' (1,2 Chronicles, Allen, p358) This chapter is one attempt at harmonisation.*

3. *Various clay bullae have been discovered from this period, including one that has the name of Ahaz. See 'First Impression: What We Learn from King Ahaz's Seal', Robert Deutsch, (Biblical Archaeology Review 24:3, May/June 1998).*

4. *In 2 Kings 16:1-4 there is a summary of the reign of King Ahaz. It states that he 'followed the ways of the kings of Israel and even sacrificed his son in*

the fire' (v3). It is not clear when that particular act happened, though the parallel verses in 2 Chronicles 28:3 imply that it occurred more than once. Given that Rezin and Pekah were planning to overthrow Ahaz, it would not seem unreasonable to link this crisis to such a heinous and desperate act. The practice of child sacrifice occurred in Canaanite and Phoenician contexts, and these offerings to the gods were seen as a means of manipulating deities.

5. *Ahaz seems to be accepting vassal status under Assyria, given the gold and silver he sent to Tiglath-Pileser (2 Kings 16:8) and his words, 'I am your servant and your son' (ESV, v7). His request for assistance is granted in the form of the Assyrian campaigns against Aram and Israel in 733–732 BC. 'Tiglath-Pileser's texts…record that Jeho-Ahaz (the longer form of Ahaz's name) was among tribute payers by about 734, probably soon after his 'bribe' following his takeover of power in Judah in 735.' (Kitchen, pp38-40).*

6. *The prophecy of Isaiah recorded in this chapter (from Isaiah 7) was not his only words foretelling the downfall of Damascus. Isaiah 17 also records another prophecy about this, together with Jacob growing lean (v4-6), which could be a reference to Israel losing territory in Galilee at roughly the same time that Damascus was defeated.*

7. *In 2 Chronicles 28:23, it says of Ahaz: 'He offered sacrifices to the gods of Damascus, who had defeated him; for he thought, "Since the gods of the kings of Aram have helped them, I will sacrifice to them so that they will help me."' The following is helpful: 'Since most wars were conducted as holy wars, credit was given to the god(s) of the victorious army… Here Ahaz is making a frank admission that since the Arameans had been victorious over him, their gods were more powerful and in the right. The gods of Damascus were from the Aramean pantheon and included Hadad (the storm deity), which was most probably the proper name of Baal, known from Canaanite sources. Ahaz also made a large altar to the "gods of Damascus" (see 2 Kings 16:9-16)… It was to replace the bronze altar built by Solomon. The temple that Ahaz visited was probably that of Hadad-Rimmon (cf. 2 Kings 5:18).' (OTBBC, p450). The 2 Kings 5 reference is to Naaman's mention of this temple.*

8. *Isaiah's prophecy in this chapter comes from Isaiah 7:4-25.*

9. *Imagined named characters introduced in this chapter are Joseph, Nethaniah, Miriam and Shaul.*

3

Shalmaneser king of Assyria came up to attack Hoshea, who had been Shalmaneser's vassal and had paid him tribute... The king of Assyria invaded the entire land, marched against Samaria and laid siege to it for three years. In the ninth year of Hoshea, the king of Assyria captured Samaria and deported the Israelites to Assyria.
(2 Kings 17:3,5-6)

Joah took the five-year-old's hand and gave a light tug. 'Come on, Zebediah.' His firstborn complied but was soon turning his large brown eyes upwards.

'Can I hold the rope?'

'No. You are not much bigger than the lamb, and I do not want you letting go of it in the streets of Jerusalem.' Zebediah opened his mouth. 'And if you are going to whine, then I will suppose that you would rather stay at home with your mother and sister than come with me to the temple.' The youngster swiftly shut his mouth and pouted instead. Joah decided that silence was victory enough.

That Miriam was, indeed, a fruitful vine had been swiftly established. Within three months of their marriage her belly began to swell, and Zebediah was born nine months after their wedding. And soon after Miriam had weaned him, she had conceived once more and now they had a daughter who was almost two. It was her arrival that had prompted Joah to leave his father's house and the crowded streets of Jerusalem and build a new house on the hill that rose to the west of Jerusalem's city walls. He was not the only inhabitant of Jerusalem to do so as the land enjoyed a time of peace, with both Judah and Israel now vassals of Assyria.

A sigh escaped from Zebediah. Joah chuckled as he found himself having to pull again on his son's hand. 'You knew that we would have to walk uphill most of the way to the temple, and you will be rewarded when it is downhill for most of the way back.'

'But it is such a long way...'

It was Joah's turn to sigh. 'Look—we are almost at the Valley Gate, and I can even see the temple from here.'

'But I can't.'

'No, but before long you will be tall enough to see it for yourself from here.'

They were soon passing out of sunlight and briefly into shadow, as their path took them through the impressive stone gate. They then continued their ascent through the streets of Jerusalem. Joah guided Zebediah and the lamb around a man lying at the side of the street. He suspected that it was an abundance of wine the previous night rather than a scarcity of silver that had put him there.

Smoke was soon drifting across their path, heavy with the scent of burning incense. Zebediah turned his nose up. Its source was soon spotted. It seemed that every street corner now had its own shrine, whether to Yahweh or Baal or Asherah. It had pleased Ahaz to multiply altars as well as gods. It had been the same throughout Judah, so that worshippers no longer needed to make the journey to Jerusalem every time they desired to offer a sacrifice.

The woman who was burning incense was clearly from one of the wealthy families. She was clad with colourful fine linen from her head to ankles, her wrists jangling with gold bangles, and her fingers and ears similarly adorned. The nearby beggar's outstretched hand went unheeded. *That was Jerusalem's way—the poor and the prosperous side-by-side in the streets, imploring and ignoring each other in equal measure, and begging or banqueting marking their days.* They passed two further shrines on their way to the temple, both with fragrant smoke ascending. Joah had also offered incense on such altars—and knew of few who didn't.

'Can I hold the rope *now*?' asked Zebediah as they finally reached the top of the steps to the temple courtyard.

'If we have to wait to sacrifice, then, yes, you may hold it.' Joah reckoned there would be little risk of losing the lamb when they were both standing still. His reward was a smile that came as readily to his son's face as ripe figs to the ground in a wind. Moments later he added, 'And wait we will have to.' Zebediah seemed happy enough at the prospect, taking the rope into his hand as solemnly as if he were holding the reins of the king's mule. Joah bent down and whispered, 'King Ahaz and his son Hezekiah are here. We will have to wait until they are finished.' Zebediah nodded, more interested in his charge. Joah straightened up and joined others standing in respectful silence. There was nothing else to do but wait and watch.

Ahaz was not at his new altar, patterned on the one he had seen in Damascus and now standing in the favoured spot, directly between the main gate and the sanctuary itself. He was at Solomon's bronze altar which he had moved to the north side of the courtyard. There was no fire on the altar, but rather a slaughtered animal. A diviner stood over it, his hands plunged into the bloody carcass. He then held up some of its entrails and started examining them whilst the king spoke to him, too far away to be heard. Joah suspected the king had lowered his voice anyway. *Maybe he was enquiring of the god Hadad over some matter, seeking his will.* Animals were not the only dead that Ahaz consulted, however. Joah recoiled.

Beyond the king, Joah could see another small altar on which incense was burning. Behind it was a sight that made the hairs on his arms prickle. *Nehushtan. Here was the bronze snake wrought by the very hands of Moses!* Joah knew the story—a snake crafted in metal at the word of Yahweh and lifted up on a pole, so that all that looked at it could be healed from the poison of the snakes that slithered among their tents. But it had gained a name since then and a new purpose as an idol to be worshipped.

Joah's eyes shifted from the seven-hundred-year-old snake to Ahaz's fourteen-year-old son, already named as his successor. His attention was fixed on neither the carcass nor the two men beside him, his face impassive. Joah followed his gaze to where the temple doors stood firmly shut. He wondered what it was like inside. *Dark.* The lamps had not been lit nor fire kindled on the altar of incense since Ahaz had closed the doors, barring the way into what was said to be the presence of Yahweh. But that and the altar were not the only changes the king had wrought there. No other king of Judah had changed the temple as he had, seemingly with the agreement of Uriah, the high priest. The huge laver which had once rested on the back of twelve bronze oxen now rested upon a stone base instead, the bronze being sent to Assyria as tribute. Being a vassal still carried a heavy price. It made little difference that their overlord now had a new name. Shalmaneser had succeeded his father, Tiglath-Pileser, the previous year.

As Joah watched the king, he suddenly became aware of the small hand of Zebediah in his own. In a heartbeat, memories were tumbling through his head like water through a breach in a dam. He remembered Isaiah with his own son confronting Ahaz, and the king's dismissive response. Then, the prophet's words that had followed soon after: *Should not a people enquire of their God? Why consult the dead on behalf of the living?* He recalled the piercing gaze of Isaiah and his equally piercing words: *If you do not stand firm in your faith, you will not stand at all.*

Joah stared at the lamb soon to be slaughtered. *Whose favour was he seeking to earn?* He was no longer sure. He had mumbled the name of Baal alongside that of Yahweh as he'd offered his incense on the street altars. But it was whispered that Isaiah spoke of Yahweh as *The Holy One of Israel*—not one god among many but the only God, angered by His people despising His laws. *What if Isaiah was right?* It was not the first time the troubling question had entered his head.

It was only days later that Joah's father met him in one of the palace corridors and pulled him to one side. 'Have you heard the rumours from the north about Hoshea?'

It had been some while since Joah had heard anything of the king of Israel. 'No. What is being said?'

Asaph glanced around. 'That he has rebelled against the king of Assyria and no longer pays tribute.'

Joah was speechless for a moment. 'Has Hoshea lost his mind? Why on earth would he do that? Wasn't it Assyria that helped put him on the throne in the first place?'

Asaph shrugged. 'But that was a different king…'

Joah frowned, at a loss to make sense of what he was hearing. 'Nothing I have heard suggests that Shalmaneser's power wanes, and Hoshea is a gnat next to the Assyrian lion!'

'Maybe, but it is also rumoured that he looks to the south for aid.'

Joah paused for a moment. 'To Egypt?'

His father nodded. 'Apparently he has sent envoys to King So.'

Joah bit his lip. *Judah lay between Egypt and Israel. What would happen to it if the Assyrian army came against their neighbours' alliance?*

His father seemed to sense his mood. 'You know that you and Miriam will always have a place to stay within Jerusalem's walls.'

Joah managed a weak smile. 'Let us hope that will not be necessary. But thank you.'

Asaph was quiet for a few moments. 'That is not all I have heard.' Joah held his peace and waited. 'The prophet has not been silent. He calls Israel a *fading flower*.' Isaiah did not need to be named.

Joah may have been more familiar with papyrus than plants, but he knew perfectly well what followed after a flower had faded.

'Who do you think they are?'

Joah studied the small family group unloading a cart not far from where he and Miriam were standing by the door of their house. 'If the king's scouts are to be believed, then they are most likely from Samaria—or one of the other towns of Israel.' Miriam, her belly swollen once more, left him and disappeared inside.

Several months had passed since hearing of Hoshea's rebellion against Shalmaneser, and barely a week earlier, news had reached Jerusalem that the might of Assyria had been seen near Damascus, moving south. It did not take much imagination to guess the army's destination. Joah's gaze shifted slightly to his own children who were standing at the gap in the low wall that enclosed their tiny plot of land. He smiled. *Both clearly eyeing up possible friends amongst the newcomers!*

'Here.'

Joah pushed himself away from the doorpost on which he had been leaning and turned. Miriam was holding out some bread and cakes of raisins.

'If they have travelled from the north, they will be weary. I would take it myself, but—' She drew out the word. '—if I get talking…' She raised her eyebrows, cocking her head slightly.

'If my wife gets talking, then by the time she comes back, our evening meal will have boiled dry and burnt.' He took the provisions, grinning.

'And if my husband takes his children with him…' She leant over and gave him a long, lingering kiss.

'Yes?'

'Then the stew will be even less likely to be burned.' And with a mischievous smile she disappeared back into the dim room inside.

Joah shook his head and chuckled. He walked towards the opening in the wall, paused, and looked down. 'Zebediah, Jerusha—would you like to make some new friends?' No persuasion was needed.

One of the strangers, whom Joah took to be the father, was by now banging a tent peg into the ground. He looked up as Joah approached.

'Greetings, my friend. My wife thought you might need a little food to refresh you after your journey.'

The stranger smiled, laying his mallet on the ground. 'Yahweh bless you for your kindness.'

Joah was surprised by the greeting but kept it hidden.

The man glanced over his shoulder. 'Jael!' Almost immediately a woman emerged from the tent. 'Look,' he said, nodding towards Joah, 'we are already being made welcome here.'

Joah smiled and held out the food towards her. 'You *are* welcome.' He wondered, however, given the man's remark, if she had expected it to be otherwise.

She took the bread and raisins from his hands, returning the smile. 'And you are most kind.'

After Gamaliel had introduced his family, he turned to Joah as his eldest daughter fetched a large jar from the cart. 'Where does the city draw its water?'

'Zebediah can take your daughter there.' He turned to his seven-year-old, whose face had become uncharacteristically solemn with the weight of the duty now upon him. 'Zebediah—show your new friend the way to the Lower Pool.' The youngster nodded and was soon heading towards the city walls with three of Gamaliel's offspring, eating bread or raisins as they went. Jerusha sat nearby with Gamaliel's youngest, both playing with stones, as Jael made a fire for cooking. Gamaliel's elderly grandfather sat on a stool, eyes closed, as the sun disappeared behind the hill.

'Here—let me help you.' Joah tightened the knot on the next tent rope as Gamaliel hammered its peg into the ground. 'What brings you to Jerusalem, my friend?'

Gamaliel, his face grim, pulled on the tent peg. It didn't move. 'I did not wish to see my city overrun by Assyrians and my family slaughtered or carried far away to some distant land.'

'We had heard of the army coming south.'

Gamaliel straightened up. 'If Shalmaneser is marching on Samaria, then Dothan will almost be in his path, and it does not have Samaria's fortifications.'

'Is Dothan your home, then?'

'It *was*. I am from the tribe of Manasseh, and I do not lightly leave the inheritance of my ancestors. It is only the sheer folly— or madness—of our king that has compelled me to do so. Rightly is Israel likened to a senseless and silly dove, turning to Egypt, to Assyria—to anyone but its true God. But if it is the will of Yahweh, we will return one day.' Gamaliel moved on to the next rope.

Joah followed him, intrigued by the newcomer's words but unsure of how to voice the questions stirring within. 'You speak of Yahweh…' He left the words hanging, inviting Gamaliel's response.

Gamaliel inspected the ground for a suitable place for the peg. 'That surprises you?' He glanced up. 'Not all in Israel bow down to Jeroboam's calf-idols.' His eyes returned to the task. 'It is true that the land is strewn with high places and altars to the gods of Canaan, Moab or any other land you care to name. It is also true that many worship foreign gods and treat the God of Abraham, Isaac and Jacob as just one deity among many. But that is not the way of *my* family.' Without looking up he added, 'But from what I hear and what I have seen so far, I wonder if Judah is so different under your king…' For a few moments, the only sound was that of mallet upon wood as the peg was driven in. Gamaliel straightened up once more and nodded towards the elderly man seated on the stool. 'You should listen to the stories my grandfather tells. His own grandfather lived during the days of Elijah and Elisha, and passed on to him tales of the great wonders that Yahweh wrought through the hands of his prophets. He tells of fire falling from heaven, of the dead raised, and of how Yahweh struck the whole army of Aram blind when they sought Elisha in my own city of Dothan.'

Joah was silent for a moment. *How much easier it would be to believe in Yahweh as the true God if he could see such wonders with his own eyes!* 'But we see no such signs today.'

Gamaliel shrugged. 'But did not Yahweh Himself strike King Uzziah with leprosy?'

'True, but it is hardly fire from heaven or the miraculous defeat of an army.'

'Maybe. But even seeing the works of the Almighty does not ensure that the heart will change. King Ahab saw the fire but still followed idols. But even if Yahweh's hand remains unseen, His voice has not been silent.'

'You mean the voice of prophets?'

Gamaliel took the final rope in his hand and gave it a quick tug before inspecting the ground once again. 'In my father's time, a prophet named Amos was accused of conspiracy against the king, because he spoke not only of the sin of the people but prophesied that Israel would go from its land into exile. In my own days, there is a prophet with a different name but the same message. This prophet, Hosea, calls Israel a whore because of its idolatry, and it was he who also spoke of her as a senseless dove. He even gives his children strange names as part of his message.'

'He is not alone in that,' murmured Joah. 'There is a prophet in Jerusalem who named his firstborn *A-Remnant-Shall-Return.*'

'At least there is hope in the word *return*. Hosea named his later issue *No-Mercy* and *Not-My-People,* and his firstborn *Jezreel.*'

121

'*Jezreel*? Why name him after the city?'

'To you it may be just the name of a city,' answered Gamaliel. 'To us it is a place of bloodshed.' He squatted again by the final tent peg, hammered it, and then stood straight once more. He flicked the taut rope. 'Well, at least our tent will not fall upon us as we sleep. Thank you for your help.' He turned to Joah. 'And what is the name of your prophet who speaks in the name of Yahweh?'

'Isaiah son of Amoz. He is one of the highborn of Jerusalem.'

Gamaliel folded his arms. 'Highborn or lowborn—what does it matter? Of greater importance is whether the people heed him or not.' He looked steadily at Joah. 'Do they?'

The question pierced Joah's soul. He looked away and fixed his eyes on the temple instead. *It was safer to speak of others and the things of which he was sure.* 'Ahaz has closed the doors of Yahweh's sanctuary.'

'Gideon's fleece!' exclaimed Gamaliel. 'It did not surprise me to see folly in the heart of the king of Israel, but in a son of David?' Joah turned back to face him. Gamaliel sighed. 'Let us be glad that your prophet did not also name his son *No-Mercy*.'

Joah was almost relieved when he caught side of Zebediah and the others. 'Ah—the children return.' He changed the subject. 'Will you travel on further south?'

'No, it was our intention to make our home for the time being in Jerusalem. I am neither a farmer nor a shepherd needing land.'

'What is your trade?'

'That of my father and his father before him—silversmith.'

'Then you will find many within the city eager for your wares.' Joah clicked his tongue. 'But not, I'm afraid, any room within its walls.' He gestured around. 'That is why I and others have begun building on this hill.'

'In that case, my friend, you may well have the family of Gamaliel as new neighbours.'

'We would be glad to have you as such.'

'And your trade, Joah?'

'I am a Levite, but a scribe—I work for the king.'

'A man of learning...' Gamaliel studied him for several moments. If he had other questions, they remained unspoken. Any further conversation was cut short anyway by the excited shouts of Gamaliel's children.

As Joah returned to his house, with his own children chattering away about their new friends, he could not shake from his mind the thought that Gamaliel knew the God of their fathers in a way that he didn't.

In the months that followed, as Joah both welcomed another son, Ethan, and watched his neighbour's house grow brick by brick, news from Israel also flowed south like a polluted river, and with it more travellers seeking refuge. There were reports of Israelite cities— including Dothan—falling to the Assyrians, and then the news that told them that the northern kingdom was a hair's breadth from disaster: Samaria was under siege.

'Do you think there is any hope for the city?' asked Joah as he stood next to Gamaliel, inspecting the newly installed roof beams.

'Samaria's only hope would be the hand of Yahweh, but if it is the hand of Yahweh that is now against them, then they have as much hope as an ant in the shadow of an ox's hoof.' He lowered his gaze and met Joah's. 'Do not tell me that a scribe within the king's palace is unaware of the might of Assyria and their means of conquest. Hmm?'

Joah sighed. He knew Gamaliel well enough by now to know when an answer was expected. He looked around, checking that neither Jael nor the children were in earshot. He lowered his voice anyway. 'It is true. They first ravage the land and then surround the main city, having cut off its sources of food and help. And then, yes, the end is inescapable, providing the Assyrians have sufficient time and supplies. They will either batter their way into the city, building a siege ramp if they must, or else they will starve it into submission. It will be a grim end, either way—and Assyria will prevail.'

'But you have left out a detail, my friend—only if it is the will of Yahweh.'

Joah fixed his eyes on the wooden beams once more and did not respond.

Even before he reached the Valley Gate, Joah could hear the wailing within the city. His first reaction was to wonder if the king had died unexpectedly during the night. There was a cluster around one of the guards at the gate and Joah joined them, tapping one of the men on the shoulder. 'What is going on?'

'Samaria has fallen. News arrived at first light.' There was little more they could add, other than to say that if more were known, it would be at the palace.

Samaria has fallen. Joah walked up the hill slowly. It had been three years since the start of the siege. *Three years! How had Samaria even survived that long?* Somehow, as the months had slid into years, what was happening to the north often slipped from Joah's mind. On the occasions he *did* remember the city, he had begun to wonder if somehow Samaria might, against all hope, survive. Gamaliel, however, had a different view. He had repeated the words of his prophet, likening Samaria to a twig floating on water, carried away by the flow. It seemed that the might of the Tigris had finally prevailed.

When he reached the palace, it soon became clear that no other matter was being discussed. Little work would be done that day. He had progressed beyond working with Shaul and now laboured alongside his father, recording more weighty matters of palace business than its number of jars.

Despite his hope of learning more, few other details were known for sure. That did not, however, still their tongues.

'I cannot begin to imagine how the city must have been at the end,' said a man named Azel.

'My neighbour used to live in Dothan,' replied Joah, 'not far from Samaria. He told me what happened when Ben-Hadad, king of Aram, besieged Samaria over a hundred years ago. Food was so scarce that even the head of a dead donkey could be sold for eighty shekels of silver.'

Azel let out a low whistle. 'That is a price that only the rich could pay! How could a normal worker pay several year's wages for something that no one would normally dream of eating. How did the poor survive the siege—or did they simply starve?'

Joah winced. 'You do not want to know what they were driven to kill and eat.' *That place was as dark as a night sky with neither moon nor stars.* He swiftly diverted his thoughts and turned to his father. 'What will happen to those in the city?'

Asaph shook his head slowly. 'I would not wish to be one of the leaders who encouraged rebellion against Shalmaneser. The Assyrians have many hideous ways of inflicting a painful death.'

Joah did not wish his dreams to be stalked by visions of horror. 'But what of the others? Will they be taken from the city?'

'Most of them, without doubt. Tiglath-Pileser's custom was to deport conquered people to a different part of his empire. It is still the same.'

'Why do that?' asked Azel.

'Their kings are no fools. They conquer a people, and then take them from their home and from all that is familiar. They plant them far away, forcing upon them different customs and languages and taking all that is dear. Then what do those conquered people have left to fight for? They are forced instead to depend upon their new rulers. Then they marry foreigners, and before too many years they belong more to Assyria than to Hamath or Damascus—or Samaria.'

'Like a single drop of ink falling into a huge bucket of water,' murmured Joah.

'Exactly.'

'But the Israelites are our brothers,' said Joah, suddenly feeling desolate. 'What will happen to the twelve tribes of Israel? Will the northern tribes cease to be part of our people?' He thought for a moment, and then spoke softly. 'We have all been in the land seven hundred years. Does the history of Israel finish now?'

But Azel had a different question. 'But what of Israel's land? What would stop Judah—or any other nation—taking it once it is emptied of its people?'

'Asaph is right about the Israelites being deported,' answered another older man, 'but that is only half the story. Shalmaneser will bring in others who have suffered a similar fate elsewhere, as surely as the sun will set in the west tonight.'

'But I have heard that Shalmaneser no longer rules,' said Joah, 'and that Sargon, his successor, took the city in the end.'

His father shrugged. 'I wish it mattered, but the truth is that Samaria has fallen to Assyria, whatever the name of its king.'

Joah wondered if Gamaliel would weep that night for the land he once called home. But there was a deeper question that troubled him. *What if the Assyrian conquest was, as Gamaliel believed and the prophets supposedly declared, Yahweh's judgment—the harvest that Israel was reaping, having sown infidelity to their God ever since Jeroboam, two hundred years earlier? What did that mean for Judah with its worship of the pagan gods that Ahaz had embraced?* Once again, the words of Isaiah haunted him: *If you do not stand firm in your faith, you will not stand at all.*

Notes

1. *This chapter starts around 726 BC and ends with the fall of the northern kingdom in 722 BC.*
2. *It is difficult to know exactly what worship within Judah would have looked like under their apostate king, Ahaz. 2 Chronicles 28:24 states that Ahaz shut the doors of the temple, although 29:6-7 implies that his people were also involved in the apostasy, abandoning worship of the God of Israel at the temple. Given the presence of Ahaz's new altar (2 Kings 16:15), it seems reasonable to assume sacrifices were being made on it to other gods, as Ahaz would have done. As priests and Levites had to consecrate themselves when Hezekiah came to the throne (2 Chronicles 29:5), it may have been the case that those performing the sacrifices were also pagan. It is unclear how many remained faithful or heeded Isaiah at this time. Certainly, the references to 'altars on every corner' of Jerusalem and to 'high places to burn sacrifices to other gods' in every town in Judah (see 2 Chronicles 28:24-25) implies widespread apostasy.*

3.   This chapter has tried to reflect some of the sins that Isaiah denounced: idolatry (Isaiah 2:8), pagan practices (2:6), bribery (1:23), drunkenness (5:11,22), living in luxury (3:16,18-23, 5:12) whilst oppression of the poor and injustice flourished (1:23, 3:14-15). Although these sins are not linked to a particular king's reign in the book of Isaiah, it is hard to imagine that they did not flourish under Ahaz.

4.   The reference in 2 Kings 16:15 to Ahaz using Solomon's bronze altar 'for seeking guidance' or 'to inquire by' seems to suggest divination (the interpretations of omens). The ESV study Bible states, 'This probably refers to extispicy, the examination of the entrails of sacrificial animals, focusing on the inspection of the liver (hepatoscopy), in order to divine the will and intentions of the gods. Extispicy is attested in the ancient Near East from early in the second millennium BC and played an important role not only at royal courts but also in the everyday life of ordinary people. The god Hadad was central to the practice of divination, along with Shamash the sun god.'

5.   There is debate as to the identity of King So of Egypt referred to in 2 Kings 17:4, but 'Osorkon IV who ruled in the eastern delta region of Egypt… from 750 to 715 BC has been considered a likely match.' (OTBBC, p403).

6.   Only a few of the prophecies of Isaiah are given explicit settings. It is assumed here that, however they were delivered, most messages would reach the people, given that Isaiah's calling was to go to the people with God's words (Isaiah 6:8-13). The words quoted in this chapter are from Isaiah 8:19 and 28:1. The same uncertainties exist regarding the specific occasions and deliveries of the prophecies of Amos and Hosea.

7.   Once again, some of the timings of these events, including the reign of Hoshea, are somewhat problematic: 'The synchronisms between the northern and southern kingdoms during this period are very complex, and there are no easy resolutions. It is generally supposed that there were several co-regencies that are one cause of the apparent confusion.' (OTBBC, p403).

8.   The population of Jerusalem has been estimated to be around 2000 under King David, expanding to around 4500-5000 at the time of King Solomon. These figures are based on estimated population densities of

cities at this time (200 persons per acre) and the areas enclosed by the respective city walls under David and Solomon. The estimates rise to a possible population of around 25,000 at the time of Hezekiah, with the building of new city walls encompassing the hill to the west of Jerusalem. It is supposed that one reason for this population growth was the migration south of refugees from Israel at the time of the fall of the northern kingdom. See 'Estimating the Population of Ancient Jerusalem', Magen Broshi, (Biblical Archaeology Review 4:2, June 1978) for more details.

9. It is not clear how many in the northern kingdom were still faithful to Yahweh. Hosea himself may have been from one of the northern tribes. At the time of Elijah and under the apostate King Ahab, there were one hundred prophets of Yahweh (1 Kings 18:13) but also seven thousand faithful Israelites 'whose knees have not bowed down to Baal and whose mouths have not kissed him' (1 Kings 19:18). Similarly, when Hezekiah later offers an invitation to the remnant left in the north to celebrate the Passover in Jerusalem, 'some from Asher, Manasseh and Zebulun humbled themselves and went to Jerusalem' (2 Chronicles 30:11). This reference to Manasseh (and its geography within Israel) was behind the choice to make this the tribe of the fictional character Gamaliel (although this was a name used by that tribe—see Numbers 1:10).

10. Whilst the only information that Scripture gives about the lineage of Joah is that he was the son of Asaph (2 Kings 18:18), both Joah and Asaph seem to be names associated only with the tribe of Levi. There are also other specific references to Levites being scribes and secretaries (e.g. 1 Chronicles 24:6, 2 Chronicles 34:13 and Nehemiah 13:13) and other officials (e.g. 1 Chronicles 26:20-32, where they are, among other things, in charge of the treasuries). It seemed, therefore, that Joah was most likely to come from the tribe of Levi.

11. There is much scholarly debate about which Assyrian king conquered Samaria. Sargon II replaced Shalmaneser V (in a coup) and claimed the capture of Samaria for himself much later in his reign. Despite the discussion, the basic events seem clear: Shalmaneser V's army besieged Samaria for three years until it fell in 722 BC. Sargon also claimed to have deported 27,290 people from Samaria, although it is not clear if these are from what remained of Israel at this time or just the city (which Sargon claimed to have repopulated with other conquered peoples).

12. *In this chapter, and elsewhere in the book, it is assumed that scouts were used to obtain information about the movements of enemy forces. This is borne out by references to this in 1 Samuel 26:4 and 1 Kings 20:17. It is not clear, however, how far scouts would be sent, particularly into foreign nations, although it has been assumed that it would be in Judah's interest to ensure some knowledge of other military movements. King Josiah knew, for example, that Pharaoh Necho was marching north from Egypt towards the Euphrates (most likely along the coast). He also knew where he could meet the Egyptians in battle (2 Kings 23:29), implying knowledge of their route.*

13. *Imagined named characters introduced in this chapter are Zebediah, Jerusha, Ethan, Gamaliel, Jael and Azel.*

4

Hezekiah was twenty-five years old when he became king, and he reigned in Jerusalem for twenty-nine years… He did what was right in the eyes of the LORD, just as his father David had done. In the first month of the first year of his reign, he opened the doors of the temple of the LORD and repaired them. (2 Chronicles 29:1-3)

The breath had barely left the body of Ahaz before the fresh breeze of his son started purging the city's stagnation. At twenty-five, Hezekiah was twelve years younger than Joah, but he did not wait to make his mark on Jerusalem.

'Joah son of Asaph!'

Joah looked up. He immediately recognised the man standing by the entrance to his small courtyard. 'Eliakim—come in.' *What had brought the palace official to his gate?* He quickly turned to Zebediah—now sixteen—who was seated on a stool with a scroll covered in Aramaic on his lap. 'Read to yourself for a while.' Joah then called over his shoulder. 'Miriam—we have a guest.'

Eliakim held up a hand. 'Alas. I cannot stay, much as I would wish to.'

Joah noticed the scroll in his other hand. 'What brings you here, then?'

'The king's business. I have your name on a list. You are a Levite, are you not?'

'Yes…'

'And you are not yet fifty, are you?'

'Do I look that old?'

Eliakim sighed.

Joah relented. 'I am thirty-seven years, so no, I am not yet fifty.'

'Then the king requires you to report to the square to the east of the temple, tomorrow at sunrise.'

Joah was puzzled. 'But you know I work at the palace. I do not serve at the temple.'

'You will tomorrow!'

'What do you mean?'

Eliakim shrugged. 'I am only the messenger.'

A voice piped up, 'I am a Levite too!'

Eliakim smiled at Zebediah. 'Indeed, but how old are you?'

'Sixteen.'

'Ah—you see, you are not of age yet. Not for temple service, anyway.' His eyes returned to Joah. 'Do not be late!' Even as Joah was opening his mouth to ask another question, Eliakim held up his hand once more. 'I must leave you. I have five more Levites to find before I can return to my own home.' And with that he was gone.

Joah suddenly became aware of Miriam standing by side.

'What was that all about?'

Joah chuckled. 'I have no idea, but I suspect I will find out tomorrow.'

Joah groaned as Miriam's finger poked him.

'Unless you wish to keep the king waiting, you will need to get up now.'

Despite his desire to remain upon his bed, Joah's drowsiness soon departed. Excitement roused him with the memory of the summons he'd received. Before long, he was leaving the house with some warm bread in his hand, and it was soon obvious he wasn't alone in being called to the temple. He joined the steady stream upwards, but none seemed to have any more idea than he did of what lay ahead.

When he reached the square by the temple, there was already a sizeable crowd near the few steps that led up to its gates. Most stood in silence, simply gazing around. Some spoke in low murmurs. Joah judged there to be well over a hundred there. *Maybe nearer two.* As he looked through the temple gates, he gasped. The doors to the sanctuary, closed for over fifteen years, had been flung wide open. He raised himself up onto his toes. There was also no fire on the altar of Ahaz. It was as cold as the early spring morning. Joah knew at that moment that the king now sitting on the throne would be unlike his father. The anticipation that had drawn him from his bed rose within him again. *Something new was coming.* Whatever it was, he was sure it concerned the God of Israel. He didn't have long to wait.

All murmuring rapidly died away as Hezekiah emerged from the temple courtyard and stood, framed by the gates, at the top of the steps. A solemn hush fell across the entire assembly as Hezekiah's gaze swept across them. The fire that was absent from the altar burned in his eyes. He did not need to wait for silence.

'Listen to me, Levites!' There was passion in his voice. 'Consecrate yourselves now and consecrate the house of Yahweh, the God of your fathers, and remove all the defilement from the sanctuary!'

Joah's eyes did not move from the king, as if he alone were there. Something stirred within.

Hezekiah continued. 'Our fathers have been unfaithful and have done what was evil in the sight of Yahweh our God…'

Joah listened, rapt, as the king recounted not only the infidelity of the people but also the anger of Yahweh—and he spoke of making a covenant with their God. *When had there last been a time like this?* After the years under Ahaz, Joah's head and heart were both reeling.

When the king finally finished addressing them, the Levites were divided into their ancestral families, with Joah joining the Gershonites. The task allotted to his particular group soon became clear: *carrying*.

'I am glad that the temple is at the top of the hill and the Kidron Valley at the bottom,' puffed the Levite with whom Joah was sharing the latest burden. 'At least we are bearing this lump of bronze downhill and not up.'

Even in the cool of the spring day, Joah could feel the sweat upon his brow. It was already his third journey to the valley to the east of Jerusalem, but this was the heaviest load yet. 'That is at least something to be grateful for,' he replied, his breath laboured. 'I am more used to lifting a pen.'

'You're a scribe?'

'Since my youth…' Despite the effort, Joah's pounding heart was lighter than it had been for longer than he could remember, and the reactions of most they passed amused him. Although he saw frowns—even displeasure—on a number of faces, many were simply mystified. Some even stopped, mouths gaping, to watch the strange procession, as bones, ash, wood, stone and bronze—anything that had defiled the temple—were borne by Levites of all professions down to a ditch in the valley. It was where much of the city's refuse and rubble usually ended up.

'Joah!'

Joah searched for Gamaliel's wife in the crowds and when he found her, he grinned. Both men stopped for a moment.

'What *are* you doing?'

'The king's bidding…'

Jael stared at the two men, bewildered. 'Carrying a piece of twisted bronze through Jerusalem?'

Joah grinned again and started moving, calling over his shoulder, 'I will explain later…'

As they neared the Fountain Gate, Joah wondered how many months or years Hezekiah had silently and secretly been planning all he would do upon his father's death. Everything seemed well-ordered.

The unmistakable sound of metal upon metal greeted them as they went out through the gate. A small circle of men were gathered around a crouching figure who was pounding an object on the ground with a heavy iron-headed hammer.

Joah was curious. 'I wonder what they're doing?'

They quickly tossed their load down into the part of the ditch where bronze was being piled up, waiting to be taken away for smelting. It clattered loudly before coming to rest. They then joined the little circle.

Joah drew in a sharp breath. A snake wrought from bronze was beneath the hammer-blows. He immediately recognised it. 'Has the king instructed *this* also?'

One of the men turned to him. 'Yes, he has given the order for Nehushtan to be broken into pieces.'

Joah whistled. 'But it was made by Moses at Yahweh's command! Is it not sacred?'

'Hezekiah says it is no longer so because it has been worshipped as an idol. He will not have one more Israelite bowing down to it, so he says it must be destroyed.'

Just then, the snake yielded to the might of the iron and broke in two. A second man took one of the pieces and began pounding that, so the sound of two hammers rang out. Joah shook his head slowly in wonder as he and his companion turned to begin the climb back up to the temple. The zeal of the new king was like nothing he had witnessed before.

As the sun rose to its zenith and then sank to the west, the work on the temple went on. The large altar in the centre of the courtyard was gradually being dismantled and broken up. Anything from the mind of Ahaz rather than the heart of David or Solomon was destined for destruction. Repairs to the doors into the sanctuary had also begun, and there was a steady stream of priests in and out, as the holiest part of the temple was cleansed.

Joah paused by one of the water jars that was kept filled for the workers. He dipped a cup into it and emptied it swiftly. Water dripped down his beard as he lowered the cup again. *The king had certainly seen to their needs.* Generous platters of bread and cheese and fruit had been brought out around noon for them all.

A priest smiled at him as he also stopped to refresh himself. 'It seems as if your labour has been heavier than mine!'

Joah drew his sleeve across his forehead, wiping away the sweat. 'I have lost count of how many times I have walked all the way down to bottom of the Kidron Valley and then back up. My wife will tell me that I stink tonight!'

The priest laughed. 'And mine will ask why my hands are blistered.' He held them up. 'Polishing gold!'

Joah refilled his cup and then gazed around the temple. 'I do not think I ever imagined my day would be like this.' He took a draught from the cup.

'Nor mine. The king has told all the priests that we are not free to worship as we choose or according to our own design. From now on, our duties will only be according to the instructions of Moses or David, revealed to them by Yahweh.'

'This will not be like the days of Ahaz…' replied Joah, his eyes turning to the open doors of the sanctuary.

'Welcome to the days of Hezekiah.'

If either Miriam or Joah's neighbours had wanted a full account that evening of all that had happened, they were to be disappointed. Joah was not used to such heavy labour, and after a good meal, all he wanted was his bed—and he slept more soundly than he had done in months. For the next seven days, with a break for the Sabbath, he returned to the temple. The work on the courtyard, started on the first day of the month, was finished by the end of the eighth. Only then did Joah return to his work as a scribe, as the priests continued cleansing the sanctuary itself.

All was completed by the sixteenth day, and early the following morning, Joah found himself standing in the courtyard once more— though not as a Levite, but as one of the city's officials. He felt a certain satisfaction as those near him stared wide-eyed around the temple, knowing that he had played a part in its transformation. Solomon's bronze altar was now in the centre of the courtyard once more, gleaming. Every mark that Ahaz had made on the temple had been erased, like ink washed from papyrus. Joah wondered if it had ever looked so clean and unblemished since the day of its consecration, over two hundred years earlier.

Joah craned his neck. He could see the king, dressed simply and standing at the bottom of the steps to the sanctuary. Every serving priest and Levite was clad in clean white linen. Near the altar was a collection of bulls, rams, lambs and goats—and soon the sacrificing commenced, with the blood of each animal sprinkled on the altar.

Joah watched in silence as atonement was made for the kingdom, for the temple, for Judah. Fire had been kindled for the first time in numerous years upon Solomon's altar, and smoke began rising upwards as the fat of the offerings crackled in the flames.

And then it began: the slow procession of every official past the seven male goats that were to be slaughtered as a sin offering for them. Joah knew what was expected of him—the act that the king had performed first and which was being repeated by every man: *the laying of his hand upon the head of one of the goats to symbolise the laying of his sin upon the animal.* Foremost in Joah's mind were the times he had taken the name of Baal upon his lips or offered incense to gods other than Yahweh. *Could that be atoned for?* He took comfort from the knowledge that he was just one among many there who had done such things.

It was only after the goats' blood had been spattered against the altar, their fat added to the fire, and their carcasses taken away to be burnt outside the city, that the sombre mood of the assembly changed. The sun had now risen above the Mount of Olives and Hezekiah, standing upon the sanctuary steps, was bathed in the morning light. Beams streamed in through the open doors behind him and Joah glimpsed the glint of glory beyond.

The king looked around the gathering and lifted his voice. 'Let the burnt offerings begin, to honour Yahweh, the Almighty, the Holy One, the God of Israel!' There were a few moments of silence and then trumpets rang out. Cymbals, harps and lyres joined them, and Levites began singing the praises of Yahweh.

Joah had never heard anything like it. His heart soared as, with every man around him, he knelt and bowed his head down to the cool stone of the courtyard. As he remained there, it was as if he had suddenly woken from a stupor. Everything suddenly felt clean and bright and wholesome, unlike the corruption that Ahaz had brought. Joah remembered it all. *The rumours of children sacrificed to the god Molech. The diviner poking through bloody entrails. The sacred wooden pillars erected on hills, before which men bowed down and near which they lay with shrine prostitutes to make the land fertile. Were not all abominations before Yahweh, deeds of darkness rather than light? How could such base acts be anything other than sinful?* With the praises of Yahweh ringing in his ears, Joah wondered how he could have been so foolish to even consider them otherwise.

When the music stopped, Joah rose to his feet. The king was about to address them again.

Hezekiah stretched out his arms, as if in invitation. 'Now that you have dedicated yourselves to Yahweh, come near and bring your sacrifices and offerings to Him.'

Joah and many others then fetched animals they had tethered outside the temple and brought them forward. The number of animals was vast, and the sun had long passed its zenith by the time that Joah drew near to the altar. The tunics of the priests and Levites were darkened by sweat. The fire on the altar was roaring, continually fed with more fuel, both wood and fat. The rich smells of blood and roasting meat mingled together. Joah could scarcely believe that so much had changed so quickly. And as he presented his own lamb, there was finally no doubt in his mind. *This was an offering for Yahweh, the God of Israel, the one true God.*

'All of you, listen!' Joah and the other scribes in the room looked up. His father, already one of Hezekiah's chief officials, stood before them, a scroll in his hand. 'I have instructions for you from the king.'

A smile graced Joah's face. It was only days since the consecration of the temple. *What would it be this time?*

'The king assigns all of you a new task. Next month, the Passover will be celebrated in Jerusalem. According to the Law of Moses, the festival should have been celebrated in this month, but neither the priests nor the people were ready. Therefore, King Hezekiah and the leaders of the city have thought it right before Yahweh to celebrate it instead in the second month. The king has decreed that letters be sent out, not only into Judah but from Beersheba to Dan, proclaiming to the people that they should come to the house of Yahweh in Jerusalem and celebrate the Passover to Yahweh, the God of Israel.' Murmurs of excitement rippled through the room. Asaph held up his scroll. 'This is the decree that must be copied, word for word, so that it can be sent out into all Israel.' He paused. 'Joah?'

'Yes, Father.'

He beckoned him forward. 'Come. You are to read these words out to your fellow scribes and ensure that every word is as it should be on every scroll. If any mistakes are made, then the papyrus must be discarded. Do you understand?'

'Yes, Father.'

He held out the scroll to him. 'The king wishes riders to leave with the decrees tomorrow at first light.'

Joah's heart swelled. *Never before had he been entrusted with such a task.* He stepped forward and solemnly took the papyrus from Asaph's hand. He wondered if his father had spoken of him to the king. After further instructions, including the number required, Joah looked his father in the eye. 'I will do exactly as you have said, and all will be done by tomorrow.' He smiled wryly. 'I will write them myself through the night if I must.'

As his fellow scribes placed fresh scrolls on their tables and refilled their ink pots, Joah looked down at the words in his hand. *O sons of Israel, return to Yahweh, the God of Abraham, Isaac and Israel, that He may return to those of you who are left, who have escaped from the hand of the kings of Assyria...* Once more, his heart was moved. The room gradually became silent, all attention upon him. He drew in a breath and began to read.

Gamaliel stared at Joah, wide-eyed. 'The Passover? Here? Next month?'

Joah chuckled as the two men perched upon his low courtyard wall in the evening sun. 'We will celebrate it on the evening of the fourteenth of Ziv, as if it were the fourteenth of Nisan.'

'A wonder indeed! And you finished all the scrolls?'

'We did. And they each now carry a wax seal, bearing the king's name and his beetle emblem. They will go out tomorrow, including to your own tribal lands.' Joah met Gamaliel's eyes. 'Do you think many among the remnant of Israel will come?'

Gamaliel shrugged. 'I do not know, but I begin to think anything is possible as Yahweh stirs up the hearts of men. Is this not a new age that has come upon us?'

'And all since the new moon…'

Gamaliel let out a deep sated sigh. 'Ah! To think that I will finally be celebrating the Passover in Jerusalem. I am blessed indeed.' He studied Joah's face for a moment. 'And yet there is something that troubles my friend.'

Joah smiled. 'Can a man not hide anything from you?' He dropped his gaze and fixed it on the dirt at his feet. In the silence that followed, Joah could hear chatter from nearby houses on the hillside, faraway shouts from behind Jerusalem's walls, and a dog barking in the distance. When it became clear that Gamaliel was waiting for him to speak, Joah drew in a breath. 'Can there truly be forgiveness for those who have been unfaithful to their God, to those who have offered incense to Baal? Can they be counted worthy to eat the Passover?'

'Ah…' Gamaliel seemed to understand but he held his peace.

'Today I dictated these words: *Yahweh your God is gracious and compassionate, and will not turn His face away from you if you return to Him.*'

'But you doubt them?'

Joah waited. The distant dog barked again. 'Words are not true simply because we wish them to be.'

'Indeed. I could speak of myself as a young man, but anyone who sees my greying hair would question it.' Joah smiled. Gamaliel went on. 'I have spoken before of the prophet Hosea in the north.'

'The one who gave his children strange names and who called Israel a whore…'

Gamaliel chuckled. 'That is the one. He caused a stir among the people, not only when he married a whore at Yahweh's command, but also when he sought her out when she was unfaithful to him, even paying her lover to buy her back, again at the direction of Yahweh. Oh, how the people's tongues wagged!'

'Why would Yahweh instruct him to do such things?'

'Because there was a message in it—a message that even when we had turned to other gods, Yahweh still loved us and wanted us back.

It has been the same ever since the sons of Jacob left Egypt.' Gamaliel paused. 'Do you know the thing that often ails us?'

Joah looked up. Gamaliel was smiling. 'Tell me…'

'We think that the Almighty is like us, with our whims, our fickle hearts and our memories of those who have wronged us.' He paused. 'I do not know many of the words the prophet spoke, but I remember these: *I am God and not man, the Holy One in your midst.* He is *not* like us, and if *He* tells us that He loves us and forgives us, then we must trust Him that it is so. The words are true not because we wish them to be but because He spoke them.'

For several moments, Joah mused on what had been said, surveying the colours of the evening sky. His heart felt lighter. He lowered his gaze, raising an eyebrow. 'With such wisdom, I might think you a son of Solomon himself.'

Gamaliel laughed. 'You could say it as well if you wanted, but it would not make me any less a son of Manasseh!'

Even before the Passover was upon them and as crowds were gathering, there were further changes in the city. Joah himself helped carry one of the street-corner altars on which he had once burned incense down to the Kidron Valley. Although some scowled as they passed, clearly still adherents of the ways of Ahaz, it pleased Joah greatly to swing the altar back with his companions and then toss it into *the ditch of defilement* as he called it. It landed with a satisfying crunch and split apart. Joah dusted off his hands. *The past was behind him. The only name he would now take upon his lips was that of Yahweh.* By the time the full moon came, and with it, the Passover, Jerusalem had been rid of every idolatrous altar.

The joy in Jerusalem was like nothing Joah had ever experienced. Although there were times when it was barely possible to move through the crowded streets, the mood was one of unrelenting jubilation—for those, at least, who embraced Hezekiah's reforms. Songs of praise resounded around the temple every day, and feasting continued into each night. Joah had never eaten such an abundance of meat, much of it provided by the king himself, although Joah and other officials like him had also made modest contributions. And after the seven days of the Feast of Unleavened Bread that followed Passover, it was agreed that there should be seven further days of celebration.

'Has Jerusalem ever seen the like of this?' asked Zebediah one night.

Joah smiled at his son. 'Maybe in the days of Solomon, but probably not since then. Certainly not in my lifetime nor that of my father.'

'*In Judah God is known; His name is great in Israel!*' responded Zebediah, quoting some of the words sung by the Levites.

'It is indeed,' said Joah, 'it is indeed.'

Only a few days after their celebrations had finished, Zebediah had a very different question. 'Who are they?' he whispered.

Joah studied the back of the group of men who had swept past them in the palace, led by the official in charge of the king's household. They were clearly heading for an audience with the king. 'If I didn't know better,' he said under his breath, 'I would say by their dress they are Philistines.'

'Then what are they doing here?'

'For the answer to *that* question,' replied Joah, 'we will both have to wait.'

At the end of the day, he sought out his own father.

'You are right, Joah. They *were* Philistines—here to give the king their condolences on the death of his father.'

Joah scoffed. 'And the real reason?'

Asaph glanced around. 'They seek an alliance—an alliance against the Assyrians. They were never likely to get one with Ahaz. He was the one, after all, who made Judah the vassal of the Assyrian kings.'

Joah thought for a moment. *If the previous two months had shown him anything, it was that Hezekiah only had one thing in common with his father: his blood.* He lowered his voice. 'Is Hezekiah likely to throw off the yoke of the Assyrians?'

'Who knows? But if he does, it will not be done quickly or lightly. He may bide his time, awaiting his moment. But I *can* tell you two things: the Philistines were not the only ones to pay him a visit, and if the king does rebel, it will not be due to a Philistine alliance.'

'What do you mean?'

'The prophet has brought a message to the king—and times have changed. Ahaz paid as much attention to Isaiah as to a beggar by one of his shrines—'

'You mean he ignored him and acted as if he weren't there.'

'Precisely. But Hezekiah listens to him, as he does to words of the prophet Micah, with an open heart.'

'So what was the prophet's message?'

'I cannot tell you its exact words, but I can tell you its meaning: the Philistines should fear what is coming from the north, and it is in Yahweh's city not Philistia that His people will find refuge.'

Their neighbours to the west were not the only ones to send envoys to Hezekiah early in his reign. Others arrived from Egypt with the promise of aid for those who rose against Assyria. But once again the voice of the prophet prevailed—*it was Yahweh who ruled.*

But for Joah, Hezekiah's early years brought a new responsibility, and one in which he rejoiced—not only because of the trust the king placed in him, but because of the task itself.

He looked over the pile of old scrolls on the large table. He ran his fingers lightly over one of them. *Maybe Solomon himself had penned these words. And even if he hadn't, a scribe had written them down directly from lips! These were treasures indeed!* His task was to oversee a number of other scribes as they searched through the writings of Solomon for proverbs, so they could be drawn together into one collection with those they already had. It was a noble task.

He watched as they pored over the scrolls, reading them carefully. Whenever a scribe found what he believed to be a proverb, he hailed Joah. If he agreed, then it was copied out carefully onto a different scroll.

A hand went up. 'Joah!'

Joah made his way over to the table, looked down and read. *'Take away the dross from the silver, and there comes out a vessel for the smith; take away the wicked from before the king, and his throne will be established in righteousness.'* Joah paused. 'That will please our king—and also my neighbour.'

'How so?'

Joah smiled. 'He is a silversmith.' He determined to write the words out for Gamaliel and present them to him later. There was, however, another delight for him before the day was done.

A hand went up as the late afternoon sun streamed in through the high window. 'I'm coming,' said Joah, even before the scribe hailed him.

'There,' said the younger man, pointing to the middle of the scroll.

Joah read the words to himself—and could barely believe his eyes. 'That is a wonder of wonders,' he murmured. The scribe was puzzled.

Others looked up. 'What is it?'

'It is a proverb that I used to write out as a child—one that my father taught me.' Joah turned back to the scribe who'd found it. 'Why don't you read it out to the others. It has a lesson for us all.'

The young man lifted the scroll. *'A man's pride will bring him low, but the lowly will be honoured.'*

He caught one of the youngest scribes smirking to another, and saw a single name being mouthed: *Shebna.* Guilt immediately replaced the smirk when he realised Joah's attention was upon him, and in an instant his gaze had returned to his own scroll, nodding sagely as he studied it intently.

Joah smiled to himself. *He would let it go. After all, if there was one person within the palace whose pride was like that of a strutting cock, then it was Shebna.* Joah did also have to admit, though, that he was, nevertheless, the palace official most likely to become the next head over Hezekiah's household. He had an able mind, a smooth tongue, and was from one of the richest families within the city. He also knew it and took every opportunity to ensure that others did too. Joah found it difficult to imagine him ever being brought low.

As Joah walked through the palace at the end of the day, he felt a quiet satisfaction. *It had been a good day.* The door of one of the rooms he passed was ajar and he peeked in. He immediately paused, standing both still and silent, wishing to remain unnoticed. Isaiah was sitting at a table, wearing the customary sackcloth of a prophet. He, too, was surrounded by piled-up scrolls, with a reed pen in his hand. But Joah knew he was not copying proverbs. It was he who was writing the history of Hezekiah's great grandfather—King Uzziah.

Joah thought once more about the proverb his scribe had found. It was pride in the heart of Uzziah that had caused his own father to impress its words upon him as a child. What struck Joah in that moment was the gulf between what he had seen of Isaiah and what he knew of Shebna. Isaiah displayed none of Shebna's self-importance, and yet he spoke the words of the Almighty and had seen Yahweh Himself in a vision. *Surely that, more than anything, would give a man reason for pride!* Then Joah smiled to himself, and quietly resumed his journey home. *No, that was wrong.* He knew that mankind was the pinnacle of Yahweh's creation. *But surely standing in the presence of the Almighty would make any man realise he was also the merest puff of wind.*

The wisdom of shunning an alliance with the Philistines became clear in the fourth year of Hezekiah's reign, when their city of Ashdod fell to the Assyrians. One evening shortly afterwards, Joah found Zebediah waiting for him at the end of the day. 'Ah—am I to be honoured by the presence of my son for my walk home this evening?' Joah almost always finished later than Zebediah at the palace, ensuring that all under his charge was left orderly and that nothing had been left undone.

Zebediah grinned. 'I have not had to wait long. My tasks took longer because I was talking more.' They began walking side by side to the main palace doors. 'There was a matter we were discussing today, and you will know more of it than those I work alongside.'

'And what is that?'

'Egypt.'

'What of it?'

'Did you not say that envoys were sent from there soon after Hezekiah came to the throne?'

'They were indeed. Shebitku, the Nubian, had just taken the throne of Egypt, and wished to stir up any nation he could against the Assyrians, promising help to those who defied Sargon. But Isaiah spoke against such an alliance.'

'And Egypt sent envoys to the Philistines?'

'I believe so—why do you ask?'

'I said as much to one of the other scribes, but he said that Ashdod received no such aid.'

'Ah—and you wish to know who is right?'

Zebediah nodded as they emerged into the evening sun. 'Indeed.'

'Then I would say that you both are. What Egypt promised it did not give, and Ashdod was left to stand alone against Sargon's forces—and was crushed.'

'So it was an empty alliance?'

'The Philistines were leaning on a spider's web.'

The two men continued their discussion as they made their way down through the city, until both suddenly fell silent and stopped. Joah studied the commotion in the street ahead of them. *Whatever—or whoever—it was, was causing a stir.* Some were jeering, others gawped, and mothers were dragging children away whilst the youngsters looked back over their shoulders. Those ahead of Joah parted to let someone through. His mouth fell open, and for a moment, words left him.

'What…?' murmured Zebediah.

A naked man was walking up the street, with neither the stagger of a drunkard nor the raving of a madman. It was several moments before Joah realised with a jolt that he knew him. It was not, after all, the face of the man to which Joah's eyes had first been drawn—and he had never before seen Isaiah without his garment of sackcloth. They stood speechless as the prophet walked past, barefoot and head lowered, and continued staring until his uncovered buttocks had disappeared from view, further along the street.

'Well!' exclaimed Zebediah, eyebrows raised. 'What was that about?'

They looked back up the street again, then turned to continue their short journey home. 'I do not know.' They walked in silence for some way, Joah deep in thought. He then shook his head slowly. 'All I can think is that he mimics the shame of the conquered, being led to captivity in humiliation.'

'Like those of Ashdod?'

'But if that is his message, then he is only telling us what we already know.'

'What else might it be then?'

Joah thought hard but then shrugged. 'I do not know.' And then, as they reached the Valley Gate, he added, 'Though I am not sure I want to.' He was all too aware that, despite Hezekiah's reforms, injustice, immorality and idolatry all still festered out of sight in the dark corners of the city—like a stubborn sore than would not heal.

It was only sometime later that words were added to the prophet's message, telling them not of Ashdod's past but Egypt's future. It seemed to Joah that Yahweh was telling them once again that it was futile to look anywhere other than heaven for help. And once again, the prophet's words echoed within: *If you do not stand firm in your faith, you will not stand at all.*

Notes

1. *This chapter starts around 715 BC—the year of Ahaz's death and the start of Hezekiah's sole reign according to the dating of Thiele and others. Hezekiah may have had a possible co-regency with Ahaz from 729 BC, which would make sense of the overlap of Hoshea and Hezekiah mentioned in 2 Kings 18:1. The chapter ends in the year of the fall of Ashdod in 711 BC.*

2. *It is worth remembering that Israel was not only the name of the northern kingdom. It was another name for Jacob, father of the twelve tribes, and, by extension, for the people of God in general. Hence, for example, both Isaiah and Hezekiah still speak of Yahweh as 'the God of Israel'.*

3. *As with Ahaz, there is archaeological evidence for the reign of Hezekiah in bullae found in Jerusalem. One carries the words 'Belonging to Hezekiah, (son of) Ahaz, king of Judah' and the image of a winged*

beetle. See 'King Hezekiah's Seal Bears Phoenician Imagery', Frank Moore Cross, (Biblical Archaeology Review 25:2, March/April 1999). Even more remarkably, another clay bulla has been found alongside one of Hezekiah's, marked possibly with the seal of the prophet Isaiah. See 'Is This the Prophet Isaiah's Signature?', Eilat Mazar (Biblical Archaeology Review 44:2, March/April May/June 2018).

4. It seems from Isaiah 14:28-32 that the Philistines sent a delegation to Hezekiah to arrange an alliance against Assyria, which Isaiah warned against.

5. Proverbs 25-29 are introduced by the words, 'These are more proverbs of Solomon, compiled by the men of Hezekiah king of Judah' (25:1). This chapter imagines how this might have happened.

6. 2 Chronicles 26:22 states, 'The other events of Uzziah's reign, from beginning to end, are recorded by the prophet Isaiah son of Amoz'. Given Isaiah's seemingly easy access to the palace during the reign of Hezekiah (e.g. 2 Kings 20:1,14), it might not seem unreasonable for Isaiah to be given free access to the palace and its records to compile such a history.

7. Shebitku was an early Ethiopian pharaoh of the twenty-fifth dynasty.

8. Isaiah 20 contains the account of the prophet being instructed to go naked and barefoot. There is some debate amongst commentators about the degree (both in length of time and extent) that Isaiah went about naked, and how the three years spoken of in Isaiah 20:2 relate to the year of Ashdod's capture (mentioned in 20:1) and the message that follows the act (20:3). Also, although the reference to sackcloth in 20:2 could imply a sign of mourning for the fall of Samaria (some ten or so years earlier), it may be more likely that it was simply the normal dress of a prophet (see, for example, 2 Kings 1:8 and Zechariah 13:4).

5

*In the fourteenth year of King Hezekiah's reign, Sennacherib king
of Assyria attacked all the fortified cities of Judah and captured them.*
(2 Kings 18:13)

Excitement spilled from the king like wine from an over-filled cup.
'Shebna—come! And you, Joah—this must be written down in the
palace annals.'

'My lord?' replied Shebna swiftly, ever attentive to the king.

'The stonecutters will likely break through today. Last night,
those on one side heard those on the other through a cleft in the
rock. We must not miss this!'

Joah picked up his writing kit and followed the others. In the
time since he had risen to the rank of recorder—indeed, even in the
ten years that Hezekiah had been king—he had seldom seen him so
full of fervour. Much had changed in those years. Joah's home, like
all those built on the hill to the west of Jerusalem, was now within
a new city wall. And yet what they were about to inspect was no less
impressive—though hidden from the eyes of most.

Joah watched the two men in front of him. Hezekiah, now thirty-
five years of age, was gesturing expansively with his hands as he walked
briskly through the palace. Shebna strode alongside him, erect and with
head held high. He was clad in his beloved robe and sash that marked
him out as the royal steward—head over Hezekiah's household, and
second only to the king himself. Wherever he went, other palace
attendants would draw respectfully to one side or nod their heads. He
would smile benignly. *Basking in their deference like a lizard in the warmth
of the sun,* was how Joah thought of it. Whether the king noticed it or
not, Joah didn't know, but he *did* know he was not alone in seeing it.

Joah blinked as they went out into the bright sunlight. They would not be there long.

The king looked over his shoulder, barely slowing as he did so. 'And when did you last see the tunnel, Joah?'

'A month ago, O king.'

'Then you will not fail to notice how the stonecutters have advanced.'

As they left the palace and descended towards the tower that housed the Gihon spring, Joah recalled his previous visit. Making his way by the light of dim lamps through a damp, uneven and narrow channel cut through rock had felt like being swallowed by the earth—and more like a tomb than a tunnel. The idea had been conceived within the king's mind, and Joah had to admit that it was both a bold and brilliant one. Instead of water travelling from the spring to the Lower Pool in the channel that ran alongside the city's walls, it could flow safely under the city itself, out of reach of any enemy army, and into a new pool being dug at the tunnel's southern end. Although Hezekiah had not said as much, Joah had no doubt that one thing more than any other had prompted the endeavour: *Assyria*.

Sooner than Joah would have wanted, they were out of daylight and into the tunnel. The faint sound of iron upon rock fell upon his ears as the work's overseer began leading the king down the tunnel, followed by Shebna with Joah at the rear. Each had a small lamp in their hand. Joah wondered why on earth he had brought his writing kit; it was questionable whether he could record anything when he could barely see even Shebna in front of him. The darkness seemed to have done little to dampen the king's mood, however. Hezekiah cheerfully conversed with the overseer as they picked their way along the winding tunnel, the blows becoming ever louder.

Eventually they stopped, the tools falling silent. Although Joah could not see it in the narrow passage, he knew they were close to what remained of the rock between those tunnelling away from the spring and those tunnelling towards it. All Joah could do was listen— and try not to think of the hundred cubits of rock above him.

Hezekiah's voice rang out. 'This is the king—can you hear me?'

The reply through the fissure was more muffled but distinct. 'Yes, my lord.'

'Continue your work, and, if Yahweh permits, I will see your face soon!' The picks resumed, as did the deafening blows—but soon they stopped once more, and the king cried out, 'Yahweh be praised—I see your light!' They had broken through. The men continued working until a face could be seen through the hole in the rock. Hezekiah then seemed satisfied. 'We will return when you have hewn a hole through which I may walk, so that I may be the first to walk from the Gihon spring to the new pool under our city.

'Yes, O king.'

'Joah—you may turn and lead us back up the tunnel.'

Still clutching his unopened writing kit and lamp, Joah turned—unsure whether he was more relieved to be returning to daylight or more fearful of having no one ahead of him in the tunnel. He shook himself out of it. *No one could pass him so there was no other option.* His only consolation was that Shebna's lamp-lit face had been purged of all pomposity.

To Joah's discomfort, he discovered before sunset that he was to accompany the king down the entire length of the tunnel so that he could observe and then record the event. Shebna had excused himself, saying that the honour should solely be that of the king. Joah was sure of two things: that it was the first time he had heard those words from the steward and that it would probably also be the last. *Unless another tunnel was involved.*

Joah found his mood to be different this time, however. *Maybe it was the knowledge that there was a way through, rather than a dead end ahead.* Although there would be more work needed to turn the tunnel into a water channel, nevertheless, Joah was awed at what had been wrought. By the time they had passed through the point at which the two sides had met, he knew he was witnessing a wonder.

It was only as they were nearing the end of the tunnel and Joah passed a smoother part of the wall that he suddenly had an idea. 'My lord!'

Hezekiah stopped and turned, looking past the overseer between them. 'We are almost through—why do you stop me, Joah?'

'Forgive me, my lord the king, but would it not be fitting to record the events of this day not only upon a scroll but also upon the rock of these walls? An enduring testimony to both the vision of my lord and the labour of these stonecutters?' As Hezekiah studied him in the flickering lamplight, Joah went on. 'My lord, the rock is smooth here. Might this not be a suitable place for such an inscription?'

A broad smile broke onto the king's face. 'You have spoken well—that would be fitting indeed. I will look to you to put pen to papyrus first, and then I will see what you suggest. But now, come—let us complete our course!' And with that, he turned and forged ahead.

Joah breathed deeply of the cool evening air as they emerged into the dwindling light of the day—and hoped he never had to walk through the tunnel again. Later that evening, by the light of a lamp, he sat inside his house, a scroll on the table in front of him and pen in hand. He wanted to offer his words to the king the following morning and words were already forming in his mind. He thought for a few moments and then began: *This is the way the tunnel was cut through...* He formed each letter, whether it was the ornate *tsadeh* or the tiny *yod,* with the same care he bestowed on all royal documents. All around him faded away, even the crying of his latest grandchild. He wrote of the stonecutters wielding their picks, of the cleft in the rock, and of the voices that could be heard through it. He paused. He did not know the final length of the tunnel. *He would leave a gap in the words for now and speak of it to Hezekiah in the morning.* He smiled. He could almost imagine the king wanting to measure the length himself. There was, however, one figure that he had already been told—the one that had weighed upon his mind in the tunnel. He dipped the pen in the ink again and wrote the final words: *A hundred cubits was the height of the rock above the head of the hewers.*

The stonecutters were soon assigned another task—not by Hezekiah but by his steward.

Joah had barely stepped out into the corridor and closed the wooden door to his room when a familiar voice rang out.

'Ah, Joah—there you are.'

He groaned inwardly. All he wanted to do was return home and fill his belly with Miriam's spicy goat stew. He fixed a polite smile on his face before turning to face Shebna.

'You must come with me. I have a fine sight to show you!'

Joah was given no choice. 'And what is that?'

'You will soon see, my friend. We will ride there together.'

Joah smiled to himself. *He might have known.* Despite the short journey between his fine stone-built house and the palace, Shebna never walked when he could ride in one of his chariots. They began walking together to the main doors of the palace.

'I was speaking of Egypt to the king again,' continued Shebna.

'But you know that Isaiah speaks against such an alliance…'

'I prefer prudence,' scoffed Shebna, 'to the words of a prophet.'

'An alliance with Egypt did Ashdod no favours.'

'But that was in the days of Sargon.' Shebna turned towards Joah, smirking. 'And favour was upon us the day Sargon met his death in battle, with his body lost to the enemy. Now all the nations know that Assyria and her kings are not invincible—and that is why, as you well know, many have now revolted against the son of Sargon. Our king has chosen his moment wisely to rebel against Sennacherib and withhold tribute.'

'And now we wait,' murmured Joah, 'to see how Assyria's latest king will respond.'

At that moment they stepped out into the courtyard. Shebna's ornate chariot was waiting for him, both its horses and driver in place, with a servant holding a shade. Another servant stood ready to walk before them. Shebna waved the shade away. 'The sun is low—I will not need you now.' Shebna stepped up into the chariot and gestured for Joah to join him. He addressed the man who was to clear their path. 'I wish to see the labourers at the Mount of Olives.' The servant nodded and began walking towards the gates of the palace courtyard. The driver jerked the reins and they lurched forward.

Joah grabbed the side of the chariot. Unlike Shebna, he would rather have walked. The streets of Jerusalem were often uneven, but the swaying of the chariot seemed to matter little to its owner. The cries of *Make way!* from Shebna's servant caught the attention of those in the streets and parted them like the waters of the Red Sea. As Shebna began describing the latest decorations he had added to his house, Joah tried to look interested. After a while, Joah found himself wondering how the chariot with its ivory inlays and silver trims would fare in battle. *But then, neither the chariot nor Shebna were ever likely to be there.*

'What do *you* think, Joah?'

Joah froze. They had by now left the city by its southerly Dung Gate, crossed the Kidron Valley and were ascending the Mount of Olives on the other side. He wondered for a moment if he should admit to his mind having been elsewhere. Such an admission was not, however, needed.

'I, of course, would favour purple,' continued Shebna without waiting for an answer. 'I know it is far more expensive, but it is worth every shekel of silver.'

Relief washed over Joah. 'A good choice, indeed.' *Whatever it was for.*

'Ah, look, here we are now.'

Joah followed Shebna's gaze to where a tomb was being cut into the rock. It was not the only one there—this was where Jerusalem's rich carved out their burial caves. The chariot soon came to a stop and Shebna stepped out, followed by Joah. The sound of chiselling mingled with the evening birdsong.

Joah inspected the finely worked entrance. 'This is to be your family tomb?'

'Indeed, it is.' Shebna turned to face Jerusalem, drew in a deep breath and let it out slowly. They were now to the south-east of it and nearly on a level with the City of David. 'I chose this position myself. There is surely no finer view of the city, save that of the eagles.'

Joah decided not to point out that the view would be no different to that of a dung heap to the eyes of the dead. 'We are blessed with such a city.'

'Blessed indeed.' He then turned to face Joah. 'And you should consider an endeavour such as mine for yourself. There is ample room among the rock here. Is it not fitting for those who serve our king and our nation as we do to have a memorial that will outlast countless generations?' He clearly expected no dissent and turned his attention back to the cave. 'Now let us see what progress the men are making.'

Joah was glad that, unlike Shebna's house, the tomb contained only two chambers with their stone shelves and was swiftly seen. After a brief exchange with the stonecutters, they were soon back in the soft evening light.

'I have already decided the inscription that shall be carved over the entrance.' He glanced back at the cave and then surveyed the valley. 'It will say: *This is Shebna, the royal steward. There is no silver or gold here—only his bones and the bones of his handmaid with him. Cursed be the man who opens…*' Shebna's words petered out, his attention suddenly fixed elsewhere. Joah turned. Isaiah was walking steadily up the hill towards them. 'What does he want?' muttered Shebna.

Both held their silence and waited. The prophet was looking older—undoubtedly now some way beyond his fiftieth year. He finally stopped three or four paces in front of them, his back to the city.

'This is what Yahweh, Yahweh Almighty, says,' began Isaiah, addressing Shebna. *'What are you doing here and who gave you permission to cut out a grave for yourself here, hewing your grave on the height and chiselling your resting-place in the rock?'* His eyes did not leave the steward. *'Beware, Yahweh is about to take firm hold of you and hurl you away, O you mighty man. He will roll you up tightly like a ball and throw you into a vast country. There you will die and there your splendid chariots will remain, you shame of your master's house! I will depose you from your office, and you will be ousted from your position.'*

Joah could feel Shebna bristling at his side. Even as the prophet paused for breath, Joah considered whether he should hurry away. But in the few heartbeats of silence, he decided it was safer to stay both still and silent, and therefore discreet. *Maybe he would then avoid a similar fate.*

Isaiah continued, '*In that day I will summon my servant, Eliakim son of Hilkiah. I will clothe him with your robe and fasten your sash around him and hand your authority over to him. He will be a father to those who live in Jerusalem and to the people of Judah. I will place on his shoulder the key to the house of David; what he opens no one can shut, and what he shuts no one can open. I will drive him like a peg into a firm place; he will become a seat of honour for the house of his father. All the glory of his family will hang on him: its offspring and offshoots – all its lesser vessels, from the bowls to all the jars.*' Isaiah paused again and drew in a deep breath. '*In that day*, declares Yahweh Almighty, *the peg driven into the firm place will give way; it will be sheared off and will fall, and the load hanging on it will be cut down.* Yahweh has spoken.' And without another word he turned and left.

Joah breathed freely once more. *He had escaped Yahweh's displeasure!* He stole a look at Shebna. He was seething but did not speak until Isaiah was out of earshot.

'How dare he come here and speak to me like that?' he spat out. '*I* am the royal steward—second only to the king. How dare he!' He turned, and it was only then that Joah realised that the workmen had stopped and were standing at the entrance to the tomb. 'Get back to work!' bellowed Shebna, before turning his back on them.

For a few moments they stood and watched Isaiah disappearing down a path to the city. Joah had no desire to be subjected to Shebna's ire on the way back nor to be asked to agree with it. *Besides, maybe some time to think about Isaiah's message would do him good.* He could not meet Shebna's eyes, however. 'I will walk back and see you at the palace in the morning.' Without waiting for an answer, he began making his way downhill. He only went a few paces before he was stopped.

'Joah!'

He turned. Shebna was breathing heavily and shaking.

'You will not speak of this to the king nor to any other! Do you hear me?'

Joah nodded, and with that, he continued down the path. His mind was like wine being swirled in a cup. *Was Shebna to cease as royal steward—and what did it mean that he would be thrown like a ball into a vast country? Were the words final or was Shebna being warned?* Joah knew the

Eliakim of whom Isaiah had spoken—he was another official at the palace. *But if he was to replace Shebna, what about the words of him being like a peg that gives way? And if these things were to come to pass, when would that be?*

By the time he had entered the city and walked up the western hill towards his house, he was only sure of one thing: if Yahweh *had* indeed spoken, then *He* would bring these things to pass and would do it in His own time.

Miriam looked up from the cooking pot as he entered the courtyard. 'Ah, there you are! You are late tonight. Did the king keep you?'

'No, Shebna took me to see the tomb he is carving for himself upon the Mount of Olives.'

'And was it worth seeing?'

Joah pondered for a moment. 'The view of Jerusalem was splendid in the setting sun.' Miriam laughed as Joah walked over to the pot. 'Is the stew ready? I could eat an ox.'

Eliakim handed Joah a scroll. 'Make sure these judgments are entered in the palace annals.'

Joah opened out the papyrus and glanced at its contents. 'It will be done before the day is out.'

'Good. I will go now to see if the king's condition has improved overnight.'

'Do send word to me of what you find.'

'I will tell you myself.'

Joah watched as Eliakim, dressed in the robe and sash of royal steward, turned and left. He had never discovered the reason why Hezekiah had lowered Shebna to the position of secretary and replaced him with Eliakim, but it was just as the prophet had said. The words *royal steward* had, however, already been carved into the rock above Shebna's tomb. It had amused Joah but also impressed yet again Solomon's proverb upon his mind: *A man's pride will bring him low, but the lowly will be honoured.* He wondered what went through Shebna's mind every time he saw his beloved robe and sash upon another.

He fingered the scroll, his thoughts with the king. A sore had formed upon Hezekiah's skin and become inflamed, steadily growing worse as the days went by. He took comfort in Hezekiah's faithfulness. *Surely Yahweh would not allow harm to befall his devoted servant?*

'Joah?'

He looked up at the scribe who had just entered the room, and with that, his attention returned to the day's affairs.

He and the scribe were still poring over a papyrus when Eliakim reappeared at the door. 'Joah—you must come now.' There was calm in neither his speech nor his stance, and Shebna was with him.

Joah immediately rose, putting the scroll into the hands of the scribe. 'Find Zebediah—he has mastered Aramaic and will help you with the words.' He joined the men, but it was only when they were hurrying down the corridor towards the king's chambers that Eliakim spoke, his voice lowered.

'The king now has a fever that rages. Nothing the physician does seems to abate it.'

'When did it start?' asked Joah.

'As the moon rose—and he was in great pain all night.'

'Does the fever confuse him?'

Eliakim shook his head, 'No—he is still in his right mind. But as the king's chief officials, we must discuss with the physician what must be done.' He then fell silent, leaving only the sound of their sandals' swift steps upon the stone floor.

Had the king's death been in Eliakim's mind?

A guard by the door to the king's outer chamber opened it for them, shutting it again once they were inside. The physician joined them from the inner room, pushing its door to. 'Is the wife of the king still with him?' asked Eliakim, his voice still lowered.

The physician nodded. 'Yes, she will not leave him.'

But the physician had barely begun to answer the men's questions when the door behind them opened. 'I told you that no one was to…' The words died on Eliakim's lips when he saw that it was not the guard but Isaiah.

157

'I bring Hezekiah the words of Yahweh.' There was neither question nor request in his utterance, his demeanour as sombre as a herald of loss.

Joah's hairs bristled. Isaiah might not bear Moses' staff nor wear Elijah's cloak, but to Joah he was just as much Yahweh's prophet. Joah hurried to the inner door and opened it for Isaiah, following him in as the others did, but all holding back as Isaiah approached the king. Hezekiah's head turned toward him, and relief seemed to flood his face.

Isaiah stopped by the bed. 'This is what Yahweh says,' he began softly, laying his hand upon the king's arm. 'Put your house in order, because you are going to die; you will not recover.' Hezekiah's wife gasped and began to sob. The physician swore under his breath. The king and the prophet shared words, spoken too softly to be heard. Then Isaiah nodded, turned, and without another word made his way towards the door. The men parted for him, and for a moment, Joah's eyes met those of Isaiah. They brimmed with sorrow.

The king's wavering voice broke the silence. 'Leave me—all of you.'

They hurriedly retreated into the outer room, the king's wife with them, tears on her face. 'I will return shortly,' she sobbed before hastily taking her leave.

Joah looked from one face to another. No one spoke. From within the king's chamber came the sound of bitter weeping—and then a voice. Even through the closed door, Joah could tell that the king was entreating the God of Israel.

Eliakim, clearly shaken, whispered. 'We will mourn the king when that hour comes, but now we *must* ready ourselves and ready the palace. A kingdom in disarray is a kingdom ripe for conquest.'

Joah nodded. 'You are right, Eliakim. Sargon's sudden death weakened Assyria greatly. We must not be caught unprepared.' The face of the king's young son rose in Joah's mind, but Shebna named him first.

'But Manasseh is only six! How will putting him on the throne appear strong?'

'Shh. Keep your voice down.' Joah thought for a moment, ploughing the field of the palace annals within his mind. 'Joash was only seven when *he* came to the throne. He ruled under the instruction of the high priest Jehoiada until he was old enough to bear the mantle alone.' Joah was about to add that the kingdom had been no worse for it when the outer door opened again.

Eliakim drew breath, but before a word was even on his tongue, Isaiah had entered. The royal steward shut his mouth again.

The solemnity of death was no longer upon the prophet. 'Yahweh has sent me back. He has heard the king's prayers.'

Once more Joah opened the inner door for Isaiah. The sound of weeping became louder and then abruptly stopped. Joah's heart was pounding as they followed him in, remaining near the door once more. *Would the king yet live?*

Hezekiah was silent, his fevered face fixed on the prophet.

'This is what Yahweh, the God of your father David says,' began Isaiah. *'I have heard your prayer and seen your tears. I will heal you. On the third day from now you will go up to the temple of Yahweh. I will add fifteen years to your life. And I will deliver you and this city from the hand of the king of Assyria. I will defend this city for my sake and for the sake of my servant David.'*

Hezekiah's eyes remained fixed on him. 'What will be the sign that Yahweh will heal me,' he said, his breathing still rapid, 'and that I will go up to the temple of Yahweh on the third day?'

But instead of answering him immediately, Isaiah turned to the physician. 'Prepare a poultice of figs and apply it to the boil, and he will recover.' He then turned back to the king and paused, as if listening. 'This is Yahweh's sign to you that He will do what He has promised: shall the shadow on the staircase go forward ten steps or back ten steps?'

A bead of sweat rolled down the king's face and into his beard. 'It is a simple matter for shadows to lengthen. Let the shadow go back ten steps.'

Isaiah nodded. 'It will be.'

'Then let me see this sign,' said Hezekiah.

The physician stepped forward. 'You are not strong enough, O king.'

'Then send for my litter whilst you prepare my poultice!' Despite his fever, the king's spirit seemed to have suddenly risen within him.

Eliakim stepped forward. 'We will see to it, O king.' He immediately turned to Shebna. 'See that it is done—and done quickly.'

Shebna visibly bristled at being ordered by the one who had replaced him, but he had no choice but to obey. Joah smiled to himself. He had no doubt that Hezekiah would be healed and the shadow would shorten—but that in no way diminished his desire to witness both. *Especially the latter.*

'*Surely it was for my benefit that I suffered such anguish,*' dictated Hezekiah.

Joah carefully began writing the next line of the king's words, composed to honour Yahweh for his healing. He had just begun the seventh word, when Hezekiah continued.

'*In your love you kept me from the pit of destruction.*'

'Please, O king, a little slower. I wish your words to be neither amiss nor a mess upon the scroll.'

Hezekiah put his head back and laughed. '*Amiss nor a mess!* Well spoken, Joah.'

Joah flushed. 'I will admit, O king, that it is not the first time I have used the words. My own sons heard them many times when I was teaching them to write.'

'Ah—and how are Zebediah and Ethan?' asked Hezekiah. 'I see them often around the palace.'

Joah opened his mouth to reply, but never got any further. There were three sharp knocks.

Hezekiah looked towards the door. 'Enter!' Eliakim appeared, bowing low. 'Why such an interruption, Eliakim? What brings my steward here?'

'You have visitors, O king.'

'Visitors? I was not told to expect any.'

'They have travelled far, my lord—sent by Merodach-Baladan.'

Hezekiah's eyebrows lifted. 'Envoys from Babylon?'

'Yes, my lord. The king of Babylon heard of your illness and recovery—and of the miraculous sign that Yahweh performed for you. He has sent letters and a gift by the hand of his envoys.'

'And you have received them according to our customs?'

'Yes, O king. Their camels have been taken to the stables and the men have been shown to the guest rooms. They are being provided with bowls of water to refresh themselves, and I have told them that when they have changed their garments, the guards will escort them to the Hall of the Throne. If it please your majesty, we will then serve food and drink as you receive them there.'

'Good. You have done well, Eliakim.' He thought for a moment. 'Set out chairs that I may sit with them, rather than above them on the throne. Tell me when they are ready, and I will come with Joah. Make sure that Shebna is also ready to join us.'

'As it pleases you.' And with that, Eliakim bowed once again, turned and left.

Hezekiah was silent for several moments, clearly deep in thought. The news seemed to have pleased him greatly. Then he smiled. 'Where were we?'

It was only when Joah was in the middle of reading back to Hezekiah the completed song of praise that Eliakim returned with Shebna. The scroll was set to one side, and Joah was soon following the king to the hall.

The Babylonian envoys rose when Hezekiah entered the room, bowing low to him in respect. Soon, however, all were seated together, with Eliakim at the king's right hand, and Joah and Shebna seated behind them, both with writing tablets in their hands. There were scrolls in the envoy's laps.

After greetings were exchanged and the good wishes of Merodach-Baladan conveyed, it swiftly became clear that the king of Babylon did not wish peace and prosperity for Hezekiah alone. Both kings knew what could stand in the way: *Assyria and Sennacherib*. The envoys had come with more than a letter of greeting.

Joah's marks were hastily impressed upon the wax of his tablet as the discussions continued late into the evening. On the morning that followed, Hezekiah personally showed the Babylonians both the wealth and strength of the kingdom, and (to Joah's mind at least) it seemed to bring him great pleasure. Eliakim, Joah or Shebna were often asked to supply figures of whatever lay before them—whether weights of silver and gold, measures of spices and fine oil, or numbers of swords and shields.

'They are impressed, are they not?' whispered Shebna to Joah as they stood on the city's ramparts, the sun high above them. The envoys were praising Hezekiah for the devices designed in the days of Uzziah, both for shooting arrows and hurling stones from the walls.

'They seem to be.'

'The king has every right to be proud of the city.'

'Hmm.' Joah was less sure of the wisdom of such pride—though it was almost impossible to avoid seeing it in the king. *Had Yahweh's promise of fifteen more years made him feel unassailable?*

Shebna went on in a lowered voice. 'Merodach-Baladan will be told of all that Judah can bring to an alliance against Sennacherib. And if Egypt were to join such an alliance, Assyria will see that their might wanes and that their arm can no longer reach to Jerusalem.'

Joah held his tongue. It was not only the promise of fifteen years that he remembered from Isaiah's words. *Had not Yahweh also spoken of delivering the city from the Assyrians?* He was not persuaded that such a deliverance would be in accordance with Shebna's notions.

It was only when the Babylonian camels had disappeared out of sight that Hezekiah received another visit. Joah's pen was poised over the papyrus on the table as Isaiah entered the room unannounced. Hezekiah lowered the scroll in his hand. Eliakim appeared nervous—despite being the king's steward, Isaiah was the one man he would not or could not command.

'What did those men say, and from where did they come?'

Joah's eyes flitted between the king and the prophet, standing only a few paces apart. Although he couldn't be sure, Joah suspected that Isaiah already knew the answer to his own question.

'From a distant land,' replied Hezekiah. 'From Babylon.'

'What did they see in your palace?'

The prophet's question seemed as needless as his first. Joah shifted uneasily on his stool and rolled the pen rapidly back and forth between his fingers.

Hezekiah looked steadily back. 'They saw everything in my house. There is nothing in my treasuries that I did not show them.'

The reply seemed to bring the prophet no joy. 'Hear the word of Yahweh Almighty: *the time will surely come when everything in your palace, and all that your fathers have stored up until this day, will be carried off to Babylon. Nothing will be left, says Yahweh. And some of your sons who will come from you, whom you will father, will be taken away, and they will become eunuchs in the palace of the king of Babylon.*'

The silence and stillness of the dead descended upon them. Several moments passed. Once again, Joah's eyes darted between the one who wore the crown and the one clad in the sackcloth of a prophet. Eventually the king spoke. 'The word of Yahweh you have spoken is good.'

To Joah the words sounded anything but good, and it was only after Isaiah had left that the king revealed his mind.

He looked at Eliakim and then Joah. 'Do not Isaiah's words speak of peace and security in our day?'

Eliakim bobbed his head. 'May the wisdom of the king be proved true.'

Joah repeated the gesture—but wondered what it would mean for his own sons. And why those who came to forge an alliance were cast as their conquerors.

Notes

1. *This chapter covers roughly 705-703/2 BC. The earlier date is accepted for the death of Sargon. The exact date of Hezekiah's water tunnel is not*

known but has been assumed to be around this time. Regarding the later date, Merodach-Baladan was, for a second time, on the Babylonian throne for several months around 703/702 BC.

2. *The exact nature of the roles of Eliakim, Shebna and Joah are not clear. The titles of royal steward, secretary and recorder have been chosen here, through translations of the terms used for them in 2 Kings 18:18 (and the parallel passage in Isaiah 36:6) vary. Their roles have, therefore, been kept vague, although it has been assumed that Eliakim managed the palace as the king's 'right-hand man', that the secretary arranged for all royal edicts, and the recorder kept the palace records. It seems that Shebna, who had previously held the higher post of royal steward according to Isaiah, was demoted for some reason and replaced by Eliakim (as predicted in Isaiah 22:15-20). Hobbs states, using the term 'archivist' for Joah: 'Scribal activity was a skilled enough art to require special training… The function would have been a necessity in any court at this time… 'the archivist' is clearly connected with the root 'to remember' and the context clearly identifies some court official. If, as the etymology of his title suggests, he 'remembered' or better 'brought to memory' events of national importance, then it is perhaps to Joah ben Asaph that we owe the substance of the record of the meeting between the Assyrian delegation and the Judean officials' (p256).*

3. *The exact timing of Hezekiah's rebellion against Assyria (referred to in 2 Kings 18:7 and presumably involving stopping the payment of tribute) is not clear. It has been assumed here as shortly after Sennacherib came to the throne, when Assyria was somewhat weakened and there were rebellions across the Assyrian Empire. Although Hezekiah blocked off streams and repaired walls when Sennacherib finally attacked, the water channel must have taken some considerable time to plan and construct, so may have been in his mind before he rebelled.*

4. *Some think that Hezekiah's tunnel followed the line of a natural karst (i.e. a system of caverns and channels caused by the flow of ground water) – see for example 'Jerusalem's Underground Water Systems. How They Met: Geology Solves Long-Standing Mystery of Hezekiah's Tunnelers', Dan Gill, (Biblical Archaeology Review 20:4, July/August 1994). Others, however, believe it was 'an authentic engineering project, without any*

pre-existing natural conduit that could have guided its excavators', guided rather by 'acoustic communication between hewers and the surface teams'. See 'Tunnel engineering in the Iron Age: geoarchaeology of the Siloam Tunnel, Jerusalem', Amos Frumkin and Aryeh Shimron, (Journal of Archaeological Science, Volume 33, Issue 2, February 2006, Pages 227-237). Hence the manner of tunnelling has not been specified.

5. *The Pool of Siloam is mentioned in Nehemiah 3:15 and described as being next to the King's Garden. It is probably the same as the King's Pool mentioned in Nehemiah 2:14. This is assumed to be the new pool that Hezekiah made, mentioned in 2 Kings 20:20.*

6. *Isaiah's word to Shebna is recorded in Isaiah 22:15-25. According to Oswalt, the setting for this could be any time between 711 and 701 BC but has been assumed here to be shortly after 705 BC. The fulfilment of Isaiah's word to Shebna concerning his faraway death (Isaiah 22:18) is not recorded in Scripture. A tomb was found in 1870 in the district of Silwan (ancient Siloam) in Jerusalem, whose inscription was only deciphered in 1953. Although the name in the inscription is incomplete, it is thought that it may well be that of Shebna, as it has a Hebrew title that matches the position of royal steward, is of the right period, and fits the description in Isaiah of a grave cut into the heights. Further research has concluded that the inscription is from the time of Isaiah, given the similarity in letters and writing styles with that in Hezekiah's tunnel. Clay bullae have also been discovered bearing Shebna's name, identifying him as a 'servant of the king'. See, for example, Biblical Archaeology Review 35:3, May/June 2009. It is not clear at what point Eliakim replaced Shebna as royal steward, only that it had happened by the time of the Assyrian invasion (2 Kings 18:18).*

7. *Although the Assyrian invasion (generally dated to 701 BC) is recorded before Hezekiah's illness in 2 Kings, 2 Chronicles and Isaiah, commentators suggest that the events happened the other way around. Ancient writers were not constrained by chronological order in the same way as modern historians. The text may also imply this: (a) Hezekiah's treasuries were full at this point whereas he had to empty his treasuries of silver and strip the temple doors of gold in an attempt to pay off the Assyrians (2 Kings 18:15-16); (b) the promise of healing that Isaiah brought to Hezekiah*

also contained God's promise to deliver the city from the hand of Assyria (2 Kings 20:6), implying the event lay in the future; (c) Merodach-Baladan, the king of Babylon mentioned in 2 Kings 20:12, reigned from 722 BC to 710 BC, and from 703 BC to 702 BC. This would put him before the time of the Assyrian invasion, and in his short second reign he may well have wished to enlist the support of Israel against Assyria. The miraculous sign mentioned by the envoys (2 Chronicles 32:31) seems to refer to Hezekiah's healing and the movement of the shadow.

8. The 'machines' made by Uzziah, referenced in 2 Chronicles 26:15, are thought to be some form of protective shielding devices (rather than catapults), allowing defenders on the cities to hurl stones and shoot arrows at the enemy with a measure of protection.

6

After all that Hezekiah had so faithfully done, Sennacherib king of Assyria came and invaded Judah. He laid siege to the fortified cities, thinking to conquer them for himself. (2 Chronicles 32:1)

For a while, the king's attention turned westwards. The army of Judah that marched out at his command defeated Philistine cities loyal to Assyria, strengthening Hezekiah's hand. But his joy was short-lived.

Joah scanned the scroll delivered to the palace by a rider. He clicked his tongue, then responded to the servant who had placed it in his hand. 'I must take this to the king immediately.' He hurried off, only stopping to summon Shebna. Eliakim was elsewhere in the city.

'What is it?' asked Shebna. Joah was already two paces ahead of him. 'And why the urgency?'

'News from Babylon.'

'Good or bad?'

'It will not gladden the king's heart.' Joah then remained tight-lipped until they were in the king's presence. They found him sitting in the courtyard, instructing his son Manasseh. They did not approach but waited for his invitation.

As soon as the king looked up, his smile faded. He rose, laying a hand on his son's shoulder. 'Keep reading. I will be back after I have spoken with Shebna and Joah.' He hastened over. 'Why such a lack of cheer? What has happened?'

'A letter has arrived, O king,' began Joah, 'with news of Merodach-Baladan.'

'Go on...'

'He was defeated in battle by the Assyrians and has fled. Babylon has surrendered to Sennacherib and the whole land has been subdued by him.'

'How recently?'

'Maybe two months ago.'

'And what of the Assyrians now?'

Joah shook his head. 'I have told you all we know.'

Hezekiah was silent for a few moments. 'Sheba—see to it that extra scouts are sent out. We must learn what we can of Sennacherib's movements.'

'Yes, O king.'

Hezekiah dismissed them, but Joah glanced back before leaving the courtyard. The king was walking slowly back to his son, but as if he now wore a mantle with the weight of iron. *If Babylon were an ally, it was now a defeated and impotent one.*

The early news gleaned from scouts and merchants cheered Joah, with Sennacherib's army marching away from them, east beyond the Tigris. But as the months passed, the storm clouds began to gather in the north.

Joah scanned the hall. The palace officials were all known to him, as were some of the armed officers. The faces of others were unfamiliar. Joah's attention returned to his writing tablet as Hezekiah began questioning the high-ranking officer who had brought the news of the fall of Sidon.

'And what of the city now?'

'Sennacherib has installed a noble loyal to him as their vassal king.'

'And you say there are other cities that have fallen to the Assyrians?'

The officer listed an ominous number. It sounded like most of Phoenicia. 'Any cities that will not pay the heavy tribute are conquered.'

'And the size of the army?'

'Vast.'

The single word dropped like a heavy stone into still water. Murmuring erupted around the room, disturbing both its order and Joah's mind. *Hezekiah had ceased sending tribute to Sennacherib—and now Assyrian boots were trampling all who opposed them.*

The murmurs only died away when the king drew breath and raised his head to speak again. 'We can do nothing to lessen Sennacherib's numbers, but we can increase our readiness to face them. We are already fortifying the cities of Judah.' He addressed his head of works. 'What progress has been made?'

Joah recorded every place whose walls and towers had been reinforced, whether it was Libnah or Lachish, Bethlehem or Beth Shemesh. The recent months had seen new towers erected in Jerusalem, like sentinels upon the city's walls. But the strengthening of the land was not solely with stone.

Hezekiah turned to his steward. 'Eliakim—what of our stores? What grain and oil do we have if the Assyrians march south?' Both Joah and Shebna wrote furiously as the king responded to the report, his commands as swift and numerous as a swarm of bees, with supplies to be sent to any city that might face a siege. As the sun rose higher, plans were drawn up to stop up streams and springs throughout Judah, cutting off any water that could quench Assyrian thirsts. Then, as the shadows lengthened, orders were given to forge further weapons and shields. But it was the final decision of the day that still weighed heavily upon Joah as he returned home that evening, pausing at the house of Gamaliel first.

The two men sat upon stools in the courtyard, cups of beer in their hands. Gamaliel sucked on his teeth after Joah had relayed the news from the north. 'It is indeed disturbing.'

'Assyria's king has only one name for those who withhold tribute—rebel. And only one remedy—defeat. And yet that is not all that disturbs me…'

'There is more?'

Joah took another sip of beer. 'Some insisted that an alliance with Egypt must be forged.'

Gamaliel shook his head. 'But Hezekiah knows that Yahweh's mouthpiece speaks against it!'

'I know, and yet the voices urging reliance upon Egyptian chariots prevailed.'

'Was Isaiah even consulted?'

'No...'

'And Hezekiah heeded these others instead?'

'There were many, believe me.' Joah sighed. 'I do not pretend to know what was in our king's heart, whether he agreed with them or felt he had no choice—'

'There is always a choice!'

'Maybe. But at first light tomorrow envoys *will* ride south with payment for a pact with Egypt.'

'*Woe to the obstinate children*, declares Yahweh, *to those who carry out plans that are not mine...*'

Joah winced as Isaiah's words rang out across Jerusalem's crowded street.

'*...forming an alliance, but not by my Spirit, heaping sin upon sin; who go down to Egypt without consulting me; who looked for help to Pharaoh's protection, to Egypt's shade for refuge.*'

Joah glanced around. Some stood and listened, open-mouthed, whilst others pointedly turned away.

But the prophet had more to say, his gaze sweeping the street as intently as a lion seeking out prey. '*But Pharaoh's protection will be to your shame, Egypt's shade will bring you disgrace.*'

'He does not hold back,' whispered Zebediah.

'With good reason.' Both father and son fell silent once more, listening until the oracle was over and the prophet had moved on.

'*Rahab the Do-Nothing,*' echoed Zebediah as they resumed their walk. 'Do you think the king knows that Isaiah gives Egypt that name?'

'Not Isaiah—Yahweh. But as to the answer you seek, if Hezekiah does not know already, I'm sure he soon will.'

'Will *you* tell him?'

Joah cocked his head. 'It is my job to record the affairs of the city. I should, therefore, report what I hear.' He bit his lip as the palace gates came into view. 'But even if the king receives the words, there will be those who oppose them.' Joah hoped his courage would not fail him.

It was not the only oracle against Egypt to be delivered by Isaiah.

Joah took comfort, however, from the threads of promise woven into the rebukes: *that when his people were ready to cry out to Yahweh, He would then deliver them.*

Joah watched the setting sun. He shivered but not from the waning of the day. *What had the Assyrian army looked like as it had marched south?* Its path had taken it closer to the Great Sea than to where they now stood atop Jerusalem's western wall.

Eliakim broke the gloomy silence. 'What should we do now, O king?'

Joah glanced at Hezekiah. His eyes were also set westwards. It was little surprise. In that direction lay not only Eltekeh, where Sennacherib had repulsed the chariots of Egypt, but also Ekron, which had only weeks before bowed to Assyria. Joah had had little doubt then that it would be towards Judah that Sennacherib would look next. He had been right. Hezekiah blocking the water supplies had done little to prevent Sennacherib beginning to ravage the land.

Hezekiah tapped the top of the wall several times. He then brought his hand down hard, as if his mind were finally made up. 'There is only one arm that can save us, and that is the arm of Yahweh. For too long we have looked elsewhere for hope, and I fear that my heart has been proud. The prophet Micah has warned of Jerusalem becoming a heap of rubble. We must trust Isaiah, that the Holy One of Israel will even now hear us.'

Joah paused and then spoke up. 'Surely there is wisdom in what you say, O king. Have not Isaiah's words prevailed in the past? In my youth, he prophesied the overthrow of the kings of Aram and Israel, and it came to pass within two years. And in the year your father died, he foresaw the king of Assyria leading away Egyptian captives. That too, has now come to pass.' He left the prediction of Shebna's demise unsaid.

'I chose well when I made you my recorder.' Joah flushed slightly at the king's praise. 'And you have not even spoken of my own healing or the miraculous sign that Yahweh wrought for me.' Hezekiah paused, nodding, as if to himself. 'I will speak to the officers of the army in the morning and tell them that we do not stand alone. I will tell them that there is a greater power with us than with the Assyrians. That we must be strong and courageous and trust in Him.' He paused, and then added, 'Yes, that is what I will do. Come, Shebna—I must prepare. And you will need to summon the officers.'

Hezekiah departed leaving Joah and Eliakim upon the wall. They looked to the west once more. 'It is said,' began Eliakim softly, 'that Sennacherib executed all the officials in Ekron who'd opposed his rule, and hung their corpses on the watchtowers around the city walls…'

Joah flinched. 'They are not the first to do so. The Philistines did the same with Saul and his sons after they fell on Mount Gilboa—'

'But Hezekiah at least has a promise from Isaiah that he still has years ahead of him.'

'Indeed. But do not suppose our king has nothing to fear if he is delivered alive into Assyrian hands.'

'You bring me no cheer!' Eliakim's words brimmed with despair.

'But there *is* hope.' Joah wished his voice sounded more confident. 'Saul did not trust in Yahweh, but King David did, and the Almighty delivered the Philistines into his hands.'

'The Philistines were not the vast army of Assyria—'

'Do numbers matter to Yahweh?' Once again, he drew on what he had both read and heard. 'Many scrolls have passed through my hands. Our people have always recorded and retold our stories, so that we do not forget all that Yahweh's arm has wrought in the past. Gideon defeated the hordes of Midian with just three hundred men, and my neighbour Gamaliel tells me that when Samaria was besieged in the days of Elisha, Yahweh caused the entire Aramean army to flee without the thrust of a single sword.' Joah paused for a moment. Eliakim was still looking west. 'Hezekiah speaks of being strong and courageous. His words are well chosen for they were spoken by Moses to Joshua when the conquest of the land lay before him. Yahweh has fought for His people many times. Can He not do the same for us now, if we put our trust in Him?' Joah knew the words were as much for himself as Eliakim.

The steward was silent for several moments then turned to face Joah. 'We now have nowhere else to put our trust anyway.'

The guard who had come from the watchtower bowed low before the king.

Hezekiah stood with his arms folded. 'What news?'

The guard straightened up. 'The Tartan is calling for you.'

'I will not be summoned by Sennacherib's commander as if I am his underling, and neither will I put myself in his power!' Hezekiah thought for a moment and turned to Eliakim. 'But we do need to hear what he has to say.'

'But you sent Sennacherib the three hundred talents of silver and thirty of gold that he demanded—' began Shebna.

'And yet *he* has not done what I asked,' replied Hezekiah angrily. 'He has not withdrawn from Judah, and he still besieges Lachish. He certainly does not send his officials to thank me, if he sends a large army to camp outside Jerusalem's walls!'

Hezekiah paused, tapping a finger on his lips. Joah's gaze darted this way and that. The recent news had been grim. The Assyrian army had swept into Judah like a plague of locusts, attacking and stripping their cities, and Hezekiah's trust in Yahweh had wavered. As the army had begun their siege of Lachish—Judah's second most important city and not much more than a day's march to the south-west—he had sent a message to Sennacherib, offering whatever payment was demanded in return for their withdrawal. Hezekiah had emptied the treasuries and stripped the temple doors of their gold. Yet apart from the city's riches, nothing had changed. Gold had proved as ineffective a saviour as Egypt.

The king broke his own silence. 'Eliakim—go out to the Tartan with Shebna and Joah. He will want me to hear his words so he will let you report them back to me.'

Joah bowed his head with the others. 'I will record the message for you, O king.' His mouth was dry.

'Very good. But do not answer him.' Then Hezekiah added, 'In fact, no one should give him *any* answer.' He turned to the guard.

'Let it be known to any upon the walls that the king commands every person to remain silent, with neither insult nor answer upon their lips. If we speak, it will only be as Yahweh directs us.' It seemed that Hezekiah was finally looking only to their God.

'Yes, O king.' The guard bowed again.

'Now go—all of you. And Yahweh be with you.'

Joah hurried out with the others, his heartbeat as swift as his feet. 'Have you seen the army yet?'

Eliakim glanced back. 'Only from afar. I was with the king upon the walls as they drew near to Jerusalem.'

'And you say it is not the whole army?' asked Shebna.

'Not according to the scouts,' replied Joah. 'Sennacherib is still besieging Lachish and building a siege mound there. But be in no doubt, the numbers outside Jerusalem's walls are still far greater than our own.'

'But why does Sennacherib not withdraw?' protested Shebna. 'Hezekiah paid him the tribute he required!'

'A mouse may offer all it has to the lion in whose paws it is held,' replied Eliakim, his face grim. 'The lion may take it and yet still decide to devour its prey. The lion will care little if the mouse complains.'

They were then left to their own thoughts as they hurried through the palace and out into its courtyard. Joah knew Eliakim was right. *Sennacherib would want to show what happened to kings who rebelled against him. Why stop at Hezekiah's gold when he could have his city and his people as well—and maybe even the king's lifeless body suspended upon a wall?*

They made their way through the streets towards the gate nearest the Assyrian camp. Joah's mouth was dry. He dreaded the moment when the city's gates would be opened for him to go out— and then shut tightly again behind him. He was glad of the silence. It both concealed his terror and gave time to pray. *Hear me, Holy One of Israel!* His soundless lips formed Isaiah's name for their God. *Let your prophet's words be true. Deliver us from our enemies. Save me from my foes!*

All too soon they had reached the city walls. They stopped in front of the thick wooden gates, strengthened by iron across their width. 'On the orders of the king,' began Eliakim, his voice quivering slightly, 'open the gates that we may speak with the Assyrians.'

The heavy bars were drawn and the inner gates opened. They walked through into the gap between the gates. Normally it would be bustling, but now it stood empty aside from the guards. The inner gates closed behind them and for several moments they were captive. Joah swallowed as he heard the bars being slid back into place. Eliakim nodded to the guards. Joah's clammy hands tightened their grip on the writing tablet clutched against his chest, his heart thundering beneath it, like galloping hooves upon hard earth. He stole a glance at Eliakim. He was pale and tight-lipped. As they waited for the opening of the outer gates, Joah mined what he could from his memory of the mighty deeds of Yahweh. 'Let us put our trust in Yahweh,' he whispered as the bars were pulled back. Light flooded in as the gates swung open, and before them was the Assyrian army. For a moment, all in Joah's mind drained away as swiftly as water poured out onto a ploughed field. He began to doubt whether his legs would carry him forward.

'Let us go,' said Eliakim, his voice wavering. 'Remember, it is not our place to answer them.'

Joah began walking, every step a small victory. It was made no easier by the attention of the Assyrian horde turning toward them, or by the sight of their spears and sharpened swords. Joah had never been so close to the strange-looking men from the east. They were clad in short tunics, the fringes of which fell just above their high laced boots. Some wore a further tunic of mail, but all had wide belts around them and conical helmets of bronze that glinted ominously in the sun. Three men, dressed in full-length garments that set them apart from and above the rest, were talking together, as if unaware of their presence. Then together they turned their gaze on Joah, Shebna and Eliakim, looking them up and down as if they were misshapen pots in the market-place, to be bartered down to the lowest price. The ample curls of their long hair and beards were carefully groomed into numerous tight twists, seemingly not a single lock out of place. They began sauntering towards them, their short-sleeved tunics brightly patterned and richly embroidered. The long fringes and tassels of the shawls that were wrapped and fastened over them further marked them out as Sennacherib's highest officials—those bearing the Assyrian titles of *Tartan*, *Rab-saris* and *Rabshakeh*. Their elaborate garments only served to demean Eliakim's robe and sash. Both parties stopped several paces apart. Joah opened his writing tablet, and he and his companions held their peace and waited for the others to speak.

As Joah stared down at the tablet a memory suddenly rose in his mind, unbidden. *He had stood here once before with a writing tablet! Then, he had accompanied his father in the days of Ahaz, and the prophet Isaiah had come with a message for the king. If you do not stand firm in your faith, you will not stand at all. Yes, that was it.* Then the silence was broken and the memory gone.

The Rabshakeh, clearly their spokesman, raised his voice. 'Tell Hezekiah,' he began, 'thus says the great king, the king of Assyria.'

The words took Joah by surprise. He spoke not in Aramaic, as Joah had expected, but in Hebrew. It took a moment to realise why. *The Rabshakeh was not only addressing the three of them, but also those upon the walls behind them.* He had no more time to think. He began jotting down the words from Sennacherib spoken by his mouthpiece.

'On what do you base this trust of yours? You say you have the counsel and strength for war, but they are only empty words.' He spoke with derision. 'On whom do you rely, that you have rebelled against me? Behold, you are relying now on Egypt, that splintered reed of a staff, which will pierce the hand of anyone who leans on it. Such is Pharaoh king of Egypt to all who depend on him.'

The words stung, the Assyrian taunting them with the recent defeat of their ally. Joah wrote furiously, only glad that he did not have to suffer their faces too.

The Assyrian continued, 'But if you say to me, *We trust in Yahweh our God,* is it not he whose high places and altars Hezekiah has removed, saying to Judah and to Jerusalem, *You shall worship before this altar in Jerusalem?*'

The words unnerved Joah. *What else did they know of the affairs of Judah?* He had no time to ponder the question.

'Come now, make a bargain with my master the king of Assyria: I will give you two thousand horses, if you are able on your part to set riders on them.' *He was mocking them—and Sennacherib was no keeper of bargains.* 'How then can you repulse a single captain among the least of my master's servants, when you trust in Egypt for chariots and for horsemen?' He paused, as if to let his words sink in. 'Besides, is it without Yahweh's approval that I have come up against this place to destroy it? Yahweh himself told me to go up against this land and destroy it.' He fell silent.

Joah lifted his head. The Assyrians were sneering. He suddenly felt uneasy. *Had Yahweh spoken to Sennacherib somehow?*

'They are trying to dismay those upon the walls,' hissed Eliakim under his breath. 'Joah—you speak Aramaic better than Shebna or me. Tell them to use our own language whilst in earshot of the city.'

Joah swallowed and tried to look steadily at the Assyrians. 'Speak now to your servants in Aramaic, for we understand it.' His voice sounded weak in his own ears compared to the confidence of the Rabshakeh. 'Do not speak to us in Hebrew in the hearing of those on the wall.' He knew his words were futile but deferred to Eliakim.

The Rabshakeh's eyes poured out their scorn upon him, his words dripping with the same derision. 'Has my master only sent me to say these words to your master and to you?' He lifted his gaze above and beyond them. 'Are they not also for the men who sit on your wall and who, like you, will have to eat their own dung and drink their own urine?' Joah's heart sank as the Rabshakeh's attention remained on the walls and he called out even louder and in Hebrew to all within earshot. 'Hear the word of the great king, the king of Assyria! Thus says the king: do not let Hezekiah deceive you. He cannot deliver you from my hand. Do not let Hezekiah persuade you to trust in Yahweh when he says, *Yahweh will surely deliver us, and this city will not be given into the hand of the king of Assyria.*'

Joah was finding it hard to keep his hold on the stylus as the words seemed to sap the strength from his grip. But he recorded, as best he could, Sennacherib's offer of peace and prosperity—and life—if they surrendered. But the Rabshakeh's final words were the greatest insult and the greatest threat, for they spoke of Yahweh as no more able to deliver them than the gods of the conquered nations.

The Rabshakeh fell silent, and Joah looked up. The arms of the Assyrian were folded. *He had finished.* The Tartan and Rab-saris were smiling at them contemptuously. He dared not look at the army again.

'We do not answer them,' whispered Eliakim. 'Let us return to the king.'

Following Eliakim's lead, Joah turned his back on the Assyrians. He scarcely dared breathe, and silently prayed that an Assyrian arrow would not embed itself between his shoulder blades. He glanced up. His fellow Judeans upon the wall were watching them. All had held their silence as the king commanded. Joah heard the bars being drawn, and the gates swung open before them. Only when they had clanked shut behind him, did he begin to breathe freely again, drawing in great gulps of air. Joah could think of only one thing. Despite the Rabshakeh's smooth words offering peace, unless Yahweh acted for them, his own body would soon be hanging from Jerusalem's walls. The sound of ripping cloth filled his ears, as Eliakim rent his steward's garment. Joah gripped the edge of his own tunic and gave a sharp tug, his anguish even greater than the grief at his father's death.

After the inner gates were opened for them, they began hurrying back to the palace. 'Do you think they have spies among us?' asked Shebna. 'How else would they know of the king's reforms?'

Now within the safety of Jerusalem's walls, Joah could think more clearly. 'It does not have to be spies. All Judah heard of Hezekiah's reforms, and one captured Judean with a sword to his throat could have told the Assyrians all there is to know.'

'And they now have an abundance of captives to choose from,' added Eliakim grimly.

The light of dawn, however, began to break in Joah's mind. 'But they do not understand what they have been told.'

Shebna glanced at him. 'How so?'

'To the Assyrian, as to King Ahaz, more altars to their gods could only be good. Sennacherib believes our king has angered Yahweh by removing altars throughout the land, insisting instead that all worship at the temple—'

'But we know that to Yahweh, it is an act of obedience,' said Eliakim.

'Exactly.'

Eliakim then shook his head. 'But maybe he knows that not all were pleased by what the king did.'

'But the Rabshakeh was right about one thing,' added Shebna, 'that Hezekiah has told us to trust in Yahweh.'

Joah's features creased in concentration. 'The Assyrians may have been seeking to weaken the people's loyalty, sowing seeds of doubt about all that Hezekiah has done.'

'Not once did they even refer to him as king,' added Shebna.

'Unlike Sennacherib—*the great king.*' Eliakim shook his head again. 'Oh, I am in no doubt that the Tartan and his mouthpiece would rather the city rebelled against our king and surrendered rather than face another lengthy siege. How *that* would please their master!'

All stared at them as they passed. *News of their meeting with the Assyrians had surely spread throughout the city already.* Joah's stomach churned. *Was each person destined to eat and drink the filth from their own bodies, as the Rabshakeh claimed? Was that what was happening even now in Lachish—or did grain supplied by Hezekiah yet remain?* They hurried into the palace, and soon the doors into the great hall were being opened for them.

Hezekiah turned, the strain on his face easing before their very eyes. 'Yahweh be praised! You are back safely.' Those around the king parted to let them pass. He stared at their torn clothes. 'What did they say to you?'

Joah opened his writing tablet and began to recount all they had heard. No one spoke when he finished. Then the king tore his robes, rending the silence as well as the cloth. Others followed him.

'This is a day of distress and disgrace,' began Hezekiah, shaking his head slowly.

Eliakim bowed slightly. 'Indeed, O king. But what of their offer of peace?'

'Peace?' spat out Hezekiah. 'All he offers if we surrender is an exile from which there will be no return—and that will only be for those whom he does not slaughter with a slow death first.' His gaze swept across the officials. He had no need to say any more. 'He holds out a hand laden with bread and olives, wine and honey, to tempt us out. But make no mistake: he also holds a sword in the hand behind his back.' He fell silent again, seemingly studying the floor beneath his feet. Then he raised his head. 'But he has ridiculed the living God. Rightly he has said that the gods of the other nations have not saved them—but they are only wood and stone, fashioned by the hands of men. We worship Yahweh, the creator of heaven and earth who alone is God over the nations.' His voice seemed to strengthen as he spoke. 'Every one of you must exchange your clothes for sackcloth, and I will do the same. Then return here. We will humble ourselves before Yahweh and pray that he will rebuke the king of Assyria for the words he has spoken to ridicule our God.' He paused and then turned to his steward, 'And you, Eliakim, will take a message from me to Isaiah son of Amoz, asking him to pray to Yahweh for the remnant of His people who yet live.'

The coarse cloth chafed against Joah's skin. *But then, that was the intent.* The stone of the temple courtyard was cold and unyielding beneath his knees. The king knelt nearby, now stripped of his royal clothes and clad, like Joah, in sackcloth alone. Sometimes Joah caught words of anguished prayer, as Hezekiah petitioned heaven—more for the honour of Yahweh's name than his own deliverance. Joah's mind returned to the words he had remembered earlier: *If you do not stand firm in your faith, you will not stand at all.* There was nowhere else to stand now anyway. His lips began to move in silent prayer—but not for long.

'O king!'

It was Eliakim. The king turned and then rose to his feet. Joah followed his lead, and was soon by Hezekiah's side, facing those who had been sent to the prophet.

'Is there a word from Yahweh for us in our plight?'

'Yes, O king.'

'Then tell me.'

Shebna opened his tablet. 'The prophet told us to give you these words. Thus says Yahweh: *Do not be afraid of the words you have heard, with which the underlings of the king of Assyria have blasphemed Me. Behold, I will put a spirit in him so he will hear a rumour and return to his own land, and there, in his own land, I will cause him to fall by the sword.*' Shebna shut his tablet and looked up.

'That is all?'

'Yes, O king. That was the message.'

Joah stared up into the darkness that night from his bed, Miriam's arm across him. He pondered the events of the day, related to the family over a meagre evening meal. The possibility of a lengthy siege still hung over the city like an ominous thundercloud.

'Do you really believe, Joah, that the Assyrians will withdraw from us as Isaiah has said?'

He did not need to ask if she was afraid. He thought for a moment, and then recounted the deeds of Yahweh as he had done to the king some weeks earlier, though now including the story of Shebna's demise. 'Isaiah's words have never yet fallen empty to the ground.' He paused. 'Today, the Rabshakeh multiplied his words to instil fear, and yet Yahweh's answer was both simple and short. If I were to say that there is only peace in my heart, I would be speaking falsely. And yet there is now less dread than when the sun rose this morning. I have seen for myself Yahweh turn back the shadow of the sun, and I *do* believe that turning back the Assyrian army will be no more difficult for Him.' He rolled over onto his side to face Miriam. He could not see her but could feel her warm breath upon his face. He wrapped his arm over her and drew her closer. 'Yahweh tells us not to be afraid,' he murmured. 'We must do our best to do what He says.' He fell silent, and soon had slipped into a sound sleep.

Only a matter of days later, Joah found himself upon the walls of Jerusalem once more with the king. No longer were they looking west, but out over the camp of the Assyrian army. The bustle there was unmistakeable. Since being summoned to the Tartan, nothing had changed—until that morning.

'What is happening, O king?'

'Unless my eyes are mistaken, Eliakim,' began Hezekiah, 'they are breaking camp.'

'For what reason?'

'Unlike Yahweh, Eliakim, I am not all-knowing,' answered the king drily. 'But I will say this—I believe it is the hand of Yahweh.'

For several moments they watched in silence. Assyrian tents were being collapsed everywhere. *As if an unseen foot were trampling them down.* A different movement suddenly caught Joah's eye. He waited until he was sure he was not mistaken. 'Look, O king.' He pointed. 'Assyrian messengers are approaching the city.'

Eliakim turned to the king. 'Should we go out to meet them?'

Hezekiah did not hesitate. 'No—they can come to us.'

Soon the messengers were within earshot, and this time they spoke in Aramaic. 'We have a message for Hezekiah from the Rabshakeh.'

Rather than reply to them, Hezekiah turned to Joah. 'Tell them—in Hebrew—that they may bring their message to me in my palace. Shebna—go down to the gate and escort them to me with guards that are double their number. And Eliakim, come with me.' With that, he departed, the others following, leaving Joah on his own. He drew in a deep breath and called out in Hebrew. He didn't give them the chance to reply.

If the messengers were nervous, they did not show it. They held their heads high and showed the king no deference. One of them marched straight up to where the king was sitting on his throne and held out a scroll. Hezekiah took it, broke the seal and unfurled it. He scanned its contents without a word, rolled it up again, and then addressed the three Assyrians. 'You may go. Guards—show them out.'

One of them tossed his head and blew out his breath between his teeth in contempt, but all went without another word. Joah watched them go. It was only when they were out of the room and the door closed behind them that Hezekiah spoke again, handing Joah the scroll. 'Read it out.'

Joah unfurled it again and began reading. '*Say to Hezekiah king of Judah: do not let the God you depend on deceive you—*' He paused, looking over at the king.

Hezekiah nodded. 'Yes, I know—it is blasphemy. But continue…'

'*Do not let the God you depend on deceive you, saying, Jerusalem will not be given into the hands of the king of Assyria. Surely you have heard what the kings of Assyria have done to all the countries, destroying them completely. And will you be delivered? Did the gods of the nations that were destroyed by my predecessors deliver them?*' The short message ended with a list of places and kings that had been defeated by the Assyrians. Joah looked up again when he had finished, waiting for the king to speak.

Hezekiah clasped his hands together in his lap. 'Eliakim—keep watch on the Assyrians from the walls. And Shebna—arrange for scouts to be sent out as soon as it is safe to do so. I wish to know where they are going—and what has happened to Lachish. We have been without news and shut up in this city, liked a caged dove, for too long.' They nodded their obedience. The king's gaze then fell on Joah. 'Joah—make sure that this is all recorded in the palace annals.'

'Yes, O king.' Joah rolled up the scroll and held it to his chest.

The king, however, extended a hand. 'No—I will take the scroll to Yahweh at the temple.' Joah returned it to him. 'I will place these blasphemous words before Him and ask for His deliverance. The king of Assyria is right when he says the gods of the nations did not deliver them, for those gods are only the creations of men's hands. But he is utterly mistaken to think the same of our God, the Creator of heaven and earth.'

As the king rose, Eliakim suddenly blurted out, 'Is the departure of the Assyrians, O king, the fulfilment of Isaiah's word?'

Hezekiah paused and smiled weakly. 'I dare to hope it is, Eliakim, but I will not presume anything that Yahweh Himself does not tell us.'

Joah dipped his pen into the pot of ink and lowered it carefully onto the papyrus once more. *Samekh, Nun, Heth...* The letters flowed neatly onto the scroll like a tiny, winding black stream, as he began writing out the name of Sennacherib. He only noticed the lengthening of the day as the page gradually started to dim before him, the letters no longer standing out boldly. He had wanted to finish before a lamp was required—and he had succeeded. He blew gently on the scroll to dry the final letters. He then straightened his back and groaned. *He ached.* His only interruption had been when Eliakim had put his head around the door to inform him that the last of the Assyrians had left. They had seemingly been in a hurry to depart.

Just as he was beginning to pack up his pens and ink, there was a sharp knock on the door. Joah glanced up, but even before a summons was on his lips, the door was opening.

'Father! The king wishes to see you.' Zebediah's eyes were shining.

'Is he back from the temple, then?'

'He is.'

Joah looked over his work and then up. 'See to my things and roll up the scrolls when you're sure they are dry.'

'Yes, Father.'

'Do not wait for me if I have not returned by the time you have finished.' He rose. 'And do you know why the king sends for me?'

'No, but you are not alone in being summoned.' Zebediah held his eyes. 'But it is the best news we could have hoped for, is it not, that the Assyrians have left? Has Yahweh not delivered us?'

Joah smiled and sighed. 'It is good news, indeed, but I will wait to hear the words of the king before I say more. Where is he?'

'On his throne.'

Joah hurried through the corridors of the palace. Servants were beginning to light the lamps with the approach of dusk. A clutch of officials were already gathered around the throne by the time he arrived. When the king caught sight of him, he beckoned him. His face seemed devoid of the anxiety that in recent months had seemed etched as firmly into his features as words carved into rock.

'Yes, O king?'

Hezekiah placed a scroll in his hands. 'I wish you to read this, Joah, when all are assembled.'

'Yes, O king.' Joah stepped back and opened out the papyrus. He glanced down at it. It was not the one delivered by the hand of the Assyrians earlier in the day. He drew in a sharp breath. The hundreds of words he had written that day were as nothing compared to the first three words upon the scroll: *Thus says Yahweh...*

The voice of Hezekiah suddenly rang out, stilling any murmurs. 'Today, the king of Assyria insulted our God. In the eyes of Sennacherib, Yahweh is no different to the dumb idols of the nations. But the Almighty is the true and living God—the God who hears His people's prayer and who speaks to them. And today Yahweh has answered us by the mouth of His prophet. So hear now the message that He sent to me today at the temple.' He nodded to Joah.

Joah drew in a breath. 'Thus says Yahweh, the God of Israel: *I have heard your prayer about Sennacherib king of Assyria. This is the word that Yahweh has spoken against him...*'

It was dark by the time Joah left the palace and walked down through Jerusalem. It was as if the city had suddenly come alive again, with men and women out on the streets rather than shut away for safety in their homes. And there was only one matter on the lips of those out in the cool of the evening—the departure of the Assyrians.

Joah suddenly felt tired, but it was the pleasing tiredness of a long and gruelling journey home finally completed. His stomach growled, and he wondered what Miriam had cooked—and whether they had waited for him before beginning their meal. He pulled himself up through the streets of the western hill and towards the family house. Light streamed out from the open door of their courtyard. Gone was the large plot of land they had once enjoyed when their house was first built. Now the hill was covered with houses with narrow alleys between them, and his home resembled the one he had grown up in, with a courtyard enclosed by a high wall. He smiled as he heard the familiar voices and then paused for a moment in the doorway. The whole family were waiting for him, and the smells from the cooking pots told him it would not be another meagre meal.

Miriam rose swiftly and threw her arms around him. She kissed him and then whispered, 'Is it true? Have they finally gone?'

He kissed his wife back. 'If you feed me, I will tell you all I know.'

The patterned rugs of their main room were soon covered in baskets of bread, a dish of lentils and onions, and a steaming pot of lamb stew flavoured with garlic and coriander. Joah sighed with deep satisfaction after his first mouthful. Between those that followed, he related the message sent by the Rabshakeh, Hezekiah's response, and the departure of the Assyrian army.

'But what of the gathering of all the officials?' asked Zebediah with some impatience. 'What did the king say to you?'

Joah chewed on some bread soaked in the juices of the stew. He swallowed. 'Ah—it was not so much what the king said to us, as what Yahweh said to the king.'

'Another message from Isaiah?' asked Ethan, his eyes shining.

Joah kept his second son—and the others—waiting for the answer as he took another mouthful. 'It was. The prophet had written the oracle on a scroll and at the king's command, I read it out to all assembled.'

'What did it say?'

Joah smiled at Ethan. 'It said everything my heart would have wished it to say—though most of it was directed to Sennacherib.'

'Sennacherib?' echoed Miriam. 'What did Yahweh have to say to the king of Assyria?'

'That he had, in his arrogance, ridiculed and blasphemed the Holy One of Israel, and that Yahweh had heard all his proud boasting about his achievements.' He paused, shaking his head slowly in amazement. 'And do you know what Yahweh said then? He said that Sennacherib had only done those things because He, Yahweh, had ordained it long ago.' He let the words sink in. '*In days of old I planned it; now I have brought it to pass, that you have turned fortified cities into piles of stone.* Those were His words.'

Ethan cocked his head slightly, clearly bemused. 'But why would Yahweh have plans for such a godless nation?' The room fell silent, waiting for an answer.

Joah stroked his beard for a few moments. 'I have spoken about such matters before with my wise friend Gamaliel. Is it not true that our God used the Assyrians to bring judgment against Samaria a score of years ago? Surely it is a measure of His power that He reigns even over nations that do not acknowledge Him and do His bidding unawares. In my youth, Isaiah referred to the king of Assyria as a razor that Yahweh Himself would use to shave His people.'

'But what about their cruelty?' asked Miriam softly. 'We have all heard the stories…' She left the details unspoken.

'That Yahweh may wield Assyria as the instrument of His purposes does not mean they will go unpunished.' Joah then drew from his memory other words of the prophet. *'Woe to the Assyrian, the rod of my anger, in whose hand is the club of my wrath!* Those words were also spoken many years ago. Isaiah's oracle that followed spoke of Yahweh punishing the king of Assyria for his pride.' Joah then smiled. 'And even in the words I read today, Yahweh spoke of putting His hook in the nose of the king of Assyria and leading him away.'

Miriam laid a hand on that of Joah. 'And was there anything for Jerusalem in the message?'

'We have the promise of the Almighty that He will defend this city and save it, that Sennacherib will neither enter Jerusalem nor lay siege to it but will rather return to his land, and that soon we will be harvesting again crops that our own hands have sown.' Joah picked up his cup of wine. 'Including the fruit of the vine.'

'Are the Assyrians returning to their own land, then?'

Joah drained his cup before answering Zebediah. 'We have been as good as blind whilst Sennacherib's army camped outside our city walls, unable to see anything beyond the near hills. But Hezekiah is sending out scouts. Soon we will know more—of both the fate of the Assyrians and that of Judah.'

'But we have the words of Yahweh!'

Joah smiled. 'You are right, Ethan. And what He has said is worth far, far more than what our eyes can see. And for now, His words are enough.'

'What happened?'

Hezekiah's question went unanswered for several moments. One of the scouts scratched his head. 'We do not rightly know, O king.'

Joah stared at the small group of men, still dusty from two days on the Judean hills.

'Yet you report to me,' continued Hezekiah, 'that a good part of the Assyrian army lies dead south of Libnah and that you believe Sennacherib is now hastening northward with what remains of his army, seemingly to return to Nineveh.'

'Yes, O king.'

'Was there a battle, then?'

'There were no signs of one.'

'So how did they die?'

There was another pause. 'We do not know, O king. All we can tell you is that there were bodies everywhere, as if asleep. Except it was the sleep of death. The Assyrians must have left in haste, for they neither stripped the bodies nor buried them.'

Hezekiah suddenly put his head back and laughed. 'It is the hand of Yahweh!' The room erupted in shouts of triumph and joy.

Joah's heart soared like an eagle. *Surely there could be no other explanation!* He lifted his voice. 'Yahweh be praised! Yahweh be praised!'

But the joy was not unsullied. After the clamour died away, Hezekiah addressed the scouts again. 'So what of Libnah and Lachish?'

'Libnah still stands and we spoke to its officials. Sennacherib had been fighting against it but turned south when the rest of his army arrived from Jerusalem.'

'Is it possible, O king,' asked Joah, 'that he faced another threat?'

Hezekiah looked at the scouts. 'Do you know of one?'

'No, my lord.'

'Maybe it was the hand of Yahweh again. But what of Lachish?' The room was suddenly still.

'It fell and now lies devastated, its people deported.'

Gasps, murmurs and anguished cries filled the room. Hezekiah lowered his head. It was a bitter blow, with many thousands living there, and its defences Jerusalem's equal. The grief of the gathering gradually subsided as Hezekiah eventually looked up, the recent triumph in his eyes now traded for deep sadness and unspent tears.

'I will offer sacrifices to Yahweh at the temple for our deliverance, but then I will see Lachish with my own eyes—whatever the story it tells.'

Joah suspected its tale would be a terrible one.

Joah had never beheld a sight so bleak, made all the more terrifying by the knowledge that, without Yahweh's intervention, Jerusalem's fate would likely have been the same. Hezekiah's chariot had stopped and he had stepped down from it without a word. He was now gazing towards Lachish. None of the other officials or soldiers spoke. Even from where they stood, to the north-east of the city and on the opposite side to its main gate, they could see its charred devastation. The city lay eerily quiet, like the bones of a corpse, picked clean of flesh—a hideous shell of what it once was.

'Come,' said Hezekiah eventually, 'let us see what has been done.'

The party walked along the eastern side of Lachish, mostly in silence. The city rose above them on a large mound with its two walls—an outer, lower one and then an inner one, higher up the slope. Both seemed largely intact. A different sight soon greeted them, however, at the most southerly corner of the city. A vast heap of rocks and earth had been piled against the mound to create a smooth slope leading directly up to the city walls.

'A siege ramp,' murmured one of the soldiers. 'It must have taken them months.'

But it had clearly worked. Joah kept the words to himself. The walls at the top of the ramp had crumbled—presumably under the battering of the rams of the Assyrian siege engines, reports of which had reached his ears. Then the king stopped. Joah's stomach lurched and one of the others vomited. Despite the horror of it, Joah's gaze was held by what he feared were the remains of three of the city's officials—their bodies not hung from the walls but impaled on tall wooden stakes near the bottom of the ramp and now food for ravens and vultures.

'Take them down and bury them.' Joah glanced at the king—his eyes were fixed on the same point. 'Sennacherib has paid dearly for such vile deeds with the lives of his own men.' Soldiers moved forward to carry out the king's orders. As they walked closer to the bottom of the ramp, they all covered their mouths and noses against the stench. Other corpses of their brothers were strewn everywhere, some without heads. Joah suspected the latter had not been killed in battle but executed. Numerous arrows and slingshots lay scattered across the ground, like ripe fruit fallen from some vast and terrible tree.

'This must have been where the fighting was fiercest, O king,' ventured Joah.

'Whether it was or not, all these will need to be buried.' Hezekiah stopped and turned to one of the army officers. 'You will need to find a cave or dig a pit for all the bodies. The city will no doubt yield further dead.'

'Yes, O king.' The officer chose two other men and headed off.

Joah then followed Hezekiah up the steep track leading to the main entrance to Lachish. The sight at the top was dismal. All that was left of the massive outer gates was twisted bronze fittings laying amongst charred pieces of wood. They went in and picked their way through the ruins of the city. It seemed that anything that could burn had been set alight, and that fire had blackened the rest. Ash covered every surface, and what had been the city's fort and stables were no more.

Hezekiah said little, and Joah forced himself to take in every sight as they walked around. *It was a bitter cup.* The two of them finally left the way they had entered, and stood together looking out to the west, where the land dropped down to the Great Sea.

'We will rebuild Lachish,' said Hezekiah eventually, his eyes still set westwards towards the setting sun. They would camp overnight nearby before returning to Jerusalem. 'You will record the city's fall in the annals, but I will not have the abominations of Assyria sullying any scroll.'

'Yes, my lord.' Joah paused, hesitant, before adding, 'I have a question, O king…'

'Ask it freely.'

'Why deliver Jerusalem and yet not Lachish?' The soldiers below them were now bearing bodies for burial to a point on the city mound a little north of where they stood. It seemed strange to Joah in the moments that followed that sweet birdsong was mingled with the murmurs of the men.

Hezekiah then sighed. *'These people come near to me with their mouth and honour me with their lips, but their hearts are far from me.'*

'My lord?'

'Words spoken by Yahweh through the mouth of Isaiah. And on that scroll you read, Yahweh said that He would save Jerusalem for His own sake and the sake of my father David—not because the city deserved to be saved. I may have rid the land of many idols and their altars, but I could not rid the hearts of my people of their idolatry—or their pride or dishonesty or any of their other sins. I would be a fool to think that all in the land have been in favour of what I have done. I know that corruption clings to Jerusalem as stubbornly as my great-grandfather's leprosy clung to him.' He sighed once again.

'Do you mean, O king, that my question should not have asked why Yahweh did not save Lachish, but rather why He *did* spare Jerusalem?'

'Indeed. That Yahweh yet shows mercy is both our salvation now and our only hope for the days to come.'

Joah thought back to what he knew of Israel's history and turned to Hezekiah. 'But has that not also been the story of our people's past, O king?'

A wry smile broke upon the king's face, bathed in the mellow light of the evening sun. 'Always.'

Notes

1. The events of this chapter are widely dated to 701 BC and are well documented in Assyrian accounts.

2. Although Assyria and Nineveh are geographically north-east of Judah, the Arabian desert meant that those from either Assyria or Babylonia were far more likely to travel along the fertile crescent to Carchemish or Aleppo and then come south. Hence the references in the prophets to disaster coming from the north (Isaiah 14:31, Jeremiah 1:13-15). The prophecy about the alliance with Egypt is from Isaiah 30.

3. According to Kitchen (p53), at Lachish 'many scores of storage jars exist from [the end of the 8th century] bearing the royal stamp l-mkl, "Of the King", indicating that Hezekiah had provided supplies for the city.

4. It is not clear exactly at what point an alliance with Egypt was made. Although it is mentioned only indirectly in 2 Kings 18:21 in the words of the Assyrian official, Isaiah denounces the alliance in Isaiah 30:1-7 and 31:1-3, although again it is not clear exactly when and how these oracles were delivered. Isaiah 30:6 records that this was an alliance for which payment was made. Oswalt suggests that, since Hezekiah's name is not mentioned in the oracles, he may not have been the instigator of the alliance but may have been forced into it by his officials (p544).

5. Although the historical accounts in 2 Kings 18-19 and Isaiah 36-37 are largely identical, harmonisation with 2 Chronicles 32 provides some challenges, particularly determining the point at which Hezekiah's encouragement to his military officials (vs 6-8) occurs. It does seem that the king's faith may have wavered at times, but Jeremiah 26:18-19 tells of how Hezekiah responded to the prophet Micah's words in Micah 3:12, probably delivered around this time.

6. The terms for the Assyrian officials referred to in 2 Kings 18:17 are variously translated. 'The Tartan (Assyrian turtanu) was one of two persons in the Assyrian army with this title who often led campaigns on behalf of the emperor, and the Rab-saris was himself often dispatched on campaigns at the head of Assyrian forces. The Rabshakeh, or 'chief cupbearer,' would have accompanied the emperor as a personal attendant. His presence in this delegation is no doubt to be explained in terms of his linguistic abilities.' (ESV Study Bible)

7. *The historical reconstruction of this chapter follows that of Kitchen (pp40-42). A withdrawal of Sennacherib's troops from Jerusalem to aid him against Tirkanah, the king of Cush (not referred to in this chapter but referenced in 2 Kings 19:9) seems to make most sense of the letter sent by Sennacherib to Hezekiah (2 Kings 19:9-10) and Isaiah's words in 2 Kings 19:32-34. The deaths in the Assyrian army may have occurred at the place to which they withdrew.*

8. *The description of Assyrian costumes in this chapter is based on a paper by Kim Moonja, Prof. Dept. Clothing & Textile, Suwon University, Journal of Fashion Business, Vol. 14, No. 3, pp1-19 (2010).*

9. *It is not clear who buried the bodies at Lachish (Hezekiah's men or Sennacherib's), but a large pit or cave was discovered on the northwest slope of Lachish's mound which was a mass grave containing over 1500 bodies (ESV Bible Atlas, p164).*

7

*Manasseh was twelve years old when he became king, and he reigned
in Jerusalem for fifty-five years…He did evil in the eyes of the LORD,
following the detestable practices of the nations the LORD had driven
out before the Israelites. (2 Kings 21:1-2)*

Joah stood at the entrance to the court of the temple and stared. *What
was this new abomination?* He knew, of course, exactly what the wooden
pole was—a representation of the Canaanite goddess and mother of
Baal. *Did the son of Hezekiah imagine that somehow Yahweh needed a consort
or company?* Worshippers were, however, bowing down to Manasseh's
latest idolatrous innovation. Joah glanced around the courtyard.
There were altars to Baal, and altars to the gods of the sun, the moon
and the stars—and on each there were fires burning, devouring the
offerings of those nearby. A fire was also lit on Solomon's altar, which
had once again been moved away from the centre—but there was
little on it beside the smouldering wood. The air was heavy with
incense, and some were seeking omens in the livers of slaughtered
beasts. The Asherah pole was more than Joah could take. *How could
his own sacrifice to Yahweh remain clean in the midst of such corruption?* He
turned and led away the goat with a whispered prayer: 'Forgive me,
O Yahweh, but I cannot worship You where You are dishonoured so
greatly. Please accept the devotion of my heart instead.' He began his
journey home.

The streets now seemed alien to him. If the throne of Hezekiah
had brought a cleansing breeze, the accession of Manasseh had brought
a putrid stench. The young king had reigned alongside his father for
ten years, until Hezekiah had lived out the last of the additional days
granted to him by Yahweh. Manasseh had never witnessed the days

of Ahaz, yet the sins of his grandfather flowed from him just as truly as his blood flowed within. In the few years since Hezekiah's death, it was as if his father's reforms had never touched Jerusalem and the apostasy of Ahaz had blossomed instead into a bigger and deadlier bloom. There had been rumours that some who had spoken against Manasseh had been murdered—if not by the king's own hand, then at his command. And Joah had no reason to doubt the whispers that a son of David had once again offered his child in the fire of the accursed altar rebuilt in the Valley of Ben Hinnom.

Joah led the goat past the idols that once more nestled in the dark corners of Jerusalem's streets. They seemed to multiply as readily as the city's rats. He had presented offerings on their altars as a younger man but had vowed never to do so again, even if the sacrifice was to Yahweh. *How could incense offered to Yahweh be mingled with that being burned to Baal?* Raucous laughter spilled out from an open door. One glance was enough. Harlots plied their trade openly, whatever the hour of day. Silver could now buy you sin with ease: a naked body or a concealed bribe, the words of the dead or the silence of the living. If Hezekiah had been a dam, holding back the wickedness of the people, then Manasseh was a wide channel. Iniquity flowed freely until it was a foul torrent, engulfing the land and all but drowning devotion to Yahweh. Manasseh's gods seemed to demand very little beside incense and obeisance.

As he came to the Valley Gate, he caught sight of one of the city's destitute, hand outstretched with begging bowl. Joah paused and looked down at the goat. *Yahweh—accept this as my sacrifice to You.* To the astonishment of the beggar, Joah put the animal's leash in his hand, murmuring, 'Yahweh bless you.' Without another word, he went out through the gate. Once across the valley, he dragged his aging body up the hill towards his house. He would reach his three score and ten the following year. Gamaliel had reached the age the year before, and Joah counted it a mercy that he still had a trustworthy friend. He suddenly decided to pay a visit.

Gamaliel had buried his wife some years earlier, adding further grey hairs to his head and deeper lines to his face. Yet he still had a ready smile for Joah—as he did now. He called out to his daughter. 'Abigail—bring some refreshments. We have an honoured guest.'

Joah smiled weakly. 'A weary guest.' He picked up a small wooden stool and set it down beside the bench on which Gamaliel was sitting in the courtyard's shade, his great-grandson on his knee. Joah lowered himself onto the stool and sighed deeply.

Gamaliel studied him. 'What ails you?'

'I have just come from the temple, and my heart is heavy.' He lowered his voice. 'The king adds an Asherah pole to both the temple court and the list of his abominations.' Gamaliel muttered something under his breath. Joah didn't catch it—his hearing was no longer as sharp as it had been. 'Are we now no different from the nations around us?'

Gamaliel lifted the child down from his knee. 'Go and play.' The youngster took a few steps and then sat down on the dirt of the courtyard beside a collection of stones. He began moving them around. Gamaliel shook his head slowly. 'If we *are* different, it is in but one respect—we are *worse*.' He, too, lowered his voice. 'I heard that the king had made such a pole, but to put it in the temple…? Is nothing sacred to Manasseh?'

Joah glanced over to the doorway. *There was no one outside.* 'Sennacherib may have blasphemed Yahweh with his words,' he whispered, 'but Manasseh seems to do it with his every deed.'

Gamaliel shook his head again. 'How quickly the people forget Yahweh's deliverance.'

Abigail appeared with a wooden tray bearing a jug of beer, two cups and a small basket holding wafers. She set the tray down on the bench beside Gamaliel, and then returned inside. He poured a cup of beer for them both. For several moments they sat sipping it in silence and watching Gamaliel's great-grandson as he tried to build a tower out of the uneven stones. The third stone teetered uncertainly before tumbling back down onto the dirt, the second stone with it. He began building again. The same thing happened. He started a third time, then a fourth.

'Is that not like Judah?' murmured Gamaliel.

'In what way?'

'It stands upright for a season, and yet always seems to fall back into sin as inexorably as those stones topple to the ground.' He lifted the beer to his mouth, took a sip and then returned the cup to his lap. 'The land moves to the steady beat of summer and winter, seedtime and harvest. And yet there is a darker turning of the seasons also. As surely as the arid months of summer follow the spring rains, so Judah's infidelities follow its devotion.'

Joah watched the pile of stones collapse once again. 'Caught in sin's grasp like a bird in the fowler's snare.' He took a bite of one of the wafers. It had the sweetness of honey. He then sighed again. 'And yet I know its grasp upon my own heart too, but when I took a goat as a sin offering to the temple, I could not offer it alongside the idolatry.'

'What happened to the goat?'

'I gave it to one of the city's poor…'

'Well, do not the prophets say that with such sacrifices Yahweh is pleased?'

'I know, and yet my sin still needs to be atoned for.'

'And far more so, the sin of the whole land.' Gamaliel dropped his voice again. 'The people not only follow the king in abandoning the Almighty but also His laws.'

'It makes me afraid.' Joah drained the beer. 'The people not only forget Yahweh's deliverance, they forget his judgment too.' He left the word *Samaria* unspoken.

The door to Joah's courtyard burst open. He looked up, but even before he could speak, Zebediah swiftly pressed his finger to his mouth. His eyes darted around. He then hurriedly beckoned in what appeared to be a family, all with shawls over their heads. He immediately closed and barred the door behind them. All of the strangers were bearing baskets or bags. Two carried a wooden box between them. Joah glanced over to Miriam who was kneeling by the cooking pot. Her hands were frozen, mid-air, her eyes wide with fear. Without a word, Zebediah gestured for Joah to go inside.

He waited in the house and was joined shortly by Zebediah and another man—now carrying the box between them. As soon as the door was closed, the stranger lowered his shawl. He seemed vaguely familiar in the dim light. Zebediah lowered his voice. 'Mother is taking the others to one of the upper rooms.' He gestured towards the stranger. 'This is Amoz. At least that is what he will be called from now on.'

'That is the name of my grandfather,' said the man, 'and it is an easier and safer name to call me. My father named me *A-Remnant-Shall-Return*.'

It took a moment for Joah's mind to catch up. 'You are Isaiah's son!'

'One of them.'

'Ethan is even now taking the other to the house of Gamaliel,' continued Zebediah. 'He was the only other one we knew we could trust completely.'

Joah stared at his son. 'What has happened?'

'It is what *might* happen,' replied Zebediah. 'There is a rumour at the palace—Ethan heard it—that Manasseh now intends to put to death any prophets who speak in the name of Yahweh.'

Joah's mind reeled. 'And you think he would kill even Isaiah?' His words sounded distant to his own ears, and yet even as he said them, he knew that one who had defied and blasphemed Yahweh so openly was unlikely to have any fear of murdering His prophets.

'The city flows with innocent blood at the command of the king.' Zebediah paused. 'We had to act.'

'But what of Isaiah?'

'He sent us away.' Amoz' voice trembled. 'He is almost eighty. He says he will not fear any man, and I worry he will flee only if Yahweh instructs him to do so.'

'Then he is in danger,' replied Joah.

'I know, but my father has spoken.'

Joah's mind raced. 'You are welcome to stay in my house for as long as you wish, but little goes unseen in this city.'

'And that is why he is now Amoz, my cousin, who is visiting the city on business with his family. It gives us time to decide where else they can make a home.'

Joah sighed. 'There are precious few cities left to choose from in Judah now.'

'It also gives us time for another task…'

Joah stared at the prophet's son. 'What is that?'

He knelt down by the wooden chest, opened the latch and lifted the lid. It was full of scrolls. 'There are few greater treasures in all of Israel,' he murmured. 'These are the oracles of Yahweh, given to my father, and written down by his hand.'

Joah stared at them for several moments, speechless. 'Treasure indeed. But you spoke of a task.'

'They must be copied—carefully. I will take the copies with me, but these must remain here in Jerusalem, stored where they will be safe and out of both the sight and the reach of the king.'

'And you wish *me* to copy them?'

Amoz fingered one of the scrolls and then looked up. 'My father's eyesight begins to fail him, but he speaks of you as a faithful scribe who served Hezekiah well as his recorder. There is no one in the whole of Jerusalem better suited for this task.'

Joah thought for a moment. 'The Sabbath begins tomorrow evening, and we will rest in obedience to Yahweh. I will begin the day after.'

Zebediah's brow furrowed. 'Why not tomorrow?'

A faint smile lightened Joah's face. 'Tomorrow I will grind gum and make the ink, and *you* will acquire the scrolls. We will need plenty of both.'

The days that followed the Sabbath followed a similar pattern. Joah would sit in the courtyard while there was good light, but out of sight of any on neighbouring roofs. He did not wish to invite unwelcome questions. His table bore only three things: a pot of ink, one scroll written by the hand of Isaiah, kept flat and open by clean stones, and a fresh scroll for writing upon. Each day Joah summoned a lifetime of skill and as much care as he could muster for the task. His right hand, marked by the lines and wrinkles of seventy years, needed frequent breaks, so that his letters became neither laboured nor error-laden.

Some of the oracles were known to him. He paused when he came upon words that had been impressed upon his heart over fifty years earlier: *If you do not stand firm in your faith, you will not stand at all.* He had been raised to remember Solomon's proverb on pride, but the prophet's decree had shaped his life more profoundly. He silently thanked Yahweh for graciously helping him as he'd sought to live by those words. Other oracles were unfamiliar. When each scroll had been filled, however, Amoz would carefully scrutinise every word, alerting Joah to any corrections needed, until both men were satisfied that the text was true.

The evenings were also part of the repeated daily pattern, with discussion on the meaning of what had been written out that day. By the time another Sabbath had passed, it seemed that every oracle was new, its words loftier, Joah's questions deeper.

'Despite all the scrolls that have passed through my hands,' murmured Joah, 'I had never read the like in all my lifetime. This day, I have written of Yahweh as a shepherd who gently carries the lambs of His flock in His arms. Yet a few words later, I was writing of Him as the One who has measured the waters of the earth in the hollow of His hand, marking off the heavens by its span!' His eyes shone as he regarded those sitting hushed as they listened intently, the evening meal for the moment forgotten. 'Yahweh is the Holy One, the Everlasting God who knows every star by name.' He shook his head slowly. 'And yet He also gives strength to the weary. No other nation has such a God.'

Amoz nodded. 'Their idols are nothing, merely a craftsman's work.' Joah pondered the words, the light in his eyes dimming. 'It makes Manasseh's lumps of wood both more ridiculous and more repugnant—and your father's words of Yahweh's coming judgment more daunting.'

'Might Yahweh yet stay His hand?' asked Ethan hesitantly. 'After all, Isaiah's words often call the people to turn to Yahweh. What if Manasseh repented?'

Zebediah laughed bitterly. '*Manasseh repenting?* That would indeed be a wonder of wonders.'

Joah turned to the prophet's son. 'What do you think?'

He shrugged. 'Yahweh told Hezekiah that both this city's wealth and its sons would be carried off to Babylon…'

'But surely the Assyrians are the ones we should fear?' interrupted Miriam.

'For my father, Assyria was never the one to be feared—just as Egypt was never the one to be relied upon.'

'You are right,' replied Joah, nodding. 'The Assyrians were only ever a tool in Yahweh's hand—and He has been faithful to His word of judgment. Even this very year, merchants from Nineveh have brought news of how sons of Sennacherib struck him down in the temple of his god. It was only days ago that I copied out words uttered by Isaiah twenty years ago, that Sennacherib would fall by the sword in his own land. If Yahweh fulfils His words against Assyria—just as He fulfilled His earlier words against Aram and Israel—will Judah escape His judgment, however long it is in coming?'

No one answered.

Eventually Ethan took a piece of bread and dipped it in the cooling stew. 'But surely there is still hope?'

The deep lines on Joah's forehead shallowed. 'Yahweh speaks of scattering Judah but also of gathering them—'

'Of a remnant returning,' added Amoz. 'After all, is not my own name a testimony to that?'

'But when?' asked Miriam quietly. 'Will my sons or grandsons be taken from this land—and, if so, for how long?'

Joah laid his hand over hers. 'I do not think we know. At least, I have not written of it yet—'

'And I do not believe Yahweh has revealed it to my father.'

'But we *will* stand firm in our faith in Yahweh, and trust that He will fulfil His word with mercy.' From his memory, Joah drew out once again words that had flowed through his pen, not only onto the papyrus but also his heart. '*He will be the sure foundation for your times, a rich store of salvation and wisdom and knowledge; the fear of Yahweh is the key to this treasure.'*

Amoz nodded slowly. 'So we fear neither Assyria nor Manasseh but only our God—not the fear of terror, but of trembling in awe at His greatness.'

Joah smiled. *'In quietness and trust is our strength.'*

As the third Sabbath approached and Joah's task neared its end, there was one question that burned within more than any other. As Amoz scrutinised the final papyrus put into his hand, Joah fixed him with his gaze. 'Who is the Servant of Yahweh spoken of in the oracles?' Amoz looked up. 'I have come to the end of the scrolls and yet I still do not know. I have asked myself whether it is your father, or even Yahweh's people, but it seems an ill-fit—' He searched for the right words. '—as if they are a sandal that is far too small for a foot.'

'My father has spoken of him as someone else—'

'Then who?' Without waiting for an answer, the questions flowed from Joah liked water from a raised sluice. 'The servant is spoken of as establishing justice and being a light to the nations, so how can he also be described as despised? He is the one in whom Yahweh delights, so why would Yahweh also crush him? And how can a mere man bear the iniquity of us all? I do not understand.' He looked at Amoz but the other man still held his peace. 'I have written of a child being born who will sit upon the throne of David and yet he will be called *Mighty God* and *Eternal Father.* How can that be? How can any of these things be? It makes little sense. Yet again and again I have seen with my own eyes the words of Isaiah—Yahweh's words— proved true.' He paused. 'I would put my faith in these oracles, but they feel like swirling waters, and I cannot find the bed of the river on which to plant my feet.'

Amoz shrugged. 'My father does not know either. He does not know whether he has seen the hills of Judah or the mountains at the end of the earth. But he believes the world will one day see the fulfilment of every word that Yahweh has spoken through him— and that they will be, as Yahweh has said, *awesome things that we did not expect.*' A few heartbeats passed. 'You spoke recently of a sure foundation—a foundation that is Yahweh Himself. Maybe we have to hold to what we know of Him and trust Him for the things we cannot yet see. *We are so small and the Holy One of Israel is so great.* That is what my father used to say to me when I was a child and asked him so many questions.'

'Hmm. If the nations are *dust on the scales,* what are we?'

Amoz thought for a moment. 'His beloved.'

'Are you coming to bed?' murmured Miriam.

'Shortly.' The whole house had fallen silent, and in the dim light of the one remaining lamp, Joah stared down at the unfurled scroll in his hand, covered with the same sort of ink lettering he had learned in his youth. His advanced age had added some variance to his letters that had not been there before. *But the words were clear enough—and correct—and that was all that mattered.* He had never lost his sense of wonder at how a mere twenty-two characters could capture any and every thought—and those on the papyrus even held those of the Holy One of Israel.

A fresh question now troubled him. He stared up into wooden beams above him. *Where to store the scrolls so they would be safe from Manasseh? He had spurned the sanctuary and closed its doors—could a trusted priest hide them within? Or might even the Holy Place yet be desecrated by their idolatrous king?* He sighed. *He was too tired. He would think about it in the morning after Amoz and his family had departed.* He wondered for a moment about the fate of Isaiah and mouthed a silent prayer. His eyes then returned to the scroll. '*The grass withers and the flowers fall, but the word of our God endures for ever,*' he murmured. *The ink letters would outlast both himself and Isaiah, but even if the papyrus eventually crumbled, the words of the Almighty would somehow yet remain—whatever Manasseh did.*

A smile played on his lips. He had been amazed to find that Shebna was not the only official to be mentioned in the oracles. When Isaiah had written of Sennacherib's assault on Judah and Jerusalem, he had named not only the steward and the secretary, but the recorder as well. *If, therefore, the word of Yahweh, was to endure, then so would the name of Joah son of Asaph.* He rolled up the scroll and laid it down gently. He blew out the lamp—and chuckled.

Notes

1. *The relevant dates for this chapter assume a co-regency between Hezekiah and Manasseh from 696 BC (when Manasseh would have been twelve) to 687/6 BC (the presumed date of Hezekiah's death, fifteen years after Isaiah's prophecy). Sennacherib was murdered by his sons in 681 BC.*
2. *The events of this chapter, beyond the apostasy of Manasseh, are imagined. We do not know how the words of Isaiah were preserved, although the fact that Jeremiah's words were written on scrolls (and that Isaiah himself wrote the history of Uzziah) would seem to imply that Isaiah also wrote out the prophetic messages that were given to him. Somehow the words were preserved, and it would not seem unreasonable to imagine that at least one copy was made.*
3. *In Jewish tradition, Isaiah was martyred by Manasseh, with commentators generally agreeing that the description in Hebrews 11:37 of those who 'were sawn in two' is a reference to this tradition. There is, however, no explicit Biblical record of Isaiah's death, so it is left ambiguous here.*
4. *According to Wikipedia, 'For an adult population (age range 18–60) the average speed of copying is 40 letters per minute (approximately 13 wpm), with the range from a minimum of 26 to a maximum of 113 letters per minute (approximately 5 to 20 wpm).' In Isaiah there are just over 25,600 words in Hebrew. Assuming 10 words per minute (there are no vowels, so the words might be quicker to write, but copying Scripture would require greater care), that might imply around 42 hours of work to copy the whole book of Isaiah. Given the exacting nature of copying, and the need for breaks, maybe 6 hours a day would be possible, and therefore 7-8 days of writing. Given a break for the Sabbath and possible mistakes, two weeks seems a reasonable estimate. John 12:41 says, after quoting Isaiah 53:1 and 6:10, 'Isaiah said this because he saw Jesus' glory and spoke about him.' It has been assumed here that the prophet therefore had some understanding that the Servant Songs applied to a future individual.*

5. *The verses of Isaiah quoted in this chapter are as follows: 'If you do not stand firm in your faith, you will not stand at all.' (7:9); 'He will be the sure foundation for your times, a rich store of salvation and wisdom and knowledge; the fear of Yahweh is the key to this treasure.' (33:6); 'awesome things that we did not expect.' (64:3); 'dust on the scales,' (40:15); 'The grass withers and the flowers fall, but the word of our God endures for ever,' (40:8).*

6. *The only imagined named character introduced in this chapter is Abigail.*

Nehushta

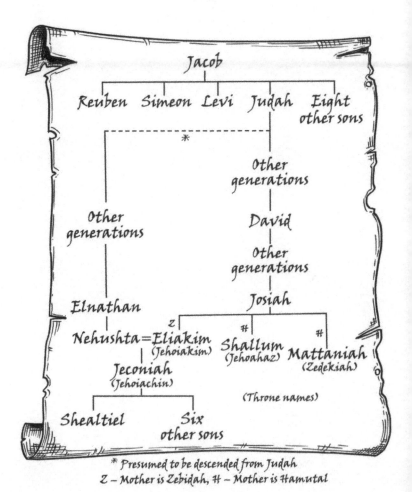

Jacob

Reuben Simeon Levi Judah Eight
other sons

*

Other
generations

Other
generations

David

Elnathan

Other
generations

Josiah

Nehushta=Eliakim
(Jehoiakim)

Shallum
(Jehoahaz)

Mattaniah
(Zedekiah)

Jeconiah
(Jehoiachin)

(Throne names)

Shealtiel   Six
other sons

* Presumed to be descended from Judah
Z – Mother is Zebidah, H – Mother is Hamutal

I

After all this, when Josiah had set the temple in order, Necho king of Egypt went up to fight at Carchemish on the Euphrates, and Josiah marched out to meet him in battle. (2 Chronicles 35:20)

Nehushta knew how to speak with her eyes. She could feign meekness, contrition, compliance, respect. But it would be none of those that day. Her father, Elnathan, had told her to keep her eyes lowered and fixed on the floor. *To display your modesty to King Josiah,* he had said. She stared at the cold stone slabs near her feet but had no intention of keeping her gaze there. *Not that she planned to look at the king, for that would have been folly. No, her deep brown eyes would speak to his son—the one whose exploits elicited the whispered gossip and to whom she might be given. Maybe Josiah believed that a daughter of a trusted and godly official might tame him.* Nehushta's lips quivered slightly at the thought. She kept her head bowed but raised her eyes slightly under her dark lashes. She waited for her moment. She did not have to wait long. Out of the corner of her eye she saw the king turn towards her father, addressing him in a low voice. She knew her father's attention would be fixed on him—and she raised her eyes. They met those of Eliakim. He held her gaze as their fathers continued their exchange. She let her eyes speak a single, silent word: *desirable.* It was the sort of look her father might have called *brazen.* But she had been blessed with beauty and intended to use it. Eliakim's eyes wandered down her and up again, and when they met hers once more, the corner of his mouth twitched. *They were playing a similar game.* She then lowered her gaze again—not swiftly in discomfort, but slowly, steadily, deliberately, her beguiling complete. She smiled to herself. *If Eliakim had any say in the choosing of his own wife, then she would be his.*

The servant-girl giggled as she helped Nehushta out of the embroidered and beaded dress she'd worn to the palace. 'When are you to wed the king's son?' asked Peninnah, pulling the garment of deep orange carefully up and over her mistress. The veil that had covered her head already lay discarded on the floor.

Nehushta's face was triumphant as she emerged. 'At the new moon. My monthly bleed will have finished by then.' She picked up a green tunic from her bed. It was less ornate but still made with the finer weave that the richer families of Jerusalem could afford. She slipped it on. 'Bring me the yellow fringed scarf, Peni.'

Peninnah went over to a large carved cedar box and lifted its lid. 'He won't be king, though, will he? That's what the others are saying.' She pulled out the long piece of tasselled cloth, its colour that of saffron, and presented it to Nehushta.

'If Josiah has chosen one of Eliakim's younger brothers to be the next king, what is that to me? It matters not.' She tossed her head and tied the scarf around her waist, drawing in the tunic to call attention to her womanhood. More than once her mother had loosened such scarves. She turned to face her young maid. 'I would rather be married to an ox that runs free than to one that spends its days yoked to a cart, hauling burdens!'

Peninnah giggled again. 'You mean a wild one.'

A smile played on Nehushta's lips. 'His eyes danced when I looked into them. I knew I pleased him—and I think he will please me.' She picked up her brush. As she raised it, the thick gold bangle etched with a pattern of leaves that Eliakim had placed on her wrist slid down her arm. 'Moreover, the king is only thirty-two. If he lives as long as his grandfather Manasseh, it could be more than a score and ten years until *any* son of his sits on the throne.' Peninnah dutifully reached for the polished bronze mirror but frowned as she held it up. 'What is it?'

'Is Eliakim not eighteen?'

'He is. My parents tell me the king fathered him at fourteen by his wife Zebidah.'

'That is young for one of noble birth…'

'But then Josiah came to the throne when he was only eight after his father was murdered.' She shrugged and then began brushing her thick, dark hair. 'Maybe the high priest or some palace official thought it wise that he should have a son as soon as he was able…should anything happen. Besides, I was as much a woman at fourteen as I am now at sixteen.' She gazed at her image. 'A little higher…'

Peninnah raised the mirror. 'What do you know of the king's family—and where you will live?'

Nehushta paused her brushing, lifting her chin and moving her head from side to side slightly. 'Josiah has three sons—he had a fourth who died young. Shallum, who is sixteen and is to be king one day, is of a different mother to Eliakim. *Her* name is Hamutal, and she also bore the king another son, Mattaniah, two years ago.'

'What of Eliakim's mother?'

Nehushta shrugged again. 'Zebidah's eyes bore into me today, looking over every handbreadth from the top of my veil to the sole of my sandals, clearly weighing if I was good enough for her son.' She chuckled. 'I wore deep respect upon my face for her. And I will wear it again when I need to.' She resumed brushing. 'As to where we will live, we'll have a large room to ourselves on the top floor of the palace with a smaller room leading off it. I am told it is bright and faces south. I may even be able to see this house from its window. And I do not doubt, Peni,' she said with relish, 'that it will be richly furnished and that I will fill it with fine garments to wear and patterned sandals for my feet.'

The maid's eyes sparkled. 'And you will have more gold upon your arms and your fingers!'

There were two swift knocks upon the door. Before Nehushta could say *enter,* it opened and her mother walked into the room, another servant-girl by her side.

'I am glad to see that you have changed already.' She glanced down at the floor. 'Peninnah, pick up Nehushta's veil please and put it away before one of you walks upon it. Then you may leave us.'

Peninnah hurriedly lowered the mirror. 'Yes, Mistress.'

As soon as Peninnah had closed the door behind her, Sarah continued. 'You did well before the king today, my daughter. You listened well to all we had told you.'

She clearly had not seen the way she had looked at Eliakim.

Her mother continued. 'And I have decided that I can give no greater gift to you, as you wed the king's son, than Dinah to be your maid.' She smiled at the girl by her side. 'She will serve you well, as she has done me since the day she arrived.'

Nehushta's heart sank. To her, Dinah was dull—a piece of plain woollen cloth to her own bright colours—and as likely to help her find amusement as a slug was to fly. Dinah had been orphaned four years earlier, and her father's pity had brought the impoverished girl into their house. 'But I thought Peninnah would come with me.'

Her mother took a breath. 'Peninnah is only twelve, and you are going to be a daughter-in-law of King Josiah. Dinah's years match your own, and she has shown herself not only to be faithful but also to have good judgment. That is a quality that will be worth more to you at the palace than a maid who will simply do your bidding.'

'Peninnah will be *so* disappointed…'

'She will still have a place here.'

Nehushta thought swiftly, then feigned concern. 'Mother, I know that all that you have spoken of Dinah is true, but she is *your* maid and to take her with me would leave you the poorer. It is too generous of you. It is too much. I will be content to take Peninnah and will be happier if Dinah can still serve you!'

Sarah smiled again. 'That is kind, Nehushta. But a mother wants the best for her daughter, and my mind is settled.'

As soon as she was wed, maybe she could ask Eliakim to send Dinah elsewhere in the palace.

'Your father is also pleased by it, and he will commend her to the king when he next speaks to him.'

Nehushta groaned inwardly. *Her fate was sealed.*

There was light tap on the door as Nehushta stared up at the ceiling. 'Enter…Dinah!' There was a pause and then the door slowly opened.

Her maid entered, pushing the door with her elbow as she carefully carried a tray with curds, fruit and fresh bread, and a small jug of water. Nehushta rolled over onto her side and propped herself up on the bed. 'I have told you already, if you can't knock any louder there is every chance I simply will not hear you.' She made no effort to hide the annoyance in her voice.

'I am sorry, Mistress. I will do better next time.'

Nehushta waved in the general direction of the cedar chest. 'Put it down over there.'

'Your mother asks that you dress for outside, as your parents wish you to go with them to the temple to present a fellowship offering.'

Nehushta found any such trip tedious. 'Tell her that I still have my monthly bleed.'

'I have already told her that it finished two days ago—'

'Why did you do *that*? I didn't ask you to!'

'But she asked me to let her know.'

'I thought you were meant to be serving *me* now,' muttered Nehushta. She rolled onto her back again. 'Then tell her I have an ache in my belly. No, better—tell her I couldn't sleep last night because I was worried about the wedding, and that I am too tired to go and must sleep now so that I do not appear worn when I wed. Tell her that.' When she heard no movement, she turned her head. Dinah was staring at her. 'Go. Now!' Without another word, Dinah lowered her eyes, turned and left her. Nehushta sighed and stared up at the ceiling again. *She would need to teach Dinah her ways.*

Nehushta's mind turned to the wedding garment she would wear in a few days, and to the jewellery that would adorn her arms, her neck, her ankles. She had breathed in the heady scent of the myrrh from the perfume bottle her mother had bought for her. And she thought of Eliakim and began to imagine what it would be like to be lying in his bed instead. Her thoughts were abruptly ended by two sharp knocks on the door. She traded her sunshine for a clouded day, then called out softly, 'Come.' But it was Dinah who entered and not her mother. She was carrying a bowl of water with a towel over her arm.

'I told your mother you would wash when you had had your breakfast and would be with them as soon as you were dressed.'

Nehushta stared at her, open-mouthed. Then her eyes flashed. 'How dare you! Why didn't you say what I told you to say? You are *my* maid now and you obey *me*!'

Dinah lowered her head as she set the bowl and towel on small olive-wood table. She spoke softly. 'But Yahweh has told us not to bear false witness. My parents taught me that and to obey Him first. So I cannot lie for you, Mistress.' Dinah finally met Nehushta's gaze. 'But I will not lie to you, either, whether for my own benefit or that of others.'

Nehushta was still seething. She wished she could think of something clever—something cutting—to say. But she could not, so held her tongue and continued glaring.

Dinah looked away, but not in shame. She crossed to the chest and picked up the tray of breakfast, bearing it to the bed. 'You should eat, Mistress. I will fetch whichever tunic you desire to wear and will find a scarf and veil to complete it.' She set the tray down by Nehushta and waited. 'Mistress?'

Nehushta had no reply beyond an answer to her maid's question. 'Bring me the pale green tunic with the dark green embroidery around each hem.' Her words were still clipped.

'As you say…'

As Nehushta began scooping out the curds with the bread, she noticed that the dish had been drizzled with honey. Each of the dates had been carefully cut and its stone removed. She was not about to thank her maid, however. She ate in silence, missing her usual chatter with Peninnah but having no desire to be on more familiar terms with the maid who had defied her. She glanced at Dinah. She had already laid the correct dress out and was searching carefully through the carved chest. The silence was only broken when the tray had largely been emptied. 'Here.' Nehushta gestured at the tray. 'Take it away and when you come back you will brush my hair.'

She sighed as much in relief as in resignation when Dinah was out of the room. She dropped her legs over the edge of the bed and lifted the cloth from the bowl. She squeezed it out and began running the cool cloth up and down her arms. She paused. *Maybe a servant who would not lie to her could be useful. She had known Peninnah fib to save her own skin many times. And surely there would also be other servants at the palace who would be more compliant to her wishes, even if she had to suffer Dinah's pious presence for a portion of each day.* She then studied the garments set out on her bed. *For one who dressed so plainly, Dinah did at least seem to have some understanding of how to blend colours in a way that pleased the eye.*

The silence was only broken on Dinah's return by Nehushta directing her to the brush.

'You have beautiful hair, Mistress,' began Dinah as she gently pulled the brush downwards. 'The light catches its red tinge.'

Her hair had borne that hint of colour since her birth. It was why her parents had called her *Nehushta*, with her name's likeness to the word *bronze. Not that she would tell her maid that.* She remained aloof, only speaking to tell Dinah to bring her the mirror. As she scrutinised her reflection she smiled. *She could surely endure a dull maid if she had a husband who was all that Dinah was not.*

It felt strange to wake up with a man next to her. But then everything felt strange—as if she had awoken in some distant land, unfamiliar and yet enlivening. The bed was large, and the sheets had been perfumed for their wedding night. They were of fine Egyptian linen and coloured brightly, but not of a depth that might mask the evidence of her virginity. Eliakim's arm lay across her. He was breathing slowly and steadily still. The room was still dim, though shafts of morning light were finding their way in past the heavy curtains over the windows. She breathed in deeply and Eliakim's arm, cloaked in a mass of dark hair, rose with her. She could still smell the myrrh on her neck and the aloes on the sheets. She breathed out slowly and his arm fell again. She repeated the action and then giggled.

Eliakim stirred, opened his eyes and gazed into hers. He then yawned loudly and proclaimed, 'I have a woman in my bed!' He disappeared under the sheets, causing her to shriek with laughter.

'My lord…!'

He emerged, an eyebrow raised. 'Did your parents tell you to address me like that?' It was the first time they had spoken properly in private.

'Is it not right to do so?' she said playfully.

He propped himself up on an elbow and began twisting a lock of her hair around his finger. 'I have no interest in what either father or mother tells us of what is right or wrong in their eyes. I will do as I please, as often as I am able! So call me Eliakim or Eli or both. Just not *my lord*.'

'Very well.' She thought for a moment. 'And what happens now? How will you spend your day?'

'Doing as little as I can.' He paused. 'But first…' He looked over at the door and bellowed. 'Shimron!'

The door immediately opened, and an older man entered. 'Yes, my lord?'

Eliakim turned back to Nehushta. 'He is a servant not a wife,' he whispered. He winked at her before addressing Shimron again. 'We wish to eat.'

The servant nodded. 'I will see to it, my lord.' He left as swiftly as he'd entered.

Nehushta stared at the door. 'Does he stand out there, simply to do your bidding whenever you call?'

'He does so, for as long as I am in the room.'

She returned her attention to him and rolled onto her front. 'That sounds far more pleasing than having a servant sent in to wake you when all you wish is to sleep on.'

'It is. And *you* are no longer in your parents' house.'

'But do you not have royal duties?'

'Not today.' He ran a finger down her back. 'But I am famished. We will eat before I drink of my wedding cup again.'

She thought for a moment. 'Then, while we wait, tell me, *Eliakim*, what I need to know.'

'And what is that?'

'The women in the palace—especially the king's wives and his

216

mother: whose path should I avoid and whose favour should I seek? And how should I do both?'

Eliakim put his head back and laughed. 'If I had known the answers to those questions ten years ago, I might have saved myself much grief.'

'Then tell me *now*.'

He then nodded to himself, amusement still in his eyes, and leant in towards her, as if to share a secret. 'Our ancestor Jacob and his wife Rachel both used guile with their parents. So why should we not do the same? I will tell you, then, how to walk within the palace walls to both our gain.'

Eliakim told her not only of the women she had named, but also of the officials who *stalked the palace*. Nehushta listened carefully, storing every detail, and asking questions when she needed to know more. 'And if those I have named in the palace for you to avoid are not enough, then I will add one more name: *Jeremiah*.'

'The one they call a prophet?'

Eliakim nodded. 'Yes. Even if the sun is shining in all its brilliance, he will still cloud your day.'

'You have heard him speak?'

'I have been told his words. He called the nation of Israel a harlot and says that Judah is worse.' He paused. 'He is as bad as my relative Zephaniah, who declares himself to be a prophet too, but speaks only of destruction. If I were king, I would muzzle them both!'

They suddenly fell silent when Shimron returned with a large tray loaded not only with bread and fruit, but also with meat, cheese and sweet cakes. He went to set the tray down on the large cedar table, but Eliakim halted him. 'No, Shimron. Set it down here on the bed.'

'As my lord wishes...' They waited until he had left the room.

As Eliakim threw a grape up and caught it deftly in his mouth, his new wife pondered another question. 'You spoke of doing what you please when you are able...'

Eliakim nodded, looking impressed. 'You were listening well. Go on...' He started on the round of bread.

'What are those things, then, that do not please you and yet must be done?'

He didn't wait until his mouth was entirely empty before answering. 'It is another good question…' He left his words hanging whilst he swallowed the bread and then picked up a roasted quail and began tearing meat off the bone with his teeth. She waited whilst he both chewed on the meat and deliberated. He lowered the small carcass. 'And it is one with a ready answer. My father requires me to attend all the meetings of his council—to know what happens within the palace, this city, our land and beyond its borders. But I do not see the point if I am not to sit upon the throne.'

'But are there not times when knowledge can be used to one's advantage?'

'True—especially within these walls.' He raised the quail to his mouth again and ripped off some more flesh.

Nehushta nibbled on a sweet cake, thinking. 'You have told me what happens within the palace walls, but what about outside them?'

Eliakim raised an eyebrow. 'You wish to know such things?'

'I only wish to know more than the other women!'

He laughed out loud. 'I have found a wife after my own heart. Well then, I will tell you.' He thought for a moment again. 'As for what happens within the city, my father carries on the reforms he began when I was five. The work to cleanse (as he calls it) the temple and to repair it is almost finished—or so he tells me—and you will know of the Passover that was celebrated here. *What*? Seven years ago?'

'Six…all Jerusalem knew of it.'

'As did Judah and the parts of Israel that he seeks to bring under his rule, be it Bethel or Samaria. His desire for reform seems to know no bounds. He has certainly done much beyond this city. Not only has he removed from Jerusalem all the altars to Baal, to Asherah and to the host of heaven—and with them, their priests—he has also sought to do the same throughout the land. He has destroyed, wherever he has found them, the high places dedicated to the gods of Moab and Ammon, caring not whether they were set up by his own grandfather

Manasseh, Jereboam of Israel, or the mighty Solomon himself.' He took another mouthful, leaving the tiny bird almost devoid of meat.

She waited again and studied him. There was much in his tone that made her suppose that Josiah and his son walked different paths. But she held her peace.

'He has even slaughtered the priests of the high places on their own altars, burning their bones upon them to defile them. He also removes any mediums and spiritists he finds from the land.' He tore a final piece of flesh from the carcass and tossed it down. 'And so the land is *cleansed*.'

Nehushta decided not to question him more on the reforms—*at least, not directly and not until he knew he could trust her with his secrets*. 'My father says that the king's zeal flows from his reading of Yahweh's Book of the Law—the one that was found when the temple was being repaired.'

Eliakim flicked the quail's carcass. 'Your father is correct.'

'And beyond the borders of our land? What do I need to know?'

'I can answer in a single word: *Babylon*.' He tossed another grape into the air, but this time towards Nehushta. She leaned forward to mimic him, but the tiny fruit bounced off her chin and onto the floor. He roared with laughter. 'She has not my talent!'

'Yet! Such things would have been frowned upon in my father's house.'

'Not here—at least, not in *this* room. You will need to practice then.'

She grabbed another grape and tossed it at him. It veered to his left, but he still caught it and grinned. His approval drew out a boldness she scarcely would have imagined only a day earlier. 'My husband's peculiar talents amaze me, but he should now impress me with what he knows of Babylon.'

'My wife's peculiar *questions* astonish me, but—' He drew out the word. '—I will please her so that she will, in return, please me.' He leaned back against the pillow on the bed, tilting his head back to look at the ceiling. 'Babylon,' he began slowly, 'may change everything.'

'How?'

219

'Ten years ago, a Chaldean named Nabopolassar defeated the Assyrian army—or a portion of it—outside Babylon. He seized the city and set up a throne for himself there. Ever since then, the Assyrians have tried to take the city back. But they do not succeed. Instead, Nabopolassar attacks other cities nearby to take yet more from the Assyrian king.'

'Are you saying that the power of Assyria wanes?'

'Exactly that—it has been doing so ever since the death of Ashurbanipal, its last king. My father says that unrest now weakens their empire, and that no king can fight an enemy outside if there is also one within. It has given Judah greater freedom and allows my father to extend our borders.'

'But can the Babylonians ever topple Assyria?'

'Maybe, if they form an alliance. There may be others to the east who would be glad to see the end of the Assyrians.' He reached for a plump date and popped it in his mouth.

Nehushta pondered the words. Assyria had been a dark cloud over their nation for more than a hundred years. Her eyes narrowed suddenly. 'But what if the Assyrians form an alliance of their own?' Eliakim let out a low whistle which swiftly rose and then fell again. *She had impressed him once more.*

'Ah, my wife learns swiftly!'

'Only if it pleases her to do so!'

Eliakim lifted the tray and set it down on the floor, propelling, as he did so, the date stone from his mouth and onto the tray. *Their meal was clearly over*. For a moment, Nehushta wondered where Dinah was. She had forgotten all about her. *No matter*. For now, it was a question to which she did not need—or wish—to know the answer.

After one year of marriage, Nehushta had borne Eliakim a son whom he had named Jeconiah. After two years, another power—the Medes—had risen in the east and taken the ancient Assyrian city of Asshur after a siege and a bloody battle. After another two years, the heart of the Assyrian empire—the city of Nineveh—had fallen. An alliance of the Medes and Babylonians had left the city in ruins, its

220

king dead, and the remnants of the Assyrian army fleeing west to the city of Harran from which Abraham had once set out for Canaan. Between raising Jeconiah and pleasing herself, Nehushta followed what she could of such news, which flowed through the palace corridors like a mountain stream—waxing or waning in strength with the passing seasons. It all felt distant, however—a cloud over a far hill whose shadow never reached Judah or her life as Eliakim's wife.

But the sky finally darkened when Nehushta turned twenty-three and Jeconiah six.

The loud rhythmic clash of wood upon wood stirred Nehushta from her nap. 'Coniah!' Her exclamation from the bed where she lay sprawled was edged with exasperation. 'I have told you before: the table is not a tent peg, and your toys are not mallets.' The six-year-old looked crest-fallen. Nehushta didn't care. She stared up at the ceiling, turning her sharp tongue upon her maid. 'Dinah—if he must play with his wooden animals, then find him some shade upon the roof. It is not beyond even your wit to do so!' She lowered her gaze but still couldn't be bothered to raise herself. The early afternoon sun had just begun to stream in through both windows.

'Yes, Mistress.' Dinah held out her hand to the boy. 'Come, Coniah, we will gather up your animals as if they are entering Noah's ark, and we will take them on a journey.'

Nehushta rolled her eyes but had to admit, *Dinah was good with the boy—as she was with every duty.* It was she who rose during the night if he needed food or comfort, and she who often spent the larger portion of the day amusing him—when she wasn't running errands for her mistress or tidying up after her.

Dinah paused, however, a cedarwood bull in her hand. 'Mistress—something stirs in the city.'

Nehushta finally propped herself up. 'What do you mean?'

'I do not know, but there is a different noise within its walls today.'

'Tell me if there is anything I need to know.'

But there was no opportunity for Dinah to even acknowledge her order. The doors flew open, turning fully on their hinges and crashing into the walls behind them. Eliakim strode in, cursing, a dark look upon his face that was utterly unfamiliar to Nehushta. Shimron was hurrying behind him. Her son's lip began to quiver. She rose swiftly. 'Dinah! Leave the rest of the animals where they lie and take Jeconiah to the roof *now*.' Her maid immediately heeded the command, sweeping the child up into her arms. 'And close the doors behind you.'

'Where are my winter boots?' demanded Eliakim as he sat down on the bed, his face drawn and his mind clearly elsewhere. 'And the thick embossed belt?'

Nehushta knew better than to point out that they would be where they always were. 'Shimron will fetch them for you.' The servant disappeared into the adjoining room. 'Whatever has happened, Eli?'

'Word arrived at first light from scouts near the Egyptian border that Pharaoh Necho and his army are marching north.'

Nehushta stared at him, incredulous. 'Here?'

Eliakim swiftly pulled his sandals from his feet and threw them across the floor. One of the sandals careered into an abandoned wooden horse, knocking it over. 'No. My father believes that they are marching to the aid of the Assyrians at Carchemish.'

'To what end?'

'To help Assyria regain Harran from the Babylonians and re-establish their rule there—or so the king believes.'

'But what is that to us—and to you, Eli?'

'My father intends to ride out in his chariot with the army to meet Necho in battle at Megiddo…'

She could barely take in the words that she was hearing. 'But why, if they are not coming here?'

'Shimron!' bellowed Eliakim. 'I need my boots! NOW!'

The servant emerged only moments later, the boots in his hands. 'They are here, my lord.' He hurriedly knelt by Eliakim and began to help him on with them.

Eliakim looked up at her, his face grim. 'Why? Because he believes he is invincible and can stop the Egyptians reaching northern Aram. He wishes to see an end to the Assyrians and means to help the Babylonians achieve it.' He spat on the floor in contempt. 'It is madness! My father should leave them to their own battles.'

'And you?' Her voice sounded very far away and small.

'The king commands me to ride with him in my chariot.'

'When?' The single word was all she could manage.

'This day. Stores and weapons were being gathered all morning.'

Nehushta opened her mouth to speak but there were no more words. Her thoughts and fears spun through her mind like leaves caught in a swirl of wind. Her mouth, which she closed again, felt suddenly dry.

'My belt, Shimron. MY BELT!' The servant nodded and rose swiftly, returning to the inner room. 'Why must I have to endure such hopeless servants!' he muttered, rising to his feet. He caught sight of one of his son's wooden animals near his feet. He cursed loudly. 'And why this childish nonsense in my bedroom?' He kicked the small ox with such force that it bounced back half the distance after hitting the wall, two of its legs sheared from its body. As soon as Shimron reappeared, holding out the belt to him, Eliakim snatched it from his hand, not waiting to put it on or to bid his wife farewell before striding towards the door.

Nehushta finally found her voice. 'When will you be back, Eli?'

Eliakim paused in the doorway and looked back at her, his face a thundercloud. Whatever answer was in his mind remained unspoken. His eyes darted instead to his servant. 'Come on, Shimron!' As he turned and left, she heard him mutter *madness* once more. Then she was alone, the room suddenly silent, left with one answer to her question forcing itself upon her mind: *never.*

The sounds of the city slowly flowed in on her, rising ominously like a river in flood. *Dinah was right.* Barked commands, clattering, shouting, a multitude in the streets. Even closer, within the palace, she could hear movement and voices. It was as if she suddenly awoke. She hastily slipped on her sandals, and then snatched up the mirror. *Good enough.*

She hurried into the corridor and towards the door that opened onto the steps to the roof. She made her way upwards. For a few moments, the only sound was that of the leather of her sandals slapping against the stone like the first patter of large drops of rain at the coming of a summer storm. She soon emerged onto the flat palace roof and glanced around. Dinah was standing by the south parapet with Jeconiah balanced on an up-turned clay pot next to her, his hand in hers. With her free hand, she was pointing down into the city streets. An elderly male servant was standing on the other side of Jeconiah holding a shade over them against the afternoon sun. For a moment, anger replaced her fear. She strode over to them.

They heard her approach. 'Leave us!' The older man immediately thrust the shade into Dinah's hand and bowed to Nehushta before hastily departing. She glared at Dinah. 'I told you to play with Coniah in the shade of the wall—*not* to gawp out over the city at the young men.' Her slur was deliberate. *She was not to be defied by a low-born servant!*

Dinah bowed her head. 'I am sorry, Mistress. I had no intention of displeasing you.' She raised her head slightly. 'But the young one will fear what he cannot see,' she said softly, 'more than those things that he can.'

Nehushta's anger subsided but she refused to acknowledge the wisdom of her servant's words. Her own fear, momentarily supressed, began to rise to the surface again, like a dead and rotting fish within a pool. 'And what can you see?' she asked in a strained voice.

'I can see soldiers!' Jeconiah's excited reply only proved the truth of Dinah's words. 'And chariots and shields!'

For some while they watched the preparations for war. Men were now armour-clad, bearing either spear or bow together with a sword. All carried round shields, and with helmets upon their heads all looked alike. Dinah suddenly pointed to a chariot pulled by horses that had come into view in one of the streets. 'Is that the master?'

Jeconiah waved madly. 'Father! Father!'

Nehushta pushed his arms back down. 'If it is your father, he will not see you with his back to you and will not hear you in all the clamour.' Her eyes, however, were fixed on the figure until the chariot, also bearing a driver and armour-bearer, disappeared around a corner. She continued staring at the stone wall, a puzzle rising in her mind. She turned slowly to Dinah. 'Before he left,' she began, speaking quietly above her son's head, 'Eliakim said that his father, the king, believes himself to be invincible.' She paused. 'It was a strange remark.' She left her words hanging, inviting her servant's thoughts.

'Eliakim may know of the words spoken by the prophetess Huldah to his father.'

The servant's answer needled her. She hated Dinah knowing something she didn't. *But then again, Eliakim rarely, if ever, conveyed to her anything from the mouth of a prophet. He held them in contempt.* Her curiosity overcame the pride that abhorred admitting ignorance. 'And what were the ravings of this woman?' It was language she had learned from her husband.

If her words shocked Dinah, she did not show it. Dinah looked beyond the city, and when she answered, it was slowly and deliberately. 'I was told by some of the older servants that when King Josiah found Yahweh's Book of the Law in the temple, he grieved and wept when it was read to him, because he knew that the people of Judah had not acted in accordance with Yahweh's laws written there. So he sent his officials to Huldah, knowing she was a prophetess. She told him that the God of Israel was going to bring disaster on this place and its people, but that Josiah would not see it but would be gathered to his grave in peace.'

Nehushta stared at Dinah as the words sank in like water upon dry sand. 'So our king may believe he cannot fall in battle.' She gave a little snort. 'And you believe these words—and of disaster to come?'

Dinah turned back to face her. 'If Yahweh spoke them, they are true.'

Notes

1. *The events in this chapter take place in 616-609 BC, which are roughly the 22nd-26th years of the reign of King Josiah in Judah.*
2. *Nehushta's father is named as 'Elnathan of Jerusalem' (2 Kings 24:8).*

It will be assumed in the story that this is the same person as 'Elnathan the son of Achbor' (Jeremiah 26:22, 36:12,25), a palace official. It seems feasible that Josiah could choose the daughter of a senior official for the wife of his son, particularly if Elnathan respected the words of Jeremiah the prophet (Jeremiah 36:25). The mother of Nehushta is not referred to, so the name Sarah has been given to her.

3. It is not clear at what point it was decided that Eliakim (Jehoiakim) would not be the immediate successor to Josiah, or why. Both Kings and Chronicles attest to 'the people of the land' making Jehoahaz (Shallum) king after Josiah. Here it is assumed that it was Josiah's known wish (in the same way that David designated Solomon as king after him, over his older sons), and was due to Eliakim's unsuitability. Given his later behaviour, the latter may well be the case.

4. The extent to which Judah may have expanded under Josiah is not known. There are certainly references to his influence in Bethel and Samaria—both in what had been (before it fell to Assyria) the northern kingdom of Israel (see 2 Kings 23:15-19). John Bright writes the following in 'A History of Israel' (p317): 'Josiah both launched a sweeping reform and moved to take possession of appreciable portions of northern Israel. The extent of Josiah's annexations is, however, uncertain. That he controlled the erstwhile province of Samaria seems clear, for, as we shall see, he carried his reform into that area. He also, at least for a time, held a corridor reaching to the sea, as a fortress of his own on this coast south of Joppa indicates. Some believe that he gained control of the provinces of Megiddo (Galilee) and Gilead as well. But we cannot be certain… When, and by what steps, Josiah enlarged his domain is unknown; but since Assyria was no longer in a position to oppose him, and since most northern Israelites probably welcomed the change, it is unlikely that he encountered much resistance… By the time Josiah's reform reached its climax (622) Assyria was in extremis, leaving Judah both in name and fact a free country.'

5. There doesn't appear to (necessarily) have been a long period of betrothal in the Old Testament (cf. David marrying Michal and Abigail, 1 Samuel 18:27, 25:39-40).

6. We are not told whether adult sons of the king lived in the palace or elsewhere. Although David's sons seem to have had their own houses (cf. 2

Samuel 13:7), Jerusalem was much smaller then, as would have been the palace. It is assumed here that Josiah's sons still lived in the palace, given the extensive nature of the one Solomon built (if it was still being used at this time).

7. *Scripture does not give an explicit reason as to why Josiah engaged Necho in battle, but many commentators conclude that it was to thwart assistance for the Assyrians. It is also an assumption here that Josiah wrongly presumed upon the promise delivered to him by Huldah. It is also not clear if any of the king's sons would have accompanied him to the battle, but here it is assumed that at least Eliakim was also there.*

8. *Imagined named characters introduced in this chapter are Peninnah, Sarah, Dinah and Shimron.*

2

The people of the land took Jehoahaz son of Josiah and anointed him
and made him king in place of his father. (2 Kings 23:30)

The city reeled like a drunkard in the streets at the news from Megiddo and the return of its fatally wounded king. Even before the tap on the door, Nehushta knew that Josiah had died, the wailing seeping in from the streets a more eloquent herald than any official.

She rose from her seat before answering. 'Enter.'

The door opened and a palace servant stood in the doorway. He bowed. 'Your presence is requested in the courtyard, my mistress.'

'By whom?'

'Your father.'

'Tell him I will join him.'

'Very good.' The servant hesitated.

'And has the end now come upon our king?'

The servant lowered his head. 'It has, my mistress. I am sorry.'

She nodded a dismissal and with that he was gone. Nehushta made her way to the corner of the room where Dinah was seated on the floor with Jeconiah. Her maid's eyes brimmed with unspilled tears. The six-year-old's innocence was, as yet, unsullied. He had seen his father briefly on his return, though Eliakim had only been in the room with them long enough to change his clothes, before joining his brothers at the king's side.

'Coniah, I want you stay here with Dinah. I am going to see your grandfather.'

'King Josiah?' His young face was open and his question offered in the cheerfulness of ignorance.

'No, your other grandfather.' She turned to her maid. 'Tell him what has happened—' Nehushta had no desire to see her son's tears, though she wondered how much he would understand anyway. '—and control yourself.'

Dinah pressed her lips together tightly and nodded, blinking.

Nehushta left them and made her way down the stone steps to the halls and rooms where the palace business was conducted. She was puzzled—and irritated. She had known Josiah for seven years, though their paths had rarely crossed. Dinah had never spoken to him. *Why should her eyes be filled with tears for a man she did not know?* As she approached the courtyard, she put the thought out of her head and solemnity upon her face.

Elnathan was standing with his hands behind his back, staring upwards into the bright sky. 'Father!' Since her marriage to Eliakim, she saw little, if any, need to defer to her parents.

He immediately hurried towards her. 'Nehushta.' He kissed both her cheeks.

As she stepped back, she studied him. Age's brush had added more streaks of grey to his hair, and the recent days dark rings like charcoal marks beneath his eyes. She gestured to a bench nearby and they both sat. She waited for him to speak. The sound of lament was nearer now, the halls of the palace echoing with mourning for the king.

'Your mother and I pray that you know the comfort of Yahweh on this dismal day.'

Nehushta feigned pain before lowering her gaze. 'For that I am thankful. It is indeed a dark day.' There was a long silence. She looked up.

'These are uncertain times,' he began and then paused.

Nehushta was not sure what lay behind his words. 'Go on...'

'I know not whether Eliakim will tell you all that has happened, but I thought you should know.' When Nehushta held her peace, he sighed and then ran a hand through his hair. 'You know my loyalty to the king. I have served Josiah faithfully at the palace for many years. But—' He glanced around, then lowered his voice. '—I remained unsure of the wisdom of engaging Necho and his army. The king rightly knew that if the Egyptians were travelling north along the coastal route, they would have to pass through the Carmel range near Megiddo if they were to reach the Valley of Jezreel and the way to Carchemish by Galilee. But as far as I know, he had no direction from any prophet for his action.' He paused again. 'Some in the army are even saying that Necho sent a message, claiming God was with him and telling Josiah to turn back, otherwise he risked being destroyed by God.'

'And do you think Egypt's pharaoh was speaking truth?'

'I do not know. But it does seem that the Egyptians had no quarrel with us and intended only to travel north through Israel. The king disregarded Necho's words, however, and went into battle disguised so as to avoid their attention. Yet an archer shot him, seemingly by chance but wounding him mortally.' He sighed deeply once again and shook his head slowly. 'There was then no reason to fight on, and our army withdrew swiftly, returning the king to Jerusalem.'

'And now Josiah is dead.'

Pain filled her father's features. 'Yes, he is dead.'

'Eliakim *did* say that Josiah wished to stop the Egyptians aiding the Assyrians. Was he right?'

'Probably. But the Egyptians are no friend of Judah either. They have never been such and have less reason to be so now. If they can rule over us, they will—of *that*, I am sure. And I am also sure that Necho has no wish to see Babylon waxing strong and extending its empire beyond the Euphrates and into these lands.'

'And we will have to wait to know who prevails in the north?'

'We will. But whatever happens, Egypt must be watched. Necho has only been on its throne for a year, but it would not surprise me if his ambitions lie beyond his own borders, especially as Assyria's grip on these lands has loosened.'

'And what of Judah? Will Shallum still be made king?'

'He will—once Josiah has been laid to rest with his fathers and the land has mourned its king.'

If her father had any thoughts on Shallum's suitability—or Eliakim's unsuitability—he did not share them, and for some moments, neither spoke. Nehushta's mind flitted back to what Dinah had told her as they'd watched their army depart. She would never have challenged her father's devotion to the God of Israel as a child, but now all had changed—and she was emboldened by Eliakim's own contempt for those who claimed to be Yahweh's mouthpiece. 'It is said that a prophetess told Josiah that he would die in peace...'

'Be gathered to his grave in peace,' replied Elnathan, correcting her. 'Those were her words—Yahweh's words.'

'But surely there is little peace in being mortally wounded by an Egyptian arrow.'

Elnathan stared into the air. 'I have thought much about that since our king returned. All I can say is that Yahweh's promises cannot be twisted to our own ends. We can neither presume upon Him nor force His hand.' He then turned to her. 'Our king did, however, die surrounded by his sons and not on the battlefield. Even now, the city mourns for him as for an only son. He did not live to see forty summers, and yet he will be lamented with bitter tears by all Judah and remembered and honoured for all that he did for this city, for the land and for Yahweh.'

Nehushta fixed her attention on a sparrow that had landed near the base of a large clay pot holding a fig tree. Despite her father's words, she thought that *not* being wounded by an Egyptian archer would have been a better fulfilment of Huldah's words—if they truly were the words of a prophetess. She opened her mouth to declare that she was sorry but would have to return to her son, when her father laid a hand upon her arm.

'My daughter! The prophets are saying that disaster hangs over this city, and yet Yahweh tells us that, even now, if we return to Him, we may yet be saved.' It was as if he were pleading with her.

Nehushta suspected his words were the real reason he had come to speak to her. She also sensed there was more he wished to say yet was holding back. *Maybe her father had been content to see her wed to Eliakim whilst they lived under both Josiah's rule and sway. Maybe he feared Eliakim's effect upon her, now that the king was dead. But she intended to fully embrace all that her husband desired!*

Her eyes, however, feigned accord once more—if only to be rid of his concern. 'I will hold your words in my heart, Father.'

His face visibly softened. 'And your mother and I will always hold you in our prayers to Yahweh.'

'Thank you.' Nehushta rose. 'But I must now hasten back to Jeconiah. He will be grieving the loss of his other grandfather. Forgive me, Father, for having to leave you.'

Elnathan rose and kissed her once more. 'There is nothing to forgive.'

It was late in the evening when the door opened and Eliakim finally walked in, subdued. Nehushta was alone in their room. All he sought—at least to start with—was comfort in his wife. But later, sleep eluded them both. Two images vied for the uppermost place in Nehushta's mind. One was Jeconiah sobbing in Dinah's arms whilst her servant shed silent tears, when she'd returned. The other was of her father's strained expression when he had implored her to return to Yahweh—for that, she had decided, was what he had been doing. Despite her son's distress, she found the former image preferable.

She opened her eyes. All was black. She was facing Eliakim and could tell he was lying on his back—and was awake. She knew the steady, slow—and noisy—breathing of his sleep, but all was quiet. 'Eli?' she said softly. He grunted. 'You cannot sleep either, then.' Silence and darkness pressed in on her. She began to wonder if he *was* actually asleep, but then he spoke.

'My father used to tell me a story when I was younger—a story of one of the kings of Israel. King Ahab.'

'What was the story?'

'Ahab, he said, kept disregarding the words of the prophet Elijah. Both he and his Sidonian wife, Jezebel, worshipped Baal and Asherah instead of Yahweh, doing as they pleased in the land. My father said that a second prophet told Ahab that he would die in a certain battle. Ahab, however, went into the battle anyway, but disguised himself, knowing that his enemy, the king of Aram, would be looking for him to kill him.' He paused. 'Do you know what happened?'

'No, tell me.'

'An Aramean archer fired his bow into the air, and his arrow happened to find Ahab, striking him in the space where one piece of armour met another and mortally wounding him. He told the driver of his chariot to take him from the battle and he died that evening.' He fell silent for a moment and then added, 'My father said that story showed that if we abandon the God of Israel for other gods, we cannot escape Yahweh's judgment, however hard we try.' He paused and expelled a breath in a short burst from his nose. 'My father worshipped Yahweh, but tell me—how is his death any different to that of Ahab who worshipped Baal?'

Nehushta thought for a moment. 'Surely there *is* no difference...'

'Who is to say, then, that Baal—or another god—has not now brought down upon my father exactly the same judgment for his destruction of *their* altars? After all, this land belonged to the Canaanite gods before our fathers arrived here, and are they any less powerful than Yahweh? I know of many in this city who opposed my father's desecration of the land's high places, even if they did not do so openly. If my father thought he had erased the worship of Baal from people's hearts, he was wrong!' He paused. 'If I were king...' But he broke off.

'What?'

'Things would be different.'

Nehushta laid her arm across Eliakim, feeling his chest rise and fall. 'But what of your brother Shallum? Do you know how he intends to rule?'

There was a very long pause. 'I do not know. But what I will say is this: if the people desire to make him king because they believe he will be like my father, then they will be disappointed.'

Nehushta heard it for herself: a clamour within the city that grew as swiftly as the onset of a thunderstorm. Jerusalem was astir as it had been at Josiah's death, three months earlier. Every other face on the palace roof began turning, like hers, this way and that, all seeking an answer to the commotion below yet finding none.

Nehushta turned to Dinah. 'Come—bring Coniah!' Her maid lifted the boy up into her arms and followed her swiftly across the roof and towards the steps down.

'Do you think King Jehoahaz has returned from the north, Mistress?' asked Dinah, using the throne name that Shallum had taken.

Nehushta glanced back over her shoulder without slowing. 'That is more likely than anything else.'

The city had only recently received the news from Carchemish that it had been the Medes and Babylonians who had prevailed there. But whilst it had been the end of Assyria, the Egyptian army and its Pharaoh had returned and made themselves masters over the land of Judah, summoning its new king north to Riblah to stand before Necho there. None had been sure of how Jehoahaz would fare—and Eliakim had accompanied him.

Nehushta was not the first to reach the steps, but others parted to let her and Dinah pass. By the time they had descended to the level of the courtyard, the corridors of the palace resembled the tumult of the marketplace, with all surging towards the palace doors. But the river of people soon began to slow and build into a crowd, as if the flow had been dammed. Nehushta craned her neck. A greater number were coming towards them.

'Make way for the king!' The cry parted the crowd, forcing them back against both walls as the king and his officers advanced. And the clamour swiftly faded into whispers.

Nehushta stared, open-mouthed. For the man sweeping through the palace with his officials behind was not Shallum but Eliakim, the crown of Judah upon his head. It was only when those around her bowed that she thought to do the same, drawing her breath in short bursts.

'Come, Nehushta.' Her father's soft but urgent words raised her head. 'And bring Jeconiah.'

Nehushta nodded to Dinah to accompany her. 'Set him down,' she hissed swiftly, 'and let him walk. He is now the son of the king.' Nehushta took the six-year-old's hand in hers, holding her head up high as thoughts swirled through it like the turbulent waters of a river in flood. *What had happened to make her husband king—and to suddenly exalt her?* As they passed through the corridors that led to the hall in which the throne of Judah was set, she stared at the faces of those pressed against the walls. Before their heads lowered, she glimpsed, in equal measure, wonder, bewilderment and shock. If any met her eyes, they swiftly looked down. The only one who seemed at ease was Jeconiah. He beamed at the bowed heads surrounding him. Nehushta then caught sight of Shallum's mother, Hamutal, on the steps that led up to the living quarters. By her side was her other son, Mattaniah. She was holding him close, her face drained of all its colour and wet with tears, clearly already aware of what had happened to Shallum. For a moment, Nehushta pitied her. *She had suffered the loss of her husband to an Egyptian arrow, and then, for a mere three months, she had been honoured as queen mother—the foremost of the women in the palace, and the only one beside the king to wear a crown. Now it seemed she had lost both son and standing on the same day, her head already devoid of its diadem.* Nehushta deliberately looked away. Whatever her sorrow, she had no desire to share it.

There was no ceremony to place Eliakim on the throne. He simply took his seat there. That he already considered himself king was evident. The room fell silent and one of the officials stepped forward. 'Long live the king!' The cry was taken up around the room and Nehushta added her voice to the acclamation, even as she wondered for a moment if she was dreaming. All seemed so startling and strange. *Yet if it was a dream, then maybe she would rather not awake. Was she now truly the wife of the king?*

Eventually the cries died away, though Jeconiah's voice was one of the last to be heard. He was rarely, if ever, given the chance to shout with such abandon without censure. Dinah crouched beside him and swiftly put a finger to his lips. *Now was, indeed, a time for silence.* Nehushta glanced around—all attention was on Eliakim. She followed their gaze.

Eliakim drew in a deep breath. 'My brother is king no more. Pharaoh Necho deposed and imprisoned him at Riblah and he is to be taken to Egypt.' Murmurs rippled around the room, and Eliakim waited until there was silence again. 'I have been made king instead and will henceforth be known as *Jehoiakim*. Judah is now a vassal of Pharaoh, and he has laid upon us a tribute of one hundred talents of silver and a talent of gold.' The murmuring resumed. '*This*—' Eliakim looked around the room, swiftly quashing any whispers. '*This* is far less than King Hezekiah paid to the Assyrians and is a price that we will pay for peace. But be sure of this—' He paused, and none stirred. '—I will be taxing the land to exact this payment, and none will be exempt.' His eyes swept across his new subjects once more, as if he were challenging any man to defy him. No one did.

Their new king did not have much more to say. The assembly of officials and servants was soon dismissed. As Nehushta was slowly carried along by the flow of people towards the large cedar doors, Dinah whispered to her.

'The king's mother waits for you, Mistress.'

Nehushta peered between the heads around her until she spotted the woman whom Dinah, with her greater height, had seen. Zebidah was standing to one side of the doors, but clearly looking in her direction. Not for the first time she was grateful for her maid's warning—for that was how she perceived it. As they neared her, Nehushta took a deep breath and veiled her wariness with the semblance of respect. She stopped in front of the older woman, whose head now bore a crown, and bowed her head briefly. 'Queen Mother.'

Zebidah smiled down at her grandson who beamed back at her. She then looked Nehushta in the eye. 'I would like you to come with me, Nehushta. Dinah can take Jeconiah back to your room.' She didn't wait for an answer—it was not an offer. The older woman turned and walked out through the doors.

Nehushta bit her tongue. She nodded to Dinah and followed Zebidah in silence along the corridor and into the courtyard. She resented being told what to do. *She was now the king's wife!* But she knew that Zebidah, though not yet forty, was now the queen mother—and the one woman she had to defer to.

When they reached a quiet corner of the courtyard, Zebidah sat and gestured for Nehushta to sit beside her on the bench. She studied her daughter-in-law for a moment and then laid a hand on her arm. 'Much will be different for you now, Nehushta. Some of the changes may be hard for you to bear.' Although her tone was kindly, Nehushta still bristled inside. 'But you have an important part to play. You must do all that is in your power to support Eliakim now that he is king.'

'Should we not now call him *Jehoiakim?*' The words slipped out, not so much as a question but as a challenge.

If Zebidah was irritated by Nehushta's interruption, she concealed it well. She removed her hand from the younger woman's arm, however. '*I* will continue to call my son by the name his father gave him. *You* must do as he directs.' Nehushta gave a tiny tight-lipped nod. 'You must not expect to see your husband as you have done before, and neither must you expect to share his bed. He will have his own room—the king's room—and will summon you only if he desires.'

It was an unwelcome reminder of the working of the palace. Nehushta kept her discontent hidden. *It would gain nothing to rail against what she could not change.*

'You must not be surprised either if he chooses to take more wives. Such is the manner of Judah's kings. I was not Josiah's only wife, as you well know, and you must accept it if Eliakim takes others.' Her face softened. 'But you are the mother of Jeconiah, and if Yahweh wills it, he will one day become king. Do your best to prepare him for that day. I will help you with that task and you must send the boy to me often, that I too may teach him of Yahweh's ways.'

Mocking words rose in her mind as swiftly as a grasshopper into the air. *Do you not know that Eliakim rejects your ways and the ways of his father? Or do you hope that Coniah will somehow be different?* The words reached neither the courtyard walls nor Zebidah's ears. Instead, she nodded. 'I will do that.' *But it will not be as often as you may wish.*

Zebidah suddenly took Nehushta's hands in her own, meeting her gaze. 'I may not have the years of your own mother, Nehushta, but I was Josiah's wife for twenty-five. Do not be above asking for help if you need it.'

Nehushta had the impression that the other woman knew more of what was in her own heart than she wished her to know—and for a moment Zebidah's manner reminded her of her own father. She dismissed the thought and dropped her eyes. 'That is kind, Mother.' She withdrew her hands and once again used her son as an excuse to escape. 'If you will permit me, I must now return to Jeconiah. Though he is young, I do not doubt he will have many questions.'

Zebidah smiled weakly. 'As you wish.' She leant over and kissed her on both cheeks, but as Nehushta rose, she added. 'But bring the lad to me tomorrow.'

'I will. And thank you for your words of wisdom.' As she turned to leave, she determined that she would do all in her power to ensure that no other wife supplanted her—and that she would know more than Zebidah.

Nehushta was about to send Dinah away with Jeconiah to put him to bed that evening when there was a familiar sharp knock on the door. She looked up. 'Enter.' She suspected it was her husband's servant but waited to see if she was correct. She was. 'What is it, Shimron?'

'King Jehoiakim bids you to join him in his room.'

It was as she had hoped. She gave the response she had prepared. 'Tell the king I will be with him presently, as soon as I have prepared myself for him.'

'Very good.' Shimron nodded and left as swiftly as he had come.

Nehushta was ready. 'Dinah—take Coniah to his bed and let one of the other maids tend to him. Then return immediately to me.' As soon as her maidservant had left, Nehushta hurried into the smaller room. She had already set clothes aside, just in case.

By the time Dinah returned, she had poured water from the pitcher into the large stone bowl and swiftly washed. She looked over her shoulder. 'Good—now you must help me get ready.' Dinah was well-practiced at brushing and arranging her hair, and soon Nehushta was clad in a bright red tunic. She had had it made and embroidered

238

whilst Eliakim had been at Riblah—in part, simply to take her mind off the possibility that he might not return. She put on her arm the gold bangle given to her by Eliakim, whilst Dinah tied an orange scarf about her waist. The final hasty additions were a necklace set with gems and dabs of nard to her wrist and neck. Dinah then held the mirror up. Nehushta moved her head whilst keeping her eyes on the highly polished bronze. She pulled in the scarf around her waist a little. 'Will I be pleasing to the king, Dinah?'

'You will, Mistress.'

Dinah had proved herself true to her word—she did not lie. Once, when Nehushta had painted her eyes, her servant had told her that she looked like a harlot. She had been right. And now, more than ever, Nehushta needed candour not flattery from her servant. She slipped on her sandals. 'Then I am ready.'

'A moment, my mistress.' Dinah hurried to a large vase and snapped off two fresh flowers. She pushed them into Nehushta's hair. 'Now you are ready.'

'Thank you, Dinah.' Her servant flushed slightly at the rare acknowledgement.

It was not many moments later when she was knocking at the large carved cedarwood doors of the king's chamber. Instead of being called in, the door was opened by Shimron. He gestured for her to enter. Nehushta had never been in the room before. It was large and richly furnished, with colourful hangings on the wall, and patterned rugs on the wooden floor. Eliakim was sitting at an ornate table, the remnants of a substantial meal before him and a golden goblet in his hand. His eyes rested upon her.

She bowed low and lingered there. 'My king.' When she straightened up, his gaze had not moved, but he bore upon his face what she recognised as approval.

His eyes finally left her. 'Clear this away,' he said, gesturing to a servant. 'And Shimron—put the wine and the grapes on the low table.'

'Yes, my lord.' The servants busied themselves.

The king rose, goblet still in hand. He took a draught from it, and then moved towards a dark green couch. 'Come, Nehushta, and sit beside me.' He turned back to Shimron. 'Bring another goblet.' The servant obliged, filling it with wine before handing it to Nehushta. He then set the golden jug and bowl of grapes on the table next to the couch.

'I trust you ate well after your journey, my king.'

He picked up a grape and tossed it up, catching it deftly in his mouth. As he chewed, he answered. 'Very well.' He then tossed a second grape into the air, but towards Nehushta. She caught it in a similar manner. It was an art she had swiftly mastered. He grinned. He then turned towards the servants who had loaded the contents of the table onto two trays. 'Make sure we are not disturbed, Shimron.'

'Yes, my lord.'

As soon as the door closed behind them, the king turned his attention back to Nehushta and placed a hand upon her knee. He breathed in deeply, and then smiled. 'Nard.'

'Indeed, my king.'

'*My king*?'

'It is not *my lord,* but does it not fit well the one who now bears the crown?' She paused. 'But I will call you whatever pleases you most.'

'It *does* please me.' He took another draught of the wine, draining the goblet. Nehushta swiftly reached for the jug and refilled it, the aroma of the wine mingling with that of the nard. He drank again, and then cradled the goblet against his chest. 'Let us talk awhile.'

'Whatever pleases my king…'

He seemed to relish her words and the way in which she said them. 'I wonder whether my wife has one of her peculiar questions to amuse me…' He raised an eyebrow and left the words hanging.

She took a long sip of wine to give herself the chance to think. She lowered the goblet and looked at him enquiringly through her eyelashes. 'I wonder if my king has determined yet what he will do first, now that he is free to do all that his heart desires.'

He drew in a deep breath and let it out slowly. The goblet moved with his chest. For a moment, his face clouded. 'I am not completely free—Necho must be paid.' He stared into the wine. 'He had my brother imprisoned and even now takes him to Egypt, as if to both punish my father's folly and let me know what will happen if the tribute is not paid.'

Nehushta briefly wondered if Shallum would ever return, but then leant forward and ran her fingers through her husband's hair, soothing him. 'The king should not let such thoughts disturb him.'

But a sly smile stole onto Eliakim's face. 'But a new tax need not be for Necho's tribute alone.'

She paused. 'And what would the king do if he were to collect more than the pharaoh requires…?'

'If Necho could set himself up comfortably at Riblah away from Egypt, why should the king of Judah not have another fine palace to dwell in—not in this crowded city, but apart from it?'

'A palace of your own design,' she murmured. 'What would such a fine palace be like?'

The question seemed to please him. 'It will not be crowded, like this one.' She then listened whilst he spoke of spacious rooms, every one of which would be panelled with cedar. He spoke of chambers painted red, and of rich curtains and carved tables. There would be a large courtyard, and all kinds of fine stone and marble would be used.

When he finally fell silent, Nehushta smiled and nodded. 'A palace fit, indeed, for a king. It is an excellent plan.'

'But it is a plan that will take time. The gathering of the gold and silver will not be done in a day.' He paused, swirling the remaining wine around in his goblet. 'But Jerusalem need not wait until then to see what sort of king they have in Jehoiakim. They will soon know that I am not my father and will see with their own eyes a city under *my* rule. They will listen to *my* voice, not the voice of any prophet. Be sure of this—' He raised the goblet once more and drained it to its dregs. His lips glistened red for a moment with the wine, until he ran his tongue lightly over them. '—when the sun rises tomorrow, I will begin to adorn the streets of Jerusalem once more with altars to the gods who have been neglected for too many years. And I will not delay in offering them their incense, and their meat and drink. They will then make the land fertile and leave us to live our lives as

241

we please, with no book to tell us what we must or must not do. And the city will do as I do.'

'As will I.' For a moment, her father's earnest face rose in her mind. But her husband's words were as heady as the wine, and, not for the first time, she found herself drawn to what felt thrilling and new.

He took the half-full goblet from her hands and consumed its contents, before setting it down clumsily alongside the other. It teetered and she steadied it. He wiped his hand across his mouth and rose. 'Come.' The time for talking was over.

Notes

1. *The events of this chapter take place in 609 BC.*
2. *It is not clear how Egypt compelled the subservience described in 2 Kings 33:34-34, summoning Jehoahaz to Riblah and replacing him with Jehoiakim, though clearly there must have been some display of superior power. Here it is assumed that Jehoiakim (i.e. Eliakim) was made king in Necho's presence, but this may not have been the case, and Jehoiakim may have remained in Judah when Jehoahaz was summoned to Riblah.*
3. *There is a difficulty in harmonising the account in 2 Kings with the record of the sons of Josiah in 1 Chronicles: 'The sons of Josiah: Johanan the firstborn, Jehoiakim the second son, Zedekiah the third, Shallum the fourth' (3:15). As Selman comments: 'Of Josiah's sons (v15) Johanan is not mentioned in Kings and may well have died young, and Shallum, the throne name of Jehoahaz (2 Kings 23:31-34, cf. Jeremiah 22:11), is described here as the youngest of the four brothers, even though he reigned before Jehoiakim and Zedekiah. The information here cannot be reconciled with what is said about their ages in 2 Kings 23:31,36; 24:18, and it is easiest to assume some scribal error in connection with the numbers.' (1 Chronicles, p100). Here, the ages recorded in 2 Kings are followed, with Eliakim being two years older than Shallum, and with Zedekiah (i.e. Mattaniah) being younger than them both.*

4. *The title of queen does not seem to have been used of the wives of Jewish rulers—maybe because the kings often (or usually) had multiple wives. The only time the title is used in Scripture seems to be of foreign rulers (e.g. the queen of Sheba or Queen Vashti), or in 'the queen mother', used for the mother of a king (e.g. 1 Kings 15:13, 2 Kings 10:13). The exchange between Solomon and Bathsheba recorded in 1 Kings 2:19-20 gives an example of the honour accorded to the mother of the king. Jeremiah 13:18 also implies that the queen mother as well as the king wore a crown. Queen mother 'was an official title in ancient Israel. It was an office with high rank and royal prerogatives, especially when the monarch was a minor (and the queen's husband, the former king, had died). She did not just have influence over her son the king but had great authority of her own… She was probably afforded rank on the accession of her son as king.' (OTBBC, p653).*

5. *There is a reference to eye makeup being used by Jezebel in 2 Kings 9:30, and it is also mentioned in Jeremiah 4:30 and Ezekiel 23:40.*

6. *The Biblical records point to there being more than one palace in Judah (2 Chronicles 36:19, Jeremiah 33:4, Lamentations 2:5), and Jeremiah speaks out against Jehoiakim for exploiting the people in order to build his own (Jeremiah 22:13-18).*

3

Jehoiakim was twenty-five years old when he became king, and he reigned in Jerusalem for eleven years. His mother's name was Zebidah daughter of Pedaiah; she was from Rumah. And he did evil in the eyes of the LORD, just as his predecessors had done. (2 Kings 23:36-37)

King Jehoiakim was true to his word—both gods and taxes multiplied.

'Peninnah—bring the offering.' The servant, whom Nehushta had summoned to join her when her husband became king, picked up the woven basket. 'Dinah—you will stay and take care of Coniah whilst I go to worship.'

'Very well, Mistress.' Dinah paused. 'Would you like me to take him to see his grandmother whilst you are gone? It has been several days since she has seen him.'

Nehushta thought for a moment. Much as she chafed at having to send her son to see the queen mother, Dinah's suggestion would at least save her from an afternoon in Zebidah's presence. 'Yes, do that.' She picked up a small engraved gold box full of fragrant incense. Then, mindful of Dinah's tiresome (at times) fondness for honesty, she added, 'If she asks, you may tell her that I have gone to worship. And if she asks where, you may tell her that I have not told you that—for that is true.'

Peninnah's face was as full of perplexity as her basket was of cakes baked for the Queen of Heaven—just one of the gods whose altars had sprung up seemingly on every street corner. The servant looked down at the cakes, and then up again, and opened her mouth. Nehushta's severe gaze bore into her. 'And that is all that needs to be said.' Peninnah swiftly closed her mouth and fixed her attention on the polished wooden boards on which she stood.

Dinah bobbed her head. 'As you say, Mistress.' She held out her hand to the king's son. 'Come, Coniah.'

As the six-year-old started trying to cram his hands full of wooden toys, Nehushta sighed loudly. 'Just one…' The boy hesitated, and then set the animals down in a heap, save a single horse. He took Dinah's outstretched hand in his empty one. But Dinah waited. To Nehushta, she was a puzzle—a servant who defied her if her God commanded something different, but whose deference in every other respect was faultless. Dinah would never walk out of the door before her mistress, but would always follow, even if heading elsewhere. Her dedication to the smallest detail—whether flowers for her hair or perfumed sachets hanging by her bed—could, even now, take her by surprise. Nehushta had known better than to command Dinah to accompany her to any altar other than that of Yahweh, and risk others witnessing her servant's disobedience. But Nehushta tolerated it, for Dinah's truthfulness and loyalty were worth more. *And besides, there were others who would do her bidding unquestioningly—whatever her desire.*

By the time she had left the palace, she had gained two more servants, one bearing a shade and the other a jar of wine, and four guards, bearing both shields and spears. The presence of the latter ensured a clear passage through Jerusalem's streets, should any fail to recognise the finely dressed and richly adorned woman who walked through her husband's city—for that was how she viewed it—her head held high. And whichever altar she chose to receive her offering, there was never a need to wait, as other worshippers swiftly stepped aside. But that day, as the weather was pleasantly warm, she had decided to leave Jerusalem and visit the high place to the east of the Kidron Valley. It would be free from the city's noise, bustle and smells.

Peninnah, having been used to chattering to Nehushta when both were children, was oblivious to the restraint common to most royal servants—and her mistress was, in the main, glad of it. 'Have you been to the high place before, Mistress?'

'No. It has only recently begun to be used again.'

'Since Eliakim became king?'

Nehushta lifted her gaze from the path at the bottom of valley. 'What have you forgotten?'

The nineteen-year-old screwed up her face for a moment before light dawned. 'To call the king *Jehoiakim*.'

'That is better. But, yes, you are right.' Nehushta raised her eyes higher, to the hill just south of the Mount of Olives. 'The wives of the great King Solomon worshipped here, and I shall be like them!' She revelled in the thought, allowing it to elevate her—at least in her own mind—above others. 'Neither Zebidah nor Hamutal worshipped here when they were wives of Josiah. He desecrated its altars. But the king now brings his own reforms and is glad to see such places restored, as are the many who never stopped worshipping the goddess.'

Peninnah glanced down at the cakes in her basket, stamped before they were baked with the image of an amply endowed female. 'What do you know of the Queen of Heaven, Mistress?' she asked, her voice awed.

As they began the ascent on the east side of the valley, Nehushta recalled all she had learned from Eliakim. 'Her name is Ashtoreth. She is the consort of Baal, and together with him, she blesses the land and makes both womb and field fertile. She was worshipped in this land long before our people arrived here from Egypt.'

Peninnah frowned. 'But what of the words of the prophets? Does not Jeremiah say we should not offer such worship?'

Had any other servant asked such a question, it would have earned a stern rebuke—or worse—for the slur that it cast on the king. *But Peninnah was merely ignorant and looking to her mistress for enlightenment—and she would give it.* 'Just because a man claims to be Yahweh's mouthpiece does not make him so. After all, no other nation limits itself to the worship of one god—are they all mistaken to do so? We have Yahweh's temple in Jerusalem, but why shouldn't we seek the favour of other gods as well? And is it not fitting that as our men worship Yahweh and Baal, their wives and daughters offer sweet cakes and wine and incense to the Queen of Heaven?' She knew how her father or mother—or Dinah—would answer, but thrust it from her mind. She comforted herself instead with the knowledge that many, if not most, in Jerusalem willingly embraced Eliakim's changes. *Josiah's reforms had been short-lived. Now they were free to worship as they wanted!* Then she laughed, remembering her slight nervousness—as well as the thrill—when she had first sacrificed alongside her husband at an altar to Baal. 'Besides, there is no bolt of lightning from heaven nor sudden plague upon the land.' She then echoed words from Eliakim's own lips. 'And did not Manasseh sit on the throne far longer than Josiah ever did, living out his years rather than having them cut short by an Egyptian arrow?' Her husband's reasoning suited her own mind.

'Maybe King Jehoaikim will reign even longer than both!' Peninnah's doubt seemed to have been satisfied, and she was clearly happy to embrace all her mistress had told her.

Nehushta looked up the path which wound up the hillside ahead of them. 'So we will present our offerings to the Queen of Heaven today on her altar at the top of this hill and know that she will be pleased with our worship and bless our land and its king.'

There was, however, a cloud that darkened Nehushta's day as she neared the palace on her return. Something was causing a stir at the temple. Men were hurrying up the streets towards it, engaged in debate as they went. Nehushta paused—and her party with her. For a moment she studied those surging forward. She turned to one of the guards. 'Find out what is happening, and then report to me. I will be in the palace courtyard.' He nodded and left them.

Peninnah turned to her. 'What do you think is happening?'

'I am not a seer,' she replied dryly. 'But we will find out soon enough.'

Nehushta was sitting under the shade of a fig tree in the courtyard, still supping the cup of cool water that Peninnah had brought her, when the guard returned. He bowed slightly and waited for her to speak. 'What have you discovered?'

'It is the prophet Jeremiah, O Mistress. He has been speaking in the court of the temple.'

'And what of his words?'

'I did not hear them myself, but others say that he spoke in the name of Yahweh, telling the people not to suppose that His temple will save them. He said that if the people do not heed the words of the prophets and walk in Yahweh's law, then He will make the temple as desolate as Shiloh and Jerusalem a curse to the nations, casting us out of the land.' He hesitated.

'And what else did this man who calls himself a prophet of Yahweh say?' When the guard seemed to be struggling for the right words, Nehushta added, 'You will not be punished for telling me the truth of what he said. It will be worse for you to withhold his words. I would rather know by what means he seeks to deceive King Jehoiakim's subjects.'

'He spoke against the images and altars the king has set up in the temple and the building up of the high places...' His words trailed off.

Nehushta held him in her gaze. 'And?'

'And of making offerings to the Queen of Heaven.'

She snorted. 'He does, does he?' She paused. 'And is there yet more to his oracle?'

He shifted. 'I was told that he finished by saying that the bones of the people—be they of king or priest or prophet—would be taken from their graves and spread out in the open to all the gods they have worshipped.'

It was a distasteful image. She put it out of her mind. 'And how were his words received?'

'The temple priests and other prophets seized him, calling for his death. A crowd then gathered, and some of the officials from the palace—including your own father—heard of it and went up to the temple. They had just arrived when I got there. The priests and prophets continued to call for Jeremiah to be put to death, but he still maintained that Yahweh had sent him to prophesy against the city and the temple. He said that if we changed our ways and obeyed the God of Israel, walking in the ways of justice, then Yahweh would not bring misfortune on the city and would allow us to stay in the land, but that if he was put to death, then the city and its inhabitants would have his innocent blood upon them.'

Nehushta rested her cup in her lap and straightened her back. 'And whose words held sway?'

'The officials and the people opposed the priests, saying that Jeremiah had spoken in the name of Yahweh. Some of the city elders also added their voice, saying that King Hezekiah had not put to death the prophet Micah when he spoke a similar word. So Jeremiah was allowed to leave, with one of the sons of Shaphan by his side. Then the people began to disperse, so I also left to return to you.'

'Shaphan may have served Josiah well enough,' she answered sharply, 'but Jehoiakim is king now and the sons of Shaphan should think carefully about where their loyalty lies.' She did not want any of the palace guards having doubts about their loyalty either. She looked at him steadily. 'If that is all, you may go.' He bowed to her and left— and Nehushta wondered what her husband would do with the report when it reached his ears.

'He shall not die.' Eliakim drained his goblet and set it down on the table. 'Not while there are those in the palace who support him—your father included. But there are other means by which to mute a madman.'

Nehushta waited, raising her own cup to her lips. The king's next words, however, took her by surprise.

'I am sending your father to Egypt.'

The wine never touched her lips. She lowered the cup. 'To what end, my king?'

'There is another man who calls himself a prophet—a man by the name of Uriah son of Shemaiah. He has spoken in like manner to Jeremiah, and I determined to seize him, but he escaped, fleeing to Egypt.' He smirked. 'He should have fled north! If he is a seer, then he is a flawed one, for he has failed to foresee his own downfall.'

'How so?'

'Am I not a vassal of Pharaoh? It may be irksome, but it has its uses. Necho will not refuse, I think, the simple request of one who faithfully pays him gold and silver, particularly if the request is for the return of a troublemaker—' His mouth formed a twisted smile. '—and is conveyed by the father-in-law of the vassal king.' He raised his empty goblet and held it mid-air. Shimron crossed swiftly from the side of the room and re-filled it from a golden pitcher. Eliakim took a quick draught. 'And, who knows, it may be that Uriah will return more willingly if it is with your father. He will know that both Elnathan—and his father, Achbor, before him—supported Josiah's reforms.'

'And what will you do when this Uriah is brought back here.'

'His treachery will be suitably punished—and Jeremiah will hear of it.'

She cocked her head and looked at him slyly through her dark eyelashes, a beguiling smile upon her lips. 'The king is cunning as a fox! Our nation is blessed to have such a ruler.' He seemed pleased by her words. *She could still charm him! And although other women now shared the bed of the king whenever he desired it, she was the one with whom he shared his plans. She who embraced his ways more readily than some in the palace.* She decided, however, not to ask about the exact nature of the prophet's punishment. A different question would serve her better. 'And what else is in the heart of the royal fox tonight?'

The gold and silver to placate Necho—and to pay for a new palace—flowed into the king's treasuries as the new taxes were levied upon the land. But it was not all that flowed within the palace walls.

The dreamlike thoughts that drifted through Nehushta's mind as she dozed in the warmth of the early afternoon came to an abrupt end.

'Mistress!'

Nehushta gazed out from the bed through half-opened eyes. 'What is it, Dinah?' Annoyance edged her words. 'Why do you disturb me?'

'You must hear this.'

The urgency in the words roused Nehushta and raised her onto an elbow. 'Hear what?'

'What I have just heard from Shimron. Your father has returned from Egypt with the prophet Uriah.'

'So Necho *has* sent him back here.' Nehushta suddenly fell silent and sat up. Her servant was ashen. 'What has happened?'

'Uriah was taken before the king, who ordered one of the guards to run the prophet through with a sword. Jehoiakim then ordered his body to be cast down into the Kidron Valley among the graves of the common people.' She paused. 'He sheds innocent blood in the palace!'

Nehushta was suddenly aware that she was gaping at her servant. She quickly masked her shock. 'You should not speak of the king in such a way,' she answered sharply.

'But it is evil.'

Nehushta's shock turned to anger, though fuelled, in part, by her own conflicted feelings. *Was she relishing the way her husband wielded his power—or repulsed by it?* All she was sure of was the rightness of her own words. 'You will silence your tongue, Dinah!'

The servant's eyes filled with tears. 'But Eliakim is a son of Josiah,' she whispered. 'A descendant of King David...' Just as Nehushta opened her mouth to repeat her command, Dinah's voiced trailed off and a tear slipped down her cheek.

Nehushta's breath became ragged. She did not reply for several moments as she tried to control herself and think of a suitable reply. Slowly, calmly, firmly, she finally said, 'Jehoiakim is king now. You will not speak ill of his deeds to any other within the city walls—and you *will* do as I say. Do you understand?' Another tear spilled from Dinah's eyes. Her servant nodded silently. 'And that, Dinah, is for your own good.'

But against Nehushta's will, the conflict resolved within her. *Dinah was right*. She had joined her husband in mocking prophets as madmen—but even she knew that such slaughter was wrong. For the voice that she suppressed deep within told her that the guilt lay with the king and not the prophet.

Notes

1. The events of this chapter take place in 609 BC, or shortly after, being recorded in the book of Jeremiah as 'Early in the reign of Jehoiakim' (Jeremiah 26:1).

2. It is clearly more difficult for the reader to have the name Eliakim used alongside the regnal name of Jehoiakim. However, given that events here are seen through the eyes of Nehushta, it seemed more natural for her (and Dinah) to continue to think of him as Eliakim, though able to refer to him by his regnal name to others.

3. It is not clear if the rebuilding of high places (after Josiah had destroyed them) is ever explicitly linked to Jehoiakim. Both the books of 2 Kings and 2 Chronicles deal only briefly with the reigns and the deeds of the last four kings of Judah. However, some commentators have dated Jeremiah chapter 7 to the reign of Jehoiakim (see note 4 below), and that does explicitly mention the building of high places (7:31). It is certainly the case that after the death of Hezekiah, who had also destroyed the high places, his son Manasseh swiftly rebuilt them. It seems reasonable to think that Jehoiakim (roundly condemned by the prophet Jeremiah) would have done similarly after Josiah's death, including possibly the high places on the Hill of Corruption (2 Kings 23:13).

4. Worship of the Queen of Heaven is mentioned in Jeremiah 7:18 and 44:17-25. It seems to refer to the equivalent of the Assyrian goddess Ishtar (referred to as the 'queen of heaven' or the 'lady of heaven'), the consort of a male deity. The Canaanite equivalent is known as Astarte in Greek or Ashtoreth in Hebrew. From the references in Jeremiah chapters 7 and 14, it seems that the worship of this goddess was a particular form of idolatry engaged in by women (though with the knowledge and support of their husbands), and involved offering cakes imprinted with, or in the shape of, her image.

5. The events of Jeremiah 26, where Jeremiah preaches in the temple and is opposed by its priests, is thought by some commentators to be a summary and retelling of the 'temple sermon' recorded in chapter 7. Certainly, its themes are the same—condemning empty reliance upon the temple (or issuing a threat of its destruction), the rejection of Yahweh's law, and the

people's evil deeds, together with the warning of impending doom but the offer of an escape from judgment should they repent. The assumption has been made here that these two chapters are the same oracle/event, and therefore both early in the reign of Jehoiakim (26:1).

6. *2 Chronicles 36:15-16 makes it explicit that the judgment that came upon Judah was due to the sin of the whole nation and not just its kings. It is also clear from Jeremiah 44:17-18 that there were those who viewed Josiah's reforms as a mistake and the cause of the nation's calamity. Clearly many of the people were happy to embrace Jehoiakim's idolatry.*

7. *Shaphan was Josiah's secretary (2 Kings 22:3) and involved in his reforms, as were one of his sons, Ahikam, and what may well be Elnathan's father—Achbor son of Micaiah (2 Kings 22:12, cf. Jeremiah 26:22). Ahikam son of Shaphan is recorded as supporting Jeremiah and responsible (in part) for his deliverance from a sentence of death (Jeremiah 26:24). Other sons (or grandsons) of Shaphan who are sympathetic to Jeremiah are named in Scripture: Elasah (Jeremiah 29:3), Gemariah (Jeremiah 36:10), Micaiah (Jeremiah 36:11) and Gedaliah (Jeremiah 39:14).*

4

Woe to him who builds his palace by unrighteousness, his upper rooms by injustice, making his own people work for nothing, not paying them for their labour. (Jeremiah 22:13)

At one of the New Moon feasts, Nehushta found herself seated between her husband and her father. It was still early in Jehoiakim's reign. Her son, Jeconiah, sat at the king's right hand with Zebidah beyond him. Fattened calves had been roasted, as had quail and other game. Steam rose lazily into the warm room from large dishes of stew, both of meat and vegetables, and platters piled generously with bread made from the finest flour resembled a small range of undulating hills along the long tables. The room was lit by numerous lamps on the tables and on the lampstands behind the benches on which most sat. Only those nearest the king occupied carved cedarwood chairs. The wine was as rich and plentiful as the food, poured by servants into any goblet that was lacking.

The king seemed in a particularly good mood, the reason not difficult for Nehushta to guess. 'How was your visit to see the new palace, my king? Are the workmen making good progress?'

Eliakim looked pleased with himself. 'They have begun panelling the walls with cedar.' He plunged his knife into the roast calf that was nearest to him, hacking off another portion of the meat. 'The steward of the works tells me he hopes it will be ready by the early summer.' He laid down the knife and tore the meat with his fingers. He began devouring the tender morsel.

Nehushta smiled. 'In time to escape the heat of Jerusalem.'

'And it will be, if the builders keep doing as they are told.'

Nehushta's father had been leaning forward and listening to

their exchange. 'Is there any reason why they would not do so, my lord?'

Elnathan's face and tone were full of innocence, but Nehushta sensed, whether from the tiniest hint in his face or voice she wasn't sure, that her father already knew the answer.

Eliakim shrugged, as if the matter were of little consequence. 'The new tax is yet to deliver all that is needed, and Necho must be paid first. If the builders must wait for their wages, or receive a smaller pouch, then so be it. They are *my* subjects, after all, and they are doing the king's bidding, as they should.'

Elnathan's brow furrowed. 'That is true, my lord.' He seemed to be choosing his words carefully. 'But surely they will have families who are also the king's subjects and who need feeding?'

'Let them feed themselves! Wives and sons have hands that can also work. And are you not forgetting, Elnathan, that others before me have taken labour as a man's tax?'

Elnathan nodded slowly. 'The king is right again—but wasn't that just one month of a man's labour?'

'Those before me did not have Necho to pay.'

Nehushta's head turned from one man to the other—one free of care and one full of discomfort and unspoken words. Even she had heard the rumours of builders who went unpaid. She felt an oily hand rest upon hers. She turned back to the king, her smile of approval unsullied by doubt. She could still mask what lay within by her expression without.

Eliakim seemed satisfied and took a large gulp of wine. A drip escaped from his lips. She wiped it away with a finger bearing jewelled rings. His gaze then went beyond her to her father. 'But what of the Babylonians, Elnathan? Has there been any more news of them?'

'Nothing that you do not already know, my lord.' He drew in a deep breath. 'As far as the scouts can tell, Nebuchadnezzar still pushes his father's army into the mountains to the north of Carchemish, while the king remains in Babylon.'

'And do you still suppose that he intends to engage the Egyptians?'

Nehushta listened with interest. She had heard that the Egyptian army still lingered on the west side of the Euphrates at the city of Carchemish, to where it had retreated after the fall of Assyria.

Elnathan shrugged. 'If the Babylonians are wanting to expand their growing empire to the west, then that is what they will most likely have to do. But I am no seer.'

The king snorted. 'Do not talk to me of seers...' He took a long draught of wine and then chuckled. 'I have more worthy matters to spend my breath on.' With that, he turned about, giving his attention to his son and his mother.

With the king's back to her, Nehushta had no choice but to face her father. Both were silent for several moments. Elnathan then drummed his fingers on the table and stopped as abruptly as he'd started, as if he had suddenly come to a decision.

'I saw Dinah today—out near the market.'

'I sent her to find some thread for me. She has a better eye for colour than any of the other servants.'

Her father nodded slowly. 'I trust you know that you have both a loyal and resourceful maid in Dinah.'

'I know it...'

'And a wise one.' Nehushta held her peace as her father paused. 'Did you see her after her return?'

'Only very briefly. I asked her for the thread and then sent her to get Coniah ready for the feast whilst Peninnah dressed me.'

Her father nodded slowly. 'Dinah and I spoke at some length today.' His eyes then flitted to the king for the briefest of moments. Whether it was deliberate or done without thinking, she didn't know. She opened her mouth to speak but then closed it as her father placed a hand gently over hers and held it there. He smiled. 'I'm sure she will tell you about it later.' He then patted her hand. 'And now tell me what my grandson has been learning lately. Your mother will want to know.'

And Nehushta knew that something her father wished her to know had deliberately been left unspoken.

Nehushta excused herself from the feast before the wine flowing into the king's goblet turned him from the husband she'd married into the man she preferred to avoid. She had no desire to be summoned to his room later. She had said it would be better for her to take Jeconiah to his bed—which was true, as she had seen both his boredom and his yawns. And Zebidah had agreed, leaving with them and saying she would take the boy to his room. It suited Nehushta. For since the exchange with her father, she was curious to know what had passed between him and Dinah earlier in the day.

When she entered her room, the lamps were still alight, but Dinah had fallen asleep in a chair, some mending lying in her lap and her fingers still holding a needle. She swiftly roused herself.

'I am sorry, Mistress. I must have dozed off.' She laid the mending down and stood, ready to serve.

'It is no matter. I did not ask you to be awake on my return—merely to be here.'

Dinah smiled. 'Thank you, Mistress.' She followed Nehushta into the smaller room.

As Dinah helped her take off her jewellery, Nehushta related some of what had happened at the feast, but then, as the servant helped her out of the heavily embroidered and beaded green dress, Nehushta said lightly, 'My father tells me you met him near the market today.'

There was a pause. 'Yes…' She took the dress from her mistress and then handed her a simpler tunic for her bed.

Nehushta pulled it over her head and smoothed it down. 'What did you speak about?'

Dinah was silent for a moment. 'Only what has been happening in the city.'

Nehushta looked steadily at her. 'Follow me.' She went out into the larger room and sat down on her bed. 'Bring the stool and sit here.' Dinah complied without a word, though seeming hesitant, and then sat with both her hands and her gaze in her lap. Nehushta drew in a breath. 'Now tell my why my father wishes me to know of what you spoke…' Dinah bit her lip. Nehushta sighed loudly. 'It will be worse for you if you do not tell me than if you do.'

Dinah finally looked up. 'You commanded me once not to speak ill of the king, and I have obeyed you completely. So know that these are not my words but your father's. And not even your father's, for he was merely relating the words of the prophet.'

She did not need to name Jeremiah for Nehushta to know of whom she was speaking. 'What supposed oracle has he brought now?'

Dinah's gaze returned to the hands still in her lap. 'Your father told me that he has spoken of the royal house by name. He spoke of the king's brother—of Jehoahaz, though calling him Shallum...'

'That was his name before he became king...'

'The prophet said that we should weep for him, for he will never return to this land, but will die in Egypt.' She fell silent.

Nehushta had given Shallum little thought in the time since her husband replaced him as king. Besides, the thought of him in chains languishing in some Egyptian prison was not one she wished to dwell on—particularly as Necho was capable of doing the same to Eliakim, should he fail in his obligation as vassal. She guessed, however, that this was not what her father wished her to know. 'And was there more?'

'Yes, he told me that a second oracle named Jehoiakim...'

'And what was said?'

Dinah drew in a deep breath, but spoke in a lowered voice, still not looking up. 'He denounced the king for building himself a fine palace while denying the builders their wages. He said that, unlike Josiah, he acts without righteousness or justice, but with dishonesty and oppression, shedding innocent blood.'

As Dinah paused, the name *Uriah* intruded into Nehushta's thoughts.

Then Dinah raised her eyes, meeting those of her mistress. 'There was a final word. Your father told me that he prophesied that Jehoiakim would not be lamented—' She paused. '—but would have the burial of a donkey.'

It was clear to Nehushta—as clear as the waters of a mountain spring—that if the king had supposed that Uriah's death would cow Jeremiah into silence then he was very much mistaken. She held her servant's gaze for a moment. 'Do not speak of it to others, Dinah.'

'I would not, Mistress.'

'Then you may go when you have seen to the lamps.' Dinah bobbed her head. Nehushta watched as she rose, picked up her stool and put it back by the wall. She extinguished all but one of the small flickering flames around the room, and then straightened one of the mats on the floor as she went, closing the door softly behind her. Then all was silent. Nehushta sat for a moment, and then pushed back the covers on the bed and climbed underneath.

As she lay on her back, staring up into the dim light of the one lamp left burning, she found it hard to expel from her mind Jeremiah's oracle. *Why did her father wish her to hear the damning words? Did he want her to see her husband differently, in a darker light? But surely these were only the ravings of a madman. Or were they?* She was tired. She turned onto her side and closed her eyes. *It was a question she couldn't answer, and it would have to wait for the dawn of another day—maybe a distant one.*

It was not the last of Jeremiah's prophecies that were reported to Nehushta. News swiftly reached her that an oracle had earned the prophet a beating and a day of humiliation, his feet, hands and neck held fast in the stocks outside the temple. Both punishments were at the command of Pashhur, the priest who kept order in the house of Yahweh.

Nehushta's curiosity was too great—she had never seen for herself the prophet who caused such an uproar. She decided to take Peninnah with her—and not tell Dinah her intention.

When they reached the Upper Gate of Benjamin by the temple, Peninnah screwed up her face. *It was, indeed, a distasteful sight.* Nehushta couldn't help staring—fascinated and repulsed in equal measure. The prophet stood constrained, able to move neither body nor head. It was difficult to see his face, with his head bent downwards by the stocks and his hair hanging about it. His chastisement was accompanied by the unrestrained mocking of those nearby, including temple priests. Nehushta turned to one of the guards with her. 'Is one of those near the stocks the priest by the name of Pashhur son of Immer.'

'Yes, Mistress.'

Her wish to see Jeremiah was matched by a desire to know what had brought such derision and discomfort upon him. 'Summon the priest to me.' The man whom the guard approached was standing, arms crossed, ridicule upon his lips. He seemed to find pleasure in the sight before him—and further pleasure in being called over to Nehushta.

He bowed when he reached her, bearing an expansive smile. 'Mistress.'

'I understand, Pashhur, that this punishment is at your command.'

'It is—and I trust it meets with your royal approval.' He did not wait for an answer, clearly assuming her response. 'This madman is no friend of King Jehoiakim nor of the temple. He deserves no less and should be grateful he has not suffered the just fate of that other false prophet, Uriah. He must be taught not to speak his deceitful and profane words.'

She returned to the stocks, strangely drawn to the sight. She wondered if any would dare defend him. 'Do his family venture to come and speak with him when he is so humiliated?'

Pashhur snorted. 'The man has no family! He takes no wife and fathers no children—and claims that it is at the command of Yahweh. As if Yahweh would command such perverse conduct! It is yet another proof that the man is mad!'

It did, indeed, seem strange behaviour. 'And what were the words that brought this punishment down upon his head?'

'You wish to know his profanities?' There was surprise in his voice, and when Nehushta glanced back at him, he looked as if he had just bitten into a rotten fig. 'I would not wish to repeat his blasphemies to your gentle ears.'

'But is it not wise,' she murmured, 'for the king's wife to know the ideas—even poisoned ones—that may reach the ears of her servants and the king's subjects?'

There was a pause. 'As you wish. He spoke his first lies in the Valley of Ben Hinnom, condemning the very worship that our king permits. He claimed that the ground on which he stood would be

260

renamed *the Valley of Slaughter*. He claimed that the people of Judah and of this city would fall by the sword, and, if you will excuse such abominable language, their bodies would become food for birds and beasts.' He snorted again. 'It is an outrage. This city is blessed with the house of Yahweh. How can it be besieged or become desolate as he has claimed? Then the madman smashed a clay jar, supposedly as a sign that the city would be broken beyond repair. And *then*...' He paused again and Nehushta tore her eyes away from the prophet. The priest's face was sour as vinegar. '*Then* he had the impudence to stand in the court of the holy temple itself and utter his profanities there. Preaching calamity in Yahweh's name in Yahweh's own house! He called the people stiff-necked.' Pashhur's gaze fell upon the stocks. 'It is *his* neck that will be stiff by tomorrow—if it is not already.'

The image of the prophet in the merciless restraints stayed with Nehushta through the rest of the day—like the taste of rancid milk that lingers on the tongue. It also entered her disquieting dreams that night. Her troubled mind woke her, and her immediate thought was that, as she lay in comfort upon her bed, Jeremiah was at that very moment outside in the dark, his head still held bowed by iron.

After a night that brought her little refreshment, curiosity compelled her again—this time to learn what the day and night in the stocks had done to Jeremiah. She sent the same guard who had summoned Pashhur to witness the release. She waited in the courtyard for his return.

She rose as he entered, approached her and bowed. 'What happened?'

The guard's expression was one of bemusement. 'When Pashhur released the prophet, he could barely stand straight or walk, yet immediately faced the priest and pronounced an oracle against him.'

Nehushta was shocked. 'Then and there?'

'Yes, Mistress.'

'What did he say?'

'He claimed that Yahweh had given Pashhur the name *Terror on every side*. I do not claim to be able to remember every word just as the prophet uttered it, my mistress, but I can relate the kernel of it: that the king of Babylon would take all of Judah into exile and its wealth as plunder, and that Pashhur would die in captivity there. That was his message.'

She dismissed the guard and sat down slowly. *What drove the prophet to persist in saying such things when it could earn him yet more days in the stocks—or worse? It was, indeed, perplexing.*

The news from the north spread through the city as swiftly as flames through sun-baked grass. The palace corridors were astir not only with the reports of the defeat of the Egyptian army at Carchemish but also with debate of what it would mean for Judah.

Dinah stood waiting after conveying all she had gleaned from Shimron. For once, Nehushta determined to seek her father out rather than wait for him to come to her—as he often did with matters he deemed helpful for her to know. But another voice spoke first.

'Does that mean Pharaoh Necho is dead?' asked Jeconiah. 'Can we keep our gold now instead of sending it to him?'

Nehushta turned to her ten-year-old son. 'We do not know the answer to those questions yet, Coniah. But I am about to find your grandfather to ask him.'

'Can I come?'

'No, you can't. Peninnah will take you to the queen mother instead.'

'But I'd rather…'

Nehushta cut in. 'I don't care what you'd rather! You are going to Grandmother Zebidah. She will be pleased to see you. And do not pout.' Her words had little effect upon him.

'Uncle Mattaniah?' he tried again, his voice plaintive. The brother of the king, though a son of Hamutal rather than Zebidah, was little more than three years older than Jeconiah.

'No! The two of you caused chaos when you last played together, and *you* were the one leading *him* astray.' His face fell again. She sighed. 'I'm sure you will see Mattaniah soon enough.' She looked over to Peninnah. It was enough to summon her maid and send her and the boy off. She watched them go. Sending Jeconiah to Zebidah had become a useful tool for her, and she had grudgingly admitted, if only to herself, that her son always returned better mannered—at least for a short while—than after time with his father.

'Come, Dinah.' Her maid followed her out and then down the palace's wide steps. Over the eleven years that Dinah had served her within the royal household, she had become her most-trusted servant, whose good sense had saved her more than once. She was certainly not as dull as she had once supposed her, and the only matter that still needled Nehushta was her servant's stubborn refusal to embrace the king's way of worship—and the disapproval of it she could detect in her eyes.

Elnathan was not where she could usually find him—the chamber of the scribes. Nehushta hailed one of the servants nearby. 'Have you seen my father?'

'He is with King Jehoiakim, Mistress—as are all the king's officials.'

'Tell him to come to me on the roof when he has finished his business with the king.' The servant acknowledged her request and returned to his task. She turned to Dinah. 'Let us see how Jerusalem stirs…'

They were soon looking down over the roof's waist-high wall onto the bustling streets beyond the palace, with Dinah holding a shade over them both. The early summer sun was starting to wax strong. 'See how they linger together.' Nehushta watched the small groups of men, arms and hands gesturing vigorously as they talked. 'Little work will be done today.'

'They speak of only one thing, I am sure, Mistress.' Dinah paused, then looked up. 'Coniah's questions were apt, were they not?'

'Apt—but as yet without answers. Let us hope my father will know more when he comes from the king.'

'Whatever those answers, there will be change surely. Do you not think so, Mistress?'

Nehushta pondered the question. 'I cannot see how it would be otherwise…'

'But will it be for the better?'

'That, Dinah, is another question that I hope my father will answer.'

As the sun continued rising to its highest point, Nehushta began to wonder if she should return to her room. There was little left to see or say. But then a familiar voice called out behind them.

'I am sorry you have had to wait so long for me, my daughter.' Both women turned to see Elnathan approaching them. 'I was detained with the king for some time and have only just received your message.' He greeted her with a kiss on each cheek. He glanced at Dinah. 'I see you have had good company, though.'

Nehushta responded with neither accord nor dissent. 'What have you learned about the Egyptian defeat—and what it will mean for Judah?'

'All the scouts could tell us is that what is left of the Egyptian army has abandoned Carchemish and is fleeing south.'

'Back to Egypt?'

'It is too early to say, Nehushta—the Babylonians pursue them, even now. But whatever happens, Necho's arm has been greatly weakened.'

'And will that mean that Judah can now cast off the yoke of Egypt?'

'That is the king's hope.' Elnathan's eyes alighted upon the servant. 'What is it, Dinah?'

She looked to her mistress, as she always did, for permission to join the exchange.

Nehushta nodded 'Go ahead, Dinah. You may speak.'

'What if the Babylonians come as far south as Judah?'

Elnathan nodded his head slowly. 'That is the question that should concern the king most.' He looked out over the city. 'Babylon and its king have already taken much of the land over which the Assyrians held sway. If they are now seeking to expand their kingdom to the west, then the only one who knows where they will stop is Yahweh. And we are in His hands.'

Nehushta remembered Jeremiah's words to Pashhur. 'But should that bring us comfort or fear?' she murmured.

Elnathan's gaze returned to the women. 'If our hearts are humble before Yahweh, then it is always better to be in His merciful hands than outside them—whatever that brings.'

Nehushta considered his words. 'And what of the one whose heart is not humble?'

Her father looked her in the eye. 'I would not want to be that man.'

The summer brought the news that Nebuchadnezzar, the son of the king of Babylon, had successfully defeated what remained of the Egyptian army at Hamath in Aram to the north. But just when the people of Judah feared that the Babylonian army might flood their land, the advance stopped. Rumours abounded. *Yahweh had saved them. Baal had saved them. Jeremiah was wrong. The prophet was right. The king of Babylon was ill. Nabopolassar was dead.* But just as the greatest heat of the summer began to pass and the dates and summer figs were being harvested, the Babylonian army swept into the land as unstoppable as the night. With it came the truth of what had happened not much more than a month earlier—and the realisation of their worst fears.

Nehushta was terrified but feigned calm instead. She was standing once again on the roof of the palace with her father, but this time the landscape around the city was different. Instead of the hillsides being cloaked with either rocks or greenery turned yellow or brown by the summer sun, they wore the trappings of a huge army—tents, horses, carts, chariots. Its soldiers swarmed on the Judean hills, numerous as a plague of locusts and even more deadly. The city was surrounded and under siege. And their own king—an ant next to their locusts—had been summoned to stand before Babylon's newest king. The only reason for the army's earlier pause had been Nebuchadnezzar's return to Babylon to take the crown after his father's death. And he had returned to the land to the east of the Great Sea as swiftly as he had left it—to finish whatever it was he had started there.

'What will the Babylonians do with Eliakim?' The words sounded smaller than Nehushta had intended. Her mouth was dry and her throat tight.

Elnathan's eyes were fixed on the large imposing tent in which they supposed their own king to be meeting that of Babylon. It was safely beyond the reach of any spear, arrow or slingshot from Jerusalem's walls. 'I cannot be sure.' He paused. 'All I *am* sure of is that we are no longer a vassal of Egypt. Necho's power over Judah has disappeared as quickly as a morning mist, and he has been driven back into his own land.'

'So will we now be a vassal of Babylon?'

'That is the best that our king can hope for.'

Nehushta looked steadily into the distance, away from the tent. 'When Shallum stood before Necho at Hamath, Necho deposed him and deported him in chains to Egypt, making Eliakim king instead…' She left the words hanging, but then felt a hand upon her shoulder. She turned.

'And you wish to know if the same might happen to your husband?' His tone was as gentle as the touch of his hand.

She nodded, afraid her voice would betray her completely if she tried to speak. Even the word *yes* suddenly seemed an impossible feat. Her father's gaze was steady, and she had to look down.

'Nehushta—I can give you no certain pledge that that will not happen.' He had never been one to offer baseless promises. 'But our king has two things in his favour that may stand him in better stead than Shallum: our army has never gone out against the Babylonians or opposed them, and Nebuchadnezzar is far from home and only newly crowned. He will not, I think, want to risk a lengthy siege of this city.'

She couldn't bring herself to ask of the things that might stand against her husband in the eyes of Yahweh rather than those of the Babylonians. She knew the hideous rumours of his dark deeds down in the Valley of Ben Hinnom, turning children into burnt offerings on its altars as the Babylonians approached. She had never been more thankful that her own son was the king's firstborn. But now Nebuchadnezzar was a looming threat to the precious fruit of her womb. 'Jeconiah is only ten…' she finally whispered.

'I know.' He patted her shoulder. 'I know. But there is one thing of which you can be sure.' She looked up again. 'Your mother and I will not cease praying to Yahweh for you and for this land.'

Nehushta had never seen Eliakim in such a foul mood. His meal was largely untouched, and any servants had been dismissed. He clearly wanted to vent his anger but only in her hearing. There was thunder in his face, and his words came as suddenly as the rain of a summer storm, and with the same intensity. 'He humiliated me!' His fist hit the table. 'In front of not only his officers but mine also. 'He made me kneel before him, and then with the merest wave of his hand, some common soldiers stepped forward and bound my wrists and my neck with bronze chains!' He was by now shaking with rage. 'He treated me as if I were some snared wild animal, to be put on a leash and led away for sport.' The memory of it only seemed to enrage him further. The back of his hand sent his goblet tumbling across the room, scattering its deep red wine across both cedar floor and woven rugs. The force of the blow was such that it was only the wall that prevented the vessel going further.

His anger scared her, but she did not—and dared not—let it be seen by him. For the second time in the day she feigned composure, but had no idea what to say or how to calm him. The safest path to walk seemed the one of silence—at least until some notion of what to do or say came into her head.

'He looked down upon me, but only spoke through an interpreter. He said that I had a choice. I could keep the chains and go with him to Babylon—' He seethed. '—or kneel prostrate before him and pledge eternal obedience as his vassal. It was no choice! I had to kneel with my forehead to the ground and my arms outstretched on the ground towards him. And he deliberately kept me there, abased for all to see and with the chains still upon me.' He turned to her. 'How dare he!'

She summoned her courage and reached out, knowing he expected a response, and laid a hand upon his arm. It was still shaking. 'But you are safe, my king—and so is the city. You have been restored to your people and are still exalted in their eyes—'

'Except,' he interrupted, almost shouting, 'those of the army officers and officials who accompanied me and saw me degraded before the Babylonian!' He leant across and took her goblet and proceeded to empty it of its wine.

'They will think no less of you,' she said, her voice steady and soothing. She had no idea whether her words carried any truth, but if a lie calmed the wild animal within him, that was all that mattered.

It occurred to her then that her husband cared more about his own humiliation rather than the salvation of the city and its people. And then, suddenly, an image rose in her mind of the prophet Jeremiah—and the humiliation and shackles he had borne, not at the whim of a foreign king, but of their own temple priests. It was an act of which her husband would have approved, whether he knew of it or not. The distraction was short-lived.

The goblet was slammed down. 'And there is, of course, a price that the king of Babylon demands from us: gold and silver vessels from our temple—and young men from our highest families to serve him in Babylon.'

She gripped the chair, her nails digging into its cushion. 'Please, not Jeconiah!' Any pretence of composure had suddenly disappeared.

'Your son is safe, though others will not be so fortunate.'

Nehushta stood with Dinah on the palace roof once more. Her maid seemed to sense that she had no desire to talk, and so left her to her thoughts. They watched in silence as the last of the Babylonian army departed across the Judean hills. *Somewhere in their midst were the vessels from the house of Yahweh—destined for some Babylonian temple, as if to proclaim the supremacy of their gods.* But Nehushta knew that among the ranks of their new overlords were other treasures—those of bone and flesh. She wondered in how many homes of the nobles or the wider royal family there were distraught mothers and fathers—bereft of sons, some of which would be the firstborn and others of which were likely to be only sons. *There was little chance they would ever see them again or know their fate in Babylon, for good or for ill.* She flinched.

The Babylonian army receded into the distance. But it felt as if there were another threat far closer to hand. It suddenly occurred to her, like a lamp being lit in the darkness, that though she had once considered the ways of her father dull, she had always felt safe in his house. *Her parents' love for her and their faithfulness to Yahweh were as dependable and constant as the hills stretching out before her. Eliakim, however, was as unpredictable as the path of a hornet, never knowing where it might land or sting next. He could be charming or cruel, docile or deadly—the only cause guiding his path, his own wants and his alone. To him, that was what it meant to king, the throne merely a tool to deliver whatever he desired—be it a palace or a prophet's silence. He wielded power like a child with a wolf on a leash.* And it had begun to frighten her.

Notes

1. *These events largely take place in 605 BC although it is not clear when exactly Jeremiah's prophecy against Jehoiakim (in Jeremiah 22:13-19) occurred, but it is assumed here to take place earlier in his reign than 605 BC.*

2. *There are some difficulties in determining the precise chronology and harmonisation of the different accounts: (a) Nebuchadnezzar 'coming up' and making Jehoiakim his vassal for three years (2 Kings 24:1); (b) Nebuchadnezzar 'coming up against' Jehoiakim and putting him in bronze chains to take him to Babylon (2 Chronicles 36:6); (c) a siege of Jerusalem by Nebuchadnezzar in the third year of Jehoiakim's reign and the deportation of Daniel and others to Babylon (Daniel 1:1), although this is generally taken as his third year according to Babylonian reckoning, which would be his fourth year by Hebrew reckoning, i.e. 605 BC; (d) the Babylonian Chronicles, recording their victory over the Egyptians at Carchemish (605 BC), Nebuchadnezzar coming to the throne in August that year, before returning around a month later to 'Hatti' (Syria and Palestine) from where he took 'heavy tribute', returning again to the Levant the following year (604 BC) and taking Ashkelon. It is assumed here that Jehoiakim became a vassal on Nebuchadnezzar's return to the Levant after being crowned king, and that Jehoiakim was never taken*

269

to Babylon, so that putting him in bronze chains was merely a threat. *Although 2 Chronicles does not record Jehoiakim's death, 2 Kings 24:6 does, and Jeremiah's prophecy in Jeremiah 22:19 links his burial—or the absence of it—to Jerusalem.*

3. *As the Bible Background Commentary states, concerning the cedar panels and red-painted walls in Jeremiah's oracle against Jehoiakim (in Jeremiah 22:13-19): 'Cedar panelling was considered the most luxurious and expensive material that could be used. It was used almost exclusively in palaces and temples. Wall painting is not widely attested in Israelite excavations but... [other frescos] attest to the preference for red and orange in interior decoration. This characteristic is also referred to in the wall decorations in Ezekiel 23:14.' (p657). Archaeology has discovered remains of what is considered to be an ancient palace, three miles south of Jerusalem. See 'Royal Palace, Royal Portrait', Gabriel Barkay, (Biblical Archaeology Review 32:5, September/October 2006).*

4. *An assumption has been made that Jeremiah 19:1-20:6 (the prophecy heard by Pashhur) was early in the reign of Jehoiakim. This is a plausible date, given that Jeremiah was not able to enter the temple by 605 BC (see Jeremiah 36:5), and was in hiding by the end of 604 BC (see Jeremiah 36:26), although he had some freedom again later in the reign of Jehoiakim, after the Babylonian invasion (see Jeremiah 35:1,11).*

5. *Jeremiah 29:26 records another reference to the use of stocks for those whose messages were unwelcome: 'you should put any maniac who acts like a prophet into the stocks and neck-irons.' Although it is not clear precisely what it entailed, it was probably 'a restraining device of some sort in which the prophet could be held and displayed in a humiliating and uncomfortable stance.' (OTBBC, p662). Given Jeremiah's complaint in Jeremiah 20:7-8, it certainly seems to have resulted in both humiliation and mocking.*

6. *Some seals have been discovered in Jerusalem that may have belonged to the brother of Pashhur. See https://www.biblicalarchaeology.org/daily/clay-seals-give-clues-to-wealth-of-biblical-jerusalem/.*

7. *The defeat of the Egyptian army at Carchemish by Nebuchadnezzar is mentioned in Scripture in Jeremiah 46:2.*

8. *The meeting between Jehoiakim and Nebuchadnezzar described in this*

chapter is wholly imagined, but based on the premise that it was likely that they met, given what is said in 2 Chronicles 26:6 about Nebuchadnezzar binding him in bronze chains, and in 2 Kings 24:1 about Jehoiakim becoming a servant (or vassal) of Nebuchadnezzar.

9. *There is no reason to think that Jehoiakim didn't engage in the abomination of child sacrifice, particularly given the extremis he found himself in, caught between Egypt and Babylon. Jeremiah 7:31 mentions this practice (and the oracle could be dated to Jehoiakim's reign), and it was something that Manasseh, Jehoiakim's great-grandfather, had done (see 2 Kings 21:6).*

10. *'Bone and flesh' is the Hebrew equivalent of the English idiom, 'flesh and blood'.*

11. *There is no indication given of how many, if any, other wives or sons Jehoiakim may have had, though it is likely that there were a number of both, particularly with an eleven-year reign.*

5

It was the ninth month and the king was sitting in the winter apartment, with a fire burning in the brazier in front of him.
(Jeremiah 36:22)

The winter's day had dawned far colder than most. Jerusalem's elevation was a blessing in summer, keeping the city cooler than the heat of Jericho, but as the days waned to their shortest, it was more akin to a curse. Although the morning was bright, the lamps were lit in Nehushta's room, the hangings over the windows keeping out the day's light as well as its chill. She rose from the padded stool on which she had perched as Peninnah braided her hair. The long, pointed sleeves of her red and orange gown hung down in front of her as she wrapped her arms across her chest. The cloth was heavier than usual, though still exquisitely embroidered in colourful threads. She was already wearing an extra linen undergarment.

Dinah paused her task of tidying the bed. 'Would you like me to find a warm shawl? There is a tassled one whose colour and weight might serve you well.'

Nehushta nodded. 'Yes, bring it. Then we will make our way to the winter-house. The king will not begrudge us a corner of the room—one hopefully not far from the brazier.'

Peninnah placed a small cap adorned with tiny carnelians upon her head and began securing it. 'Do you think many will be at the temple today, Mistress?'

'I do not doubt it. Ever since the fast was called, people have been coming from throughout Judah. But the king will not be among them—he sees no reason. The Babylonian army may have sacked Ashkelon and deported many of its nobles to Babylon, but unlike the Philistines, King Jehoiakim is Nebuchadnezzar's vassal. Judah is safe.' Despite her own words, she knew perfectly well that the future of the nation was by no means secure. They were still caught between the Babylonians to the north and Egypt to the south.

Nehushta watched Dinah straightening and smoothing the bed covers. She would not be touching food until dusk. No such abstinence had been required in the palace, however. She had never known Eliakim to deny himself anything. As Peninnah fastened an elaborate veil to the cap, Nehushta continued. 'I will tell you who also will not be among them—the prophet Jeremiah.'

Dinah looked up. 'Is he still forbidden from entering the temple?'

'The priests desire neither him nor his denunciations in their courts,' murmured Nehushta, studying her head from both left and right sides in the mirror that Peninnah had handed her. Her reflection pleased her. 'Good. But *we* will be in the king's presence today and will occupy ourselves by observing his business.' She paused and smiled, mischief dancing lightly upon her lips. 'And if that proves dull, then we shall discuss who among the nobles have daughters who may, when they flower, make a good wife for my son!' Peninnah giggled. 'Except we will *not* be making such sounds and earning the king's displeasure.'

Once her shawl was pulled around her, they went out into the corridor. Its chill was stark. Nehushta watched her breath make tiny clouds which swiftly dispersed as they made their way towards the inner rooms of the palace. Guards opened the door to the winter-house for them. With no outside walls or windows, it immediately felt less harsh. The glowing coals filling the brazier near the king's seat ensured the room was warmed rather than filled with smoke. Eliakim acknowledged his wife with a brief nod, their son sat at his side. His attention then returned to the scribe at a table nearby, surrounded by the tools of his trade: a pot of ink, papyrus, pens, a knife.

Nehushta soon became bored with the king's business—as bored as he himself seemed. The women's whispered conversation soon turned to the merits—or otherwise—of every girl that they knew within Jerusalem's leading families. Jeconiah would be twelve in a few months, and Nehushta did not consider it too early to begin planning. *Hadassah, Merab, Abihail, Haggith, Mahalath, Tamar.* All were discussed at length.

More than once, her swift, stern glance had quietened Peninnah, always keen to express what, in her eyes, were the flaws of each girl— *ears that were too big, lips that were meagre, a face like a mouse, teeth of a rabbit, arms like sticks.* Dinah, for her part, preferred to commend what was good.

It was only when they had begun to debate Susanna, that Nehushta suddenly held up her hand, stilling the tongue of Peninnah. A group of men had entered the room, among them her father, his demeanour uneasy. *This was a delegation.* They bowed as they reached the king.

A spark of interest kindled upon Eliakim's face and that of his son. 'What tears you away from your labours to bring you here?'

Elishama, the palace secretary, stepped forward slightly and bowed again. 'If it pleases you, O King, a matter has come to our attention: a certain—' He hesitated. '—*incident* at the temple today. We felt you may wish to know of it.'

The king's face darkened slightly. 'What manner of *incident*? Does it involve that madman, Jeremiah?'

'Not directly, my lord.'

'Then how so?'

'The prophet's scribe, a man by the name of Baruch, was at the temple by the New Gate, reading words from a scroll to all who entered. When this was reported to us, we summoned the scribe to know more fully the nature of what was written.' He paused, seemingly weighing his next words.

'And…' His tone was edged with a dangerous impatience.

'It seems, O King, that the prophet dictated all his oracles to be written down in the name of Yahweh.'

'Did he now…?' The king's words bore the chill of the day. 'And do they still augur doom?'

Elishama lowered his gaze, as if he could not look steadily at the king. 'Yes, my lord. Disaster is prophesied for this land and this city.'

'And where are the scribe and his scroll now?

'The scroll is in my room, but the scribe left us. I cannot say where he is now.'

The glow of the brazier was reflected in Eliakim's eyes. His jaw twitched. They waited. He then turned to one of the other officials. 'Jehudi—go and fetch this scroll. You will then read it aloud to me, and I will be the judge of the worth of its words.' The official bowed and hurried off.

Nehushta glanced around. The attention of every person—including that of her son—was upon the king. The only sound, apart from an occasional cough, was the king drumming his fingers on the arm of his cedarwood chair. She avoided her father's gaze, smiling instead at Jeconiah, her face at odds with her racing heart and dry mouth. *How would Eliakim react to the prophet's words—if that was what they were? Would the coldness in his voice be burnt away by the raging fire of his anger?*

The door creaked and every head turned. Jehudi entered, a large scroll in his hand. He approached the king. Eliakim linked his fingers and flexed his hands. He then sat back in the chair and folded his arms. 'Let us hear, then, what this so-called *prophet* has to say.'

As Jehudi began to read, the words gripped Nehushta—as if there were no one in the room but simply a voice. A voice speaking with utter certainty, defying all challenge. *Were these really the ravings of a madman?* The words of poetry might have seemed beautiful were it not for their message. *The people of Yahweh exchanging their glorious God for worthless idols. Judah a prostitute. A corrupt vine. A wild donkey in heat. Innocent blood filling Jerusalem's streets.*

'Stop.' The sudden silence was absolute. Jehudi stood frozen, staring wide-eyed at the king. Eliakim turned to the scribe nearby and calmly stretched out his arm. 'Give me your knife.' The wooden legs of the scribe's stool scraped on the stone floor as he pushed it back and rose, flustered. He snatched his scribe's knife, hurriedly placing it in the king's open palm. Eliakim closed his fingers around its haft. He beckoned to Jehudi. 'Here. Give me the scroll.' Once in his hand, he scanned the unfurled section before bringing the blade down upon it, its sharpened edge slicing through the crisp papyrus. He then lent forward and tossed the severed portion onto the hot coals in the brazier.

Nehushta stared as it lay there for a few moments, darkening and curling. Then it suddenly flared, sending an orange flame upwards and turning it from the colour of sand to that of the ink upon it, before its fire petered out and the papyrus and its words were completely destroyed. Nehushta looked around as low murmuring replaced the sound of crackling flames. She'd heard sharp breaths drawn as the papyrus was consigned to the coals, but not all faces were as her father's. Some bore the same fascination as boys she had once seen watching a raven pecking at a dead mouse. The lips of others were twisted, as if revelling in a rival's humiliation. Both her servants, seated on a bench next to her, were open mouthed—one in amazement, the other in distressed disbelief. 'Mask your disapproval, Dinah!' hissed Nehushta. The servant shut her mouth and stared at the floor.

'And now…' Eliakim's voice rang out. He paused, commanding silence, and then returned the scroll to the official. 'And now, Jehudi, you will continue reading.' He rested the knife in his lap.

The poetry spoke again of adultery with foreign gods. Yet among the words that were as hard and unyielding as the iron of the scribe's blade were others full of tender and generous invitation to return to their God. She wondered—and the notion shook her—if this might be the voice of Yahweh Himself. But another harsher voice interrupted.

'Stop!' Jehudi looked up. Eliakim wagged the fingers of his outstretched hand back and forth. 'Give it to me.' Jehudi obeyed, though as a kid before a wolf.

'My lord!' Nehushta's eyes darted to her father. Two other officials were stepping forward with him. Eliakim glanced up, unconcerned, his attention immediately returning to the scroll, scrutinising it as before. Elnathan swallowed. 'O King…' Her father's voice was strained and quieter. '…is it not better to leave the scroll intact, even if the words are hard to bear?' He fell silent. Eliakim began slicing through the papyrus again. 'My lord?'

It was only when his knife had done its job that the king looked up. 'The only thing these words are good for is bringing us a little more warmth on a winter's day.' With that, he tossed a second portion into the brazier and handed the scroll back to Jehudi. 'Continue.'

The reading of the scroll continued with the same pattern and predictability as the waxing and waning of the moon: the power and brightness of its words growing stronger through the mouth of Jehudi, but then halted and their light quenched until all that was left was dark and lifeless ash. Nehushta had once rejoiced in likening Eliakim to a wild ox. *But was this rousing freedom or reckless folly? Would she have burned a scroll where Yahweh described His people as His beloved— even after telling Judah they had as many gods as towns, and as many altars to Baal as streets of Jerusalem?*

From time to time, Nehushta recognised oracles recounted to her by others. But when Jehudi uttered *Woe to him who builds his palace by unrighteousness, and his upper rooms by injustice,* it was as if every breath in the room was suddenly held.

Jehudi glanced up nervously. Eliakim stared back as though looking through him. Jehudi cleared his throat and returned to the scroll. '*Therefore this is what Yahweh says about Jehoiakim son of Josiah king of Judah:*

"They will not mourn for him:
    'Alas, my brother! Alas, my sister!'
They will not mourn for him:
    'Alas my master! Alas his splendour!'
He will have the burial of a donkey—
    dragged away and thrown
    outside the gates of Jerusalem."'

Nehushta stared at the floor. *It would be a brave—or foolish—person who would risk meeting the king's eyes.* But instead of an outburst, all she heard were the familiar words: *Give it here.*

There was not a single moment in the scroll's recital when Nehushta sensed either fear or contrition in her husband. Neither at the description of his own demise nor of the ruin of the land at the hands of Nebuchadnezzar. She saw only contempt and no oracle escaped the flames. Besides Dinah, only her father and those with him showed any disquiet. In her own heart, however, a battle had begun to rage—one from which she would rather retreat.

Even before the flames feasting on the final vestige of papyrus had begun to diminish, the king's voice barked a new command. 'Jerahmeel—come here.'

The official had been leaning against the wall to the king's right, his arms folded across his ornate blue robe flecked with gold thread. Among the king's servants, Shimron was his most trusted; but among his officials, it was Jerahmeel upon whom Eliakim's favour rested like a jewelled scarlet turban. And all knew it. Jerahmeel bowed low before the king. 'What does my lord wish of me?'

'One thing—and one thing only. Scour the city until you find Jeremiah and Baruch. When you find them, seize them and bring them to me.' He pointed to two other officials. 'And you will both assist him. I want the mouth of the prophet and the pen of his scribe silenced before they can poison the city further with their treacherous deceits.'

Jerahmeel bobbed his head. 'It will be done, O king, as surely as night follows day.'

'Then do not delay.'

The official bowed once more to the king, and then turned. A swift nod summoned the others appointed to the task, and all three headed out of the warm room and into the winter air.

Before the door was closed behind them, Eliakim was holding out the knife for the scribe to retrieve. 'And now I will eat.'

Nehushta placed the earring she had just removed on the carved table by her bed. It was a large disk of gold with a central carnelian ringed by smaller stones of yellow jasper. As her fingers went to the other ear, she listened to her servants whispering in the adjacent room. Peninnah had never properly learned how to lower her voice to be out of her mistress's earshot.

'What of those words about Nebuchadnezzar coming against Judah? The scroll said that we would serve the king of Babylon for seventy years. What do you think that means? Doesn't the king serve him already?'

Nehushta stood absolutely still, straining her ears. But whatever Dinah's reply, it was whispered too softly to catch. All she heard was Peninnah's response.

'Even the king?' Another reply as gentle as the breeze, then, 'If the king heard you say that—'

A sharp rap silenced Peninnah. Nehushta turned towards the outer door. 'Come.' The door opened.

Shimron stood in the doorway, still gripping the door handle. He bowed. 'The king desires your presence, my mistress.' He didn't wait for a reply, but simply pulled the door shut again, leaving her with the summons.

Nehushta bit her lip and then sighed, her breath visible in the flickering lamplight. *She had no choice.* She turned towards the other door. 'You will have heard Shimron's words, so come quickly. I will not keep the king waiting.'

Dinah appeared first, concern on her face. 'But your supper has not arrived yet, Mistress.'

'What matters most is pleasing the king.' Her eyes met Dinah's— and it suddenly struck her that she had not yet had the chance to break her fast. 'I will not starve. Now bring me fresh clothes—ones that will be to the king's liking, so choose something with a finer weave.' She picked up the earring she had just put down, threading its loop through her ear once more as Dinah disappeared into the smaller room. She called after her, 'Something red—bright red—and a shawl and necklace to match.' She turned to Peninnah. 'Unbraid my hair and brush it out—and be quick.'

Before long, Dinah was draping a heavy necklace around Nehushta's neck. It was cold to her skin, but from its chain of red and yellow jasper beads hung embossed golden leaves which followed perfectly the curve of the crimson gown's neck—a neckline that her mother would have described as *immodest*. Unbidden and unwanted, words that she had heard earlier in the day rose in her mind exactly as she had heard them: *Why dress yourself in scarlet and put on jewels of gold? Why highlight your eyes with makeup? You adorn yourself in vain. Your lovers despise you; they want to kill you.* She shook her head almost imperceptibly, as if to banish the words from her mind. But it was impossible to dispel the day's events. Unlike her breath in the air, they were solid, striking, stubborn.

'I heard Peninnah ask you about the meaning of the scroll's words.' She paused, looking straight ahead, as Dinah fastened the clasp at the back of her neck. 'What was your answer?' She waited— and knew she would be told the truth.

'I said to her what I have said to you before, Mistress: if Yahweh spoke those words, then they are true. And then I reminded her that the words we heard today prophesied the people of Judah being carried away to Babylon.' Her hands left Nehushta's skin, and the necklace held. Her voice softened. 'I said that if Yahweh could allow our last king to be exiled to Egypt, then He could allow all Judah to be taken to Babylon.'

Nehushta turned to face her. 'And she asked you if that would even be true of King Jehoiakim?'

Dinah looked her mistress in the eye and nodded. 'And I said yes.'

The battle within began again, but Nehushta's hunger and her own fear allowed the baser force the upper hand. 'Peninnah has more sense in this than you!' Her eyes flashed. 'You must keep your pious notions to yourself. Do you understand? The king called the words treacherous lies. Did you not hear with your own ears what the king intends to do to Jeremiah and his scribe?'

Dinah looked down and spoke softly again. 'I'm sorry, Mistress. Peninnah asked me a question and I only wished to answer truthfully.'

'Well, if anyone outside this room ever asks you such a question again,' she hissed, 'then do what any fool would know to do—lie!' She snatched the shawl that Dinah had found, flung it around herself and marched out of the room without another word.

The chill of the corridor swiftly cooled both her arms and the fire within. By the time she was standing outside the king's chamber, shivering, the flesh on her arms was like that of a plucked pigeon. She wished for warmth inside. The door was opened to her and she entered, her mind settled for the moment on one matter only: she had no desire—and could not afford—to lose the king's favour over the words of a prophet.

She smiled and made every effort to ensure her eyes did not linger on the tray bearing the remnants of Eliakim's meal as it was borne past her in the opposite direction. The room was, however, warmer. He rose from the table, goblet in hand. 'My king.' She bowed low to him. The expression that met her as she straightened up was one of approval. 'You must forgive me if I have kept you waiting.'

He flicked his free hand dismissively. 'It is no matter. I was still eating.' He led her to the couch and sat her down beside him, removing her shawl and tossing it aside with the same lack of care he had shown for the cut papyrus. He noticed her arms. 'Ah—you will soon be warmed by the king's company.'

She set an enticing smile on her face and her hand lightly upon his. 'I know it, my king. There is nowhere I would rather be on a winter's night—or any night.' She waited. *It was for the king to decide where their conversation would go—and it could go ill if she spoke of a day he might wish to forget.* But it seemed he could no more avoid it than she could.

'And what of being in the king's presence earlier? Did it enliven a cold winter's day for my wife?'

'It did indeed, my king.' She waited again.

'My actions seemed to draw the disapproval of your father, though.' He leaned back against the couch, lifted the goblet to his lips and drank. He ran his tongue along his lower lip and looked steadily at her. 'What does the daughter think?'

His eyes gave him away. He expected only one answer and she would give it. 'The king's actions were bold. The words were dangerous, and he was shrewd enough to do what was needed. King Jehoiakim's subjects should be pleased to have such a zealous king.' She ignored both the voice within, which told her where the danger really lay, and the powerful, compelling voice she had heard earlier that day.

281

'And when we find the source of the poison, we shall treat them as we would a brood of vipers or any other venomous snake.' He took another swig of wine and put the goblet down. He took both her hands in his and squeezed them until it was almost too painful for Nehushta. 'We will continue to worship Baal and honour the Queen of Heaven—and we will see just whose words prevail!'

As Nehushta lay in the bed, she turned over yet again, and pulled the covers up against the cold—and against the sound of snoring. But it was not only her husband's noisy breathing keeping her awake. However much she tried to suppress it, or divert her mind from it, the words on the scroll were as insistent as the crying of a hungry child, demanding attention. She wondered how Eliakim's slumber seemed so untroubled. And among the intrusive words were some that had been among the first to be burned. *My people have committed two sins: they have forsaken me, the spring of living water, and have dug their own cisterns, broken cisterns that cannot hold water.*

When she finally drifted into sleep, it was not the bliss of oblivion. Her dream was of a desert and of potsherds scattered everywhere. Whenever she came across a clay jar full of water, it shattered as soon as she touched it, its contents draining away in an instant into the parched sandy ground. And among the broken pottery were altars whose idols leered at her and from which children's arms of bones reached out, trying to grasp her as she searched in vain for water. Even when the dream forced her awake, the fear stayed with her as the darkness of the room pressed in on her. All was silent except for her husband's breathing. She told herself that all was well, that it was only a dream. She edged closer to Eliakim under the covers. *But what if she was wrong?*

Notes

1. *The events of this chapter take place in 604 BC. The fast in the ninth month of Jehoiakim's fifth year and Jehoiakim's burning of Jeremiah's scroll (Jeremiah 36:9-26) are generally taken to be in December of that year.*

2. The temperature in Jerusalem in winter can get down to freezing point occasionally, although it is more normal for it to be around 10-14 degrees C during the daytime.

3. It is not clear if women would have taken part in either the gathering at the temple or the fast.

4. Our knowledge of the clothing of the time is imprecise. The descriptions in Isaiah 3:18-23 of the finery of the women of Jerusalem give some pointers, although the Hebrew terms used for both the items of clothing and the accessories are translated in a variety of different ways. There is, therefore, a certain amount of speculation in this chapter and elsewhere.

5. Jeremiah 36:5 describes Jeremiah being restricted at this time so that he was not allowed into the temple. It is not clear in what way Jeremiah was restrained, or for what exact reason, although he may have been forbidden to enter the temple after the events of 19:1-20:6.

6. Jeremiah 36:22 speaks of the king sitting in 'the winter apartment' with a 'fire burning in a brazier'. Again, there are no additional details to allow a more precise understanding of these terms, although it is likely that the winter apartment was away from the outer walls of the palace and in a place where heat was retained more easily. The brazier could be either a portable metal container or a fixed hearth. The use of charcoal would ensure very little smoke or fumes.

7. Not all the prophecies of Jeremiah are dated, so it is impossible to know exactly which oracles were written on the scroll that Jehoiakim burned. The words that had been dictated by Jeremiah covered all his prophesies (beginning in the reign of Josiah) until that point (Jeremiah 36:2). Jeremiah was later instructed to dictate to Baruch once again all the words that had been on the scroll, 'And many similar words were added to them'. (Jeremiah 36:32).

8. Jerahmeel is described in Jeremiah 36:26 as 'a son of the king'. As Jehoiakim was around thirty at this time and Jehoiachin (Jeconiah) only around eleven, it is more likely that this term refers to a favoured or special servant rather than an actual son.

9. Bullae (pieces of clay with seal impressions) have been discovered from this period. One has been found with the name 'Berachyahu son of Neriyahu the scribe', which may be Jeremiah's Baruch as he is named in Jeremiah 32:16 as 'Baruch son of Neriah'. Another bears the name of Gemaryahu

(a variant spelling of Gemariah), the son of Shaphan—also named in Jeremiah 36:10.

10. *All the girls discussed as a potential wife are fictional.*

6

During Jehoiakim's reign, Nebuchadnezzar king of Babylon invaded the land, and Jehoiakim became his vassal for three years. But then he turned against Nebuchadnezzar and rebelled. (2 Kings 24:1)

Nehushta glided around the palace courtyard as effortlessly as an eagle riding the winds. The enclosed garden, open to the warmth and sunshine of the spring day, was filled with the chatter of women and the fragrance from small lamps burning perfumed oil. She basked in the deference that every mother and daughter afforded her—bowing and smiling, listening attentively to her every word. She had not mentioned the word *betrothal* in the invitations to Jerusalem's high-born families, but all knew why they were there. Each mother had dressed the girl at her side in a manner that proclaimed only one thing: *I am a fitting wife for the future king.*

The wife of Jerahmeel and her eldest were standing beneath a fig tree. Both bobbed their heads as Nehushta approached. They exchanged greetings and then pleasantries for as long as Nehushta could bear. *The latest child conceived, the elegance of her dress, the worth of a gifted goldsmith or a dazzling dye.* Throughout it all, she scrutinised every handbreadth of the girl: her hair, her eyes, the fullness of her figure, down to the size of her ankles and the shape of her toes. It was as Zebidah had once done with her.

As a steward refilled their goblets, Nehushta casually asked, 'And has your husband found the prophet Jeremiah or his scribe yet, as King Jehoiakim commanded?' She waited, sipping and then savouring the wine blended with honey, spices, and water from the Gihon spring.

The other woman tensed, gripping her goblet more tightly. More than two years had passed since the king had given the order.

'Jerusalem is a large city, Mistress, and there are many places to hide. If they are, indeed, still in the city.'

Nehushta cocked her head slightly. 'Two men cannot disappear like a summer mist.' She studied the alarmed face of Jerahmeel's pretty daughter. The girl suddenly seemed to find her spiced wine of great interest. Nehushta relented. 'But the king trusts Jerahmeel, I know. He will, I am sure, hunt his prey until they are both as mice between the paws of a lion.'

The other woman's face eased. 'He will not let the king down.'

Nehushta continued sifting her guests, lowering some of the girls in her estimation whilst elevating others. Both Dinah and Peninnah stood waiting in the shade of the north-facing wall should she need them. She had no doubt that Peninnah would be commenting on each garment—and the girl within.

When every mother and daughter had finally left, Nehushta sank down onto a bench on which Dinah had placed an embroidered cushion for her. She studied the two servants as they lifted another bench at her instruction to put it near hers. Dinah had served her faithfully for fifteen years now, Peninnah for longer. Although far beneath her in rank, they were, amongst the women of the city, the two whom she trusted most and with whom she could speak her mind without needing much care. Dinah had never, to her knowledge, repeated any words spoken in private to another. Peninnah had learned the lesson swiftly—and the hard way. *If they wished to discuss her, they had each other—though different as milk and wine.*

For a while, Nehushta was content to listen to her servants' views. Some of the girls had, indeed, flowered since they had first considered them in the winter-house more than two years earlier. Nehushta closed her eyes. Her mind wandered in the afternoon warmth to matters more pressing than even her son's marriage.

'Mistress?' Dinah's voice returned her to the courtyard. 'Does something trouble you?'

Nehushta breathed in the fragranced air. 'I am wondering if the scouts will bring fresh news today.'

'The palace seems to have been discussing little else,' replied Dinah. It had been that way ever since word came of the Babylonian army marching south towards Egypt.

'My father tells me that even if Nebuchadnezzar cannot make Egypt his vassal—which would certainly be to his gain—he will want to keep Necho out of these lands which he now considers his own.' Her servants waited whilst she drank from her goblet. 'He may have been the victor at Carchemish, but my father is not so sure that defeating Egypt on its own borders will be so easy.' She shrugged and gave a little smile. 'If a battle between Babylon and Egypt ends with both being sapped of strength, Judah may yet be well served by Nebuchadnezzar's ambitions.' Eliakim had told her as much.

Nehushta had rarely seen the king in such a good mood, his pleasure that of a victor, though no Judean sword had been drawn. He had summoned his officials on the last day of the month, seating Jeconiah on his right and the queen mother on his left. Nehushta, dressed lavishly at his command, stood nearby. She knew why Eliakim had assembled them. As silence gradually fell on the room, every eye turned to the king.

'As you will have heard,' he began, 'Nebuchadnezzar has returned to his own land, unable to conquer Pharaoh Necho. We now know from our scouts, however, that both armies have suffered heavy loss in the slaughter and been greatly weakened.' He let his words sink in. 'Whilst some in this city have prophesied doom at the hand of the Babylonians—' He did not need to name Jeremiah. '—their oracles have been shown to be false. Empty. Worthy of only contempt. They have wasted their breath.' He clearly relished every word. 'Rather than devastating our lands, the Babylonians have left them, defeated. Like a lion skulking away when fatally mauled by a bear. I have, therefore, decided that it is now time to throw off the yoke of Babylon. We will no longer be their vassal, sending them our gold and silver and bowing to their rule. Judah is now free once more!'

Cheering began in the great hall. Nehushta suspected that Eliakim had instructed a number to begin shouting in triumph on his words. But it mattered little. The cries of triumph were swiftly echoed by all assembled. Or so it seemed until she caught sight of her father. His eyes were firmly fixed far above them. His lips moved, but she knew it was in prayer, not in words of celebration.

After the king had decreed that the new moon should be celebrated by great feasting in the palace and throughout Jerusalem, the assembly had dispersed. Nehushta, however, made her way to the roof, sending a message to her father to join her. If she needed privacy in the palace, it was there she was most likely to find it. Looking down on the city from above, she could see the exultant mood already spilling out onto its streets, people pausing to greet one another and share the story of Judah's new freedom. Her father, however, was still the bitter gourd in a bowl of ripe, sweet fruit.

'Nehushta.' She turned. 'I am sorry to keep you waiting.'

She barely waited for her father to kiss her on both cheeks before berating him. 'I saw you in the assembly. Why could you not rejoice with all those around you? Why must you always be the lament among songs of joy? The king's own father-in-law seems incapable of loyalty to his lord!'

He sighed and took her hands in his. She tried to pull away, but he held her firmly. 'My dear daughter, it pains me to know that my actions upset you so. But I do not share the king's confidence that Babylon is a spent force.'

Nehushta's eyes flashed, her words sharp as a keen blade. 'Your own thoughts or those of the prophet?' She pulled again, and he let her go.

'Both. Nebuchadnezzar suffered great loss on Egypt's borders, but he was not shattered. It is too early to say whether he will rise in power again or not—and I am not alone in Jerusalem in thinking that. Your husband is proud but so is the Babylonian king, and weakened though he is, the reach of his hand is still greater than that of Judah.'

'You dare to think that the king is wrong to rebel?'

He sighed again and ran a hand through his greying hair. 'I fear that he may have acted in haste, but it matters little what I think.

Know this, though: just because the prophet's words are unfulfilled now, it does not mean they will remain so.'

She lifted her chin. She had no desire to continue their conversation—or for her father to be right. 'The king has shown his strength and boldness, and I intend to celebrate Judah's freedom. That is all I have to say. You may go.'

'Very well.' Elnathan leaned forward and kissed her forehead. 'May Yahweh watch over and protect you, my daughter—whatever lies ahead.'

Nehushta watched in silence as her father left her, his shoulders bowed as if bearing a great burden. She remembered her husband's rage at being abased by the king of Babylon. *It was little wonder he wished to be rid of Nebuchadnezzar's heavy hand upon him.* She did not want to think, however, of what might happen if Eliakim *was* wrong. She shivered, but then looked down on Jerusalem's streets once more—and determined to dispel any bitter taste with freely flowing sweet wine and drown out doubting voices with jubilant songs.

In the remaining months of that year and in the year that followed, the rebellion against Nebuchadnezzar appeared shrewd. Judah's prosperity stayed within its borders and in its own hands. Babylon was soon supplanted in Nehushta's mind by the matter of a wife for Jeconiah as he reached fifteen. It was also a welcome distraction from her life as Eliakim's wife. For the truth—though she could speak of it to no one—was that the longer her husband was king, the more he repelled rather attracted her, the more there was to fear than to relish. It was impossible for her to remain blind to it. Servants and officials lived in dread of his displeasure. Young women and girls existed only for his gratification and could be discarded after use. The powerless were only tools to be wielded or wells to be sucked dry. But the more his hands grasped, the less satisfied he seemed. But she could still wear the mask of approval, lavishing adoration upon him when required. In seeking a wife for the king's son, others would see only her devotion to the kingdom and its king—and she would have a more agreeable way to spend her days.

After Jeconiah's first wife was selected, a second and a third were chosen in the following two years. She was keen for the king's heir to bear his own son, and she chose well, each new wife swiftly conceiving. Her days were soon filled with grandsons—and with ensuring that her daughters-in-laws did her bidding.

'Dinah—take a message for me to each of Coniah's wives. All should be present tomorrow to celebrate the second birthday of Shealtiel, not just his mother and grandmothers.'

Dinah put down the purple garment she was mending and rose. 'It will be done, Mistress.'

'But find Shimron also. Tell him to let the king and Coniah both know that they are welcome to join us tomorrow, and we will be honoured by their presence. It will be a feast fit not only for the king's eldest grandson, but for the king himself.' Dinah bowed to her and left. Nehushta then continued her task of planning the extravagant celebration. She had already given instructions to prepare a fattened calf for roasting and a lamb for stewing. There would be breads flavoured with herbs and cheese, as well as with honey and fruits. Platters of prepared melons and figs would grace the table, all accompanied by an abundance of both spiced wine and pomegranate juice. She was determined that her every wish would be fulfilled. That day and the one after were both pleasurably passed ensuring it was so.

Nehushta led her two-year-old grandson around the tables laden with food and circled by guests. She had swiftly decided that sitting next to two empty places at her table would risk an appearance of having been snubbed by both her husband and her son. She masked her annoyance at their absence with feigned graciousness as she both greeted those at the feast and presented Shealtiel to them, his small blue robe studded with lapis lazuli. He seemed only too pleased to be the centre of attention.

'Will the king be joining us this evening?' The question from the wife of Mattaniah, Eliakim's younger brother, needled her. She cloaked it with a face of gravity.

'If the affairs of the kingdom allow him. They are a heavy burden and an unceasing one—I see it daily.' She sighed, smiled and then lied. 'I have little expectation that the king and his son will be able to join us tonight—but we will rejoice if they do so.' She decided to end the conversation. She tugged lightly at the small hand in hers. 'Come, Shealtiel. Let us greet some more of our guests.'

Nehushta had not progressed much beyond Mattaniah's wife when the room filled with the sound of chairs scraping across the stone floor. Those around her started rising to their feet. *She had her wish!* She smiled as she turned to see both husband and son enter, bowing low as her eyes met those of Eliakim. She squeezed Shealtiel's hand. 'Your grandfather, the king, is here. Let us go and sit with him.'

Nehushta swept her satisfied gaze slowly across the room as she made her way to her seat on the king's left. She kept her smile fixed even as she recognised the ill mood upon him. He already had his goblet of wine to his lips by the time she had taken her seat, with the two-year-old needing no encouragement to join his father on the other side of the king. She laid her hand on Eliakim's arm. 'The king does not look as happy as I would wish him to be.'

He drained the goblet and set it down heavily. She quickly signalled for a servant to refill it. He clenched his fist and then opened it. 'The bands of raiders.' He spat the words out. 'They come like swarms of wasps upon our land, stinging where they choose.'

'Arameans again?'

'If it was just Aram coming from the north, that would be curse enough. Now we have bands from Moab and Ammon coming against us on the east.' He jerked his arm away from hers to pull towards him a choice cut from the roast calf. He picked up the knife set for him. 'And I know what some in the palace are whispering. They see the hand of Babylon in the raids—and they blame me for it.' He thrust the blade into rich meat and hacked off a large piece. 'They suppose that Nebuchadnezzar seeks to punish us for casting off his yoke—getting his vassals to harry us whilst he remains weak from his whipping by Necho. Whether the hand of Babylon is in it or not, the sting hurts Judah the same.' He lifted the portion and sunk his teeth into it.

She tried to soothe him. 'The king mustn't let these things trouble him tonight. I took Shealtiel to the temple earlier. We offered sacrifices on the altar of Baal and burned incense for the king. Surely the raids will pass.'

'They will swarm back to their nests when winter comes, I am sure. But that is still some months off.'

She picked up the king's goblet to give it to him. His eyes were lingering on a young servant girl. *Clearly his latest whim.* 'But Judah is still free—' He turned and snatched the goblet, spilling some of its wine. '—and better times *will* come with the winter. You will see.'

His attention was elsewhere.

She had heard it first more than ten years earlier when news had reached the city of Josiah's fall in battle; then again when Necho set Eliakim on the throne in his brother's stead. Now she heard it a third time: *the city was disturbed.* The clamour was mounting, and she knew not why. The winter's day cooled her arms and face, but her growing foreboding caused a chill whose cold fingers reached far deeper within.

Dinah was staring at her. The noise and shouting were impossible to ignore. 'Mistress?'

'Go—now! Find out what is happening and tell me as soon as you are sure you have its truth.'

Even before Dinah was out of the room, Nehushta turned towards the window. She pulled back the hangings and stared out into the colourless day under the heavy grey clouds. She looked down on the streets below and saw only one thing: *fear.* Even before Dinah's return, she had caught more than once the name from which the dread sprang. Her stomach churned as the Jordan in flood.

The door opened and she turned. Dinah had not been gone long. 'Is it Babylon?'

'Yes, Mistress. Word has arrived that their army has been seen near Riblah, marching south.'

Nehushta bit her lip. 'Was there anything more?'

'That is all I heard, my mistress.' She paused, looking Nehushta in the eye. 'Might it be that they are marching against Egypt once more?'

'How should I know?' she retorted. She turned towards the window once more and made a swift decision. 'Find Peninnah and then fetch my cloak!' As soon as the door closed behind her, she rested a hand on the table to steady herself. The image in her mind was of her husband in chains, prostrate, when he had sworn his oath of loyalty to Nebuchadnezzar. Her mouth was dry. *What would be the penalty for the broken pledge?* She did not suppose it would be a second chance. It was almost exactly six years since they had received news of Ashkelon's destruction at the hand of the Babylonians—and of its nobles being deported from the land. *But might it be, as Dinah had suggested, that they were once more rising against Egypt rather than Judah?* The pit of her belly said otherwise.

When her cloak was finally around her, and four guards as well as her two maids at her side, Nehushta made her way to the temple, tight-lipped, despite the clamour in the city. She bore a casket of incense in her hands and a single intention in her heart: to sacrifice not only to Yahweh but to every god whose altar was there, be they Baal or the Queen of Heaven or any other of the gods that the city had embraced. *Had that not, after all, been the way of their people ever since they had made their home in the land of Canaan? Seeking the favour of the gods whose land it had been before it was theirs, bowing down to and honouring them alongside Yahweh?*

'How soon will the Babylonians reach the city?'

Peninnah's shrill query riled her. 'We do not know they are coming here,' she snapped, 'so do not ask questions like those of a foolish child.' She kept her eyes forward. 'If you had a gerah of sense, Peninnah, you would know that they will not be sending a herald to tell us. Until a scout sees the path they take after passing Galilee, we will not know what their intentions are.' Her scorn silenced any further conversation.

The temple was crowded. She was not the only one seeking favour—or deliverance—from those who could wield the power of thunder and storms rather than chariots and swords. As usual, a path cleared before her, but it was not just deference she saw in those around her. There was defiance. Resentment. She remembered her husband's words: *they see the hand of the king of Babylon...and they blame me.* Suddenly, it was inescapable. *If Babylon attacked Jerusalem, many would see it as the fault of Eliakim. Would she be blamed too?* She tried to put the thought from her mind and stared instead at the glowing coals on the altar to Baal, watching as her incense began to yield fragrant smoke that swirled upwards towards the grey sky, with prayers to Baal from those around her filling her ears.

Suddenly, she was beholding a brazier again, a scroll rather than incense burning upon the coals. *My people have committed two sins.* She didn't want to remember the words, but they were etched upon her mind more enduringly even than ink upon papyrus and could not be erased. *They have forsaken me, the spring of living water, and have dug their own cisterns, broken cisterns that cannot hold water.* She closed her eyes firmly. Unbidden, the words of Yahweh that her own father had impressed upon her since she was the age of Shealtiel came into her mind: *You shall have no other gods before me.*

Nehushta stared northwards. It had only been two weeks since she had offered her incense. Her hands gripped the parapet around the palace roof, her gaze fixed. 'Dinah—when Coniah was young, you once said that he would fear those things that he couldn't see more than those he could.' She swallowed. 'Such truth does not hold for those of us who have put childhood behind us and who behold the coming of Babylon.' Although the advancing army was still some distance away, the winter sun was glinting off what Nehushta supposed to be shields, helmets and chariots. Already, they were a huge swarm on the hillside, and she had no idea how many more were yet to come into view. She had touched no food that morning—and little since they had learned that the army's path was towards Jerusalem. Her appetite had dried up like a puddle in summer heat. Some moments passed. 'Eliakim says that the Egyptians will come to our aid, since Babylon is our common enemy...' Her voice sounded far away.

'We must put our trust in Yahweh.' Dinah spoke softly but firmly. 'He alone is our deliverer.'

Nehushta didn't reply. Both watched in silence as the morning continued to slip by.

'My mistress!'

The urgency of the voice tore Nehushta's eyes away from the Judean hills. She turned.

One of the palace officials was hurrying towards her, chest heaving. 'Your father bids you come. He waits at your room. You must come now!' He stood staring at her, wide-eyed. Nehushta hesitated. 'It cannot wait, Mistress.'

Nehushta's heart thundered as they made their way down the steps and towards her room, her chest tight. All she could think of was that some terrible fate had befallen her son or one of her grandsons. *Had Eliakim slaughtered one as a sacrifice to Molech as the Babylonian army approached?* She knew all too well the dark deeds of which he was capable. The corridor suddenly seemed to recede from her.

'Here, Mistress—take my arm.'

Nehushta felt Dinah wrapping her arm around her own, supporting her. She suddenly realised she was trembling.

Her father was standing outside her room, watching her approach. He seemed far older than she had ever seen him, his face grave as he opened the door for them. Dinah steered Nehushta through the doorway, and Elnathan closed it behind them.

'Dinah—take your mistress to a seat.'

Nehushta could barely breathe as she sat down. 'What has happened?' she whispered. 'Tell me. Is it Jeconiah?'

'No.' He looked straight at her. 'The king is dead.'

The words didn't make any sense. She stared at him, bewildered. She felt Dinah's hand rest lightly upon her shoulder. 'Eliakim? He can't be. I saw him yesterday. He was saying—'

Her father cut in. 'Nehushta.' He knelt before her, taking her hands in his. 'Listen to me. Your husband is dead.' He spoke the words slowly and deliberately, as if to a child.

Nehushta frowned. It was as if she was trying to grasp an oiled snake. *Eliakim was only thirty-six.* Eventually she whispered, 'How?'

Elnathan sighed and shook his head slowly. 'We're not sure.'

'What do you mean?'

He shook his head again. 'Nehushta, this will be hard for you to bear, but it is better that you hear it from my lips.'

She stared at him, feeling only dread. 'Why? What has happened?'

'It seems Eliakim was murdered, maybe by some within the palace.' She waited for him to continue. 'Whoever killed him then deposited his body outside the city gates, which are now shut tight.' He paused again. 'It may be that those who did this are seeking to appease the Babylonians, since it was Eliakim's rebellion that kindled their wrath and brought them here.'

The words finally sank in. 'And leaving his body for them to find…' she added quietly.

'That is right.'

Nehushta didn't reply. In the silence, it suddenly struck her that the city seemed unusually quiet.

Elnathan lifted Nehusta's hands. 'And now, my daughter, you must be strong. You must come with me, for Coniah must now be made king. He will be known as King Jehoiachin.' He turned slightly. 'Dinah—fetch a suitable robe for your mistress. She is now the queen mother, and the crown that was on Zebidah's head is about to be placed upon hers.' He stood and kissed Nehushta on the forehead.

She suddenly looked up—and for the first time, anguish crept into her voice. 'What about the Babylonians? How will Coniah know what to do? He is barely eighteen!'

'We cannot know what tomorrow will bring, but it is in the hands of Yahweh. We must put our trust in Him.' He let go of her hands. 'I will see you in the throne room.' He began walking towards the door but then stopped. He turned around slowly. For a moment it seemed as if he was pondering a decision. Then it was made. He looked straight at his daughter once again. 'Nehushta—the prophet Jeremiah spoke of Jehoiakim by name—and spoke of his death. It has come to pass, just as he foretold.'

The words had been seared upon her mind. *'The burial of a donkey...'* she murmured, staring at her father's face, but not seeing it. *'...dragged away and thrown outside the gates of Jerusalem.'*

'We must prepare ourselves for the fulfilment of all that Yahweh has said. There is no better way to do that than by humbling ourselves before the Almighty, throwing ourselves on His mercy—and putting away every idol that brings His judgment upon this nation.' His eyes pleaded with her. 'It is too late for Eliakim now, but it is not too late for you, my daughter. Heed the prophet's words.' He paused, then turned and left, closing the door behind him.

Nehushta sat for a moment, staring at the door. She suddenly wondered why she did not weep or wail. Despite her shock she felt little grief, her tears dried up like a wadi in summer. *Still, it could pass as being strong.*

She left her room a short while later, accompanied by both Dinah and Peninnah as well as palace guards. The corridors were quiet. She remembered how it had been when Josiah died—the weeping, the rent garments, the bare feet. She knew what else Jeremiah had foretold: *They will not weep for him.* But it was all too much to take in. *Eliakim's sudden death. A conspiracy. Coniah now king. The Babylonians approaching the city. Jeremiah's words. Her father's plea.* She took a deep breath as they walked along, lifting her head that was about to be crowned. *For now, for today, she would set her mind on one matter only: she was now foremost among the women. She was now queen mother.*

The reign of Nehushta's son was as short-lived as that of his uncle. Before Eliakim, Shallum had sat upon the throne for barely three months before his rule was cut short by the Egyptian pharaoh. The knife that severed Jeconiah's rule was wielded by the Babylonian king. Nebuchadnezzar's army had surrounded Jerusalem, like the hands of a priest around the neck of a sacrificial dove, severing it from its lifeblood. The siege lasted only from winter until early spring.

On the day that the city surrendered, Nehushta knew only terror. She watched from the palace entrance as her son left, heading for the city gates through which he would leave Jerusalem to meet both his conquerors and his fate. She wailed, caring little who saw her and clinging to Dinah as tightly as she done to Coniah as she had said her farewell to him. His face had been white, and he had been shaking as a leaf in an autumn wind. She knew that the gates would not be shut behind him, but would be left open for the Babylonians soldiers to stream in. Jerusalem and its every citizen were now at the mercy of Nebuchadnezzar—and all he desired to do to them, be they lowly servant or queen mother.

'What will…they do…to us?' Nehushta's words were shaky, formed from gulps of air between her sobs. *Rape. Slavery. Maiming. Death.* Every fear had free rein in her mind. 'We are…in their hands.'

'The hands of Yahweh are greater,' whispered Dinah. 'This is as the prophet said, so be strong, Mistress. Yahweh's words of mercy are as sure as His words of judgment.' After Nehushta's fresh sobbing had subsided, Dinah added, 'Surrendering swiftly may mean they deal with Coniah and with us less severely. But whatever lies ahead, you must eat something. It will give you some strength.'

Nehushta took a deep breath and slowly released her servant from her grip. She stared at Dinah—she was pale but calm. Suddenly she blurted out, 'Pray for me, Dinah. Pray to Yahweh for me.'

Dinah took her hands in her own. 'We will return to your room, Mistress, and we will call on Yahweh together.'

Notes

1. *The events in this chapter take place in 601-597 BC.*
2. *Jeremiah 36:26 records that neither Jeremiah nor Baruch were found by those sent by Jehoiakim to search for them: 'the LORD had hidden them.' This was most likely with the aid of human agents, given there were a number (including Elnathan) sympathetic to Jeremiah's words.*
3. *It is not clear exactly when Jehoiakim rebelled against Babylon, but the most obvious time is shortly after the Babylonians suffered great loss when they engaged the Egyptians in 601 BC. Babylonian chronicles report that Nebuchadnezzar did not embark upon any campaigns in 600/599 BC.*

Then in 599/8 BC, the Babylonians only 'flexed their muscles' against their nearer neighbours, the Syrian Arabs. It is possible that Jehoiakim also hoped that Egypt would become his ally when he rebelled against Babylon, coming to his aid, if needed, particularly as he had been put upon the throne by Necho.

4. According to Babylonian records, both the Moabites and Ammonites were subjects of Babylon. They may well have been required by Nebuchadnezzar to send raiders against a rebellious neighbour, to cause problems for them until the Babylonians were able to take direct action against Judah—although Scripture records this as part of Yahweh's punishment upon the land (2 Kings 24:2).

5. Jehoiachin is recorded as having a number of wives (2 Kings 24:15) and a number of sons (1 Chronicles 3:17-18), the oldest of whom seems to have been Shealtiel. Babylonian sources also state that five years after his exile, Jehoiachin had five children.

6. The Babylonian army marched against Jerusalem in the very month that Jehoiakim died—December 598 BC. Exactly what brought about Jehoiakim's death is not clear. The Jewish historian Josephus states that Jehoiakim was killed in Jerusalem by Nebuchadnezzar. This, however, does not accord with the siege that led up to the end of Jehoiachin's reign. Jeremiah 22:18-19 states, however, that Jehoiakim would not be mourned and would have 'the burial of a donkey—dragged away and thrown outside the gates of Jerusalem'. Jeremiah also prophesied (in 36:30), 'his body will be thrown out and exposed to the heat by day and the frost by night'. Some commentators (such as John Bright in 'The History of Israel') suggest that he was assassinated in the hope of being treated more leniently by the Babylonians. This view has been adopted here. Martin Selman also suggests in his commentary on 2 Chronicles that the lack of any mention of Jehoiakim's burial reflects these prophecies of Jeremiah and is also a regular mark of dishonour in Chronicles.

7. Kenneth Kitchen states that the Babylonian Chronicle notes that the Babylonians 'besieged the city of Judah [i.e., its capital, Jerusalem], and on second of Adar [15/16 March 597] he took the city and seized the king. A king of his own choosing he appointed (instead), received its massive tribute and sent them to Babylon.' (Kitchen, p44). This is the siege

recorded in 2 Kings 24:10-11. Regarding the short siege: 'The relative ease with which the city was captured may be explained by the fact that it was during winter and food would have been scarce. The city's population would have been much larger than normal, since those in the outlying areas of Judah sought refuge in Jerusalem... The quick surrender by Judah may be the reason why the Babylonians were somewhat lenient in their treatment of the Judahites.' (OTBBC, p411).

8. Scripture does not describe Nehushta's relationship with King Jehoiakim. However, given 'the detestable things he did and all that was found against him' (2 Chronicles 36:8), and the references to dishonest gain, shedding innocent blood, oppression and extortion (Jeremiah 22:17), it seems reasonable to imagine her coming to dislike and fear him. Although there are no explicit references to his sexual immorality, again it seems reasonable to suppose that he engaged in it, given the behaviour of other kings and the link between the worship of Canaanite (and other) gods and such immorality.

7

*Nebuchadnezzar took Jehoiachin captive to Babylon. He also took
from Jerusalem to Babylon the king's mother, his wives, his officials
and the prominent people of the land. (2 Kings 24:15)*

Nehushta opened her eyes. The light of day was already streaming
in through the coarsely woven cloth that Dinah had hung over
the window the previous night. The low bed beneath her was old,
constructed roughly of cheap wood and with sacking to lie on instead
of a mattress. Sweet-smelling cedar, carved with pomegranates and
leaves and crowned with colourful Egyptian linen, was now only
a memory from a distant land. But it was a bed, and the first one
she had slept on since they had been forcibly marched away from
Jerusalem over two months earlier.

The prone form of Dinah lying on the ground by the wall created
a small, dark hummock. It suddenly recalled the sloping Judean
hillside, the only landscape she had ever known. Until, that is, the
journey that had shown her Mount Hermon, capped with snow, the
wide Euphrates besides which the Jordan was a brook, and the flat,
seemingly unending plain between the two mighty rivers of Babylon.
It had also shown her hunger, exhaustion, blisters, shame—and was a
journey she would rather forget.

She suddenly yawned loudly. Dinah stirred, and then rolled over
so she was facing Nehushta.

'Did you sleep well, Mistress?'

The title was a reminder of a different life. 'You know there is no
need to call me that now.'

'But you are still queen mother—and that is why you have this
house.'

'Dinah—there is another king in Jerusalem now, and Hamutal will bear the queen mother's gold circlet once more.'

'But even as we travelled, people still spoke of Jeconiah as king.'

Nehushta fell silent. *Dinah's words were true.* But they had seemed like mockery every time she had heard them, though never the speaker's intention. She had seen her son from afar, utterly humiliated by the Babylonians. Whilst they walked freely, he was bound with bronze shackles—as Eliakim had once been. She had longed to run to him, but he was kept separate from them, bearing alone the fruit of his father's folly. 'I slept well,' she murmured finally, though wondering at that moment where her son was. His path had taken him—and his sons—to Babylon; theirs, further south. *Was he still wearing his shackles? Was he even seeing the light of a new day, as she was, or was he confined in some dark, dank prison? And what of her young grandsons?* Dinah's soft voice cut in on her agonised questions.

'I did too.' She smiled. 'It is a blessing to sleep without being woken by either the shout of a soldier or the first light of dawn.'

Nehushta rolled onto her back and looked up, 'As it is to have a roof over our heads—of sorts.' The ceiling above her was letting in light. She was silent for several moments, musing. She knew Dinah was right—honour *was* still afforded her and her family. When they had arrived at the deserted settlement allocated to them by the Babylonians, she had been allotted the largest house of the few that still stood, though it had clearly suffered seasons of neglect. She breathed in deeply of the Babylonian air before letting it out in a sigh. 'I have thought often of Josiah in these last few days.' She paused. 'Two of his sons ruled Judah after him, and then a grandson. Now Josiah's youngest son is on the throne, ruling over those left in Judah.' The news had reached them shortly after leaving Jerusalem that Eliakim's brother had been made king and would rule as *Zedekiah*, the new name Nebuchadnezzar had imposed upon him. 'Yet Shallum is imprisoned in Egypt, if he still even lives, Eliakim is dead, and Mattaniah only rules at the behest of Babylon. Such has been Josiah's heritage.' She could not bring herself to speak of Jeremiah's prophecy, during her son's brief reign, that Jeconiah would never have a son upon the throne. *That he and the mother who bore him would be hurled into a land where neither were born—and where both would die.* 'It is dismal,' she finally added, still staring upwards. 'And I know what you would say.'

'Mistress?'

'That it would have been different if the sons had feared Yahweh as their father had.' She fell silent, and Dinah didn't reply. They had spoken much of the God of Israel as they had trudged further and further from His temple. For the first time in her life, Nehushta had hungered to know of Yahweh. It was as if she was in deep water, unable to swim, and reaching out in desperation for a rope, a hand, a rock, to cling to. Dinah had spoken of Yahweh, the true God—*the only God.* Creator of the heavens and the earth and yet their loving shepherd. Nehushta knew she had heard such words before—from the lips of both Jeremiah and her own father. But she had chosen to forsake the Almighty, and favour instead idols that required incense but neither piety nor purity, gods who left her to please only herself. She was as an adulterous wife. And in the chill of nights under clear skies, she had stared up into the dazzling wonder of the heavens, speckled with myriad pinpricks of light, and felt herself and her guilt laid bare before Yahweh. *Naked as Eve, but lacking any leaves to shroud her shame.*

Out of the corner of her eye, Nehushta saw Dinah rise. She rolled over onto her side again and studied her. Dinah pushed back the cloth over the window. Sunlight suddenly bathed the room with its bare-brick walls.

'The day is already hot.' She turned. 'We should join your mother and father. Sarah has found an oven and is already baking bread outside.'

Nehushta sat up in her bed and shook her head slowly. 'I was so anxious for my parents on the journey. My father is fifty-four and my mother not much less. I need not have feared.' She rose and joined Dinah, looking down from the upper room of the house. Nearby was the cart they had been allowed, which had left Jerusalem piled high with grain and oil from the palace stores and whatever of their possessions they could fit in. Even before the city had surrendered, Dinah had bundled as much of Nehushta's jewellery as she could into hessian pouches, which she had then hidden deep in the sacks of barley and wheat before they were loaded onto the cart. Gold and gems were not shekels of silver, but would more than amply fill their role, wherever they ended up.

'You are right, Dinah. It is indeed already hot. Let us eat and then find water to wash. The grime of our journey feels heavy upon me and upon my tunic.' All but one of her fine garments and pairs of sandals had been left behind, Dinah having purchased simple but durable clothing and footwear for whatever lay ahead. Nehushta studied the unfamiliar landscape outside, then murmured, 'You prepared us well for the journey.' She paused, not taking her eyes off their new land. 'You believed the words of the prophet, didn't you, that we would be taken to Babylon?'

'Yes—and it seemed prudent to be ready for it.'

They were soon sitting on simple mats in the shade of the open courtyard. Nehushta tore off a piece of bread and nibbled it, staring at the brick building, abandoned at some earlier time by its previous occupants. 'Why do you think this place was forsaken?'

Her father shrugged. 'I have wondered that myself. Maybe some pestilence, or maybe the town was taken from the Assyrians and never lived in. Or maybe the settlement somehow incurred the wrath of Nebuchadnezzar. Even in our own history, entire towns in Israel have been put to the sword by their brothers.'

'And what of our future now?' The words hung in the air like a feather, though their weight bore down upon Nehushta's heart. The question wasn't a new one, but there had been few answers on their journey when so little had been known of their final destination—or their fate.

'We are in exile, not in prison,' replied Elnathan eventually. 'As you know, Nebuchadnezzar left most of our people back in Judah, to till its land and pay him tax. But when he stripped the city, the palace and the temple of their gold and their treasures, he also stripped them of their skilled workers. Think of those we travelled with—

craftsmen, metal workers, and palace officials trained in writing and keeping records, maybe as many as a thousand. And several thousand more fighting men to swell his army. He clearly intends us to work and benefit his kingdom—probably at little cost to himself.'

'There is ground here that can be planted,' added Sarah, 'with water nearby.'

Nehushta stared at her mother. 'Do you expect me to grow onions?'

For a moment there was silence, and then laughter—the first for many months. It felt like a draught of cool spring water on a hot summer's day.

Dinah's eyes sparkled. 'I could teach you, Mistress!'

When the laughter died down, Nehushta's mother placed an aging hand upon the servant's smooth arm. 'You could not have served my daughter better, Dinah. I have never regretted my decision to make her your mistress.' She paused. 'But you could have stayed in Jerusalem, as Peninnah did.'

The servant smiled. 'Peninnah had family in the city. You are mine.'

Nehushta returned the smile. During the long journey from Jerusalem, her servant had felt more like a sister. *Both a sister and a faithful friend.*

The settlement, with its few houses and multitude of tents, grew to a small town—*al-Yehuda*, as the Babylonians called it. *Judah-Town.* By the time several months had passed and Nehushta's collection of jewellery had thinned, the house had been repaired, extended and comfortably furnished.

Dinah pulled on her needle, and when the thread was tight, she bit it off, close to the cloth. She turned the finished article over and held the brightly coloured cushion up for Nehushta to see. 'There! With this, we now have a house fit for a queen.'

Nehushta looked up through her eyelashes with a wry smile. 'A queen in exile.' She then lifted her head and tilted it back. 'It is a blessing that the summer has now passed, and we can sit outside in the afternoon.' The intensity of its heat had driven them inside every day when the sun rose high. Even the slivers of shade in the courtyard had been unbearable.

'At least in the hills of Judah we had breezes even in the hottest months,' said Dinah.

'And a palace roof to enjoy them from—with servants to hold shades aloft.' Nehushta laid her needlework in her lap. 'I miss it.' Her heart suddenly ached: for Jerusalem, for the Judean countryside, for all that was familiar. And for her son and grandsons in Babylon, only a four-day journey away though it felt like the ends of the earth. She sighed. 'I wonder how Mattaniah fares as king.'

'He has the prophet Jeremiah to guide him.'

'If he will listen. His brothers didn't.' She paused. 'I didn't—at least, not until it was too late.'

'Maybe it is never too late to start heeding the words of Yahweh.'

'Maybe.' She breathed in the cooler autumn air and caught the scent of some mint planted by Dinah in a clay pot. 'What do you miss most, Dinah?'

'Will it not make you sad to speak of such things?'

Nehushta thought for a moment, staring up into the clear sky. A bird she didn't recognise flew over, alighting in a nearby tree. 'Maybe not all sadness is to be shunned. Maybe there *is* a time to embrace it.' She fell silent and then turned to Dinah. 'Well?'

Dinah gave a little laugh. 'Bread baked with honey and almonds, fresh from the palace ovens.'

The rest of the afternoon was spent sharing their memories, Sarah joining them after her sleep and adding hers. They only ceased when the evening meal needed preparing—not only for themselves, but for the other family members and neighbours who would join them, their larger house having become the heart of their new community. Although Nehushta had discovered afresh the satisfaction of kneading dough, she gained greater pleasure from watching Dinah's skilled hands working the flour and water.

'Is Elnathan not back yet?' asked Dinah suddenly, as she pushed her hair away from her eyes with her forearm. 'Has he not been gone too long?'

Sarah looked up from the cooking pot. 'He went to see Gamariah son of Shaphan.' She smiled wryly. 'And they accuse *us* of unceasing chatter!'

Nehushta knew the official her mother had named. Gamariah had stood alongside Elnathan when the king had burned the prophet's scroll—it had been his son Micaiah who had heard Baruch reading from it in the temple. 'The men will not call it chatter, Mother,' replied Nehushta. 'It is always *discussion*, or *debate*, or *reasoning*.' They laughed.

Dinah paused once again. 'But we do need the wisdom of the elders, do we not, now more than ever? They are our leaders here.'

She had barely resumed kneading when Elnathan entered the courtyard, announcing, 'I have news.' He fetched a small wooden stool and sat down near them. 'News from Babylon.'

Nehushta drew in a sharp breath. 'Of Coniah?' He nodded, and her heart began to race. 'What have you found?'

Elnathan stroked his beard. 'Micaiah travelled to Babylon to trade some gold and spoke at length with some of the merchants. One of them told him that Jeconiah and his sons are held in one of the official buildings, but are provided for. The man said one of his cousins provided them with a regular allowance of oil. And they still call him *the king of Judah*. Nehushta—your son and grandsons may not have their freedom, but they have their lives and are well.'

Nehushta let out her breath. 'Is there more?'

He shook his head. 'No, that is all I have heard of Coniah, and that will have to suffice for the moment. But I have learned more that may cause us to have hope. But—' He held up his hand as Nehushta opened her mouth to speak. '—I will speak of that later when we eat. And there will be more joining us tonight. It is news for us all.'

There were no tables bearing ornate golden dishes laden with rich food from the palace kitchens, but compared to the journey from Jerusalem, the simple food laid out on the assortment of rugs in the courtyard was still a feast. Pottery dishes of both lentil and vegetable stews steamed. All were flavoured with herbs and spices grown in their small settlement or gathered from the land around it. Unadorned wooden platters were piled with fresh bread. The surroundings were humble and the dress of those who had gathered plain, and yet the sky was ablaze with the vibrant colours of evening, besides which even her most vivid palace gown seemed dull. Swallows darted and dived above them against the background of the ever-changing oranges and pinks, seeking insects for their own supper as dusk approached. It suddenly occurred to Nehushta that the decorations of even the best of Jerusalem's craftsmen could not match the beauty of the world created by Yahweh. The far more modest life she now lived seemed to hold pleasures that were less tainted and more satisfying than any the palace had ever offered, particularly under her husband's rule.

Nehushta glanced around her. Family members and friends conversed easily. The faces of many bore more lines and their heads more grey than even a few months before. But the fear of the siege and the weariness of the journey had lifted. *There was sadness, yes, but also calm.* Those assembled soon took their places, seated on the mats around the food. Silence then fell, and Elnathan blessed the meal generously provided by the hand of the Almighty. Then the chatter resumed as the meal began. Dinah no longer stood to one side to wait upon Nehushta's needs. She now sat among them as their equal, dipping her bread in the same dishes.

'Why is it, Mistress, that food eaten under the sky has a taste which has no equal?'

Nehushta chuckled. 'I do not know, Dinah, but you are right.'

Once dishes were empty and the bread on the wooden platters replaced with dates and summer figs gleaned from nearby trees, conversation gradually died down, attention drifting to Elnathan. All had heard he had news from Babylon. By now, small lamps had been lit and scattered around the gathering. They threw their meagre and flickering light on faces that were variously curious, intense or sad, but all attentive.

Nehushta placed the stone of a date on the rug beside her and fixed her eyes on her father.

'My brothers and sisters, you will have heard maybe that Micaiah son of Gamariah has travelled to the city of Babylon recently. He has learned much that may lift our hearts in this place of exile.' He then repeated his earlier words about Jeconiah. Questions were asked to which there were no sure answers, but when all had fallen silent once more, Elnathan continued. 'But that is not all that Micaiah learned.' He paused and a strange smile played upon his lips. 'Many of you will remember the events of the third year of King Jehoiakim, when Nebuchadnezzar first surrounded Jerusalem and Jehoiakim became his vassal. A heavy price was laid upon us then, including of our own bone and flesh. Young men were taken from the nobility, including the royal family. *Our own families.*' He paused, and many shook their heads, sighing, the memory one of deep sorrow. His gaze then swept across the gathering, old and young. 'It seems, however, that the hand of Yahweh has been at work mightily, even in this forfeit.'

Nehushta stared at her father, her heart quickening. *How could it be? What did her father mean?*

'Micaiah was told by one merchant that the Babylonian king often takes into the service of his court the best young men among his captives—those who are most gifted in both body and mind, and able to swiftly learn the skills and knowledge to serve the king.' When he paused, no one stirred or spoke. 'Micaiah was also told that among those taken from Jerusalem eight years ago, there are a number who have already risen to high office. The merchant knew the name of the chief among them—Belteshazzar.' Murmuring rippled around the courtyard, but Elnathan held his hand up. 'Brothers and Sisters—I know what you will say: *that is not a Hebrew name.* You are, of course, right. But as you well know, conquering kings may impose names of their own choice upon those under their sway, to display their authority. So those who serve in Nebuchadnezzar's court no longer have names bearing those of the God of Israel but the gods of Babylon—be they Marduk, Bel or Nebo.'

One of the younger men sitting cross-legged on a reed mat spoke out. 'What of the man's Hebrew name—did Micaiah find that out?'

Nehushta's father shook his head. 'I asked him the same question, but the answer was *no*. But there *is* more.' For a few moments he stroked his beard, seemingly choosing his words. 'I wondered when Micaiah related this unexpected news to me whether, after eight years living as Babylonians, these men still consider themselves Jews—or are in any way still faithful to Yahweh. After all, the king may well have made them eunuchs, with no hope of offspring to preserve their lines or remember their names.' Somewhere in the distance the strange, almost human, cry of a fox rang out in the night. 'The merchant may not have been able to give Micaiah any names we would know, but he told him one more thing: that it is said that this Belteshazzar rose within the palace when he was able to correctly interpret a dream for the king—' He paused. '—a dream the nature of which Nebuchadnezzar had refused to reveal, demanding that his wise men not only tell him the meaning of the dream, but the dream itself.' The silence broke, as suddenly as the shattering of a clay jar.

Nehushta stared at her father, raising her voice above every other. 'But that is impossible!'

The clamour subsided as Elnathan waited for quiet. 'Impossible indeed—except by the help of Yahweh, surely.' He looked around, his eyes bright. 'Is it not like the story of our father Joseph, giving an interpretation of Pharaoh's dream?'

'But Pharaoh told Joseph his dream!' called out one of the men.

'Indeed.' He shook his head and smiled. 'Nebuchadnezzar is no fool. Any Babylonian sorcerer could invent the meaning of a dream, and how would the king know if it were true? But only the God of heaven can reveal both the dream—the dream He Himself has given—and its interpretation. If Nebuchadnezzar was told the former, he would know the latter was true. And this Belteshazzar gave him both—so it must be that he still fears and serves Yahweh within the Babylonian court, as our father Joseph did within the court of Pharaoh. So let us take heart. Yahweh has not abandoned us here. Surely, just as He was at work through Joseph, raising him up in a foreign court for the good of His people, He is now at work through another of His servants, whose true Hebrew name is not yet known to us.'

The news from Babylon, like a poker in a fire, kept conversation alight late into the evening. But before their guests left, the question of an older man stilled each tongue, as all waited for the answer.

'*What is Babylon like?*' Elnathan looked around in the dim light. '*Vast.* That was Micaiah's word for it.' He thought for a moment. 'He was in awe, saying that Jerusalem would fit within its walls maybe five or six times over. The Euphrates runs through the city, with part of Babylon on its east but the greater part on the west. They have not one temple, but many—to their many gods, whose names are given to the city's numerous gates. The largest temple is to their god Marduk.' He paused, his eyes suddenly filling with sadness. 'Maybe it is there that Nebuchadnezzar has placed the treasures of gold from our own temple.' He then shook his head. 'But there was one thing more than any other that Micaiah mentioned: *Etemenanki.* Or such it is called in the Babylonian tongue. It is what they call a *ziggurat*—a huge edifice reaching up into the sky, dominating the city and visible from afar. Micaiah judged it to be three times the height of our own temple.'

Nehushta could not conceive of a building of such a size. 'What is its purpose? Another temple?'

'Micaiah said it has a shrine at its top, a dwelling place for Marduk.'

She was puzzled. *Her father insisted again and again that Yahweh was the one true God—unlike any other. And yet the Babylonian god Marduk supposedly dwelt in a temple far grander than their own.* But it was as if Elnathan knew her troubled thoughts.

'We must never forget the words of King Solomon when he built the sanctuary in Jerusalem. Did he not pray to Yahweh, when the temple was dedicated, saying that the highest heavens could not contain Yahweh, and how much less the temple he had built?' He looked around at them. 'Never forget—it is our God who made the heavens and the earth. He does not need a house to dwell in or steps down to the earth. The temple in Jerusalem is merely His footstool.'

When all the dishes from the meal were finally taken inside or back to the houses or tents of those who had brought them, Sarah and Dinah rolled up the mats on which their guests had been seated. Nehushta approached Elnathan who was staring up at the almost full moon. It had risen above them as they had sat talking, bathing them in its brightness, and causing them to extinguish their lamps to conserve their oil.

He turned to her, his features illuminated by the moon's light. 'It is a wondrous sight, is it not?' His eyes returned to the dazzling orb hanging silently in the sky. 'The handiwork of Yahweh.'

They were both silent for several moments, and then Nehushta spoke, her voice soft. 'I have a question, Father.'

'Then ask it.'

It was a question that troubled her deeply and for which she had no answer. 'You spoke of our temple tonight.' He waited for her to continue. 'I know the temple in Jerusalem is a place for worship—a place to meet with Yahweh. But it is the only temple He has given us, and it is there alone where we may offer sacrifices for our sin. How then can we find Yahweh's forgiveness when we are so far away?'

He tore his eyes away from the moon. All she saw in them was tender love. 'My daughter, it is a profound question and a difficult one. But it brings me more joy than I can speak of to hear it upon your lips.' He held her gaze but then returned his own to the night sky. 'There is much that I do not know—like how the moon hangs up there as it does without falling. And I am not sure I know the answer you seek. If the prophet Jeremiah were here, we could ask him. But he is not, so you will only have my answer—and I am not Yahweh's mouthpiece.'

Nehushta glanced back at the moon. *It was, indeed, a wonder.*

'All I can say is this: although it was the Babylonian army that brought us here, that was only because it was the will of Yahweh. Nebuchadnezzar is but a tool in His mighty hand. So if we are here because Yahweh has decreed it, then we must trust that if we return to Him and repent of our sin, then He will not reject us simply because we cannot offer a lamb upon His altar. We must trust that He will still

312

turn to us in love—' He faced her, taking her hands in his. '—just as I do to you now, my daughter.'

Before his tender gaze, her own life suddenly seemed tawdry. It was sullied by her deceit and lies, her selfishness and pride, her impatience and spite, her care only for her own affairs. And it was stamped, like a seal upon a palace scroll, with her deliberate rejection of the glory of the God of Israel and her embrace of the grotesque idols of false gods. *The forsaking of springs of living water for empty, broken cisterns.*

The eyes which had spoken lies now welled up, and she found she could not speak. As soon as the tears began to slip down her cheeks, her father embraced her. They were no longer the strong, supple arms that had held her as a child—they were now bony, and their grip less powerful. But the love was the same. Then the sobbing came, like the breaching of a dam. If she had been able to speak, it would have been just two words, over and over again: *I'm sorry.*

As her father held her, he whispered, 'Nehushta—I spoke earlier of Solomon's prayer at the temple's dedication. But those were not his only words. His prayer also spoke of a time when God's people may sin so grievously that He sends them away to a land where they are held captive. But then the prayer speaks of them having a change of heart and repenting of their wickedness, turning back to Him even in the land of captivity, and praying towards the temple in Jerusalem. Then Solomon prayed these words to Yahweh, which are etched upon my heart: *then from heaven, Your dwelling-place, hear their prayer and their pleas, and uphold their cause. And forgive Your people, who have sinned against You.*' He kissed her head, still buried in his chest. 'Is that not the answer you seek, Nehushta? Hold on to those words. Let them be etched upon your own heart too.'

Notes

1. *The events in this chapter take place in 597 BC.*
2. *Writing of the exile presents some challenges, given the lack of general information on what it was like for the Jews. As John Bright states: 'To*

write the history of Israel in this period is difficult in the extreme… On the exile itself, the Bible tells us virtually nothing save what can be learned indirectly from prophetic and other writings of the day.' ('The History of Israel', p343). This chapter has, however, drawn upon the article, 'How Bad was the Babylonian Exile?' (Biblical Archaeology Review 42:5, September/October 2016), particularly with its reference to 'Judahtown' (possibly located in the area around Nippur), the existence of which was unknown until the publication in 1999 of a cuneiform tablet from ancient Babylon.

3. *2 Kings 24:13-14 states: 'Nebuchadnezzar removed the treasures from the temple of the LORD and from the royal palace, and cut up the gold articles that Solomon king of Israel had made for the temple of the LORD. He carried all Jerusalem into exile: all the officers and fighting men, and all the skilled workers and artisans—a total of ten thousand. Only the poorest people of the land were left.'*

4. *How long the journey to Babylon took is not known. It has been presumed that the majority, if not all of it, would have been on foot, travelling at a rate of maybe ten miles per day. On these assumptions, the approximately 650 miles would have taken around two months. Ezra's return journey from exile took four months (see Ezra 7:9), but this would probably have been slower, given it would have been less of a 'route march' and may have also involved animals and more property.*

5. *A series of cuneiform tablets have been found close to the location of the royal palace in Babylon, dated to the reign of Nebuchadnezzar. They record an allowance of oil for 'Jehoiachin king of Judah' and 'the 5 sons of the king of Judah'. Although it is unclear how severe Jehoiachin's confinement was, it has been assumed that he and his sons were under the equivalent of house arrest in Babylon (see Kenneth Kitchen, p68).*

6. *The famous Ishtar Gate and the Processional Way were not constructed until around 575 BC, i.e. over twenty years after the arrival of these exiles in Babylon.*

8

*This is what the L*ORD *Almighty, the God of Israel, says to all those*
I carried into exile from Jerusalem to Babylon: 'Build houses and
settle down.' (Jeremiah 29:4-5)

The rumours started just as their third winter of exile had passed and their fourth spring began.

Nehushta stared at her father as he placed a stool near her in the courtyard. 'Do you believe what you hear—that there is trouble in Babylon?'

Elnathan sat down suddenly and heavily, his years showing more keenly. He had just returned from a morning with Gamariah and other elders. 'What can I say? I have trusted in the past those who now tell us such things and have no reason to doubt them.' Dinah emerged from the house, a cup of cold water in her hand for Elnathan. She then returned to the bench beside Nehushta. 'It seems there is unrest not only across Nebuchadnezzar's empire but also in the city itself. Maybe the king's grip on power loosens. The more land you conquer, the more difficult it is to exert your authority over every corner of it.'

'But what could it mean for us?'

'Trouble.'

Dinah picked up her sewing. 'Why do you say that?'

'There are those among us who claim to be prophets. Two in particular: Ahab son of Kolaiah and Zedekiah son of Maaseiah. They stir up our people with dangerous words, speaking in the name of Yahweh. They proclaim that the days of both Nebuchadnezzar and our exile are numbered. That Jeconiah will return to the throne in Jerusalem and us to our land.' He shook his head, muttering, 'Dangerous words indeed.'

A fresh ache afflicted Nehushta's heart. No day passed without a thought of her son. She studied Elnathan. 'You are sure they are false?'

'My daughter—you heard Jeremiah's words with your own ears. Either he has spoken falsely, or they have. Their oracles cannot both be from Yahweh—and desiring one to be true rather than the other does not make it so.' His face darkened. 'But I will tell you another reason why Ahab and Zedekiah are liars. Because they are also adulterers! They lie with the wives of their brothers and then claim to be the mouthpiece of Yahweh!' His nostrils flared, and he spoke with a vehemence seldom seen. 'They do not speak in His name— they shame it and it is scandalous! How dare they take the holy name of Yahweh upon their lips? They break not only the commandment against adultery, but also the one against misusing His sacred name.'

It suddenly occurred to Nehushta that her father must have felt such ire many times in the palace, and yet hidden it—or at least tempered his voice.

'Why, if their words are false,' asked Dinah, her needle poised, 'are they so dangerous?'

'Because some fools are drawn to them and their seductive words, like dogs to a bitch in heat. But if any begin to speak of rebellion, it could bring down Nebuchadnezzar's wrath upon us all.' Elnathan clicked his tongue. 'Look around. We have a home and a community here. We have, by the mercy of Yahweh, begun to build a new life. If Jeremiah's words are true, that neither my generation nor yours will be the ones to return to Judah, then to speak otherwise is to stir up a hornet's nest—and to revolt is to risk destruction.'

The sun hung low in the clear sky, the heat of the autumn day over. *It was just as well.* Nehushta had not seen an assembly like it—at least not during their time in exile. The courtyard of their house was full, and the gathering extended beyond its low wall. Men of all ages were gathered there, but women too, some clutching babies born to them in the land of the Babylonians. Some were seated on mats, others stood in small huddles, talking. But all were there for one reason only: the elders had requested their presence for the reading of a letter sent to the exiles by the prophet Jeremiah.

She looked around. When others met her eye, some smiled or acknowledged her. Most bowed their heads briefly, still honouring her as queen mother, though there was no crown upon her head. She caught sight of Dinah squeezing her way through the assembly towards her. Nehushta moved along the bench slightly to make room. Once she was seated, Nehushta whispered, 'Did you have enough to offer our guests?'

'We ran out.'

'Of what?'

'Of everything!'

Nearby, Elnathan rose to his feet, a scroll in his hand. He had no need to gesture for silence; the chatter swiftly ebbed away and an expectant hush descended. He seemed calm rather than uneasy, assured rather than hesitant. 'Friends,' he began, his gaze sweeping the assembly. 'Brothers and Sisters. It makes my heart glad to see so many of you here. You were not compelled to come but have freely chosen to do so—to hear the words of Yahweh, delivered to us through the pen of the prophet Jeremiah and by the hand of Zedekiah's officials travelling to Babylon.'

Once, Nehushta would have mocked the idea that Jeremiah spoke for the Almighty. *A madman*, she had called him. But her heart as well as her circumstances had changed. Now she found herself longing to hear what the God of all the earth was saying to them— and to her. All her father had told her was it was *good. Good for those of us who will listen.*

Elnathan unfurled the scroll and began to read. '*This is what Yahweh Almighty, the God of Israel, says to all those I carried into exile from Jerusalem to Babylon.*' He paused, as if to let the words sink in. '"*Build houses and settle down; plant gardens and eat what they produce. Marry and have sons and daughters; find wives for your sons and give your daughters in marriage, so that they too may have sons and daughters. Increase in number there; do not decrease.*"' He paused again, looking around before resuming. '"*Also, seek the peace and prosperity of the city to which I have carried you into exile. Pray to Yahweh for it, because if it prospers, you too will prosper." Yes, this is what Yahweh Almighty, the God of Israel, says: "Do not let the prophets and diviners among you deceive you. Do not listen to the dreams you encourage them to have. They are prophesying lies to you in My name. I have not sent them," declares Yahweh.'*

Murmurs rippled across the gathering. 'Jeremiah knows of those here who prophecy in Yahweh's name,' whispered Nehushta.

'*Yahweh* knows of it,' replied Dinah under her breath, 'and I would not want to be them.'

Elnathan waited until he had their attention once more. '*This is what Yahweh says: "When seventy years are completed for Babylon, I will come to you and fulfil My good promise to bring you back to this place."*' He raised his eyes momentarily. Wonder shone out from them. '"*For I know the plans I have for you," declares Yahweh, "plans to prosper you and not to harm you, plans to give you hope and a future. Then you will call on Me and come and pray to Me, and I will listen to you. You will seek Me and find Me when you seek Me with all your heart. I will be found by you," declares Yahweh, "and will bring you back from captivity. I will gather you from all the nations and places where I have banished you," declares Yahweh, "and will bring you back to the place from which I carried you into exile."*'

Elnathan glanced up, but then the wonder seemed to fade. He returned to the scroll. '*You may say, "Yahweh has raised up prophets for us in Babylon," but this is what Yahweh says about the king who sits on David's throne and all the people who remain in this city, your fellow citizens who did not go with you into exile—yes, this is what Yahweh Almighty says.*' He suddenly paused, his eyes not straying from the papyrus.

Nehushta knew her father was struggling to say the next words. He took a deep breath and then started again.

'*This is what Yahweh Almighty says: "I will send the sword, famine and plague against them and I will make them like figs that are so bad they cannot be eaten. I will pursue them with the sword, famine and plague and will make them abhorrent to all the kingdoms of the earth, a curse and an object of horror, of scorn and reproach, among all the nations where I drive them. For they have not listened to My words," declares Yahweh, "words that I sent to them again and again by My servants the prophets. And you exiles have not listened either," declares Yahweh.'* When he paused, there was no longer silence but muttering.

'Not all accept it,' said Dinah under her breath.

Nehushta searched the faces around them. *Dinah was right.* 'Some wear disapproval as openly as a brooch upon their breast.'

'Has it not always been that way with our people?' murmured Dinah. 'We embrace the word of blessing but stopper our ears at admonition.'

Nehushta wasn't sure it had ever been the case with Dinah, but then Elnathan held up his hand to still them.

'Therefore, hear the word of Yahweh, all you exiles whom I have sent away from Jerusalem to Babylon. This is what Yahweh Almighty, the God of Israel, says about Ahab son of Kolaiah and Zedekiah son of Maaseiah, who are prophesying lies to you in my name.'

Nehushta sat up and leaned forward. *What word was about to be spoken about the men who had roused her father's anger earlier that year?*

"I will deliver them into the hands of Nebuchadnezzar king of Babylon, and he will put them to death before your very eyes. Because of them, all the exiles from Judah who are in Babylon will use this curse: 'May Yahweh treat you like Zedekiah and Ahab, whom the king of Babylon burned in the fire.' For they have done outrageous things in Israel; they have committed adultery with their neighbours' wives, and in My name they have uttered lies which I did not authorise. I know it and am a witness to it," declares Yahweh.' Elnathan fell silent, still staring at the scroll. Then he rolled it up.

Darkness was upon them when the final guests departed. Questions and answers had followed, and then discussion and debate, some vigorous and not all of it measured, with voices raised across the courtyard.

'There will be much talk across *Judah-Town* tonight,' said Elnathan as he watched those leaving through the gateway in the low wall. When he turned back towards Nehushta, however, a soft smile adorned his weathered face. 'But the Word of Yahweh will prevail, whatever the opinions of men. And He graciously offers us prosperity and peace in this place of exile—for those who will listen and obey.'

Nehushta breathed in the evening air, and with it the smell of the bread that Dinah was baking to accompany their late meal. 'Including praying for the city of Babylon?'

Elnathan shrugged. 'If they prosper, then so will we—according to Yahweh.'

'Except for false prophets.' Her eyes fell upon the fire over which their food was being warmed. She had once burned her hand as a child and remembered the pain. 'What do you imagine is meant by the words concerning the fate of Ahab and Zedekiah?'

'It is said that the king of Babylon can throw into a furnace any who anger him.'

Nehushta shuddered. 'Then they will have to hope that their lies do not reach the ears of Nebuchadnezzar. Though given Jeremiah's prophecy…' She left her words hanging as she followed a glowing cinder that rose from the fire, ascending into the darkness above.

The scroll was copied and passed around every place where the Jews had settled in exile, and the wisdom of its words were borne out in the months that followed as they began to take root and flourish. But with the dawning of the fifth year of their exile came the rise of a new and unexpected light in Babylon.

Nehushta stared in fascination as Dinah dangled a spindle from a length of unspun wool, spinning it around to create yarn. She had seen no reason in Dinah teaching herself to spin. *They could buy cloth from a merchant should they need it, so why go to the trouble of spinning and weaving?* She had to admit, however, that there was a certain satisfaction in watching tangled wool being transformed into slender thread. Her pleasure was increased by the aroma of Sarah's stew gently bubbling away. A movement turned Nehushta's head. Elnathan had wandered into the courtyard, but still seemed elsewhere.

'Father!'

He suddenly looked towards her. 'Hmm?'

Nehushta smiled. 'Are you back in Judah?'

Elnathan didn't reply but looked up at the sky. The sun had already dropped behind the nearby houses and the heat of the late summer's day was beginning to wane. He turned to his wife. 'Can the meal wait a while?'

The lines on Sarah's face deepened with her wry smile. 'As long as you wish to eat before it is dark.'

'We will be back well before nightfall.'

'Back?'

He turned. 'Nehushta, Dinah—come with me.'

'Where are we going?'

'Just to the Chebar…'

Nehushta's eyes met Dinah's. *She was curious too!* Dinah laid down the spindle and they both rose to their feet.

'What is this about, Father?' asked Nehushta, as the three of them left.

'Wait until we reach the canal…' he murmured.

They walked through al-Yehuda, bustling with activity now the day was cooler: goats being milked and bread baked in small courtyards. Here and there, young children played in the streets or chased chickens that were pecking around in the dust. Elnathan seemed to have no desire to stop and talk with neighbours, as was his custom. On the edge of the growing town was a collection of unfinished houses, layers of sun-baked bricks rising to form walls and rooms. Beyond them lay an area that was like a small Eden in the midst of the parched land, green with growth and with trees scattered around. One of them was their own garden: planted with onions, leeks, garlic, coriander and cumin, as well as a variety of beans and herbs. Each patch was watered by a small channel dug from the main canal. Nehushta smiled at those who straightened up from tending their plants as they passed. Many still bowed. It was only when they had reached the Chebar Canal that Elnathan stopped, choosing a spot in the lengthening shadows cast by a fig tree.

Nehushta glanced up and down its slow waters, fed from the Euphrates from which it divided to the north of Babylon, and into which it again flowed near the city of Erech to the south. The late afternoon sun glinted on the numerous irrigation streams. Her father's attention seemed fixed on the waters of Babylon. 'Well?'

'There is a new prophet in our midst.' His gaze didn't move. 'A prophet of Yahweh.'

'A true one?' The news of Ahab and Zedekiah's gruesome end—as predicted by Jeremiah—was still fresh in Nehushta's mind.

Her father nodded slowly. 'Yes—a priest who was exiled with us. Thirty years of age.' He paused. 'He would just be entering the service of the temple if he was still in Jerusalem.'

'Where is he now?'

Elnathan looked along the canal. 'At Tel-abib on the Chebar. I went there today with Gamariah to see him.'

Nehushta had been to the place. It was another Jewish settlement nearby. 'His name?'

'Ezekiel son of Buzi.'

'Has he brought a word from Yahweh for us?' asked Dinah, her voice hushed.

'It is not so much what he has heard as what he has seen.'

'What do you mean?'

He lifted his eyes to clear blue sky. 'He has seen visions, here in the land of the Babylonians—visions of Yahweh Himself.'

Nehushta stared at her father open-mouthed. *Yahweh Himself! Had the prophet Jeremiah even seen such things?* 'What do you mean?'

'He spoke of a great flashing cloud, and in its midst the likeness of glowing metal, as in a furnace. He saw four strange beings, each with four faces and four wings, and legs like burnished bronze. He said that they moved as swiftly as lightning.'

Nehushta's skin prickled, the air suddenly heavy and still. Her mind struggled to imagine what her father described. But there was more.

'He told the exiles in Tel-abib of huge wheels that moved with the creatures, rising from the ground as they rose, but without turning.' He paused. 'And above them was an expanse.'

'An expanse of what?' whispered Dinah.

'Of something that gleamed like crystal. And above it there the semblance of a throne of brightest blue, like sapphire.' His voice then softened to little more than a murmur. 'And on the throne, a figure—like that of a man, but glowing brightly like gleaming bronze or blazing fire, and surrounded by brilliant light.'

Silence.

Nehushta gazed up into the brightness above, trying again to picture what the prophet had seen. She saw no expanse—only a small bird swooping down towards the canal and the insects that hovered over it. Somewhere in the distance she heard muted hammering.

Eventually Dinah spoke. 'Yahweh rules on His throne here too.'

'He does,' Elnathan replied. 'He is the God of all the earth. We have always known that.' He paused. 'But it is not just the prophet's visions that are strange. We heard all this from the lips of the elders there. It seems that Yahweh has now struck Ezekiel mute—'

'A mute prophet!' interrupted Nehushta. 'How can he speak the word of Yahweh if he cannot speak at all?'

'He has indicated,' her father replied, 'that Yahweh will open his mouth when needed. But it seems that the Almighty has other ways to speak through him too.'

Nehushta was intrigued. 'What do you mean?'

'Each day now he lies on his left side, with a brick beside him inscribed with an image of Jerusalem. He acts as if he is besieging the brick—or rather the city.' Elnathan sighed. 'It is as Jeremiah has already prophesied—those left in Jerusalem are still under Yahweh's judgment, and there is further woe to come for them.'

Nehushta stared at the water again. *To know that Yahweh ruled over all the earth was a comfort indeed. Unless you had a heart that continued to resist Him.* A swallow swooped down over the canal to snatch an insect from the air. *Life could be taken so swiftly!* For a moment she thought of Eliakim's sudden demise and wondered how his brother now fared as Jerusalem's king. *Would his rule end as abruptly?* From the little she had gleaned, it seemed that the change of Mattaniah's name to *Zedekiah* had not been mirrored by a change of heart. For once she was glad to be in Babylon.

In the years that followed, more prophecies from the unmuted mouth of Ezekiel travelled the short distance from Tel-abib to al-Yehuda.

Oracles concerning the sin of Judah and the coming judgment. From the opposite direction—from the land of Judah—news also flowed, but as slowly as the waters of the Chebar. And the report that reached them in the ninth year of their exile was that Zedekiah had rebelled against Babylon.

'Will Nebuchadnezzar march on Jerusalem again,' asked Nehushta, the evening the news arrived.

Elnathan's sixty-two years lay heavily upon him. He sighed deeply, his eyes full of sadness. 'The prophets of Yahweh do not lie.'

Within months, the Babylonian army was indeed heading north-west, and even before reports from Judah confirmed it, Ezekiel's loosened lips announced to the exiles that a siege of Jerusalem had begun. Elnathan did not live to hear the report of the city's fall two years later—or the tales of horror that arrived with the new exiles.

'They are coming!' The young man who announced the news to Nehushta was red-faced. 'They will be here before sunset!'

Nehushta glanced at the sky—the sun was already low. 'How many?'

'Maybe forty or fifty?'

'The town can easily take those numbers—at least until they are ready to build their own homes. Do they come with much?'

'Not after a two-year siege.'

She paused. 'Go now. Take the news around the town. Each home must be ready to open its doors to our brothers and sisters.' He nodded and ran off. For a few moments, she watched him go. Although she rarely thought of it, she still remembered vividly her own journey from Jerusalem. Dinah joined her. 'I have no idea how many we should cook for tonight.'

'It is always better to cook too much than too little—and there is plenty in the stores. Anything that isn't eaten tonight will keep until tomorrow.' Dinah went over to the fire-pit and began preparing it for the evening meal. 'They may be more tired than hungry tonight anyway.'

'And who knows what they will have witnessed,' murmured Nehushta before turning to go inside.

The appetising smell of the bean stew was already rising from the large clay pot when the young man arrived back at the gate of the courtyard accompanied by eight strangers—a man, two women and five children, the youngest of whom was in the arms of one of the women. The man was holding a small bag. Nehushta froze. Each newcomer was gaunt beyond anything she had ever seen, clothed in little more than rags, and each with same empty expression in their eyes. Dinah's voice suddenly shook her out of her shock.

'Welcome—you are most welcome here.' Dinah was hurrying towards them, her arms open wide. 'Come in—we have a meal and beds for you all.'

Nehushta masked her feelings and rose. 'Yes, our house is your house.'

One of the women stared at her and then sudden recognition seemed to dawn. She bobbed her head slowly. 'My queen.' Her voice was flat.

Something about her seemed familiar. 'You need not call me that here. To you I am simply Nehushta—and you will soon meet my mother, Sarah.' She gestured. 'And this is Dinah. Come and sit down and rest, and we will get you water to drink.'

There was little conversation that night, and no one enquired. Dinah seemed to know instinctively what was needed. She showed the same attentiveness to the needs of the strangers as she had to Nehushta's own needs as the wife of the king. At one point a tear slipped from the eye of one of the women, Leah, when Dinah knelt beside her and softly asked if she would like some more water. *How long had it been since anyone had shown her such a simple kindness?* Even before the end of the meal, the younger children were already lying on the mats in the courtyard asleep. Dinah quickly fetched some blankets and covered them where they lay. Weariness weighed down upon those who were still awake, bowing both shoulders and heads, as if bearing heavy sacks of grain. All that they learned by the end of the meal was that Joshua and Abital were married with three of the children, and that Leah was Joshua's sister and mother to the other two.

As soon as it seemed that their guests had eaten their fill, they showed them the room off the courtyard that they had prepared for them, with cushions and blankets—far more comfort than they had had when they had reached al-Yehuda eleven years earlier. Dinah carried in the youngest, still sleeping, and gently lowered her onto a cushion. Joshua carried another and the other children stumbled in, barely awake and sinking back into slumber as soon as they lay down.

As they returned outside, Nehushta said in a low voice, 'They will need new clothes—all of them.'

'I will see to it,' replied Dinah, 'though they are little more than bone and skin at the moment.'

Sarah nodded. 'It looks as if they have endured a famine. Food will soon mend their bodies. It will take far longer, however, for their souls to be restored.'

Nehushta stared at the door to their guests' room. 'I wonder what happened to Leah's husband,' she murmured, then adding, 'I do not know why, but I feel that I have seen her before.'

'You have,' answered Sarah. 'She is the wife of one of the temple priests—though I cannot remember his name.'

Nehushta pondered for a moment. 'Yes, that it is.'

'But maybe she is a widow now,' added Dinah.

'They will tell us when they are ready.'

For the first two nights, the newcomers slept almost until the following noon. Their first day consisted of little more than cladding them in garments that were fresh and sound, even if not new; the second, showing them around the town. By then, rumours had started to swirl around al-Yehuha of a siege that had brought the city to its knees and its walls to rubble.

After feeding them on the third morning, the children—who had revived more quickly than their parents—had left them to join other youngsters playing in the streets and around the town. Only the youngest remained, sucking on Leah's shrunken breast as she sat beside Abital on a bench in the shade.

'We knew they were coming,' said Leah suddenly, not looking up. 'The Babylonians.'

There was a long silence, but then Joshua spoke. 'The king should not have rebelled against Nebuchadnezzar—it was foolishness.'

Abital glanced at Nehushta, her face anxious.

'Do not fear—Joshua is right. Mattaniah was just as foolish as his brother.' Abital's expression eased.

Joshua kicked the dirt by the stool on which he was perched. 'They surrounded Jerusalem, cutting off any supplies. They soon began building siege works against the city walls. And Zedekiah hoped for a miracle—or maybe deliverance by Egypt.'

Leah suddenly looked up, the baby still on her breast. 'The king sent men, including my husband Zephaniah, to see Jeremiah, to ask him to enquire of Yahweh. But the only oracle he received was one of doom, not deliverance. More than once the prophet told him that surrendering to the Babylonians was the only way to escape destruction. But the king would not listen—'

'And neither would the officials,' added Joshua. 'Instead, they threw Jeremiah into a cistern, and left him mired in the mud to starve to death. It was only a Cushite eunuch whose actions saved him. But it did not save the city.'

'The siege only got worse,' added Abital quietly. 'Until, after eighteen months, there was no food left in the city, and the children began to die.'

'And not all of them through starvation...' Joshua left the words hanging.

Nehushta had heard the terrible tales of sieges, where parents in desperation had killed their own children to eat. *Such horrors were better left unsaid.*

Joshua shook his head slowly. 'And yet still Zedekiah would not surrender. When the Babylonians finally breached the city walls, he tried to escape from them at night with his army.'

Nehushta stared at him, incredulous. 'How? The city was surrounded, surely?'

'As the wall was being breached on the northern side, with the Babylonians entering the city there, the king and his army left through the Fountain Gate to the south-east.' Joshua paused. 'They were fleeing towards the Arabah but were overtaken by the Babylonians on the plains of Jericho. And that was it.' He fell silent, each guest's head bowed under the memory of the day.

'What happened to the king?' asked Sarah quietly.

Joshua sighed, his whole chest rising and falling. 'We only heard of it once we had been forcibly led from the city and were already on our way to Babylon. When we passed Riblah, to the north of Damascus, we learned that the king had been taken there to stand before Nebuchadnezzar.' His stared at the ground. 'Zedekiah escaped with his life—though barely. His sons did not. The Babylonians slew them before the king's eyes and then blinded him, so that the slaughter of his sons was the last thing he saw.'

Nehushta was aghast, her heart aching. She had last seen Eliakim's nephews eleven years earlier. They had been small boys. *Now they had reaped the terrible harvest of their father's folly—as had Coniah. But their fate had been death.* She wiped away a tear from her cheek. *No, it was not folly alone that had done it. It had been both fathers' utter disregard for Yahweh, His words—and His offer of mercy.* Nehushta watched as Leah's child left the breast, put its feet on the ground, and began to walk around unsteadily, oblivious to the hideous story being told. Abital rested her hand gently on Leah's arm.

Sarah rose from her stool and sat on the other side of Leah. She took Leah's hand in hers, clearly understanding what remained unspoken. 'And what of your husband, Leah? Zephaniah was a priest, wasn't he? My own husband, Elnathan, knew him I think.'

Joshua answered for her. 'It was not just Zedekiah who was taken to Riblah. The captain of Nebuchadnezzar's guard took the chief priest, Zephaniah and three other temple officials, as well as palace officials and sixty other men from the city. Two of my own brothers were among them.' He finally looked up, his face drawn and full of grief. 'We have not seen or heard of them since—and do not expect to.'

Nehushta hesitated in the late afternoon sun.

'Let them,' whispered Dinah.

Nehushta smiled at Abital and Leah. 'Very well. Use whatever you wish in the store—you will find more than enough there to prepare any meal you wish.' Their guest's offer to cook that evening also allowed her the one thing she longed for. She turned to her most trusted friend. 'Come, Dinah. We will leave tonight's meal in the hands of our sisters and take a walk.' Her attention returned to the women. 'If you cannot find anything, ask my mother.' With that, she took Dinah's arm in hers, and they began to walk together. 'You were right, Dinah,' she murmured when they were out of earshot. 'How many months will it have been since they've had the chance to make a proper meal?'

'It will help them to feel that they have something to give—and it will be a taste of the familiar for them, when all else seems strange.'

For a while, neither of them spoke as they walked through al-Yehuda. Nehushta still wasn't sure she had taken in all they had been told that morning. Joshua had gone on to describe what had happened to Jerusalem—it seemed too shocking to even imagine. *Its walls demolished. The palace, as well as every important building and large house in the city, burned to the ground. Yahweh's house stripped of every item of value that remained, be it of gold, silver or bronze—from its huge pillars to its smallest wick trimmer. And Solomon's magnificent temple, like every other building of note, set ablaze and reduced to rubble.*

Nehushta steered them along the streets they had walked with her father to the Chebar Canal some six years earlier. It was a reminder of what she had heard on that day—of a glorious vision of Yahweh. When they finally reached the canal, they stopped and watched the water silently slipping by for a while. *It never stopped flowing. There was nothing any man could do to stop the waters—even Nebuchadnezzar. He could divert them, if he wished, yes. But he could not stop them.*

'I am glad,' she said suddenly, 'that my father did not live to see this day—and hear that the house in which he lived his whole life had been burned down.'

'He would have grieved even more over the destruction of the temple,' murmured Dinah.

329

'How can such a thing have even happened?' Nehushta picked up a twig and tossed it into the Chebar. They watched as it floated away.

'Remember that day when we heard the words of Jeremiah being read from the scroll? Did not Yahweh say then that because of the people's wickedness, He would do to the temple as He had done to Shiloh?' Dinah paused. 'Is that not the answer to your question?'

Nehushta stared at the water again. *It was Yahweh's purposes, surely, that were as unstoppable as the Euphrates.* She sighed. 'You are right, Dinah—as you usually are.'

'And yet the truth is still troubling. Yahweh promised King David that his house and his kingdom would endure forever—and yet there is now no king in Jerusalem.'

'No king, no temple, no city.'

'Yet, the vision of the prophet Ezekiel was of a throne—a throne in heaven.' Dinah drew in a deep breath and let it out. 'Yahweh was our king before David's line came to the throne. He is still our king.'

Her words brought Eliakim's brother to mind. Nehushta closed her eyes for a moment, and tried to imagine what it would be like never to see again. 'I wonder where Mattaniah is now,' she murmured, her eyes still shut. 'Maybe he will be allowed to be with Coniah, though he will never see him.' She remembered them playing together as children, only three years between them. Then she opened her eyes. 'It is a mercy that Coniah surrendered when he did.'

Dinah nodded. 'Yes, and maybe it is better that Yahweh is our only king now.'

'But what of Yahweh's promise to David, that his kingdom would endure forever?'

Dinah thought for a moment. 'But Jeremiah prophesied that our people would return to the land.'

'But also that none of Coniah's offspring would sit on the throne of David.'

'But even if that were the case,' replied Dinah, 'or if one of David's other offspring should rise as king—how will it be different to before?' She paused. 'Even David and Solomon—our greatest kings—both sinned greatly and brought down trouble upon themselves and upon the land.'

'We need a different sort of king.'

Both women fell silent again, but then Dinah suddenly turned towards her. 'But did not Jeremiah prophesy just that? *What was it?*' Her eyes suddenly shone. 'I remember the words now! *A righteous Branch.*'

'But he also said the human heart is desperately sick—' Nehushta knew it herself. '—so how can there be a truly righteous son of David?'

'I do not know.' Dinah then took Nehushta's hand. 'But Yahweh is a God of wonders, and if He says it, then He will do it.'

Notes

1. *The events in this chapter start in 594 BC.*

2. *There is no precise dating for the letter to the exiles in Jeremiah 29, but, as J. A. Thompson states, 'the situation is parallel to that described in chs. 27 and 28. There was a period of unrest all over the Babylonian empire, and prophets both in Jerusalem and in Babylon were proclaiming the imminent ending of the Exile, evidently believing that Babylon was on the point of collapse. The Babylonian Chronicle hints at internal troubles in Babylon in 595/4 BC in which some of the deported Jews seem to have been involved.' (Thompson, p544). Jeremiah 28:1 dates both chapters to the fourth year of Zedekiah.*

3. *Although Ahab and Zedekiah are named as false prophets (Jeremiah 29:23), the content of their lies is not specified. However, it has been assumed that their message was similar to that of the false prophet Hananiah (Jeremiah 28:1-4), who told those in Jerusalem that the yoke of the king of Babylon would soon be broken, and that the exiles (including Jeconiah) would soon return. This would accord well with the fact that there was unrest in the Babylonian empire around 594 BC and that Ahab and Zedekiah had clearly done something which incurred the wrath of Nebuchadnezzar.*

4. *It has been assumed that the letter sent from Jeremiah was copied. There is much about the transmission of the Old Testament Scriptures that is unknown. However, given the level of literacy pre-exile (e.g. in the keeping of records) and the preservation of the Scriptures during the exile, it does not seem unreasonable to assume that copies of the Scriptures were made. This may be implied by 2 Chronicles 17:9, which relates how, in the time of Jehoshaphat (almost three hundred years before the exile), Levites travelled around Judah teaching the people 'taking with them the Book of the Law of the LORD.'*

5. *The precise location of Tel-abib on the Chebar Canal (Ezekiel 3:15) is not known. It is the place after which modern-day Tel Aviv is named.*

6. *The horror of children being killed for food due to the severity of a siege is prophesied in Jeremiah 19:9 and referenced in Lamentations 2:20 and 4:10.*

7. *The reference to 'the thirtieth year' in Ezekiel 1:1 is usually taken to mean Ezekiel's thirtieth year, as it does not seem to correspond to any year of a king or of exile.*

8. *It is not known exactly when Zedekiah rebelled against Babylon, but it is likely to be after 593 BC as Zedekiah was required to go to Babylon then, presumably to affirm his loyalty. Also, shortly after Zedekiah became king, the Egyptians were active in capturing Gaza and attacking Tyre and Sidon, possibly leading Zedekiah to believe that a rebellion against Babylon would be supported by Egypt.*

9. *As the Bible Background Commentary states: 'Blinding was a common treatment of rebellious slaves (even subject kings) in the ancient Near East... Typical of Assyrian and Babylonian practice, Nebuzaradan [the commander of the Babylonian army] destroyed the major public centres in the city and the protective walls of the city to make it vulnerable to further attack.' (pp411-412). There is some debate as to whether Jerusalem fell in July 587 or 586 BC.*

10. *Imagined named characters introduced in this chapter are Leah, Joshua and Abital.*

9

*In the thirty-seventh year of the exile of Jehoiachin king of Judah,
in the year Awel-Marduk became king of Babylon, he released
Jehoiachin king of Judah from prison. (2 Kings 25:27)*

The years of exile passed slowly for Nehushta, with little to tell them
apart. The eighteenth year was notable only because Jeconiah, if he
still lived, would be thirty-six—the age of Eliakim when he had died.
The third decade brought stories from Babylon of Nebuchadnezzar's
extravagant building projects—of a splendid new gate and processional
way, covered in glazed blue bricks on which strode dragons, bulls and
lions, symbols of the Babylonian gods. Nehushta cared little for such
news. Of greater worth were the words of the Living God, whose form
could never be depicted in lifeless clay and yet had been glimpsed in
radiant glory by His prophet near the waters of the Chebar. There
were darker rumours from Babylon too—of a malady afflicting its
king, though little beyond that was known, at least to the Jews.

As the thirty-fifth year ended, Nehushta realised she had spent
half her life away from Judah. Every morning, however, she gave
thanks that, in His mercy, Yahweh had granted as long a life to Dinah
as He had to her. And although the sight of children playing in the
streets would often make her heart ache for the son and the grandsons
rent from her arms and her life, there were other mercies.

Nehushta wiped away the tiny stones from the knee of the small
boy and then a tear from his eye. 'There—is that better now?' The
child who had sought refuge in her lap gave a wordless nod. 'Then
go, play with your brother, and try not to fall over again.' Leah still
lived with them, and her children's offspring regarded Nehushta and
Dinah no different to Leah.

Dinah chuckled. 'It is a vain hope that he will stay upright for long. And if it is not him in the dirt, then it will be his brother.'

Nehushta watched the two boys chasing each other around the courtyard, screams of delight filling the air. 'Eliakim never allowed you to marry, Dinah.' It had long been in her heart to speak of it. Her eyes remained on the children. 'I have been more grateful than I can ever say for your faithfulness and friendship. But in denying you marriage, he also denied you a family of your own.' She paused. 'That must have brought you great pain.' Dinah did not reply immediately. There was a soft smile upon her face.

'Pain, yes, but Yahweh has been good to me. Did I not help you nurse Coniah when he was young, teaching him to walk and then to talk? Were we not then blessed by Coniah's own children?' She looked out at the courtyard. 'And now I find myself as much a mother and grandmother as if my own womb had borne fruit.' She laid her hand on Nehushta. 'I will not forget, either, how your own mother and father were far more than mistress and master to me.' She patted her friend's arm. 'I have a family. Yahweh has been good.'

'Nebuchadnezzar is dead!' Leah's son stood in the courtyard in the warm autumn sun, his face red and patches of his tunic darkened. 'The news has just arrived from Babylon.'

Nehushta rose to her feet. 'It is no surprise—he has been ill, has he not, for some months?'

'He must have been around eighty anyway,' added Dinah beside her.

Leah emerged from the house, clearly having overheard. 'Which of his sons succeeds him?'

'Amel-Marduk.'

Nehushta frowned. 'But were there not rumours some time ago that Nebuchadnezzar imprisoned him for a while?'

'They were more than rumours.' Leah's son then shrugged. 'But it is Amel-Marduk who is now king in Babylon, even though not Nebuchadnezzar's firstborn.'

'I wonder whether we will see anything change,' murmured Leah.

Nehushta's chest suddenly tightened. *It had been Nebuchadnezzar who had left Jeconiah and his sons alive, though in prison. What if this new king wanted himself rid of such captives?'*

'Whatever happens,' replied Dinah, 'it is in the hands of Yahweh. He is the King of *all* the earth.'

Nehushta sat with her eyes closed, listening to the sounds of al-Yehuda. She rarely made it through an afternoon without falling asleep, her seventy-one years wearying her daily. Several months had passed since the new king had come to the throne in Babylon, but nothing had changed for them. Children still ran around the streets, laughing and calling out to one another. Nearby, the cries of a baby could be heard, and in the distance, the steady *thud* of a hammer upon wood. Close at hand, she could hear the slow *pock pock* of Dinah's needle as it repeatedly pierced the taut linen she was embroidering, despite her gnarled fingers. The sound of the thread being pulled through the fabric suddenly stopped.

'Do you know who that is?'

Nehushta opened her eyes, squinting through crumpled eyelids. The orange sun had not yet fallen behind the houses. Above the low wall of their courtyard, she could see a man whom she judged to be around forty. He was talking to their neighbour. The neighbour suddenly pointed, and the man looked in their direction. 'No, but I think we soon will.' The stranger began walking towards them. Nehushta rose, stiff from sitting, as he entered the courtyard, his expression one she could not fathom. She waited for him to speak.

'Are you Nehushta, daughter of Elnathan?'

'I am. Why do you wish to know?'

A smile broke on his face with the brightness of noon. He took her wrinkled hands in his, his eyes shining. 'My grandmother!' He lifted her hands to his lips and kissed them.

Nehushta stared at him, stunned and speechless. But then a memory stirred—the memory of the large brown eyes of a small child on his second birthday. 'Shealtiel?' she gasped. 'Is it you?'

His smiled broadened. 'It is.'

335

'How?' she whispered.

'Amel-Marduk has released us from our captivity—my father and my brothers.'

'Coniah still lives?'

'He does—and he sent me to search for news of you, and to bring you to Babylon if I find you.'

'I am to see my son again before I die?' Nehushta's voice was as brittle as the finest alabaster perfume bottle. It wavered and then broke, releasing a sudden flow of tears as precious as any nard or myrrh. She threw her arms around her grandson and wept.

When her tears finally subsided, she loosened her embrace and stepped back. 'Here, let me look at my grandson properly.' Although grey streaked his beard, he appeared well and healthy, his frame strong and his face full and round. She glanced at Dinah. Her cheeks were wet, and she radiated joy. Her gaze back on Shealtiel, she drank in his every feature, as if he were offering a cup of cool water for a throat parched and dry. She suddenly laughed. 'I cannot believe it! Must I nip myself to prove that I am not dreaming?' For a few more moments, she studied him, shaking her head slowly in disbelief. Then it was as if she came awake. 'But I have not introduced you—this is Dinah.'

A burst of incredulous laughter erupted from Shealtiel. 'Dinah! Is it really you too? Now I am twice blessed!'

'I remember you, but you cannot remember me, surely?'

He shrugged. 'I cannot rightly say, but I have known your name for as long as I can remember, and my father speaks so fondly of you.'

Nehushta smiled. 'Dinah was as much a mother to Coniah as I was.'

'And she is welcome to come to Babylon, too—if she wishes.'

Nehushta's eyes darted to her companion, her heart suddenly pulled in contrary directions. But she needn't have feared.

Dinah beamed. 'You are my family—and I would not be parted from you for all the riches of Babylon.'

Relief swept over Nehushta. 'And I would never wish to lose you. But I am forgetting myself. Let us bring refreshments for my grandson, Dinah.'

'I will fetch them. You sit here with Shealtiel.'

As Dinah left them, there was one question burning in Nehushta's mind. 'When may I see my son—and other grandsons?'

'I came with a cart but left it on the edge of town when I began my search for you.' He glanced up at the sky. 'It is too late to begin our journey today, but we could leave tomorrow morning, if you can be ready by then. We should be in Babylon by nightfall on the second day.'

'I would leave behind everything I own in a heartbeat, if it meant seeing my son a day earlier.'

The meal that evening was lavish. Neighbours and friends flocked to the house, everyone wanting to hear of the release from prison of the man whom many still referred to as their king. It felt as if half of al-Yehuda was crammed into the courtyard, necks craned to catch a glimpse of his son. A calf had been killed and its meat both roasted and stewed. Bread was heaped in baskets, and numerous other pots brimmed with vegetables and beans braised with onions, garlic and herbs. Sweet breads, rich with raisins and date syrup, were passed around after the dishes were emptied. An almost full moon had risen into the sky above by the time the joyful celebration finally ended.

'We should finish packing,' said Dinah, when the only guests remaining were Leah's brother, Joshua, and his family. The two large wooden chests swiftly procured that afternoon were not yet full.

'Yes, go, Nehushta,' insisted Leah. 'There are enough of us to clear up and we can leave the men to talk.' Joshua was deep in conversation with Sheatiel.

Once she and Dinah were upstairs in the room they'd shared for so many years, Nehushta paused, looking around. 'It seems strange to think that this will be our last night sleeping here.'

Dinah chuckled. 'Who would have believed it this morning?' She then went over to a wooden box in the corner, knelt beside it and then opened it. 'But it is wonderful, is it not? Beyond any joy we could have imagined. We could never guess the workings of Yahweh, if we tried.'

'That is a truth I will not argue against. I have seen it in my own life, for what has felt like good and ill.' She paused. 'And yet it has always been for good.'

There was silence for a few moments, and then Dinah held something up. 'You should wear this—not for the journey, but for when we reach Babylon.'

Nehushta stared at it. It took a moment for her to recognise the deep orange garment that had come with her from Jerusalem thirty-seven years earlier. 'You have kept it all this time?'

'I thought that there might yet come a day when the dress of a queen might be needed once more. And that day has come, since Shealtiel tells us that Coniah is now honoured and eats at the table of the king of Babylon.'

Nehushta went over and fingered the fine linen, marvelling that it still seemed as bright and new as the day when Dinah had packed it. Its neck, sleeves and hem were adorned with beaded embroidery. 'I had almost forgotten what such finery looked like,' she murmured, taking it from Dinah and holding it up. 'I fear it will not fit me as before. My body is much diminished.'

'Maybe a scarf around your waist to pull it in?'

They both laughed. 'You remember the way that I used to dress!'

'When I packed this one for you, I chose a garment that was more modest that those that your husband favoured.' She delved into the box again and pulled out a small bundle. She unrolled the hessian and held up a pair of ornate leather sandals. 'And these will shoe your feet with elegance.'

'I have neither crown nor carnelians to wear with them, though.' All her gold and jewellery had been bartered long ago. She had seen no reason to keep any of it.

'No, but you have some lovely red and orange bead earrings that will match the tunic well.'

Nehushta shook her head in wonder. 'How many years, Dinah, has it been since we have spoken like this?'
Dinah smiled. 'Too many.'

'I feel like a queen taking her seat upon a throne,' whispered Nehushta as she sat down at the front of the cart.

'And soon you will look like one again,' whispered Dinah back, as Shealtiel helped her up.

The cart was surrounded. Many had gathered to wish them farewell. Leah was not alone in shedding tears. Then, with a swift flick of the reins, Shealtiel urged the donkeys forward. As they began to move, a strange sight met them: every head bowed.

'You are still a queen in their eyes, Grandmother,' murmured Shealtiel. 'They honour you.'

'If I am still a queen, then you are the son of the king. They honour you too.'

It was the same as the cart moved slowly through the town. Women stood in their courtyards and bobbed their heads, and even outside al-Yahuda, men stopped in the fields and bowed to them. 'The whole town has heard by now what has happened,' said Dinah.

Nehushta nodded to acknowledge those who had just bowed to her. 'It has been many years since they have heard such good news. Favour rests on our people at last.'

Soon they were out into the open countryside. Nehushta looked over her shoulder one last time. Al-Yehuda was by now a small cluster in the distance. She gazed at it for a few moments. *It had been her home for longer than Jerusalem had.* She turned forward again, her heart soaring for what lay ahead. Shealtiel began to ask them both about their life in the town—the years of confinement had not given him much of a story to tell, aside from what had been learned of Babylon.

'Your great-grandfather was an elder among our people,' explained Nehushta as she spoke of her parents. 'He was the one who brought the news of the prophet Ezekiel.'

'Ezekiel?'

'You have not heard? Yahweh raised up a prophet amongst the exiles!'

'No!'

Nehushta then related what she remembered of his oracles, starting with his vision of Yahweh by the Chebar and finishing with his vision of a new temple, filled with God's glory.

Shealtiel was silent for some moments. 'This new temple sounds as if it will rival the temples of Babylon—even the one they call *Etemenanki*. Its name means *the temple of the foundation of heaven and earth*, and it has gold in its foundations, if you believe what is said.'

'Temples may be adorned with gold,' replied Dinah, but only one temple will ever have the greatest treasure—the presence of the true God of all creation.'

After a night spent in a small town, they set out again shortly after sunrise along the flat plain that would eventually lead to Babylon. Nehushta had barely slept. If her excitement could have hastened the dawning of the day she would see her son again, the night would have passed in the blink of an eye. When they stopped to refresh themselves shortly after noon, Shealtiel assured them the city would soon come into view. Dinah insisted it was time for Nehushta to change, and she then brushed her hair, now almost entirely grey.

'Coniah will not see me as he remembers me,' sighed Nehushta.

'He will not expect to,' replied Dinah. 'But the same will be true of him. He is fifty-five now, not eighteen as when you last saw him.'

'It is a lifetime,' murmured Nehushta.

Babylon soon began to rise out of the horizon after they resumed their journey. And above it, one building rose higher than any other.

'Is that—' Nehushta hesitated. '—Etemenanki?' She said the word slowly and uncertainly.

'If you mean the ziggurat that towers over the city, then yes.'

Shealtiel spoke more of Babylon as the temple to one of its gods rose higher and higher into the sky. But he described more than just its buildings. 'I have heard their prayers. They can be pitiful, praying not just to the gods they know but to those they don't, fearing they have offended one of them but not knowing which one or why. It is like stumbling around in the dark.'

'Our God is not like that,' said Dinah softly. 'He shows us both Himself and His ways, telling us when we sin.'

'And He lights the path back to Him,' added Nehushta. *She had walked that path.*

By the time the gates in the city walls were clearly visible, Nehushta's heart was swirling like sand whipped up into the air by the approach of a summer storm. *Yearning. Nervousness. Exhilaration. Hesitancy.* All vied within her. Her eyes drank in every sight as they entered through one of the southern gates. Shealtiel assured them that they would soon see the grandeur of the Ishtar gate in the city's northern wall, but Nehushta was barely listening as they made their way along one of the long straight streets.

'Is it much further?'

He didn't answer immediately but pulled on one of the reins, turning the donkeys around a corner. After a few moments he asked, 'Do you see the house with the red canopy over the upper window?' Nehushta looked along the street. 'That is ours.'

It felt like a dream as Shealtiel finally stopped the cart and helped her down. He opened the wooden door in the wall and led Nehushta along a corridor that was dark after the brightness of the afternoon sun. Dinah followed behind. And then they were out into daylight again, entering a courtyard graced by a number of small fig trees in earthenware pots. A man sitting in the shade looked up and then rose, his face full of wonder. Even after the passing of thirty-seven years, there was no hesitation, for his features were unmistakable. 'Coniah!'

Later, after the reunions and a meal during which day had faded into night, both she and Dinah were taken to what was to be their new room. It had two comfortable beds, both bearing richly coloured pillows and coverings.

When the door was closed behind them, Nehushta sat down on one of the beds. The well of excitement that had kept her awake through the previous night and sustained her through the day had finally run dry. She yawned loudly, suddenly aware of the aches from two days upon a cart. She looked at Dinah. 'Are you not tired too?'

'I slept more than you last night. But, yes, I am.' She sat down on the other bed and patted it. 'And I have no doubt that I will sleep very soundly on this.'

Nehushta breathed in deeply and then out again. 'Coniah has changed. I remember him as a brash young man—very much like his father. He is not like that now.'

'Thirty-seven years of captivity would change any man…'

'It has changed him for the better.' She paused. 'Maybe as Yahweh has also used this exile to change my heart.'

Dinah removed her sandals, seeming deep in thought. Then she spoke, her voice soft. 'Yesterday, on our journey, you told Shealtiel of Ezekiel and some of his oracles. But there was one that you did not mention—one that I treasure more than any other.'

Nehushta was intrigued, her tiredness momentarily forgotten. 'What is that?'

'The prophet spoke of Yahweh gathering the exiles and bringing them back. But He also promised them a new heart and a new spirit, removing hearts of stone and giving hearts of flesh instead.'

'Do you think it means the kind of change of which I have just spoken?'

Dinah gave a little shrug of her shoulders. 'I do not know. But the prophet did speak, did he not, of Yahweh putting his own Spirit within His people.' She paused. 'Is that not what our people need if it is to be different when Yahweh restores them to the land?'

Nehushta thought for several moments. 'I do not know how Yahweh can do such a thing. But you, Dinah, have taught me that if Yahweh says something, then it is surely true. Even if—as we said the other night—we cannot guess how He will bring about His plans.' She paused, suddenly remembering the words of Jeremiah's letter. *'Plans to give you hope and a future.'*

'But we will not live to see it,' answered Dinah, sighing.

'No,' murmured Nehushta. 'But some of our descendants will, one day.' She then smiled as she leant down to remove her own sandals. 'But what about *this*? Could we have even dared to hope for it?'

342

Dinah looked around the room. 'The mercies of Yahweh always surprise, do they not?'

'They do, Dinah. Always.'

Notes

1. *The chapter spans the eighteenth year of exile (approximately 580 BC) to the thirty-seventh year (approximately 561 BC), when Jehoiachin was released from prison (2 Kings 25:27). Amel-Marduk (or Evil-merodach or Awel-Marduk as he is variously named in different Bible translations) ruled from 562-560 BC.*

2. *Nebuchadnezzar's seven-year madness (Daniel 4:33) is not specifically referenced in Babylonian records, although this is not necessarily surprising. As the Bible Background Commentary states, however: 'A fragmentary cuneiform text suggests the possibility that Nebuchadnezzar had some problem that caused him to become disengaged from his responsibilities for a time, during which his son, Amel-Marduk, was perhaps in control. But the text is too uncertain to draw any firm conclusions' (p737). Given that the judgment is related to Nebuchadnezzar's pride in his city (Daniel 4:30), it may have come after his construction of the Ishtar gate and the processional way.*

3. *Some commentators have speculated that Amel-Marduk may have befriended Jehoiachin when the former was temporarily imprisoned by his father, leading to Jehoiachin's favourable treatment when Amel-Marduk became king.*

4. *The prayer described by Shealtiel is based on the Sumerian 'Prayer to Every God' in J.B. Pritchard's, 'Ancient Near Eastern Texts' (pp391-392). The introduction to the prayer states: 'This prayer is addressed to no particular god, but to all gods in general, even those who may be unknown. The purpose of the prayer is to claim relief from suffering, which the writer understands is the result of some infraction of divine law...he does not even know what god he may have offended. Moreover, he claims, the whole human race is by nature ignorant of the divine will, and consequently is constantly committing sin.' Although the prayer was found on a tablet in*

343

the library of Ashurbanipal (668-633 BC), it nevertheless illustrates the problem of multiple gods.

5. Aside from eating at the king's table and being given a regular allowance (2 Kings 25:29-30), it is not known how Jehoiachin would have lived in Babylon, or for how long. Significantly, 2 Kings 25:27 refers twice to Jehoiachin as 'king of Judah', focusing hope maybe on the continuing line of David.

Uzziel

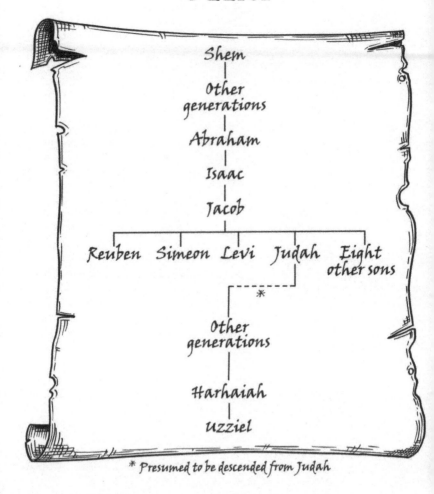

Shem

Other
generations

Abraham

Isaac

Jacob

Reuben   Simeon   Levi   Judah   Eight
                                   other sons

*

Other
generations

Harhaiah

Uzziel

* Presumed to be descended from Judah

I

'On the thirteenth day of the first month the royal secretaries were summoned. They wrote out in the script of each province and in the language of each people all Haman's orders to the king's satraps, the governors of the various provinces and the nobles of the various peoples. These were written in the name of King Xerxes himself and sealed with his own ring. Dispatches were sent by couriers to all the king's provinces.' (Esther 3:12-13)

Uzziel clambered up onto the large stone that blocked his pathway, then glanced over his shoulder. He rolled his eyes. 'Are you a snail, Han?'

Hananiah glowered as he looked up from gingerly picking his way over a pile of rubble. 'No, but neither am I a mountain goat.' His eyes returned to the stones under his feet, testing whether they would hold his weight. 'If you wish to break your bones, go ahead, but do not ask me to do the same.'

Uzziel shrugged, then jumped down, deciding to wait for his companion rather than forge ahead. He picked up a small, jagged rock and examined it. It was smooth on one side. *Another remnant of the walls.* Jerusalem's defences, razed to the ground by the Babylonians some hundred years earlier, were now the rubble over which they'd been scrambling. Uzziel drew back his arm and hurled the rock into the air. It sailed above the Kidron Valley, still graced with green before the summer heat, before descending into scraggy bushes some distance away. He smiled in satisfaction as Hananiah reached his side. 'Come on.'

The two fifteen-year-olds said little as they made their way down to where the Kidron Valley met the Valley of Ben Hinnom to the south of Jerusalem, and then headed towards the spring at En Rogel.

347

'What if she isn't there today?'

Uzziel had no need for a name. Which was as well since neither knew it. But to Uzziel, it was the face and form of the Philistine girl that mattered. He had happened upon her one day while wandering outside Jerusalem—and he'd been smitten. All he knew was that she was a daughter of a merchant from Ashdod who sold his pottery in Jerusalem and whose camp lay near En Rogel—and that she often washed clothes at the spring.

Uzziel drew a breath. 'She will be—I am certain of it.'

'You were certain of it last week, but that did not make it so then.'

But Uzziel was right. As they neared the spring, the girl was there with others. She was kneeling beside the water, her hands pushing down beneath the surface onto some garment. Her dark hair was uncovered and gleamed in the sun, her eyes sparkling and her lips full and inviting—to Uzziel at least. 'Why are the daughters of the Philistines so much more tempting than those of Jerusalem?' he murmured. He and Hananiah stopped a short distance from them. Uzziel allowed a small smile to play upon his lips as his eyes met hers. He raised an eyebrow playfully. She giggled and looked away, saying something in a language foreign to him. Another girl answered, eyeing both the visitors with some mirth.

'What do you think they are saying?' whispered Hananiah.

'They are saying that they have never seen such handsome and desirable Jews, and that their hearts burn with longing to lie with us and bear our sons.'

His friend snorted. 'More likely they are wondering why the taller one has such enormous ears…'

'My ears are no bigger than yours.'

Hananiah snorted again but didn't answer.

Uzziel groaned. A Philistine merchant had wandered out from among the nearby tents and was approaching them.

He looked them up and down with disdain. 'What do you Jewish boys want? Have you come to inspect our pottery?' His thick accent dripped with derision.

Uzziel lifted his chin. 'My father, Harhaiah, is a goldsmith and he has sent me to find a merchant who trades in gold.'

The eyes of the Philistine bored into him. 'And I am the great and mighty Xerxes. If you crave a daughter of Ashdod then maybe you should ask your father to find one for you to marry, rather than coming here to look.'

'Maybe I will…'

'Stop, idiot!' hissed Hananiah.

But it was not his plea that stilled Uzziel's tongue. A trumpet blast—some distance away, but clear and long—silenced them all. Uzziel turned towards Jerusalem, frowning, the Philistines forgotten as curiosity supplanted desire. *The start of the third month had been the previous week.* For a second time he uttered 'Come on.' Without a backwards glance, he started walking back to the city.

Uzziel quickened his pace. 'Why should they sound the trumpet when it is neither the New Moon nor a festival?'

Hananiah shrugged. 'Maybe an army has been spotted…'

'The Persians have no reason to be here, and the Egyptians are now under their rule, as we are.'

'Maybe, then, Xerxes has died.'

Uzziel scoffed. 'He's not yet fifty.'

'You asked the question!' replied Hananiah, exasperated, as they scrambled over the mass of rubble once more.

'More likely he has been killed in another of his stupid battles against the Greeks.'

When it eventually arrived in Jerusalem on the lips of merchants or travellers, news of battles won or lost by powers far greater than their own always fascinated Uzziel. He had been born the year after the Persian king, Darius, suffered a punishing defeat far away across the Great Sea in Greece at a place that bore the name *Marathon*. He was only three when Darius died and was succeeded by his son Xerxes. Later, his nine-year-old's imagination had been filled with the story of another Persian defeat by the Greeks, though as he had seen neither sea nor ship, the battle at the distant *Salamis* was harder to picture.

The boys fell silent, in part due to their exertion, but also because Uzziel had no further ideas about the trumpet blast. But when they finally entered the city through what had once been the Fountain Gate, what met them was neither the joy of a festival nor animated discussions of a distant war. The mood was far darker—bewilderment, panic, fear.

Uzziel had never seen the city like it, and though he would not have admitted it, dread rose within. 'What has happened, Han?' He neither expected nor received an answer.

A familiar voice suddenly made itself heard above the clamour. 'Uzziel!'

Uzziel craned his neck and found his father's stern features in the crowd. He was pushing through the throng towards them.

'Where have you been?' He didn't wait for a reply. 'Hananiah—your father is waiting for you at your house. I told him I would send you back if I found you.' He turned and began walking back up the hill, the command to follow left unspoken.

'What's happened, Father?'

'An edict has come from the Persians.'

'What sort of edict?'

His father stopped abruptly and rounded on them, eyes blazing. 'One that spells death!'

It was only when he and his father Harhaiah were sitting in their small courtyard that Uzziel received answers to some, though not all, of his many questions.

'But why?'

His father ran a hand through his greying hair. 'I do not know—none of us do yet. I have told you all I know—that news has come from the governor of Judah of an edict issued by the King of Persia, bearing the seal of Xerxes himself. A copy of that edict was read when the leaders of Jerusalem had been assembled, and it stated that on the thirteenth day of Adar, Jews everywhere are to be destroyed and their goods plundered. Neither young nor old, women nor children, are exempt.' He sighed. 'But why Xerxes should issue such a decree throughout his empire when we have neither rebelled nor risen against him…' His voice trailed off as he shook his head slowly, before drawing a deep breath. 'None in Jerusalem know.'

Uzziel's thoughts tumbled through his mind like the stones of a tower crashing to the ground. *Young and old? Women and children?* He pictured his grandmother who lived with them and his younger sisters, one of them barely a year old. *Would his grandmother's life end in violence and his sister lie slaughtered before she had spoken her first word?* And his mouth became dry as he thought of suffering the same bloody fate. *And all by the end of the year.* 'But why the twelfth month?' he asked suddenly, bewildered. 'Why, if Xerxes wants us dead, does he wait until then? And why set a particular day?'

'Surely you know enough of the Persians. They will have cast lots, believing their gods will direct them to an opportune day. But we must believe that it is Yahweh who has determined the outcome, giving us nine months to find some way to escape this evil.'

'But if an edict bears the king's seal it cannot be changed.' His mind was racing faster than a Persian horse. 'Maybe we could flee the slaughter…'

His father raised his eyes to the blue sky above. 'Where to? Is there any part of the world *not* under Persian rule? Even Egypt is now subject to them—and the decree has gone out to the entire empire.'

'What about Greece?'

'Even if that were possible, would they let us flee to their enemies?'

'Then we will defend ourselves!'

'In a city with neither walls nor gates?' Harhaiah shook his head slowly once more. 'Every person in the empire will soon know, if not already, that Xerxes is against us. What better way to show their loyalty to him than to kill us, without fear of punishment? And as a goad, he gives permission to take all we own as plunder.'

Uzziel stared at the ground. *Were they no more to the Persians than dirt to be walked over and trampled underfoot?* He eventually looked up. 'What are we going to do?'

His father sighed again and shrugged. 'I do not know. But the elders will meet tomorrow—and we will pray and trust Yahweh.' His gaze met that of Uzziel. 'As you know, your grandfather was born in exile, but travelled here as a child when Cyrus issued his decree to allow the exiles to return—and I was born to him in the year when the rebuilding of the temple was complete. Surely Yahweh has not brought His people back to the land to see us destroyed now.'

But Uzziel wondered what even the Almighty could do in the face of such an edict.

Later, as he lay in bed, wide-awake, his mind took him to places he would rather not go. *What would it feel like to be run through with a blade? Would death come swiftly in a few heartbeats? Or would he lie in agony as the day dragged on until darkness finally engulfed him forever or a faceless enemy finished him off? Would he have courage to fight, or would he flee in fear from the edge of a sword or spear?* The stories of far-off battles had fascinated him. It was another matter to face warfare himself. *They were a lone lamb on the barren hills, encircled by a pack of rapacious wolves, with no escape.* For a moment, the surly Philistine whom he had met that afternoon came to mind. *Would the man remember that his father was a goldsmith, and even now be planning to kill him and his family so that he could seize their gold on the appointed day?* The outing to the spring at En Rogel already felt like a different life—one that he feared had gone for good.

Notes

1. *The events of this chapter take place in 474 BC.*
2. *Some Bible translations use the Hebrew name for Xerxes, i.e. Ahasuerus. However, for ease of recognition, the more usual name of Xerxes is used here.*
3. *It is assumed that news of battles between other nations would eventually spread throughout the known world, probably along the trade routes.*
4. *Although many critics have raised doubts about the historicity of the Biblical book of Esther (mainly because of a lack of external historical confirmation), there are many others who see no compelling reason to discount its veracity, given the gaps in our knowledge of ancient history.*

The book also provides a reason for the very real Jewish feast of Purim, and there are parts of the story that accord well with what is known of the history of the time (see point 5 below, for example).

5. We cannot be sure how long it would have taken for Haman's edict (Esther 3:12-15) to reach Jerusalem. Darius I, who died in 486 BC, rebuilt an ancient highway called 'The Royal Road', running between the capital, Susa (in modern-day Iran), and Sardis (in modern-day Turkey), to allow for rapid communication with the west of his large empire. Apparently, mounted couriers were supposed to travel its length (1,677 miles) in nine days—a journey that would take months on foot. The Greek historian Herodotus, writing around 440 BC (i.e. around these times), wrote of these couriers: 'Now there is nothing mortal which accomplishes a journey with more speed than these messengers, so skilfully has this been invented by the Persians: for they say that according to the number of days of which the entire journey consists, so many horses and men are set at intervals, each man and horse appointed for a day's journey. These neither snow nor rain nor heat nor darkness of night prevents from accomplishing each one the task proposed to him, with the very utmost speed. The first then rides and delivers the message with which he is charged to the second, and the second to the third; and after that it goes through them handed from one to the other, as in the torch-race among the Hellenes.' (The History of Herodotus – Book VIII, translated by G. C. Macaulay.) Compare this with Esther 8:10: 'Mordecai wrote in the name of King Xerxes, sealed the dispatches with the king's signet ring, and sent them by mounted couriers, who rode fast horses especially bred for the king.'

6. There is debate as to whether the edict was issued to all people (and was therefore a general invitation to massacre the Jews) or to portions of armed men in each province. It is also not clear how widely it was proclaimed by the couriers to 'the general public' beyond 'the king's satraps, the governors of the various provinces and the nobles of the various peoples' (Esther 8:12). Here it is assumed that the decree went to the governor of Judah (referred to in Nehemiah 5:14-15) and was then promulgated to Jerusalem.

7. The month of Adar corresponds to February-March and is the twelfth month of the Hebrew calendar.

2

*King Xerxes replied… 'Now write another decree in the king's name
on behalf of the Jews as seems best to you, and seal it with the king's
signet ring—for no document written in the king's name and sealed
with his ring can be revoked.' (Esther 8:7-8)*

The second edict, when it came, was no less unexpected and just as
bewildering.

In the weeks since the decree, Uzziel's days had been transformed.
Each morning, he found himself wielding, not a delicate tool to shape
fine gold, but a heavy sword to end a life—or prolong his own. Even
if there seemed little hope of survival, a determination burned to defy
their doom. Maybe some would survive so that utter destruction
was not their end. Either way, they would not sit idly waiting for the
worst.

Sweat ran down Uzziel's forehead. He and Hananiah were
fighting each other with crude wooden swords under both the early
summer sun and the watchful eye of a burly soldier whom Uzziel
had named *Goliath*. They and others like them were scattered over a
level patch of dirt just outside the city. Uzziel lunged but Hananiah
swiftly side-stepped the rough blade. Previous failures to do so had
drawn loud protests and left angry red welts (which later turned
purple or black). Uzziel's response each time had been that it would
better teach him to avoid the sharp edge of real metal.

Uzziel swiped wildly once more but found only air. He dodged
Hananiah's blade and drew his own back—but then froze as a
trumpet blast split the air. Every student stopped, each head turning
towards the sound.

Goliath's stern gaze returned to them as the sound faded to nothing. 'This will not concern you,' he barked. 'Keep on practising.' No-one did, but rather stood watching as he strode away.

Uzziel waited until Goliath was nearing the gateway into Jerusalem. His curiosity would not be refused. 'Come on, Han!' They hurried across the dirt, others joining them, as they followed Goliath several paces behind. Every muttered question was the same: *why had the trumpet sounded this time?*

They were not alone in making their way up through the city streets towards the temple. Some faces wore eagerness, others unease, but most, a grim determination. When Goliath reached the edge of the gathering crowd, Uzziel did not hold back. He only stopped when directly behind his instructor. He stood listening as Goliath began a conversation with the man next to him.

'Why the signal, Imri?'

'It is another edict from Persia—but a courier has come to Jerusalem this time. They are assembling the elders and Levites here for its reading.'

Uzziel suddenly blurted out, 'What's the edict about?' Hananiah punched him.

Goliath turned around slowly. 'I told you to stay. Since when were you appointed a leader...or suddenly discover you're of the tribe of Levi?'

Uzziel decided it would be unwise to point out that neither were true of his instructor either. 'But it *is* likely to concern my fate as much as theirs.'

Imri raised an eyebrow and nodded. 'Our young friend has a point.'

Goliath looked at Uzziel evenly. 'Our young friend is *meant* to be practising his skills with a sword...'

Imri ignored the objection. 'We do not yet know the content of the edict—other than it is from the Persian king.'

Goliath pointedly turned his back on them, making it clear that the short conversation was now over. Uzziel stood up on his toes, trying to get a better view. The upwards slope of the ground made it almost impossible to see what was happening beyond the crowd. He glanced around, and then turned to his friend. 'Let's go.'

'Where?'

'Somewhere where we can see better.'

He threaded his way through the growing throng, Hananiah following closely. When he reached what was left of the wall nearby, he looked for the lowest point and pulled himself up onto it, grazing a knee as he did so. He stood and looked down. 'We'll be able to see better if we go up the wall.'

Hananiah rolled his eyes, shook his head but gave in when Uzziel reached down to help him up. They then clambered carefully upwards along the uneven top of the wall. They were soon above the level of the crowd, and when they reached a flat section of stones, Uzziel sat down, dropping his legs over the edge. Hananiah followed his lead. For a while they remained silent, simply taking in the scene before them. Uzziel picked out both their fathers among the men gathered there, too engaged in their conversation to notice their sons upon the wall. But his eyes were soon elsewhere.

Uzziel pointed. 'That must be the courier seated on the horse.' He paused. 'I wonder why he has come to Jerusalem this time. The last edict was delivered only to the governor of the region.'

'What does it matter? All that matters is what's on the scroll.' For a few moments neither spoke. 'Maybe Xerxes has had a change of heart,' offered Hananiah suddenly, 'and has revoked his first edict.'

'He cannot do that—'

'But he is the king!'

'It is their custom. They say that once a law is written in the king's name, it cannot be changed.'

'It is a stupid custom,' muttered Hananiah.

But suddenly the murmuring of the crowd began to subside. An elderly man dressed in a clean linen tunic with a colourful sash and white turban appeared, accompanied by several older men. 'Look!' whispered Uzziel. 'The high priest is here. They will read the edict now.'

One of the men at the high priest's side nodded to the mounted courier, who then unfurled a scroll. The barking of a dog in the distance could be heard—but that was the only sound. All was still.

He spoke in their own language. *'The words of Xerxes, the great king, king of kings, king of all kinds of people, king on this earth far and wide, the son of Darius the king. Xerxes the great king proclaims: "The Jews in every part of my kingdom and in every city are given the right to assemble and protect themselves, to destroy, kill and annihilate the armed men of any nationality or province who might attack them and their women and children, and to plunder the property of their enemies. The day appointed for the Jews to do this in all the provinces of my kingdom is the thirteenth day of the twelfth month, the month of Adar." This edict is written in the king's name and bears his seal.'* With that, he furled the scroll, lowered it and held it out to an official who stepped forward and took it from his hand. The courier then wheeled his horse around, urged it forward through the crowd, and with that he was gone.

The gathering suddenly came to life, as if they had suddenly been thrust into the midst of a New Moon festival. Some were engaged in urgent discussion, but the mood was mostly that of celebration.

'I don't understand,' murmured Hananiah. 'Why the rejoicing? Xerxes decrees that we can defend ourselves, but we would have done that anyway. What's different this time?'

Uzziel scratched his chin. 'I don't know. Let's go down and find out.' He had no choice but to follow Hananiah down the narrow uneven wall at a slower—if safer—pace, groaning impatiently more than once. Hananiah either didn't hear or simply ignored him.

'This way,' said Uzziel, when they were both finally on the ground. He had kept his eye on their fathers as long as he could, and—although now out of sight—knew where they'd been. He forged forward, craning his neck. As the crowd began to thin, he spotted them both, now in conversation with a number of others. 'Father!'

The small knot of men looked towards them. Both fathers smiled broadly.

'Were you here to hear the good news?' asked Haraiah.

'We heard what the courier said, Father, but what has changed? We would have fought those who attacked us without such an edict!'

'You are right, my son. But what has changed is where the king's favour lies.'

'What do you mean?'

'For reasons we do not know, the king in his last edict ordered that the Jews be annihilated, and their goods plundered. The whole empire knew that was the king's desire, and those who carried it out would gain his favour. But now, for some reason, Xerxes appears to have changed his mind—'

'But couldn't change his own law,' interjected Hananiah.

Hananiah's father smiled. 'That is right. So now, by giving us the same permissions against those who might attack us, it announces whose side the king is on, and it is not the side of our enemies. Some may have been planning to attack us only through fear of appearing disloyal to the Persian king if they did not. Now they may pay no heed to his first decree with no such fear.'

'The hand of our God is in this turn of events,' added Harhaiah. 'Of that, I am sure.'

'But what of our enemies?' asked Uzziel. 'Will they still attack?'

His father smiled. 'If they do, then be sure of this: Yahweh's hand will give us victory over them!'

The thirteenth day of the month of Adar was clear when it finally dawned. Uzziel lay staring at the rafters after he woke, feeling neither fear nor agitation. Exhilaration coursed through him. The assurance of many in Jerusalem that the hand of Yahweh was with them had worn off onto him—and it was easier knowing he would not have to bear a sword. Soon after the second edict, it was decreed that, in accordance with the Law of Moses, only those aged twenty or above were now to be included in the fighting men. Men, like his father, with little or no experience of handling a weapon were also only required to be ready if called upon. Uzziel did not, however, intend to stay at home—despite what his father had asked of him.

Having slipped away whilst his mother wasn't looking, Uzziel hurried the short distance to Hananiah's house. He did his best to silence the inner voice that reminded him that he was both disobeying his father and likely to cause his mother worry. He told himself that the real command was to stay safely away from the battle—and he could do that well enough without having to remain at home.

Hananiah was seated in the courtyard, pushing a pestle around a stone mortar. It was a familiar sight. His father was a perfumer, and the need to grind the likes of myrrh or cassia was a frequent one. But his friend was not alone, however. Uzziel kept out of sight, found a small stone, and threw it towards Hananiah when no one was looking. It landed near his feet. He looked up. Uzziel mouthed, *Come on,* jerking his head. The other youth glanced around, put his implements down and rose. Whatever excuse he gave to his mother appeared to be accepted.

Hananiah was soon beside him. 'Where are we going?'

'To see what happens.'

It was not long before they were both sitting upon the ruins of Jerusalem's walls once more—but this time facing outwards, towards the rocky ground to the north of the city. The rains of winter—now almost behind them—meant that the landscape was dotted with lush greenery. There was no grazing of animals that day, however. The sheep and goats that would normally have been out on the hillside were nowhere to be seen. Instead, armour-clad men stood in groups, alert and ready—swords in their belts, spears in their hands, or bows slung over their shoulders. Watchmen ringed the city, atop the remains of the walls, looking out in every direction and equipped with trumpets to sound a warning to gather the fighting men should enemies approach.

Despite surveying the horizon constantly, Uzziel still started when a loud blast sounded nearby. His eyes darted to the watchman to his left. His free hand was pointing. Uzziel looked out in the direction indicated, squinting. He then saw what the watchman had spotted but he had missed: faint glinting on the hills. He shaded his eyes and stared. *There! Movement in the distance!*

'Is it our enemies?'

'I can't tell, Han...'

But below them, the armed men of Jerusalem were readying themselves, with others running to join them. Uzziel then tried to judge the number that had come over the distant ridge. The sun reflected intermittently from what he guessed to be armour or weapons. 'How many do you think?'

There was a pause. 'One hundred... or maybe as many as two?'

'It is no huge army, however many,' murmured Uzziel before glancing down. The group of armed men below them had grown considerably since the alarm sounded. *Goliath* had joined them. 'Our own numbers match them now, surely, especially given those who have joined us.'

Three days earlier, armed men from the governor of their region had arrived to aid them, much to the surprise of the city. But with them had come the reason for their deliverance. A Jew named Mordecai, they were told, had risen to prominence in Susa and the favour of Xerxes was upon him. It was because of him that the second edict had been issued, and the governor now sought his goodwill by sending warriors to stand with their own.

Two men, seemingly in command, were in urgent discussion. When one of them nodded, the other addressed the men, pointing to groups of their own men, then to the approaching enemy. The instructions were out of earshot. What was not, however, was the cry that followed, swords and spears lifted high: *Let God arise, let His enemies be scattered!* The hairs on the back of Uzziel's neck bristled.

They watched, enthralled and in silence, as the men moved forward and then stopped, far enough away to keep the city out of range of hostile arrows, but close enough to be seen should others be needed to strengthen their arm. Even though he did not bear a sword, Uzziel's heart still thundered as the enemies drew closer. And then noise filled the air: hundreds of feet moving swiftly upon earth, iron striking iron, loud cries, shrieks of pain—though the sounds were diminished by distance.

His gaze did not leave the scene as the sun rose higher. It was only the sudden sound of his father's voice that drew him away.

'Why do I see my son upon the walls when he is meant to be at home?'

Uzziel looked down. He had been too gripped by the battle to notice his father's approach. He was not chided further, however.

'What do you see?'

Uzziel looked out again. 'I see our enemies falling…'

His father smiled. 'They fight only because they hate us and wish to take what is ours. We fight for our survival and for our God—and that puts a strength in our souls and our swords that theirs will never have.'

Uzziel returned the smile, and then his attention was back on the battle. *His father was right.*

And as the sun set upon the thirteenth day of the month of Adar, the sound of celebration across Jerusalem proved his words true.

With both winter and the threat of doom behind them, Uzziel's mind flitted back to the Philistine girl. He knew his father had begun to give serious consideration to finding a suitable wife for him. He waited for his moment.

Uzziel stared hard at the gold wire in his hands, his brow furrowed and his lips tight, oblivious to all else. The metal was bathed in the light streaming in through the large window of their small workshop. His fingers gently twisted the wire this way and that, trying to match perfectly the intricate pattern that his father had already created for an earring. It was only as he completed the final tight spiral that he began to be aware of the sounds of Jerusalem once more: *the footsteps passing in the street, the cries of traders, the bleat of a goat.* He felt his father's hand upon his shoulder.

'It looks as if you have done your job well.' His hand left Uzziel and he picked up the piece, holding it up to the light to inspect it. 'Hmm. It *is* good. Well done.' He laid it down on the bench again. 'You may cut off the remaining wire now.' It was the sign it was finished. His father drew in a deep breath and let it out. 'You are almost ready to make one of the daughters of Jerusalem a fine husband, skilled in a profitable trade.'

Uzziel paused, his mind racing. *He would tread carefully, with lightness in his voice.* 'And for such a diligent son, would you limit your choice only to those in this city?'

Harhaiah laughed. 'The lords over our lands may have such luxuries, but we do not. Besides, there are many fine young women here.'

'Well, what about those who may be *just* outside it?' He kept his eyes on the gold wire as he gently severed it with cutters. 'May not the daughter of a merchant from, say, Ashdod or Moab also make a good wife, and bring skills into this family that might prosper it.' He took the excess wire and put it in a little pot, from where it would be taken and melted down again. When his father didn't immediately answer he looked up. His father's arms were folded, his expression firm rather than cross.

'No son of mine will wed a daughter of one of our ancient enemies, be they Canaanite, Moabite or Philistine.'

Uzziel had planned his next words. 'But did not Salmon marry Rahab the Canaanite, and their son Boaz marry Ruth the Moabite.' He had decided against mentioning the disastrous marriage of Samson to his Philistine wife. 'Did *they* not become the ancestors of our father David by doing so?'

'You are right, but by the time they wed, both Rahab and Ruth had shown great faith, not in the gods of their own nations, but in the God of Israel. They had already joined our people. But what is also true is that by intermingling with such nations, we adopted their practices and their gods—and were exiled from the land by Yahweh.'

Uzziel had suspected his father might say as much. But he had a final stone in his sling with which he was sure he could fell the giant standing in his way. 'But a number of the sons of priests—Hanani, Shemaiah, Nethanel and others—are already pledged to be married to Hittites or Ammonites or Egyptians. If priests can marry outside of Israel, surely we are free to do the same?'

His father's eyes pierced him. 'We are never free to disregard what Yahweh has said, whatever our hearts desire—or whatever others do.'

Uzziel sighed. *His dreams of the Philistine girl were over.*

His marriage to Susanna happened the following autumn.

362

Notes

1. *The events of this chapter take place in 474/473 BC.*

2. *In the book of Esther, the second edict of Xerxes on behalf of the Jews was made 'on the twenty-third day of the third month, the month of Sivan' (Esther 8:9). This was two months and ten days after the previous edict (Esther 3:12). The month of Sivan would have run from around mid-May to mid-June. It is not clear how long it would have taken for news of this edict to reach Jerusalem (though see note 5 at the end of the previous chapter). Here it is assumed that the edict was sent directly to the Jews in Jerusalem, and therefore would have reached them much more quickly. This seems likely, given that Esther 8:9 specifically states that Mordecai's orders were sent to the Jews as well as to the satraps, governors and nobles who alone were mentioned in relation to the previous edict in Esther 3:12.*

3. *Although we do not know the exact wording of the edict, archaeology has uncovered an inscription in cuneiform in present day Turkey of a pronouncement made by King Xerxes. The way in which he refers to himself in the inscription has been replicated in this chapter as a basis for the edict. More details about the inscription can be found at https:// en.wikipedia.org/wiki/Xerxes_I_inscription_at_Van*

4. *It is assumed that Jerusalem would have been attacked by its enemies, although the book of Esther merely states that 'The Jews assembled in their cities in all the provinces of King Xerxes to attack those determined to destroy them.' (Esther 9:2). It also records that they were helped by others because of the fame of Mordecai (9:3-4).*

5. *Some details of later defensive strategies (Nehemiah 4:16-20) have been incorporated into this chapter.*

6. *It is assumed that a goldsmith would have had some form of workshop, but would it be in their home or elsewhere in Jerusalem? Would they sell their wares in a market or from the place where they worked? In the absence of such information, the details are left deliberately vague.*

7. *The imagined named characters introduced in this chapter are 'Goliath', Imri and Susanna.*

3

After these things, during the reign of Artaxerxes king of Persia, Ezra
son of Seraiah... came up from Babylon. He was a teacher well versed
in the Law of Moses, which the LORD, the God of Israel, had given.
(Ezra 7:1,6)

'Look!'

Uzziel followed the direction of his friend's gaze.

'Does that not stir memories?' asked Hananiah, laughing.

Uzziel smiled wryly. His two sons were making their way up
the wall behind them, the younger scurrying up the uneven slope
with the speed and agility of a lizard, the older following more warily.
'How can I chide them,' he murmured, 'for something their father
did before them?'

'Their father *and* his friend—though Daniel seems to have
inherited my caution and Uri your haste!'

'His mother calls it recklessness. She finds it best not to watch.'
Uzziel called up to the nine-year-old. 'Uri—if you cannot take more
care, you will have to come and stand here with Naomi. You have
gone far enough. Just sit and watch from where you are—and where
I can see you.' Both sons complied. 'And no, Uri—do not take your
scarf from your head. The sun is too strong.' Uzziel turned to face
north once more. 'There—I can now await the newcomers without
fearing yet another broken bone. I have paid enough physicians' fees.'

'At least neither of us, by some mercy of Yahweh, ever fell off.'
Hananiah glanced up at them again. 'How long has it been since we
sat there, watching the victory on the thirteenth of Adar?'

Uzziel thought for a moment. 'I was almost sixteen then, so over
fifteen years.'

364

A plaintive voice interrupted them. 'Will they be here soon?'

Hananiah looked down at his firstborn, a year younger than Uri. 'Soon enough, Naomi.' She seemed satisfied for the moment and began twirling her hair around a small finger. He whispered to Uzziel, 'She is convinced that she will soon have other girls to play with—rather than just her young brother.'

Uzziel looked up at the sky from where they stood in the shade just outside the city's northern walls, grimacing slightly. 'But what a time to travel, in the height of summer.'

'It will not have been summer when they left.'

Uzziel considered it his sacred duty—as did most—to be ready to open his home to those who had made the long, long journey from Persia, at least until they could find or build their own places to live. A few days earlier, a small company of men had arrived, announcing that they were travelling ahead of a very large number of Jews who had been granted permission to return to the land. The news had been like a spark to tinder, kindling both elation and hope, as well as endless discussion. A larger population for Jerusalem meant greater security, as well as better trade and increased wealth. It also indicated that the Jews had found favour with the latest Persian king. Artaxerxes had come to the throne seven years earlier when his father, Xerxes, had been slain by the commander of his own bodyguard.

The sun had passed its zenith by the time the first travellers appeared. What first seemed as a small stream soon became a broad river—a steady, unrelenting flow of people, animals, and possessions piled high upon carts. When they were finally close enough for faces to be seen, they bore wonder rather than weariness, their eyes feasting for the first time on the city they had always heard of but never seen.

As the sky began to set fire to the clouds, Uzziel was welcoming a family into his home. Their guests, a Levite named Azariah and his family, again seemed more overjoyed than overwhelmed. When all had refreshed themselves with cool water and changed into borrowed clothes until their own were washed, Susanna set out a generous meal in the courtyard, the heat of the day now passed. The familiar smell of fresh bread mingled with the rich aroma of a lamb stew cooked slowly over the courtyard fire. Other steaming dishes of vegetables seasoned with caraway or cumin were laid out on the large rug on which they were seated.

Uzziel smiled. *He had married well.* Susanna had learned much from not only her own mother but also his whilst she was alive. He looked around the gathering, ready to ask his aging father to say the prayer over their food. Then a sudden idea rose in his mind. He turned to Azariah. 'My brother—would you do the honour of blessing our meal?'

The Levite's eyes welled up and he lifted them to the heavens where the first star had now appeared. 'To think that we are sitting within Zion, *the city of Yahweh Almighty,* and that I am able to give thanks for His gracious provision in the place where His holy temple stands!' He returned his gaze to Uzziel. 'My friend, you could not have granted me a greater gift this evening!' And from his lips flowed the most heart-felt prayer of gratitude that Uzziel had ever heard— and his own heart stirred. When Azariah fell silent, his cheeks were wet with tears, but his eyes shone.

'Thank you, my friend. Our food has rarely been blessed with such an eloquent prayer—and from the lips of a Levite!' Uzziel gestured to the food. 'Now eat—you must be hungry.'

'You have lavished a feast upon us, Susanna!' said Azariah's wife, Hadassah, with a shy smile. 'We have not eaten like this since leaving Susa over four months ago.'

Azariah took a sip of wine from his cup. 'It was worth every step.'

Uzziel picked up the basket of bread and offered it to Azariah. 'We are eager to hear your story, but I do not wish to ask a thousand questions that will keep good food from the mouths of our guests.'

Azariah took bread and passed the basket on. 'Then tell us of Jerusalem and of the temple! We long to hear more. And tell us about yourselves.'

Uzziel thought for a moment. 'My father is not just a goldsmith. He crafts words as well, and there is no better storyteller in our family.' He looked across the gathering. 'Father, tell our guests of how the temple was rebuilt.'

Uzziel had heard the story many times, most often from the lips of his grandfather who had witnessed it himself. But the mantle had passed to his father, and with it, the tale. How Cyrus, the Persian king, had given permission for the Jews to return to Jerusalem, also issuing a decree that the temple be rebuilt, and its gold and silver articles returned. How the work had started under the leadership of both Zerubbabel, a descendant of the kings of Judah and the appointed governor of the land, and Joshua the high priest, building first an altar on which to offer sacrifices to Yahweh. How the foundation of the new temple had been laid. How there had been songs of praise and shouts of joy, but also the weeping of those old enough to remember Solomon's temple of gold, destroyed fifty years earlier. Then how the rebuilding was opposed by the enemies of the Jews, causing it to cease for over ten years. And how finally through the encouragement and support of two prophets—Haggai and Zechariah—the work recommenced under a new Persian king. A king who decreed that the royal treasury should support not only the rebuilding but also the worship of the temple, so that sacrifices and prayers could be offered for the well-being of the Persian king. And so, fifty-eight years earlier, on the third day of the twelfth month of Adar, in the sixth year of King Darius, the work had been completed.

Uzziel watched his father retelling the story—not as a lesson from history, but as if he had been there, using his arms and face and voice to bring it to life. All the children—even those who had heard it before—sat listening, rapt, as they continued to eat, their eyes barely leaving Haraiah until he finally fell silent, smiling.

'The hand of Yahweh is yet upon us,' murmured Azariah.

Uzziel chuckled. 'And you must eat, Father. The bowls are almost empty!'

'Ezra will wish to hear this story too,' said Azariah suddenly. 'We knew it only in part.'

'Ezra?'

'Ezra the priest. The gracious hand of our God is upon him, and it is because of him we are here.' He paused. 'I have never known a man whose heart burns so fiercely for the Law of Moses. He knows it, but also understands and lives it, and teaches others to do the same. I hope one day, as a Levite, that I too may teach others of the wonders of Yahweh's Law.'

'I, too, have heard him teach,' added Hadassah. Her youngest child was already asleep in her lap. 'What my husband says is true.'

Susanna rose and fetched a platter bearing small cakes of dried figs. She began handing them around to those sated with stew. 'You say it is because of this Ezra that you are here. But was it not the king of Persia who gave you permission to return? That is what we were told.'

Azariah stroked his beard. 'Both things are true. It was to Ezra that Artaxerxes granted permission to return, but he also granted everything that Ezra requested.'

Uzziel was intrigued. 'But why did the king show such goodwill?'

'It would not be the first time that a Jew has found favour within the citadel at Susa,' smiled Azariah. 'But Ezra has a better answer. He says Yahweh has moved the heart of the Persian king, just as He did with Cyrus.'

Susanna stayed Uri's hand. The youngster's eyes moved from the platter of figs to his mother's face. She shook her head, silently mouthing, *No more,* and then turned to Azariah, ignoring her son's pout. 'What else did Artaxerxes decree?'

'That the treasurers of the province Beyond the River should provide, within generous limits, whatever silver, wheat, wine or oil Ezra requests for the temple, and that all those who work at the house of Yahweh should be exempt from taxes.'

Uzziel stared at Azariah, stunned. 'A king of Persia decreed that?'

The Levite nodded. 'Yes, and more. Ezra is to teach God's laws to the people and appoint magistrates and judges to uphold that law.'

'That is, indeed, a wonder. Yahweh's hand is at work!'

Harhaiah looked up sharply. 'It is—but not all may welcome a reminder of His ways.'

Uzziel began to shiver. The paved ground on which he was sitting was as cold as it was hard, and much of his tunic was already darkened by the winter rain. He grimaced. 'I hope it will not be much longer until Ezra addresses us.'

'Just be glad that you are not married to that Philistine girl you once desired so much,' replied Hananiah, his face bleak. 'Your trembling would be even greater.' The arrival of Ezra over four months earlier had not only brought rejoicing. He had been as unbending as the stone beneath when it came to the Law.

Uzziel glanced around at those seated in the large square in front of the temple. The substantial gathering comprised not only men of Jerusalem but also those from throughout Judah. 'I wonder if any have failed to heed the call to assemble today.'

'They are fools if they have. Would you risk forfeiting not only all your property but also your place amongst God's people? Ezra's warning was clear.' The proclamation had been sent out three days earlier, after Ezra had led the people, weeping, in confession for the guilt of the land.

A trickle of water ran down Uzziel's back inside his tunic. The month of Kislev, one of the coldest, was often also the wettest. He looked upward, blinking as a raindrop splashed upon his eyelid. 'Maybe heaven weeps too for the people's sin.' He shivered, then lowered his gaze, puzzled. 'It is strange. I heard Ezra's words the other day and saw his grief. He confessed the sin of intermarrying with those who worship other gods and corrupt the land with detestable practices. He acknowledged that it had led to the exile yet is happening again. But he spoke of *our* sin and *our* guilt, though he himself is innocent of such things.'

'It is indeed strange. But maybe that is the heart of a true shepherd of Israel.'

Uzziel's attention returned to his discomfort as the rain strengthened. *It was a miserable day in every respect.* But then the assembly stirred. Ezra had risen to his feet to address them, soaked as they were. The rain did not subside.

The priest cast his eyes around the gathering, then lifted his voice. It was clear and strong. 'You have been unfaithful; you have married foreign women, adding to Israel's guilt.' He paused, letting his words,

369

like the rain upon their garments, sink in. 'Now make confession to Yahweh, the God of your fathers, and do His will. Separate yourselves from the peoples of the land and from your foreign wives.'

Uzziel knew the words with which he was to respond. They all did. They rose as one man, and he joined his voice to the loud chorus. 'It is so! We must do as you have said.' But then one of the leading men stepped forward. Uzziel craned his neck.

'You *are* right,' the leader began, so that all could hear, 'but the people are many and it is the season for rain. We *cannot* stand in the open like this, and this is not a task that can be done in one day or two, for we have sinned greatly in this matter. Let the leaders act for the whole assembly. Then let all in our towns who have taken foreign wives come at a set time, along with the elders and judges of each town, until the fierce wrath of our God is turned away from us.'

Uzziel's eyes had been flitting between the speaker and Ezra, trying to judge the latter's response.

But before it was given, murmuring suddenly rippled across the gathering. Hananiah whispered, 'They are not pleased.' He bobbed his head towards the right of the square.

Four men were standing slightly apart from the assembly, arms crossed, faces like thunder, passing comments between themselves. Suddenly, as if moved by some unseen signal, they all turned and walked away, heads held high and without looking back. Uzziel wondered if any of them—or their sons—were married to foreign women. The murmuring quickly subsided, all eyes on Ezra once more.

He addressed the man who had spoken. 'Let it be so. I will choose men from the heads of your houses, and we will be ready to begin examining this matter by the first day of the next month.' He nodded and turned to leave. It was the sign that they were dismissed.

Despite Uzziel's longing for dry clothes, a warm cloak and hot food, his mind flitted elsewhere as he and Hananiah walked back through the heavy rain to their houses. 'You were right.'

'About what, my friend?'

'I would be facing a disaster now if my father had bowed to my wishes and allowed me to marry that Philistine girl—'

'—whose name you never discovered.'

'Hmm. I have been married to Susanna for over fifteen years. I could not countenance having to send her away.'

'And maybe your children with her?'

'It is unthinkable. I have never been more grateful for my father's adherence to the Law of Moses.' He cast his mind back again. 'I remember mentioning several priests who were betrothed to Canaanite women. Hanani was one of them, I think.'

'He has an Ammonite wife, to be sure.' He paused. 'Or is she a Moabite? Either way she is certainly foreign.'

The door of his courtyard came into sight, gladdening Uzziel's heart. 'I thought the example of the priests might sway my father. But not all priests are to be followed.'

Hananiah stopped by the doorway to his own house. 'Unless they are like Ezra?'

Uzziel nodded, pausing before taking the final paces that would see him home. 'Unless they are like Ezra.'

As the new year dawned, Jerusalem could finally consider the matter of the foreign wives closed. It was not without grief, however, as foreign women and even children departed for their hometowns. But with the days warming and the darkness of winter behind, the spirit of Jerusalem was stirred again. Ezra explained the Law of Moses to them with a clarity they had never encountered, like a clear mountain stream after the muddy waters of a flood. But hearts were also fanned into flame by the desire to restore the walls and repair the foundations of the city. And there were willing hands.

Uzziel watched closely, Hananiah at his side, as their neighbour Joel turned over a misshapen stone on the dirt. He was a stonemason and had taken them to one of the piles of rubble outside the city, intending to show them how to take broken stones and fashion them for use in the city walls. Daniel and Uri had joined them. The sound of iron upon iron rang out, sharp and loud, as the mason brought down an unyielding hammer upon a similarly unyielding chisel. He repeated the action until the stone finally succumbed to the blows, splitting cleanly.

371

'There!' said Joel. 'That is how it is done.' He held out both hammer and chisel to Uzziel. 'Now you try.' He went over to another stone, examining it briefly. He put his finger upon it. 'See if you can split it here.'

Uzziel positioned the chisel upon the rock and raised the hammer.

'No,' interjected Joel. 'Not like that.' He adjusted the angle of the chisel. 'There. Now try it.'

Uzziel tried to ignore the mirth of his sons and brought the hammer down. It gave an uncertain ring as the chisel slipped, leaving a trail of white dust along the stone.

Joel brushed the dust away. 'Try again.'

But before Uzziel could strike a second time, Hananiah asked, 'Who are they?'

Uzziel lowered the hammer. All were looking to the north. It was not often that they saw either men upon mounts or armed soldiers. This was no army, but enough to be a show of force. Although still some distance away, they were clearly heading for Jerusalem.

'Whoever they are,' said Hananiah, 'it is trouble. Of that, I am sure.'

Uzziel was just about to return the tools to Joel, when a strange determination settled upon him. 'We are here to learn how to build Jerusalem's walls. Why should these men, whatever their purpose, stop us?' He set the chisel against the stone once more and raised the hammer.

'Can we go?'

He lowered the hammer again, looked at Uri and sighed. *Better maybe for others to occupy and amuse his sons, rather than his own imperfect attempts at masonry.* He turned to Daniel. 'Take your brother to see what the excitement is. Do NOT lose him in the crowds.'

Daniel grinned. 'Yes, Father.'

With that, the two scampered off like rabbits escaping the paws of a lion. Uzziel watched them for a few moments, shaking his head. He then turned his attention to the tools once more.

After five unsuccessful attempts to split the stone and one

wounded thumb, Joel sighed. 'Maybe I am expecting too much of hands that lack a lifetime's labour...'

'Unless it is a delicate gold necklace you want.' Uzziel glanced at his friend. 'Or a vial of myrrh.'

Joel suddenly seemed to brighten. 'There is, though, another way—not so elegant, but it will serve. I will show you how to make a good mortar that can fill the spaces around rough stones and enable a fit that way.'

The task of mixing lime, mud and water proved a simpler one to learn, particularly for Hananiah who was used to binding together different elements to make ointments. Joel was just showing them how to pack the mortar between stones, adding smaller fragments of rock, if necessary, when the brothers returned. There was no mistaking it.

'You must stop!' yelled Uri, hurtling across the ground, his brother struggling to keep up. He was red-faced by the time he reached them, repeating his words. 'You must stop!'

Uzziel folded his arms. 'Upon whose order?'

Uri looked up, his chest heaving and his face free from guile. 'The king!'

Daniel reached them, his expression pained. 'What does Uri mean?' asked Uzziel.

Daniel did his best to explain between gasping for air. 'The men...came from Samaria... They say...they have a letter...from Artaxerxes himself...ordering us...to stop any work...on rebuilding the city.' His words delivered, he bent over, breathing heavily and his hands upon his waist.

'Why would Artaxerxes stop us,' asked Hananiah, 'given the favour he bestowed upon Ezra?'

Joel turned to them, his lips tight. 'All I hear from Samaria tells me they are no friends of the Jews—and have no desire to see us prosper. They are making mischief for us, I'm sure. How else would the king know about our work?'

Uzziel turned to his son. 'Daniel—did the men say any more?'

Daniel glanced up, his face still contorted. 'Only that if we did not stop, they would use the edge of their swords or the tip of their spears to compel us.'

Hananiah laid down the trowel in his hand. 'Then we have no choice.'

Uzziel thought for a moment, remembering what he had learned from Ezra and Azariah, and almost surprising himself by his next words. 'Maybe for now. But is not the hand of Yahweh upon us? Have we not seen that in our own lifetimes, even before the coming of Ezra? We saw Him change the heart of Xerxes. May He not do the same with Xerxes' son?'

Hananiah smiled. 'Well spoken, my friend.'

Joel clapped them both on the shoulders. 'And when He does, be sure of this: I will make builders yet of this goldsmith and perfumer!'

Notes

1. *The events of this chapter take place in 458/457 BC. The dating of Artaxerxes' letter, stopping the work of building the foundation and walls of the city, is not specified. The text merely says, 'In the days of Artaxerxes...' (Ezra 4:7). However, Rehum's letter (Ezra 4:11-16) refers to 'the people who came up to us from you', implying this is after the return of Ezra to Jerusalem. The permissions that had been given by Artaxerxes to Ezra (in Ezra 7:12-26) related only to the functioning of the temple and the teaching of the law. It should be noted that the events of Ezra 4:6-23 (in the reigns of Xerxes and Artaxerxes) occur much later that the events in the rest of Ezra 4-6 (during the reigns of the earlier kings Cyrus and Darius). They are simply later examples of hostility inserted into the narration of the rebuilding of the temple and its opposition. Here it is assumed that the first attempt at rebuilding the walls, and the stopping of it by their enemies, occurred shortly after Ezra's return.*

2. *It has been estimated that around 5000 Jews (men, women and children) returned to Jerusalem and Judah with Ezra. Approximately 1500 men are numbered in Ezra 8:2-14, and a further 258 in 8:18-20.*

3. *It is not known how Ezra came to be in a position of influence with King Artaxerxes.*

4. *The enmity between Judah and Samaria began when the kingdom divided, with the Assyrians settling many non-Jews there after Samaria fell in 722 BC.*

5. *The main administrative district of the Persian empire was the satrapy (under a satrap). There were twenty-six satrapies established by Cyrus, with Darius increasing the number to thirty-six. 'Beyond the River' was the designation of one of the Persian administrative areas, translated variously as Trans-Euphrates, West-of-Euphrates, or by similar phrases. It included both Samaria and Jerusalem, and seems to have had either a single governor (such as Tattenai, in Ezra 5:3 – clearly with authority over Jerusalem) or a plurality of governors (see Nehemiah 2:9). It seems that Judah was some sort of administrative area in its own right (but within the larger area of the Trans-Euphrates), and had a governor of its own (e.g. Ezra 2:63,6:7)—a role to which Nehemiah was appointed (Nehemiah 5:14).*

6. *Although sending wives (and possibly children) away may seem harsh, it must be remembered that foreign wives had been taken in direct disobedience to God's Law (e.g. Deuteronomy 7:3, Exodus 34:15-16). The reason for the prohibition was not racial but spiritual: 'for they will turn your children away from following me to serve other gods, and the LORD's anger will burn against you and will quickly destroy you' (Deuteronomy 7:4). This had been borne out in practice (e.g. Judges 3:5-6, 1 Kings 11:1-8), with disastrous consequences, although even in the book of Ezra, there are indications that foreigners who had embraced the God of Israel became part of the worshipping community (Ezra 6:21). Although we are not explicitly told, the likelihood is that foreign wives who were turned away would have gone back to their non-Jewish families (as the Moabite widow Orpah did in Ruth 1:8-15).*

7. *Imagined named characters introduced in this chapter are Daniel, Uri, Naomi, Azariah, Hadassah and Joel.*

4

Uzziel son of Harhaiah, one of the goldsmiths, repaired the next section; and Hananiah, one of the perfume-makers, made repairs next to that. They restored Jerusalem as far as the Broad Wall.
(Nehemiah 3:8)

The walls of the city may have been left in ruins, but Uzziel's own life was being rebuilt and shaped by the teaching of Ezra. He had witnessed within his own home the dedication of Azariah to Yahweh's Law, finding it not a burden but a delight. Azariah knew not only the commands of the Almighty but also the stories of their people—of how the hand of Yahweh had led, guided and provided over hundreds of years. Here was a God who acted and spoke—not far off or unknowable but graciously revealing Himself. A God who disciplined His errant people but was also *Yahweh, the compassionate and gracious God, slow to anger, abounding in love and faithfulness.* For Uzziel, the God of Israel was now not just the God of Abraham, Isaac and Jacob—the God of their people—but *his* God.

Hananiah had been similarly stirred, and both men were often found on the Sabbath listening to Ezra teach at the temple. The more Uzziel knew of God's Law as the years went by, the wider its glorious light fell. It illuminated his daily life: ensuring the weights he used with his wares were true, that his children knew the commandments, that he shunned his workshop on the Sabbath. He discovered, too, that their God was neither constrained nor concerned by the span of days or years.

Uzziel looked up as the daylight in his workshop dimmed.

'Susanna said I would find you here.'

Uzziel smiled at the familiar face of Shekaniah as he stood in the doorway. The leader had arrived in Jerusalem with Ezra. 'Have you come for your bowl?'

'Uri said it was finished.'

Uzziel turned to his son. 'Daniel—it is on the shelf above you. Lift it down, please.' Daniel did so and handed him the ornate golden dish. 'Come, let us step outside—you will see its workmanship better. And bring the scales, Daniel.' Once in the sunlight, Uzziel handed the bowl to Shekaniah. It caught the sun's rays, sending them dancing upon the wall. He watched as his buyer carefully examined the delicate work.

'Beautiful,' he murmured.

'It is Daniel who embossed it. And I am not ashamed to admit that his hand is steadier than mine.' Uzziel waited until the inspection was complete, and then held out the scales, its pans perfectly level. Shekaniah placed the small bowl on one side, and Daniel held the weights out to him. 'Please weigh it yourself—or bring your own balance if you'd rather.'

Shekaniah smiled as he placed three of the weights from Daniel's hand on the other side. 'I have never heard any complaints about the honesty of either your shekels or your scales.' The bowl rose up as the two sides became level once more. 'And your price?'

'Twenty-five darics.'

Shekaniah sucked in air sharply through his teeth and pulled on his beard. 'It is more than I was hoping...'

'...says every buyer in Jerusalem!' laughed Uzziel. He turned to his son. 'Tell Uri to bring us whatever his mother or wife have to hand to refresh our guest.'

By the time the usual drawn-out task of determining a price acceptable to both buyer and seller was completed, a dish of dates had been consumed—and twenty-two darics changed hands.

Shekaniah picked at a tooth trying to dislodge a morsel of date as they perched on stools in the sun. He looked down at his finger, seemingly satisfied. 'And have you heard about the latest visitor to our city?'

Uzziel leaned forward, intrigued. 'No.'

Shekaniah raised an eyebrow. 'An official of the king of Persia—and an important one. He arrived just before noon with soldiers and horsemen.'

'Who is he?' asked Daniel.

'Nehemiah son of Hakaliah—'

'But those are Jewish names.'

'Indeed, and what is more, it appears he is the cupbearer to Artaxerxes himself.'

Daniel whistled. 'Did you know of him in Persia?'

'No, but much can happen in thirteen years.'

'But what brings him to Jerusalem?' asked Uzziel, stroking his chin.

'That, my friend, we are yet to discover.'

'Uzziel son of Haraiah!'

The shout drew Uzziel out into the courtyard. Both Daniel and Uri followed. Joel the stonemason was standing in the entrance, Hananiah and his eighteen-year-old son, Michael, at his side.

'We have work to do, my friends.'

'*We*? What sort of work?'

'Rebuilding the walls of Jerusalem!'

Uzziel stared at him, his mind flitting swiftly as a hornet in flight. 'Does this have anything to do with our visitor from Susa?' By now, the whole city had heard of the arrival of Nehemiah a few days earlier.

'It has everything to do with him! He has been appointed governor of Judah by Artaxerxes. What is more, he called a meeting with the priests, nobles and officials, proposing the rebuilding of the walls and gates. He told them that he came not only with the permission and blessing of the king of Persia, but also with letters instructing the keeper of the king's forest to supply timber for the rebuilding.' He paused. 'He also speaks of the gracious hand of our God being upon him.'

'And the leaders have agreed that the work begin immediately,' added Hananiah. 'All who are able may help.'

Uri turned to Uzziel, his eyes bright. 'We *must* join them, Father!'

'We will! We have waited long for this.' He placed a hand on the shoulder of each son. 'Neither I nor my sons will let this great honour slip through our fingers.'

'And the family of Hananiah will work at your side!'

Uzziel's heart soared. 'Surely, we see the hand of Yahweh at work once more.'

Joel nodded. 'Indeed. A plan will follow, but I must go. The need this day is to establish how many will offer the strength of their arms for this great work.' He paused in the doorway, however, a wry smile upon his face. 'You do remember how to make mortar, don't you?'

Uzziel and Hananiah stood side by side, facing west with the early morning sun on their backs and their sons at their sides. Uzziel ran his eyes up and down the section of ruined wall that they had agreed to repair. He grimaced. 'It will not be easy. If we were stonemasons like Joel it would seem, I am sure, as simple as a meander down the Mount of Olives.' He clicked his tongue. 'But to a goldsmith and perfume-maker...'

'More of an upwards climb?' offered Hananiah.

Uzziel cocked his head. *It looked no easier.* 'Or the path of a mountain goat.'

'We can do it, Father!' said Uri, going over to the remains of the wall and bracing his hand against it, as if to test its strength.

'But pushing over what yet stands,' said his brother dryly, 'will not help!'

Uzziel chuckled. 'Well, we will only complete it if we make a start. Let us begin by gathering the first stones.'

Together they crossed the nearby square and walked out through the Gate of Ephraim, Daniel and Uri pulling a handcart behind them. It was then only a short walk to the Broad Wall. It had once enclosed the dwellings on the Western Hill built under later kings. All now lay abandoned.

'At least Nehemiah is not asking for *this* wall to be repaired,' said Uzziel, his eyes wandering along the long line of stones, some standing, some scattered.

'It would take an army,' agreed Hananiah. 'He is wise to seek the defence only of what is now occupied. The walls of David and Solomon will suffice when repaired.'

Uri walked to one of the stones on the ground. 'And it means there are plenty of good stones that we can use.' He tried to lift it, but with little success.

His brother laughed. 'Stones are only of use if we can lift them—both here and onto the wall.' He and Hananiah's son, Michael, added their strength. Even then, it was only with difficulty that they heaved the stone onto the cart.

Uzziel frowned. 'If you are not to break the cart, and still wish to be able to pull it back into the city, I would not add many more stones of that size.'

In the end, four stones were hauled on the back of the cart, which was also used for the mud and lime to make mortar. It was only when the sun was at its height that they stopped for both rest and food, the latter brought by the wives and daughters of both families and set out in the shade of a nearby house. Their own stretch of wall, running north to south, offered little shielding from the summer sun.

'Are you feeding an army?' asked Uzziel as the women unloaded piles of bread and rounds of cheese from baskets, together with olive oil into which the bread could be dipped. Cakes of pressed figs and raisins as well as cool water from the Gihon spring also appeared.

Susanna lifted a water jar. 'I know how swiftly my sons and husband empty a dish when all they have done is lift a small hammer to decorate gold—'

'*All they have done?*' interrupted Uri, holding up his cup.

His mother filled it with water. 'You know what I mean. After all, is your tunic usually drenched in sweat after making a necklace?'

Uri looked down at his garment, grinning. His wife added, 'His face is only ever that red from a crucible of gold.'

It was mainly left to the women and girls to talk as the five men began devouring the food, their hunger sharpened by the morning's labour.

'Do you feel it?' asked Daniel's wife, her face shining. 'The whole city brims with new life. I see men everywhere working on the walls with fire in their eyes!'

Susanna moved around, re-filling the already-empty cups. 'It is not only men. Further down the wall, the daughters of Shallum are helping their father.'

Uzziel's fifteen-year-old daughter looked up suddenly. 'Maybe Naomi and I could help too, Father.'

'You already are, Jemimah—the builders need feeding!'

'But if the daughters of the district ruler are allowed to repair the walls, can't we have a part in it too?'

Hananiah looked over to his own eldest daughter. 'When Naomi was younger, she sometimes helped me with mixing ointments and balms. Maybe she and Jemimah, if their own chores are done, could help with mixing mortar. It needs some strength, but neither of them lacks that.'

Uzziel thought for the moment and then looked at Susanna. His wife was smiling. 'Why not, indeed? Is it not Yahweh Himself stirring up our hearts to be part of this great work? Why, then, should our own daughters not have the privilege of saying with the daughters of Shallum that they helped, too, with the rebuilding of Jerusalem's walls.' Jemimah beamed.

Uzziel groaned as he lay next to Susanna that night. 'My whole body aches and my fingers hurt. I have never done a day's work like it.'

Susanna leaned over and blew out the small lamp. 'You should try childbearing…'

He chuckled in the dark and then grimaced. 'Ow!'

After several moments, Susanna added quietly, 'But maybe your labour is not so different. Is not the sweat of your brow and your painful toil to bring to birth something noble? Did not our own daughter-in-law speak earlier of the new life in our city?'

'Hmm.' Uzziel heard no more of his wife's words that night.

The days that followed soon fell into a steady rhythm of collecting stones, carting supplies, mixing mortar, and lifting—by whatever means they could—the stones into place. They swiftly learned that Joel had been right. It was far easier to pack mortar around ill-fitting pieces of rock than shape them to match each gap in the wall. Even smaller stones could be packed in with the mortar to fill any spaces. It was *not* elegant, but it worked. And slowly the wall grew.

But then after two weeks, the city was suddenly stirred again. Uzziel and Daniel were pulling a cart with mud and lime up the hill when Uri came running towards them. 'There is something you must see.'

They set the cart down. 'What is it?'

'Jerusalem has some unwelcome visitors.'

'Who?'

'Sanballat.' Uri began heading back up the hill and they followed.

'The Horonite?' asked Uzziel. 'The governor of Samaria?'

Uri glanced back. 'Yes, he has come with soldiers.'

Uzziel frowned. 'Those in Samaria stopped the building once before. They will find it harder to do so again when Artaxerxes himself has given permission for it—'

'*And* his cupbearer is now our governor,' added Daniel.

Uzziel quickened his pace to keep up with Uri. 'What is this Sanballat doing?'

'It is more what he is saying.'

They approached a small gathering. Most were now familiar to Uzziel—men from the towns of Gibeon and Mizpah who were working on the next sections of wall, a little further up from their own. Many were leaning upon lower parts of the wall or sitting upon it, all looking out. Others were murmuring. All wore the same look of disquiet. A loud voice rang out from beyond the walls.

'What are these feeble Jews doing? Do they think they can restore Jerusalem themselves?' The mocking tone turned the words to daggers.

Uzziel craned his neck, trying to see the speaker. He had never set eyes on Sanballat, but he was not hard to spot. He was the one at the centre in the fine clothes. The one to whom the others gave their attention. The one with the sneer on his face.

Sanballat cried out again. 'Can they bring these heaps of rubble back to life?'

There was a chorus of jeers. The man next to him continued the taunting. 'If even a fox jumped on it, their wall would fall down.'

Laughter rang out, but every Jew remained tight-lipped—until Shekaniah's calm but firm voice pierced their discomfort. He had drawn alongside them. 'We are not alone in this work—the favour of Yahweh rests upon us. When they mock us, they are also mocking our God.' His face was determined. 'But Nehemiah has already told those men that the God of heaven will give us success. They will see that with their own eyes if we ignore their insults and press on with our labours.'

One of the men from Gibeon named Neziah peered out again. 'Who are the men with Sanballat?'

'He has drawn supporters from the whole region of Beyond the River: Arabs, Ammonites, men from Ashdod—'

Neziah folded his arms. 'So enemies from the south, east and west, as well as Samaria to the north.'

'We may feel surrounded,' replied Shekaniah, 'but there is a psalm of the sons of Korah that speaks of Zion: *God is in the midst of her, she will not be moved.* Let us, then, return to this great work!'

Murmurs of agreement rippled across the men. Uzziel turned and the others followed him down the street.

'Is it not true,' said Hananiah suddenly, 'that the Jews have always had enemies?'

Uzziel thought for a moment. 'Maybe it is truer to say that Yahweh's work has always had enemies.' His mind pondered the stories of their people. 'Egyptians, Canaanites, Philistines—not to mention the Assyrians. Maybe we should now add those from Samaria.'

'What about the Babylonians?' asked Michael, forging ahead.

'Ezra speaks of them as a tool in Yahweh's hand through which He brought judgment upon Judah.'

'But one which also came under God's judgment,' added Hananiah. 'The nations are nothing compared to our God!'

Their own section of wall came into view. Michael glanced back. 'Then let us irritate our enemies and sour their faces with our progress!'

Uri chuckled. 'Let our vigour be vinegar in their cup.'

After some twenty-five days—and numerous bruised fingers, cuts and grazes—their repairs had restored the wall to half its height. Similar progress was made around the city. But the clouds from the north soon darkened.

Uzziel looked up at the sky, both squinting and wiping sweat from his brow. *At least the women would be coming with food soon.* The heat of the days had strengthened, with the height of the summer upon them and no rain to cool them. Movement in the corner of his eye lowered his gaze. A group of soldiers, clad in armour and carrying both shields and weapons, were approaching. 'Han...' He then straightened up to face them, Hananiah joining him.

'Trouble?'

'Must be...' They waited in silence as the men drew closer.

The soldiers stopped. 'We bring word from Judah's governor. He has been told of a plot to attack us.'

'A plot by whom?'

'Sanballat, Tobiah the Ammonite, and those who bind themselves to them. Nehemiah thinks it more than an empty threat.' The soldier paused, surveying for a few moments the progress of their work. 'He therefore calls all those working on the walls to cry out to the God of Israel—and lay down their shovels and take up swords.'

'When?' asked Hananiah.

'Immediately—an attack could be any time, day or night. We are to defend the city at all points where the wall is lowest or there are open spaces, such as where gates are yet to be hung.'

Uzziel glanced at their repairs. *It would not take much for an enemy to scale the wall as it stood.* 'We must defend this point, then.'

'You will not do so alone. Those of us in the governor's guard will be posted around Jerusalem, too. Do your families have swords, spears or bows?'

For a moment, Uzziel was fifteen again, with the threat of destruction hanging over them. 'We do—or at least, our fathers do.'

'Good. Ready yourselves and your sons for action.' And with that, they were gone.

Uzziel and Hananiah watched them making their way to the next section of work, passing Daniel, Uri and Michael as they pulled a heavy cart up the street. 'Does not the governor of Samaria fear the wrath of the king if he attacks us?' murmured Hananiah. 'The work has his blessing.'

'The city of Susa is far away. Maybe he thinks he can avoid the king's attention—or deny any part in this hostility later.' Uzziel sighed. 'But he is getting his wish in some measure already, by stopping the work.'

'It was going so well…'

'Which must be why our enemies intend to trade words for weapons—to attack the city before its defences are complete.'

They both fell silent, watching their sons labour towards them with the cart. All were breathing heavily when they arrived, sweat upon their brows.

Uri looked down the street in the direction the soldiers had gone and then wiped his forehead. 'Has something happened?'

Uzziel nodded. 'A change of plan…'

Uzziel stood on a stone, looking out over the section they were defending. He could just see the thin crescent moon hanging low in the sky to the west. It would soon drop below the hills as the sun had done, leaving the night sky dark but the stars' brilliance above them more clearly seen. He looked up into the vast expanse and uttered a silent but urgent prayer for protection. He then sighed. A long and anxious night lay ahead. *At least it was warm.*

The two fathers and three sons had decided to divide the night into watches between them, with two awake at any time—though judging the length of each watch would be difficult without the moon's progress across the sky. Besides, Uzziel had no idea if he would sleep anyway. *What if theirs was the stretch of wall attacked first?*

Uri climbed up onto another stone beside him. 'Do you suppose they have chosen a night close to the new moon so they can approach without being seen?'

Uzziel shrugged in the twilight. 'We do not know if they will attack tonight—or any night. We were told to be on guard both night *and* day.' He swept his eyes across the deepening hills. 'Darkness is a double-edged sword to them. We may not see them, but neither will they see us, particularly as we have no need for braziers for warmth.' He was silent for moment. 'But we have a plan—or rather, Nehemiah has one—that will triumph over theirs.' He said it to reassure himself as much as his son.

'What do you mean?'

'Both setting a guard *and* praying.' Despite the threat they faced, he forced a smile. 'When Azariah and his family stayed with us, he retold the story of Joshua and the walls of Jericho, and how Yahweh by His own power brought those walls down. I do not doubt that by that same power he could perform a miracle and suddenly raise up these walls. Yet the Almighty grants us the honour of being part of His work—work that *He* has brought into being. Do we not see that again now? We put our trust in our God, praying and calling on His name—'

'—whilst staying awake with swords in our hands.'

'Exactly.' Their conversation stopped, however, as for the second time that day movement further up the street—and a flaming torch—caught Uzziel's attention. He suddenly stiffened. The soldiers were returning, but with another. 'It is Nehemiah,' he breathed, his heart quickening. He quickly dismounted the stone and Uri followed. The others, who had been sitting on mats across from them, also rose to their feet. All waited in silence, their eyes fixed upon Nehemiah. He strode towards them, a light cloak billowing behind him. Uzziel expected him to sweep by. He didn't.

'May Yahweh bless you all.' They all murmured a similar greeting in reply. Nehemiah turned towards Uzziel. 'Uzziel son of Harhaiah, I understand.' He studied Uzziel for a moment and smiled. 'Shekaniah tells me you and your sons make a fine golden bowl.'

Uzziel flushed, his fear forgotten. 'Thank you, my lord.' For a moment, his eyes met those of the governor. He saw only a quiet confidence and determination.

Nehemiah turned slightly. 'And you must be Hananiah the perfume-maker.'

'Yes, my lord.'

'I hear good things of your ointments too—' He glanced up at the walls. '—and that both of you with your sons have worked hard on your repairs. And now I see your good work for myself.'

Even in the twilight and the light of a flickering torch, the uneven layers of the wall and excesses of mortar were easily seen. Uzziel winced slightly. 'Though Joel the stonemason is right, my lord, when he says it lacks any beauty.'

For a moment, amusement softened Nehemiah's features. Then he braced his hand against the wall and gazed up again. 'Strength and swift progress are of far more value to us than perfection.' He turned back to them. 'A city wall is to protect its people. As long as it stands strong, that is all that matters.' He paused. 'But I did not come here tonight to inspect your work. I came to bring you one of my own men and to tell you what I am telling everyone—regardless of whether they are nobles, officials or men like yourself.' He nodded towards the gap in the wall and the Judean hills beyond. 'Do not be afraid of our enemies. Remember the Almighty, who is great and awesome, and fight for your families, your sons and your daughters, your wives and your homes. And Yahweh *will* be with you.' With that, he uttered a few words instructing one of his soldiers to stay, then left, walking down the street.

Uzziel's eyes did not leave him until he disappeared into the dusk. He then turned to the guard. 'Does the governor know *everyone's* name?'

'When people matter to him, their names do too.'

The night passed without incident, as did the days and the other nights that followed. All that came were pleas from places nearby for their men to return, fearing attacks on their own towns.

Uzziel stood in the courtyard of his house and splashed water on his face in the bright morning light. He groaned. He wasn't sure which was worse—the aches from lifting stones, or those from sleeping on a mat on the ground under the stars. He wiped the cool water from his skin, then slapped both his cheeks lightly with his hands. They took it in turns to refresh themselves, albeit briefly— and it was his turn. But it was short-lived.

'Father!'

He picked up the towel and turned. 'What is it, Daniel?' He began drying his face.

'We are to return to repairing the walls! Nehemiah is saying that our enemies know their plans have been frustrated since they cannot now attack us unawares. We are to continue working on the walls, whilst remaining vigilant. If we go outside the city where we are more exposed, we are to do so with a sword in one hard. And if we are building the walls, we are to keep a sword on our belt.'

Uzziel laid the towel down, suddenly eager to see the work finished. 'That is good news, indeed!'

'Nehemiah has also said that half his men will remain armed and ready, and that he will have a trumpeter with him at all times. If there is an attack, an alarm will be sounded in that place, so that every man can rally there to fight.' Then Daniel's eyes shone. 'He said that our God will fight for us!'

Uzziel picked up his sword from beside the bowl. He tied the leather thong on its sheath to his belt. 'Then let us build!'

As the walls continued to rise, every moment of daylight was used, like a cup being drained to its last drop of wine. Uzziel rose with the dawn and only returned home after the sun had set and the stars had begun to appear. Even when the final bucket of mortar had been mixed, and the last stone lifted onto their section of wall, there was still work on the gates to be done to complete the city's defences. Stone was exchanged for wood, shovels for saws and hammers, and mortar for nails. Constant toil, swift meals and sound sleep were all he knew—with one exception. The Sabbath had never felt so precious to him. Both Ezra and Nehemiah had insisted that, whilst they could defend themselves if attacked on the Sabbath, Yahweh's command to rest on the seventh day still stood. Their God would honour such obedience, even though their task was urgent.

Uzziel closed his eyes as he stood before the temple in the early morning summer sun. He drank in the psalms being sung by the Levites and the pleasing aroma of the Sabbath day sacrifices upon the altar fire. He moved his aching shoulders backwards and forwards, silently thanking Yahweh for allowing him and the sons at his side to live through such days—for the privilege of being part of it. The singing stopped and he opened his eyes. As the crowd began to disperse, Uzziel glanced around. Shekaniah was making his way towards him. He smiled broadly as he greeted them all. They then joined the flow of worshippers streaming out of the temple.

'Now tell me, Uzziel: how is your work going? Is the gate nearing completion?'

'It is! Progress is swift, now that we use all the light that each day brings and there is no sign of any attack.'

'Our enemies have not given up quite yet. Sanballat may have failed to stop the walls by scorn or sword, but he now uses guile instead as the gates are built.'

'What do you mean?' asked Daniel.

'Two weeks ago, Nehemiah received a message from Sanballat, inviting him to meet them at the plain of Ono.'

'Halfway to Samaria,' replied Uzziel, grimacing.

Uri looked horrified. 'Surely he didn't go!'

Shekaniah shook his head. 'Only a fool would have done so. It may have had the guise of a fair place to meet, but it would have been an easier place to cut Nehemiah down. He had no doubt that their intention was to harm him, and simply told them that he would not be taken away from this great work. Four times Sanballat sent the same message and four times Nehemiah sent back the same reply.'

'Good!' Uzziel thought for a moment as they crossed the large square outside the temple. 'Our governor's trust in Yahweh goes hand in hand with the sense the Almighty gives him.'

'And that is not all.' Shekaniah slowed his pace. They would soon have to part and go their separate ways. 'Only a few days ago, Sanballat sent an open letter to Nehemiah, accusing him of leading a rebellion against Persia and intending to be our king. The letter even claimed that Nehemiah has appointed prophets to proclaim him as king.'

'Anyone in Jerusalem knows that is a lie!' exclaimed Uri, as they came to stop.

'But by leaving the letter unsealed,' replied his brother, 'Sanballat knew it would almost certainly be read by every person who handled it on its journey.'

'You are right, Daniel,' replied Shekaniah. 'Sanballat stirs up rumours to discredit or to frighten Nehemiah.'

'And how did Nehemiah respond to the letter?' asked Uzziel, curious.

Shekaniah chuckled. 'He sent a reply telling Sanballat that nothing of the sort was happening, and that he was imagining it.'

Uzziel shook his head, smiling. 'I trust his letter was also unsealed!' The smile faded. 'But what if those rumours reach Susa?'

'The king hopefully knows Nehemiah too well to believe such tales. But I must go.' He turned to leave, then paused. 'Some of Jerusalem's influential families, however, are bound to the family of Tobiah the Ammonite by marriage. And he openly sides with Sanballat. It gives our enemies a foothold in this city, and they may not have finished their attacks. But Nehemiah prays that our God will strengthen his hand.' He smiled. 'And Yahweh will. It is He, not Nehemiah, who started this great work—and it is He who will bring it to completion. The nations will yet hear of the powerful hand of the God of Israel!'

Uzziel, Hananiah and their families stood together in the large crowd that had gathered to witness the last gate being hung. The ropes creaked as they took the strain, the faces of the teams pulling them contorted and red with the effort. The heavy wooden door began to rise, its timber beams cut from the king's own forests and low blocks ready to support its base. It was strengthened with bars across it, and bolts were ready to make the gates secure when closed. Slowly, one handbreadth at a time, the thick door edged closer to its post. Uzziel held his breath. The murmuring of the crowd died away, every eye upon the door. It met its upright and its pair perfectly, resting for the moment on the blocks beneath it. Uzziel breathed again. The sounds of hammers securing hinges suddenly replaced the cries of instructions and the creaks of rope and wood.

The mood was jubilant, and when the blocks were finally pulled away, allowing the gate to hang freely and be opened and closed, a deafening cheer rose from the crowd, drowning out all other sounds. Uzziel, with tears in his eyes, caught sight of the face of Nehemiah amongst the throng. It was lifted to heaven, radiant, his lips moving in what Uzziel could only think were words of praise to Yahweh. *It had all been done in fifty-two days.*

That night the wine flowed, as the two families that had laboured side by side on the walls celebrated together.

'I wonder whether my hands will remember how to twist gold wire,' said Uri grinning, as he dipped a piece of bread into the rich lamb stew.

'And *I* wonder,' laughed Michael, 'whether my nose will still tell me which is cinnamon and which calamus!'

Susanna shook her head, laughing. 'It has not been two months since you laid aside your crafts. Your fathers will despair of you both if you have forgotten your skills in so short a time.'

Uzziel chuckled and then cast his eyes around both families, beaming. 'And yet is that not part of the wonder, that such a mighty task should be accomplished so swiftly?'

'And in the face of our enemies!' added Hananiah.

Uzziel mused for a moment on what had been accomplished. 'Shekaniah was right. It was Yahweh who both laid a burden on Nehemiah's heart to restore the walls and then brought him here.

It was Yahweh's gracious hand that both protected and provided for this work. And our God always completes what He starts.' He lifted his eyes into the evening sky, tinged with gold, and echoed the words that Shekaniah had shared from the psalms. *'God is in the midst of her, she will not be moved.'*

Notes

1. *Although this chapter starts some indeterminate time after Ezra's arrival, it swiftly moves to Nehemiah's arrival in 445 BC.*

2. *Although Ezra arrived in Jerusalem in 458 BC, his public teaching is not mentioned until Nehemiah chapter 8 (the events of which were in 445 BC). However, given that Ezra 7:10 states that, 'Ezra had devoted himself to the study and observance of the Law of the LORD, and to teaching its decrees and laws in Israel', it is hard to imagine that he would not have been teaching God's law in the intervening thirteen years. How this teaching would have happened is not apparent. There is, however, precedent for Levites having this role. In the reign of King Jehoshaphat, Levites were sent out: 'They taught throughout Judah, taking with them the Book of the Law of the LORD; they went around to all the towns of Judah and taught the people' (2 Chronicles 17:9). It has been assumed that Ezra and other Levites would have been fulfilling a similar role, possibly teaching at the temple on the Sabbath (as became the norm in synagogues by New Testament times—a practice that may have started during the exile, when the Jews were not able to worship at the temple).*

3. *A daric was a gold coin introduced at the end of the 6th Century BC by Darius I, for use throughout the Persian Empire. It weighed 8.4 grams. Obviously, there is limited archaeological information about how much a daric would have bought! However, there is a reference in Ezra 8:27 to '20 bowls of gold valued at 1,000 darics', implying that one bowl was worth 50 darics. Clearly, there is no comment on how big these bowls were. The bowl in this chapter is assumed to be smaller.*

4. *There is no indication in Scripture of how the sections of the wall were allocated to different individuals or groups for repair (as detailed in*

Nehemiah chapter 3), and whether the work was allocated or volunteered for. It has been assumed that whole families would be involved in the task. Certainly Nehemiah 3:12 records that 'Shallum…repaired the next section with the help of his daughters.' Presumably this has a special mention because Shallum had no sons to help him. Although commentators vary, it has also been assumed that the Broad Wall (referred to in Nehemiah 3:8) was not part of the repairs. It was probably a wall that had enclosed the Western Hill from around the time of Hezekiah, and which abutted the older N-S wall enclosing the smaller city of Solomon's time. However, as the ESV Bible Atlas states: 'Archaeology…has unearthed little from this period of settlement in Jerusalem. It appears that much of the remains were obliterated by later massive building programs, such as those conducted by Herod the Great… Jerusalem during the Persian period is not well known to modern historians.'

5.   It is assumed that lime mortar was used in the repairing of the walls, as it was a durable mortar used in ancient times.

6.   A Biblical Archaeology Review article by Eilat Mazar, dated March/April 2009, and entitled 'The Wall that Nehemiah Built', reports on an archaeological dig that uncovered a section of wall ('Wall 27') and a tower, both dating to around the time of Nehemiah (i.e. 445 BC). The article comments on the rapid nature of the project, given the opposition from Judah's neighbours. It then states: 'But there was a price to be paid for the speed of the work. It was shabby workmanship. This is amply reflected in the poor quality of the Northern Tower and Wall 27. Macalister and Duncan, the tower's first excavators, aptly described it: "The interstices [between the stones of the tower] are very roughly filled up with chips and with large quantities of mortar. The stones have no smooth finished face, and the filling of interstices is so carelessly done that the wall face presents a series of openings and cracks …"' This archaeological evidence has been incorporated into the story. It also accords well with the work being done by men unskilled in building or masonry and may explain the words of their enemies that 'even a fox climbing up on it would break down their wall of stones' (Nehemiah 4:3).

7.   When the work was verbally attacked by Sanballat (as recorded in Nehemiah 4), it is not clear where this took place. It is assumed here that

Sanballat went around the city, mocking the different builders with the same sort of words, given Nehemiah's comment in 4:5 that 'they have thrown insults in the face of the builders', or, as the ESV renders it, 'they have provoked you to anger in the presence of the builders.'

8. Given Nehemiah's severe response later when the Sabbath law is broken (see Nehemiah 13:15-21), referring to work on that day as 'wicked' and a 'desecration', it seems reasonable to assume that rebuilding would have ceased on the Sabbath. Corporate work on the gates after the work on walls was finished is also assumed, given that there is no list (in Nehemiah 4) of those responsible for the gates as there is for the different sections of the wall.

9. In Nehemiah 5 there is an outcry about the financial difficulty being faced by many in Jerusalem. It is assumed that this happened after the rebuilding of the walls but is within the narrative to illustrate other difficulties (in much the same way as Ezra 4 inserts later events into that chapter). Commentators come to different conclusions: on the one hand, the extra financial burden caused by having to set aside 'normal work', where the story is placed in the narrative, and the reference to the rebuilding of the walls (in 5:16) may imply that it happened at that time. On the other hand, the improbability of calling a large assembly (5:7) in the middle of an urgent building project, and the chapter's reference to a point twelve years after Nehemiah's arrival (5:14), may imply it was later. The latter view has been adopted here.

10. The imagined named characters introduced in this chapter are Michael, Jemimah and Neziah.

5

A prophecy: the word of the LORD to Israel through Malachi. 'I have loved you,' says the LORD. (Malachi 1:1-2)

Uzziel looked up at the wall, patting its stones with hands that were both creased by age and calloused by a lifetime's work.

'So it hasn't fallen down, then?'

Uzziel looked over his shoulder, amused by his friend's jest. 'No, Han, it has not—at least, not yet!' He returned to his scrutiny of the uneven courses of stone and mortar they'd laid almost twenty years earlier. 'Maybe it is another of Yahweh's wonders.' His lifted his eyes to its uppermost level. 'Do you remember when Nehemiah directed that large choir to process along the top of the walls at their dedication—'

'With the governor himself and half the leaders of Jerusalem behind them? I could hardly forget it…'

Uzziel chuckled. 'I prayed so hard that our wall would not collapse beneath their weight!'

'And it didn't.'

By the time both men turned to continue their walk up the street, their families were some distance ahead. Uzziel tugged on the rope in his hand. At the other end of it was a lamb they were taking to the temple. The creature obliged and trotted forward, oblivious to its fate.

'Do you think Nehemiah will ever return?' asked Hananiah. 'It's been seven years.'

'That was his intention, was it not, when he went back to Susa? But he can only return with the king's permission.'

'It is not the same without him—'

'Or Ezra.' The priest had died some time earlier. Uzziel sighed. The lifting of his heart as they'd looked at the wall hadn't lasted. All had not been well since the governor's departure. 'Why must the people of Yahweh always stray back into sin, as surely as winter follows summer? Why, after light seems to dawn upon us does dusk follow so swiftly behind?' He shook his head. 'After the walls were finished, the whole city took a solemn oath to walk according to God's law. How is that promise so readily forgotten or set aside when the gaze of a godly leader is not upon us?'

Hananiah was silent for several moments, the only sound that of the lamb's hooves upon the ground. 'Maybe it is the same in every generation. Was not King Josiah followed by godless sons like Jehoiakim? And the same before him, with Hezekiah followed by Manasseh.'

Uzziel cast his mind back further. 'The mighty Solomon himself also sinned grievously, despite his wealth and wisdom.' He paused. 'But maybe we should say, *As with the father, so with the son*? There was grievous sin in David's own life, though we still exalt him as our greatest king.'

'And even as Moses was receiving the Law from the hand of Yahweh, what were our forefathers doing?'

'Bowing down to a golden calf.' Through the faithful teaching of Ezra and other priests like Azariah, the stories of their people had become familiar. 'But go back further. Even after the flood, there was still sin in the heart of every person in the line of our father Shem. He was, after all, not only a son of Noah, but also of Adam.' The temple came into view. Their families were waiting for them by the gates. 'It is as well, Han, that Yahweh is slow to anger. We have provoked Him often enough.'

'Slow to anger *and* gracious. Even now, he still sends prophets to call us back.'

'You mean Malachi?' The voice of the young prophet had risen among them in recent years.

'Yes—and he tells us that Yahweh loves us.'

Uzziel looked down at the lamb as they approached those waiting and tugged on the rope again. 'Maybe that is why our God allows us to bring a sacrifice for our sins.'

The families walked together into the temple court but had to wait.

'Where are all the priests?' murmured Uri, peering around.

'Azariah told me,' replied Daniel, 'that many of them—and Levites with them—are having to go back to their fields because the tithes they receive are so diminished. There is simply not enough for them and their families to live on.'

'Malachi has spoken against the people because of it,' added Hananiah.

'And that is not the only thing he speaks out against.' Uzziel lowered his voice. 'Look at some of the animals being offered...'

'Lame or diseased,' answered Michael under his breath. 'How does that honour Yahweh?'

'Exactly.' A weight of sadness lay on the scale-pan within Uzziel's own heart, tipping it towards despondency.

Eventually a priest approached them. 'You wish to sacrifice the lamb?'

Uzziel nodded. 'Yes—as a sin offering.' The priest held out a knife to him, its blade stained. Uzziel took it, then turned to Hananiah.

'No, you do it for all of us, my friend.'

'So be it.'

The priest led the animal to a small post and tethered it there. Then, one by one, they laid a hand upon the animal's head, the oldest to the youngest among them. A swift slash of the blade took the lamb's life. It crumpled to the ground.

They watched in silence as the priest then performed the ancient duty of smearing the lamb's blood on the corners of the altar. He then offered its choice portions upon the fire, the flames immediately beginning to feast on the fat.

After a while, Daniel spoke. 'We should take the young ones back.'

Uzziel glanced down at the youngest of the grandchildren, aged four and five. They were already on the verge of squabbling, their faces pouting. *The sin within remained.* 'You go, but I will stay until the offering is consumed.'

Hananiah smiled. 'And I will stay with you, my old friend.'

After the others had left, Uzziel's eyes returned to the smoke curling up from the altar. He followed it upwards. 'Do you think there will ever be a time when there is no longer a need to offer such sacrifices?'

There was a pause. 'How could that be when corruption continues clinging to us all?'

Uzziel thought of his own life. *How indeed?* But as the pleasing aroma from the altar drifted over to them, the sight and smells—with no more weight than the air—seemed to tip the balance of Uzziel's heart once more, this time towards hope. He remembered words read to them by Ezra from the law of Moses. '*The priest shall burn it on the altar,*' he murmured, '*as an aroma pleasing to Yahweh. In this way the priest will make atonement for them, and they will be forgiven.*' He paused. 'We do not stand alone, Han. Our people have always offered sacrifices to Yahweh—whether Abraham or Jacob on altars of stone, Moses or David at the tent of meeting, or any of us since Solomon at a temple in Jerusalem. All of us sinful yet finding forgiveness. All of us loved, as Malachi says.' He tore his gaze away from the altar and turned to Hananiah. 'Are those not wonders immeasurably higher than that our wall still stands?'

Their eyes met. 'Higher than the heavens are above the earth.' Hananiah looked back at the dying flames. 'Malachi also speaks of Yahweh as a refiner's fire—a fire that will purify the priests.' He paused. 'Maybe one day all Yahweh's people will be purified.'

Uzziel's gaze then drifted around the temple court as he pondered the words, imagining the priests that had served there in the days of Solomon. *But that temple had been glorious. There was no gold now as there once had been. Would the glory of Israel—and with it, Yahweh's honour—ever be restored when they were yet under Persian rule?* The face of another priest came to mind. 'Azariah once told me of a promise God gave to David, that the throne of his son would be established forever.'

'Hmm. Yet the kingdom split under Solomon's son.'

'But Azariah believes that the promise may yet be fulfilled—a descendant of David yet arising to take the throne of Israel once more.'

'Then we will wait for such a day.'

The men stood in amiable silence for a while. Uzziel then turned to Hananiah, smiling. 'Maybe *you* will make the fragrant anointing oil for his head…'

Hananiah raised a greying eyebrow. 'Hah! That will be the preserve of the priests, not a humble perfumer from the tribe of Judah. Not unless there is also a need for perfume for his feet! No, more likely he will need your services for a crown of gold.'

Uzziel's mind wandered as his eyes drifted back to the altar. *It would have to be made of the finest gold, engraved or embossed, maybe with fig or vine leaves symbolising Israel. Or should it have gold filigree settings, like those on high priest's ephod? Settings on which would be mounted the twelve gems that represented the twelve sons of Jacob—the ancient tribes of Israel. What were those stones? No matter. Either way, it should be a broad polished band of gold, easily seen and which would dazzle in the sunlight…*

'You are quiet.'

'Hmm?' Uzziel was suddenly back in the temple court. 'I was just wondering about the sort of crown such a king would wear.' He sighed. *Such a king seemed distant.* The fire on the altar had dwindled to glowing embers. 'Let us go.'

They turned and walked towards the gateway, beyond which lay the rest of Jerusalem and their homes. It was a short walk, but his ankles already ached. 'I am glad that it was my grandfather that had to make the journey from Persia to Judah and not me.'

'I share your gladness.' Hananiah then pulled on his beard. 'Sometimes it seems as if the people of Yahweh have always been on a journey—and maybe we still are.' He lifted his eyes to heaven. 'I wonder where the God of Israel may yet take us?'

'Yahweh alone knows.' As they passed through the temple gates, Uzziel's mind returned to the walls they'd restored. 'Maybe our story is also like Jerusalem itself—unfinished. Maybe Yahweh is still building something glorious.' He fell silent, but then a memory stirred. A memory of what he had said on the night they'd celebrated the restoration of the city walls. He murmured the words again. '*Our God always completes what He starts.*'

Notes

1. *This chapter is set around 426 BC. Scripture doesn't indicate how long Nehemiah was away in Persia; only that he had returned there in the thirty-second year of Artaxerxes (i.e. around 433 BC). Presumably, given the distance and his responsibilities, he may have been away several years, which seems likely, given the time needed for the significant moral decline in his absence (as recorded in Nehemiah 13). It is probable that Ezra was no longer living. He had previously dealt with some of the same sins listed in Nehemiah 13, and it is hard to imagine he would not have addressed them again in Nehemiah's absence. Ezra must also have been a reasonable age when he led the exiles to Jerusalem around 30 years earlier. Nehemiah's return to Jerusalem occurred 'some time later' (Nehemiah 13:6). This must have been before Artaxerxes' death in 423 BC.*

2. *Scholars usually date Malachi to around the same time as Ezra and Nehemiah, given the temple is standing (see Malachi 1:10) and they deal with similar issues, e.g. a corrupt priesthood, intermarriage, failure to pay tithes. The ministry of Malachi would also fit well into the more specific period of Nehemiah's absence. The people had covenanted in Nehemiah 10 to walk according to God's law, not intermarrying, keeping the Sabbath free from work, and contributing money and tithes to the work of the temple. All these things had been neglected in Nehemiah's absence (see Nehemiah 13:10-27), and Malachi had much to say about the people's deviation from God's law.*

3. *It is not clear how much the forward-pointing promises of the Old Testament would have been in the minds of those who had returned from exile—or even how widely they would have been known before the Hebrew Scriptures came together. Artistic licence (if it is required) has allowed for it here. A final comment from the essay 'The Messianic Hope' by Dr T. Desmond Alexander, a senior lecturer in Biblical studies at Union College*

Belfast, may be pertinent (see www.thegospelcoalition.org/essay/the-messianic-hope). 'The consensus of modern scholarship is heavily weighed against tracing messianic ideology back into the Old Testament. Yet, belief in a future, unique king lies at the heart of the Old Testament story. There is an expectation that a future Davidic king will play an important role in the fulfilment of God's redemptive plans for the earth. These expectations form the basis of the claims made by New Testament writers that the messianic hope finds its fulfilment in Jesus Christ.'

BIBLIOGRAPHY

Leslie C. Allen, *The Communicator's Commentary – 1,2 Chronicles,* (Word Inc, 1987).

Clive Anderson, Brian Edwards, *Evidence for the Bible*, (Day One Publications, 2013).

A. Boyd Luter & Barry C. David, *Ruth & Esther: God Behind the Seen,* (Christian Focus, 2003).

John Bright, *A History of Israel: Third Edition,* (SCM Press Ltd, 1986).

John D. Currid & David P. Barrett, *ESV Bible Atlas,* (Crossway, 2010).

Dave Ralph Davis, *1 Kings: The Wisdom and the Folly,* (Christian Focus, 2008).

Dave Ralph Davis, *2 Kings: The Power and the Fury,* (Christian Focus, 2005).

Simon J. DeVries, *Word Biblical Commentary – 1 Kings,* (Word, 1985).

J. D. Douglas (Ed.), *The Illustrated Bible Dictionary,* (IVP, 1988).

J. D. Douglas and Merrill C. Tenney, *Zondervan Illustrated Bible Dictionary,* (Zondervan Academic, 2011).

Bob Fyall, *Teaching 1 Kings,* (Christian Focus, 2015).

E. W. Heaton, *Everyday Life in Old Testament Times*, (Batsford, 1966).

E. W. Heaton, *Solomen's New Men*, (Pica Press, 1974).

John A. Heck, *Everyday Life in Bible Times*, (BakerBooks, 2013).

T. R. Hobbs, *Word Biblical Commentary – 2 Kings*, (Word, 1985).

Derek Kidner, *Ezra and Nehemiah,* (Tyndale, 2007).

Philip J. King and Lawrence E. Stager, *Life in Biblical Israel,* (Westminster John Knox Press, 2001).

K. A. Kitchen, *On the Reliability of the Old Testament*, (Eerdmans, 2006).

John L. Mackay, *Haggai, Zechariah and Malachi,* (Christian Focus, 2010).

J. G. McConville, *The Daily Study Bible: Chronicles,* (The Saint Andrew Press, 1984).

Alec Motyer, *The Prophecy of Isaiah,* (IVP, 1994).

Lorna Oakes, Philip Steele, *Everyday Life in Ancient Egypt & Mesopotamia,* (Southwater, 2005).

John N. Oswalt, *The Book of Isaiah, Chapters 1-39,* (Eerdmans, 1991).

Nick Page, *The One-Stop Bible Atlas,* (Lion Hudson, 2010).

J. B. Pritchard (Ed.), *Ancient Near Eastern Texts, 3rd Edition,* (Princeton University Press, 1969).

Martin J. Selman, *1 Chronicles,* (IVP, 1994).

Martin J. Selman, *2 Chronicles,* (IVP, 1994).

J. A. Thomson, *The Book of Jeremiah,* (Eerdmans, 1989).

J. A. Thompson, *Handbook of Life in Bible Times,* (IVP, 1986).

John H. Walton, Victor H. Matthews, Mark W. Chavalas, *The IVP Bible Background Commentary – Old Testament* (OTBBC), *(*IVP, 2000).

Various authors, *Explore Bible Notes,* The Good Book Company.